Bard   FICTION PRIZE

Bard College invites submissions for its annual Fiction Prize for young writers.

The Bard Fiction Prize is awarded annually to a promising, emerging writer who is a United States citizen aged 39 years or younger at the time of application. In addition to a monetary award of $30,000, the winner receives an appointment as writer-in-residence at Bard College for one semester without the expectation that he or she teach traditional courses. The recipient will give at least one public lecture and will meet informally with students.

To apply, candidates should write a cover letter describing the project they plan to work on while at Bard and submit a C.V., along with three copies of the published book they feel best represents their work. No manuscripts will be accepted.

Applications for the 2015 prize must be received by July 15, 2014. For further information about the Bard Fiction Prize, call 845-758-7087, or visit www.bard.edu/bfp. Applicants may also request information by writing to the Bard Fiction Prize, Bard College, Annandale-on-Hudson, NY 12504-5000.

Bard College PO Box 5000, Annandale-on-Hudson, NY 12504-5000

COMING UP IN THE FALL

Conjunctions:63
SPEAKING VOLUMES
Edited by Bradford Morrow

Cormac McCarthy said it best: "Books are made out of books." Whatever is written, be it a novel, a poem, a story, a play, an essay, even a work that defies categorizing, depends upon novels, poems, stories, plays, essays—humankind's vast athenaeum—that have been written before. Books, in other words, beget books. *Conjunctions:63, Speaking Volumes*, is a library of ideas on the book as a portal of the imagination, a gateway of language and imagery. In it the reader will discover meditations of every sort on historic books, secret books, imaginary books, ghostwritten and pseudonymous books, books translated and books banned, rare books and forged books. Books that break new ground, books that put words under the microscope, books that signify and those that defy interpretation. Books made of paper or parchment, e-books, poems both about and on Greek urns, narratives tattooed on skin. The book that is a memory jug.

Speaking Volumes encompasses them all, with writing about writing itself and the books that are home to the written word. Among the provocative and innovative contemporary writers who address this most fundamental and rich subject are Samuel R. Delany, Jorie Graham, Melissa Pritchard, William H. Gass, Peter Gizzi, Cole Swensen, Benjamin Hale, Joyce Carol Oates, and Peter Cole.

CONJUNCTIONS

Bi-Annual Volumes of New Writing

Edited by
Bradford Morrow

published by Bard College

EDITOR: Bradford Morrow
MANAGING EDITOR: Micaela Morrissette
SENIOR EDITORS: Robert Antoni, Peter Constantine, Benjamin Hale,
    J. W. McCormack, Edie Meidav, Nicole Nyhan, Pat Sims
COPY EDITOR: Pat Sims
ASSOCIATE EDITORS: Jedediah Berry, Joss Lake, Wendy Lotterman
PUBLICITY: Darren O'Sullivan, Mark R. Primoff
EDITORIAL ASSISTANTS: Kelsea Bauman, Emma Horwitz, Ariana
    Perez-Castells, Leah Rabinowitz, Jackson Rollings, Benjamin Wiley
    Sernau, Thatcher Snyder, Maggie Vicknair, Tina Wack

NATIONAL ENDOWMENT FOR THE ARTS
A great nation deserves great art.

CONJUNCTIONS is published in the Spring and Fall of each year by Bard College, Annandale-on-Hudson, NY 12504. This issue is made possible in part with the generous funding of the National Endowment for the Arts.

SUBSCRIPTIONS: Use our secure online ordering system at www.conjunctions.com, or send subscription orders to CONJUNCTIONS, Bard College, Annandale-on-Hudson, NY 12504. Single year (two volumes): $18.00 for individuals; $40.00 for institutions and non-US. Two years (four volumes): $32.00 for individuals; $80.00 for institutions and non-US. For information about subscriptions, back issues, and advertising, contact us at (845) 758-7054 or conjunctions@bard.edu. *Conjunctions* is listed and indexed in Humanities International Complete and included in EBSCO*host*.

Editorial communications should be sent to Bradford Morrow, *Conjunctions*, 21 East 10th Street, 3E, New York, NY 10003. Unsolicited manuscripts cannot be returned unless accompanied by a stamped, self-addressed envelope. Electronic and simultaneous submissions will not be considered. If you are submitting from outside the United States, contact conjunctions@bard.edu for instructions.

Cover design by Jerry Kelly, New York. Cover photograph is a detail of the installation "Accumulation—Searching for the Destination," from Chiharu Shiota's solo exhibition *Where Are We Going?* at the Marugame Genichiro–Inokuma Museum of Contemporary Art, Kagawa, Japan, 2012. Image is reproduced with the kind permission of Chiharu Shiota. © 2014 Chiharu Shiota; all rights reserved by the artist.

Retailers can order print issues via D.A.P./Distributed Art Publishers, Inc., 155 Sixth Avenue, New York, NY 10013. Telephone: (212) 627-1999. Fax: (212) 627-9484.

Printers: Edwards Brothers Malloy

Typesetter: Bill White, Typeworks

ISSN 0278-2324

ISBN 978-0-941964-78-4

Manufactured in the United States of America.

TABLE OF CONTENTS

EXILE

Edited by Bradford Morrow

EDITOR'S NOTE. 7

H. G. Carrillo, *Splaining Yourself*. 8

Aleš Šteger, *Three Berlin Essays* (translated from Slovenian
  by Brian Henry) 18

Christie Hodgen, *Customer Reviews*. 23

Peter Straub, *The Collected Short Stories of Freddie Prothero,
  Introduction by Törless Magnussen, PhD* 37

Laura van den Berg, *Havana* 45

Lance Olsen, *Dreamlives of Debris*. 63

John Parras, *Song of Magsaysay* 78

Marjorie Welish, *Folding Cythera* 103

Paul West, *Omobo* 112

Charles Baudelaire, *Poor Belgium: The Argument* (translated
  from French with an Introduction by Richard Sieburth). 125

Maxine Chernoff, *Five Poems*. 146

Brian Evenson, *Cult* 151

Robin Hemley, *Celebrating Russian Federation Day
  with Immanuel Kant*. 161

Edie Meidav, *Dog's Journey*. 177

Stephen O'Connor, *The Zip*. 190

Gillian Conoley, *Preparing One's Consciousness for
  the Avatar* 215

Can Xue, *Coal* (translated from Chinese by
Annelise Finegan Wasmoen) 227

Martin Riker, *Samuel Johnson's Eternal Return* 241

Wil Weitzel, *The Gujjar at the River*. 263

Matthew Pitt, *A Damn Sight* 281

Arthur Sze, *Water Calligraphy* 296

Gabriel Blackwell, *The Invention of an Island* 302

Robyn Carter, *Aftershock* 316

NOTES ON CONTRIBUTORS. 329

EDITOR'S NOTE

FEW SUBJECTS ARE AS RICH, complex, and profound as exile. This is especially true if one allows its definition to venture beyond the political, religious, or cultural, so that it embraces the deeply personal, psychological, and emotional terrains in which individuals inhabit a place of self-exile, or even exile from sanity and surety.

From Africa to China, Pakistan to the Philippines to locales that are not to be found on any map, this issue examines exile as both a literal expulsion or ostracism and, as Primo Levi has it, "the prevalence of the unreal over the real." H. G. Carrillo's "Splaining Yourself" explores, with an incandescent ferocity of bilingualism, the difficulties of living on the racial, ethnic, linguistic divide between two cultures, a member assimilated into and yet estranged from both. Aleš Šteger investigates the sensibility of exile in Berlin. Edie Meidav offers a boxer's-eye view of postrevolutionary Cuba, whose system of privilege and constraint under Castro drives a gifted fighter from his homeland across the waters to Miami, where he is a man finally without a country. Robin Hemley's "Celebrating Russian Federation Day with Immanuel Kant" delves into that singular world of exclaves, with its own highly individual problems about nationality and cultural identity.

The permutations of our theme are extensive. Here is an agonizing story of love that impels a man far from the precincts of rational decision making, exiling him to a locus where all that remains is a guarantee of personal destruction. Here is an orphan who exiles himself from his home to live in makeshift proximity and spy on those who move in to take his place. Here is Charles Baudelaire's proposal for a book excoriating Belgium, a country to which he has grudgingly fled after abandoning his native France—a vitriolic, painful, and hilarious document appearing for the first time in English in a superb translation by Richard Sieburth.

We hope this issue provides some fresh insights into the exiles' worlds, and makes a modest contribution to a literature that is ancient, essential, and multifarious.

—Bradford Morrow
April 2014
New York City

Splaining Yourself
H. G. *Carrillo*

You throw the sand against the wind,
And the wind blows it back again.

—William Blake

OYE ESE, BEFORE YOU set sail to your black male body with its Spanish-speaking tongue across El Estrecho de Florida into the arms of the country you believe will understand you, you will need more than that electronic pocket translator you wrapped in plastico for the journey. Although it is only a ninety-mile stretch between La Habana y the Bay of Biscayne, there is something in the air, in the water over which you have to cross, that performs an alchemy for which there is no limpia that will mark you forever as "the unknown."

Aquí, with the free and the brave, history is short, though its emotive states are long. Therefore, the majority of questions that you will be asked will be more about your body than your personhood. As if in a protracted game of Cowboys and Indians, "what" you are rather than "who" you are is the average height of the hurdles set in the circuitous series of marathons you are about to run.

Walk into a department store in an Armani suit or throw up the arm with which you are holding your briefcase in an attempt to hail a cab headed southward on Michigan Avenue and you are likely to make yourself invisible. Automatic car doors will lock as you stand or cross intersections, women will clutch their handbags as you enter public transportation and elevators. Assume the discussions you have with men in airports, train stations, and at adjacent urinals that seem to begin midthought—"Kobe was looking good last night, no?"—to have something to do with the NBA, because you have inherited a historical lineage in which Michael Jordan endorses underwear on television, Tupac has been elevated to sainthood, and the mention of someone like Percival Everett or André Watts can turn a listener's eyes to *X*'s.

Abre la boca, y porfa, you will just as easily be assumed African as you will be told that you look like some celebrity. Claim Latino identity and nonhispanoblats will request a demonstration of your native language even though they have no idea what you are saying. You will find, though, that they like to use the term "Latino"—particularly in statements like "Our department is very diverse; we have a number of African Americans, Asians, and Latinos"—although they have no idea they have conflated cultural background with notions of race. Y entonces, try to explain that the term "Latino" in English is representative of the intersection of both Latin and Anglo colonial enterprises in the United States, and you will be told, "But you don't look Latino."

"Cuban" is much more difficult. Even though the *I Love Lucy* show first aired over sixty years ago, Ricky Ricardo is hard to shake. As you try to explain that when Arnaz's character on the show sings *Babalú . . . Babalú ayé,* he is not singing exclusively in Spanish, but something that is representative of the mingling of African and European cultures on the island; that the chorus, which was never translated on the show—*Quiere pedi / Que mi negra me quiera / Que tenga dinero / Y que no se muera / ¡Ay! Vo le quiero pedi a Babalú 'na negra muy santa como tú que no tenga / otro negro / Pa' que no se fuera*—not only references the blackness of the deity he is evoking, but does so in what Arnaz believed to be an Afro Cubano dialect. Even your dentist, first generation from Greek immigrants, will stop to ask, "Are you Cuban or are you black?" and will not put his hands back in your mouth until you suggest he think of major league baseball or the Buena Vista Social Club. Clearly, even though Santiago de Cuba is at the southernmost tip of North America, the *Asiento System* is not a term given to memorize for North American middle-school exams.

There appears to be only one Cuban tale of immigration allowed here, despite the collectors of Celia Cruz and La Lupe albums on vinyl you will meet at cocktail parties who will accurately chronicle the careers of both musicians from beginning to end, and then admonish you for not knowing "your own heritage."

Oye, hombre, aquí en los Estados Unidos de América, the story of Cuban immigration must begin with the loss of a finca—a great main house, land as far as the eye can see—that culminates in a flight in the middle of the night, and ends in Miami with a hatred, and a painful longing for a place to which you can never return. Apparently, here, Jefferson never attempted to negotiate Cuba away from Spain and adopt it as a state with the hope of reducing the cost and expediting the traffic of the US slave trade, José Martí never made a landmark visit that challenged US scholars' notions of color, and Saturnino Orestes Armas "Minnie" Miñoso Arrieta was never signed to the Cleveland Indians in 1949.

It also seems that on this side of the bay, it's easy to forget that up until Castro's 1959 revolt, there was what can only be defined as "a shuttle" that traveled daily from Manhattan to La Habana that—in addition to offering sultry tropical nights, gambling, and inexpensive entertainments—provided enough distance from scrutiny to those who had a penchant for las negras they couldn't find in Harlem. Which could be why, with a population of over eleven million, the fact that over 38 percent of Cubans might be nonwhite seems disruptive to the concept of Ricky Ricardo or, por ejemplo, the newer model of Cuban American male identity, the dark-eyed, olive-skinned Richard Blanco—both of whom, as you know, asere, are considered white only on the island. Pero, you will need to abandon the question *¿Quién se hubiera imaginado que Desi Arnaz no era blanco?* They don't nor do they want to hear it, y they will make sure you look like a comemierda for asking. It will only make you sound silly in your failure to recognize the cost for both Arnaz and Blanco of crossing el Estrecho de Florida was a racial claim to whiteness. They are the Cubans, you are black, and everyone knows who everyone is just by looking at each other. Y, ahi-nama, pendejo, is the subtle difference between *who* you are and *what* you are. Aquí, they insist there is a difference between *who* and *what*, but it is unclear and le ronca el mango, the way you could spend a lot of your time trying to figure it out.

Unlike during any trip you may have made to Paris, Istanbul, Caracas, Buenos Aires, Mexico City, Vancouver, Amsterdam, Warsaw, St. Petersburg, or Dublin, in the States your body will always be an obstacle to articulating the differences between race, ethnicity, space, place, and culture. Pues, you will need to stumble upon *A Dialogue* (1973) based on the November 4, 1971, conversation James Baldwin had with Nikki Giovanni in London, in which Baldwin asserts, "The reason that people think it is important to be white is that they think it's important not to be black." Pero, you will find even you will elide the most salient portion of his proclamation for the safety of the established racial binary that divides the country between white and black. You will hold fast to this reading of Baldwin's statement until you attend a Latino literary conference in California, where you will be introduced by brown Latinos to other brown Latinos as an Afro Cubano, a black Latino, an Afro Cubano Americano writer and scholar, as if to somehow explain away your blackness. To segregate your latinidad from theirs, because after all, the *afro* they can see, ¿no?, the *americano* can be assumed, and your Hispanic surname should be enough to tell your lineage, if that is important. Why, you'll ask, can't you be a writer and a scholar in the same way they are? Pero, ese, if you can't recognize ellos no tienen dos dedos de frente, your mamá did not raise you right.

On the same trip, you will be in casual conversation in Spanish with other Latinos—what to eat, where to shop, what movies you should see, what book to read next—at the end of which someone will ask, "Where did you learn to speak such good Spanish?" Pero, it is a series of events and a question that will confuse you until you get back to your hotel room, where you will realize it is not the black/white binary Baldwin is talking about, but the anxiety of blackness. Nonetheless, in these circles, get used to the floating terms "Latino" and "Hispanic." Because even though these same scholars will talk about the imperfections of using "Hispanic"—defining it as a marker of linguistic or colonialist historical origins rather than race—they are as quick as the federal government to categorize, introduce, and regard you as "black Hispanic."

You will meet other black Latinos who carefully differentiate and segregate themselves from African Americans. You'll know them because they are the ones who will only speak to you in Spanish and will not look or speak to the African Americans in the room. The same way other Latinos speak of "los otras" to mean "white people," "los otras" between Afro Latinos is code for "African Americans." At first it is a difficult concept to understand, but it should be implicit if you were raised in an Afro Latino household or have the privilege of watching Afro Latino mothers attempt to scold away laziness, provocative behavior or dress, and slovenliness by suggesting la vida "como los otras" is far less desirable and therefore unacceptable.

"Do you want to end up como los otras?" is thrown into the air like an incantation—set out like a vela—meant to ward off poverty, ignorance, incarceration, unwanted pregnancy, drug abuse, and—possibly the most important—misidentification as non-Latino. Por si las moscas, jefe, see it long and often enough and you will find yourself quoting from the same Baldwin essay that illuminated US blackness for you: "You know, it's not the world that was my oppressor, because what the world does to you, if the world does it to you long enough and effectively enough, you begin to do to yourself."

Entonces, it is when you are looking directly at a face and a body that looks so much like yours it could be your brother's that you are told what it is you have inherited. Rarely, when he asks you where you are from, is it not presented at the level of a challenge. It is a question about what you got that he didn't, what is more available to you and less available to him. Chico, he is checking your tongue—your background, your cultural heritage—because if it is not as black as his, he is looking for an opportunity to remind you that everything else about you is, as if you didn't know.

Concede a body suspended in a space, pedestalized and policed for the suspicions it generates independent of itself. Imagine a space in which "suspicions" are only mediated by "innocence." Pero, the difference between the two—"suspect" and "innocent"—is marginal at best in the ways in which they need each other to exist, and the mediation between the two is enacted on the body without ever engaging it. Therefore, the possible innocence of any black male infant is floated as suspect of what it might grow into. Por cierto, as the boy grows, it is a body that will be more likely than others to be asked if it knows anything about missing wallets, televisions, petty cash, and cars; more likely than others, it will be asked where to buy reefer even if it doesn't smoke; more likely than others, it will be expected to know where to procure a prostitute.

Claro, in fact, it is a body more often than not associated with most notions of criminality, unless of course the offense could cause the country to change its political direction, bring a Fortune 500 company to its knees, or otherwise be defined as a "white-collar" offense. Toss all caution to the wind and contemplate a country in which black male bodies only constitute approximately 6.8 percent of the total population, yet nearly 40.1 percent of the prison population, and according to the US Criminal Justice System, one in every fifteen men and one in every thirty-six "Hispanic" men are incarcerated in comparison to one in every one hundred and six white men. According to the Bureau of Justice Statistics, one in three black men can expect to go to prison in their lifetimes. Not terribly dissimilar to Cuba, the United States you will find is a country that can attribute—but doesn't—its entrance into modernity on the backs of slave labor, though at the same time it is a country in which more black men are incarcerated than were slaves. Yet their violence, their vitriol, their anxiety, their fear, and their anger are more often described when linked with their criminality—their rebellion and distrust and tears—as being generated from what will be named in the media as "senseless." As with US slave heritage, hip-hop music, poverty, welfare, poor education, float yourself over the Bay of Biscayne and "senseless" too becomes part of the lack of agency that is assumed of your body until you prove otherwise.

Even with a body that looks like yours in the White House, you will meet other men who share bodies similar to both his and yours who still speak of "the man." Y, cuídate ese, you will need to learn that it means "white," you will need to know that it is the stealth signifier of your oppressor as well as your ignorance. Because the same brothers who will tell you that you are being "brought down," "kept down," "kept in your place by the man" will ask you if you think you are "better" or somehow more privileged than they are because your tongue does not operate the same way theirs do. They are the

13

ones, not "the man," who will tell you that you are not black enough when you reveal your mamá did not put the same dishes on her dinner table as theirs, or your musical tastes fall into categories they don't recognize. They are the closest monitors and police of your body, and they will tell you "You need to choose" whether you are black or Latino as if you could separate the two. They will school you on what "the man" says, tell you what it means, warn you about being hauled into jail just for walking down the street, chained to a truck and dragged down a dirt road in the South, and derided and infantilized for "the man's" entertainment when you work alongside him even if you are his supervisor. And they will teach you the ways of "the man" the same way they teach their way to their sons and nephews—the way they learned it—by using the same language they heard from their fathers and their fathers' fathers, who learned it from "the man."

Unlike actresses like Melissa De Sousa, Lauren Vélez, Esperanza Spalding, Zoe Saldana, or Rosario Dawson, por ejemplo, because, as a man, you will be sexualized differently, you too will regard them as beautiful—without regard for their accomplishments—just for existing in the world, and without needing to recognize the line that marks that which is perceived as domitable from the indomitable. And unlike the scores of white male celebrities of negligible talent, an accomplishment as great as consistently hitting from the three-point mark in the NBA will be required of you before you too can be listed as one of *People* magazine's Most Beautiful. And the moment you begin to question why the value placed on the performances of black male bodies is lower than those placed on black females, remember, Jessye Norman has sung the roles of Aida, Alceste, and Ariadne on the stage of the Metropolitan Opera Theater in New York; in the 1990s, Kathleen Battle gave highly critically acclaimed performances of Mozart, Handel, and Donizetti on the same stage; however, ese, you are moving to a country in which, on the same stage, the title role of Verdi's *Othello* has a tradition of being sung by tenors in blackface. Assume, in this country, that the combination of your body and your voice, even when you are silent, arouses suspicion. And, black as you are, you bring no translatable experience with you that explains the possibilities of something different to "the man" or those who reify what "the man" says. There is no cognate, no comprehendible similar experience here where you will be told you can't do something new because it has never been done before, and that misremembering seems to be the same as dis-remembering.

It is similar to *negro*, which you only know to mean *love* in the Caribbean, never quite finding a place here without an explanation. Here, all that is heard when you say it is what your body was called before it was "black," which it was called before it was called "African American." The difference, mi negro, between our *negro* and their *negro* is the line of demarcation between *love* and *hate, affection* and *derision, the past* and *the present*. It's black and white.

Oye, negrito, you will need to learn *nigger* in all its valences, acclimatize yourself to be prepared to know when it is calling you to fight, fuck, or just go out and play pool and get drunk. Pero, without a lifetime of hearing it—like American football will seem to you— understanding it or getting a clear explanation of what it is may be as illusory and abstract as attempting to describe to a yanqui who is trying to learn Spanish the differences between *por y para*.

Unless you choose to settle outside Miami or parts of Manhattan, the majority of your experiences with your native language will be had with non-Cubans. The need to have some part of yourself that is never expressed or never can be expressed, something that you will never find the words for in English, will outweigh your cultural and political differences, and the outcome is a coalition politic that is helpful in the event that you need to lobby a congressman or a cable company to consider Spanish to be as important to their overall success as English. If you live in an area where winters are unimaginably cold—por ejemplo, Chicago or Ithaca, New York—you will take turns banding together in one of your homes; you will crank the heat up until you all can pretend it's a balmy afternoon and share each other's music, cook flautas y tortas y tortillas of your own countries and compare them; you will watch boxing and futból, and stand up at each other's weddings and become the godparents of each other's children; you'll sing the songs and tell the stories that have always seemed part of your life, and you will do it all in a language that is neither Cuban nor, for that matter, Spanish. It is something that sounds

15

more like what you hear on Telemundo or Univision, and will not make a whole lot of sense to you at first—particularly if you have an argentino or two in your group—but eventually it will start to sound like home.

If you live in California around chicanos, you will find you will start to sound like a chicano, and their social concerns will become yours. Move to San Juan de Puerto Rico or Lorraine, Ohio, and the same will happen. It all changes—nearly every sound that comes out of your mouth will. Abre la boca, and need to change in a way that you are not quite prepared for because at no time when traveling from Oriente to Pinar del Río with your major amigo would you say, "Necesitamos parking," nor would you need to have a friend who understood both what you meant and why you were saying it that way. And at no time in English could you translate "me emocionan" for someone who will also never understand, no matter which language you're speaking, why you will always have a *corazón* instead of a *heart*.

Live here long and you will understand it so well that you will be leaving friends at a bar late one night and you will find yourself saying, "Ya, me voy home," simply because there is no expedient way of saying it in Spanish. Or, possibly, because it has become a separate place from where you started. Open your mouth and, sometime afterward, you will be asked, "So, where is home?" And you'll find you hesitate, and what sticks in your throat is no longer limited to English. And you will find that it is not just a predilection discrete to yanquis.

Go back to La Habana o Santiago o Mala Noche o Holguín or wherever you set sail from, mi negro, and you will find things may have changed—buildings may have come down, the Swiss may have erected a tourist resort, a palma may have grown through the roof of what your mother may have told you was the grandest house she could imagine when she was a girl—but the air will feel the same. Smell the same. You will remember a way of walking and holding yourself that until you are back on the island you have reserved for the island. You will speak to everyone in a normal voice, without ever thinking to remove its natural basso as you open up your face and raise your eyebrows because you found that it calms white girls who are waiting on you in restaurants and grocery lines in Harrisburg, Pennsylvania, and Middlebury, Vermont. And you will find yourself in the middle of a conversation with a man who looks so much like you, with whom you have felt so comfortable you will have begun to call him primo or tío. He'll say something like, "¿Qué es lo que te gusta major, Tupac o Biggie?" Just say, Tupac es depinga, because his next question is to ask you where you are from. If you tell him "here," he'll tell you, "No . . . it's close," meaning your Spanish, "but it's not from here."

Oye, negro, you'll tell yourself that it's your shoes, that the Nikes that you hadn't thought anything about had given you away. Or the Levi's you wore or your haircut. But if it is a legal trip—one in which you cross back through US Customs—you will recognize the same face you met at José Martí Airport as you and others who looked like you were ushered through Special Customs designated for those who left the island. It is a scan that moves over you head to toe before it meets you in the eye and, coño, waits for your narrative.

Three Berlin Essays
Aleš Šteger

—*Translated from Slovenian by Brian Henry*

CRACK BERLIN

WHEN SOMEONE'S PRESENCE on the street becomes imperceptible as the presence of the street becomes imperceptible in this person. Mommsenstraße, Kastanienallee, Akazienstraße have moved to the shady side, to the side of obvious everyday life, going from admiration of exceptional things to inventory. Within the least expected lurks alienation, which demonstrates that it is only for the illusion of tradition, the illusion, that keeps my attention on a short leash. Sometimes it is enough that some bored dog barks. Midflinch I see at the intersection an excursion bus. A tourist guide with microphone in hand eagerly explains. I cannot hear the words, but I have a feeling I know everything she relates. Facing forward alongside the driver, with a gaze firmly directed through the front pane. This guide is me. Since I left the apartment, this continuous speech is performed in me. I speak and speak, without a dictionary and a map, aimlessly loafing. Only when the bus moves forward do I notice that it's empty, except for the driver and guide in the bus there is no one the relating would be intended for, no one in this city of three and a half million who would hear what I speak and speak, only my footsteps and my monologue. To be discovered by the feeling of home in some foreign city? I lie in an empty room. Only one door, one window, one bed, me lying, naked walls, the space around me. Four meters above me the ceiling, on it a map of cracks, leafing through paint. As if names would fall off the streets, which I walked during the day, bringing me a child's fear before the unknown. The slow sliding of white vowels in the light, which is falling through the window. The slow sliding of me, who is falling through the crack in the ceiling, through the crack with the name Berlin. But I am not hit, am not broken, not this time, as the alcohol and pills and depression trembled the hands of Ingeborg Bachmann, here somewhere, in 1963. Slightly dazed but safe I slip through the crack of my monologues, words turn in me like the heads of newborns sleeping in an unknown place. In the dark hallway I grope for a light switch. As if seized by my hand itself, I am guided over the house's creaky steps to the large door to the study. I turn on a light and translate: *Daß es gestern schlimmer war als es heute ist,* That it was worse yesterday than it is today, *wieder kein Anschluß, die Anschlüsse sind da,* again no connection, the connections are here, *aber es wird nicht angeschlossen,* but no one connected. Berlin is a monster. Berlin is the most beautiful city in the world. Both sentences are valid and at the same time are not valid. Like spoiled children they lean on me and demand, demand. I am still a tourist guide who talks and talks to an empty bus. But with weeks, with months of strolling around Mommsenstraße, around Kastanienallee, around Akazienstraße beside a babbling guide I also became this void in the bus, this hollow, unknown law surrendered to stillness, by which words spread without leaving some trace. Domestication? Home? *In der Mauerritze habe ich,* In a moment of terror, *in der Schrecksekunde,* in the crack in the wall, *einen schwarzen Käfer gesehen,* I saw a black beetle, *der stellt sich tot,* pretending it was dead, *Ich möchte sprechen mit ihn,* I want to speak with him, *aus diesem feinen Haus ihm den Ausweg,* show him the way out of this fine, *zeigen, ihm einen Ausweg zeigen,* house, show him out, *oder ihn gleich zertreten,* or just trample him on the spot, *Ich lerne von ihm, ich stelle,* I am learning from him, I pretend, *mich tot, in diese Ritze Berlin fallen,* that I am dead, am falling into this crack Berlin, *verlaufen auf diesem Planeten,* am lost on this planet. Translating words, I carry them from German into Slovenian, break them, spin them, just like I spin the map of Berlin, it turns me, searches me, moves me from place to place. The words of someone who died the year when I was born. Words of despair and loss in some city, which has the same name as the city in which I am now alone. Words of despair and loss, which could also be mine, which could be from everyone. In the middle of the night I lie down in them, in these words, and next to my whispering of Slovenian verses in these words lies also a quiet music. It penetrates from the floor above, now I recognize it, light as May air, it is "The Girl from Ipanema" who in the middle of the night penetrates through the crack Berlin, through the terrible, through the loveliest crack Berlin.

NOTE. The German phrases are from poems by Ingeborg Bachmann. The English translations that follow are translated from the Slovenian, not the original German.

Aleš Šteger

DRAGONS AND TRANSVESTITES

Above the entrance it says RUSSIAN BOOKS, but inside in the half
light a leg immediately stumbles against Chinese pots, packages of
Taiwanese plastic pistols, and heaps of socks *made in India*. Grab
what you want, it reminds everyone who wanders into this place, so
that some of the Slavic brothers from the taiga receive very specific
socialization, in which a child places his melancholic head in the
lap of Mother Rossi, while small sickles and hammers, which push
against her apron, cause chronic allergies. Slovenians don't really understand Polish, Czech, or Baltic *ressentiment* for a Slavic Gulliver.
We were not close enough to hate. Thus, with unnecessary justification I pay for Russian vodka in a Finnish bottle, and while leaving
the caravan get caught in the strings of a sailing dragon, which hangs
from the ceiling, as if I were caught in the trap of national stereo-
types. Already the display window of the neighboring sex shop cor-
rects the design of the labyrinth in which the thought trudges. A
plastic doll of a man dressed in women's underwear. Who is a Slav,
who German? Berlin is the city of national transvestism. With Prussian fastidiousness the Russian arranges his own boutique with
select haute couture, the German grows a beard like some Orthodox
priest and goes on foot to Moscow. Isn't the most awful notion of
death death by drowning? And isn't language teaching us that the
bodies of two during lovemaking are decanted? If water is a metaphor
for annihilation and love, then Berlin is bound to its mirror image
by the Marzahn well, discovered at the site of the first Berlin settle-
ments. It is inconspicuously located in the dusty ground floor of the
Märkisches Museum by the Chinese embassy. The yawn of a guard
and the solitude of a visitor, who first followed his every step, as if
the guest wanted to demonstrate in vivo the methods of the East
German secret police Stasi. The Slavs who settled this area placed
the well on the remains of a German well. The stones are loaded and
broken, dilapidated wood replaces the arm of now one, now another
tribe. Only water in the well remains, water, which turns Berlin into
a city of transformations and changed identities. Water, for he who
comes to Berlin for the first time, is the greatest surprise and revelation. Berlin floats on rivers and lakes, though never boastfully, rather
timid. Unlike the swaggering water of Venice, St. Petersburg, Amsterdam, this city isn't standing on its toes, so that it's leaning over its
extreme edge to better see Narcissus's face. History, the movements

20

of nations, forced relocation, today's newcomers, tomorrow's losers, and yesterday's winners have shattered the mirror of this city. Only water, in which a fractured face looks, now and again pours together shattered pieces, but not in the majesty of harbors, fountains, and central promenades, rather in the lake, bordered by willows and lindens, ponds, beside which children play, banks of dreamy rivers with stalls with drinks and deck chairs arranged on the packed sand. Berlin has changed. From a man it became a woman, from a woman a man. From the capital of the world, from the Nazi capital Germania it became a group of suburbs, full of residents who are self-ironic and skeptical toward definitions of identity. Generation P is in Berlin a generation who still has a *P* in the word Prussia. Let the paws of plastic bears in Berlin amble up and down, the name of the national capital of transvestites comes from behind the Urals.

NEXT, PLEASE

Someone who sits in the first S-Bahn car, which runs west, will see at the Tiergarten station the mighty six-lane June 17 Road, how it slices up the city as if on command and vanishes beneath his knees. The widest road of Berlin, once Allee nach Berlin, after 1933 the east-west axis of the Reich's capital. June 17 was attributed suppressed demonstrations by residents of the capital of the German Democratic Republic against their government in 1953. The avenue is bordered by imposing cast-iron lanterns. This is all that remains in Berlin of Albert Speer, the Führer's architect and engineer of the conversion of Berlin to the capital of Germania. The marble that once covered Hitler's government palace designed by Speer now clothes the imposing monument of wings of Soviet victory in Treptow and columns of memorials to Soviet honor in Tiergarten, but the street lights apparently do not bother anyone. A bird's-eye view of the road's axis is like a length of taut elastic around a child's legs, jumping wide-eyed over it in a game of rubber twist. I had just jumped, but stumbled at the next figures, in front of the memorial to murdered Jews. The double brick trail in the asphalt, a pair of student's fingers raised during history class in a question mark, climbs from the river, rises by the stairs next to the Reichstag, and, by the inconceivable logic of liberation and zigzagging negotiations in the middle of the road, jumps onto the sidewalk. As if they hadn't torn down the wall, but

21

only sunk it into the ground. For some time I stood in western Europe, then my feet pushed simultaneously from the ground, as if jumping over more than four decades, in lingering waves from the past and attentiveness and play. I jumped over the trace of the Berlin Wall on the east, like some Peter Schlemihl who nearly tripped over his shadow and fell. Where? Perhaps into the white zone, which not long ago on the city plans, hanging in underground stations in western Berlin, was labeling eastern parts of the city. But rather than ride the underground or S-Bahn I take a bus. When a literary colleague and I get off some evening near Kaiserdamm, she looks down June 17 Road, where clouds have decorated with April's evening colors the Siegessäule with its golden Elsa and Bruno Ganz on top. I walked here in the eighties nearly every day, she says, but not until 1989 did I notice the tall red-brick city hall, which burns brightly in the evening light in the east. The building stood equally visible twenty years earlier, but I didn't see it because it didn't belong to my hemisphere. The wall does not divide only what we can and cannot see, it divides primarily what we want to see and what we do not. A little later, like the second in line in a bank, I reach the red stripe on the ground. It is a pleasure not standing behind it as behind a barrier. I stand with both feet on it and take a breath like a child in the instant of excitement and concentration before a crucial combination of jumps. When I hear, *Next, please,* my feet are again entangled, red tape on the floor has stuck to my soles, we don't want to let go of each other.

Customer Reviews
Christie Hodgen

(★★) IN A WORD: DISAPPOINTING by Nathan W.

DATING CHRISTIE HODGEN was OK, though not as great as I hoped. First of all, she doesn't look anything like the picture she posted, which is quite a few years old and taken from a forgiving angle with a forgiving lens. In the picture she's smiling—laughing, really—her head angled away from the camera toward someone she loves, probably her ex. But in real life, straight on, she's got a humorless face, long and narrow and pale, the kind of face you'd expect on a librarian. And not only is she not smiling in real life, she looks like someone who hasn't smiled in a long time. She looks like the director of a national campaign against smiling.

Conversation was OK, though again I was expecting better. The first two dates were fine, because we'd read many of the same books and pretty much stuck to talking about those. But we were just saying all the obvious things, recycling what we'd learned in school, or the opinions we'd heard at parties and on the radio. Ayn Rand? *Oh, please.* Hemingway? *Sort of/mostly.* Kafka, Woolf, Faulkner? *Well, duh.*

One thing that really bothers me about Christie Hodgen is that she tends to start her sentences with phrases like *It's commonly held that . . .* and never really puts forward an opinion of her own. I asked her once what she thought about all of these supposed memoirs on the market—this whole genre of apologia full of drug addiction and abusive relationships and mental illness—that in the end turn out to be bullshit. *Is it fraud?* I asked her. *Is it artistic license?* And she was like: *That's the question. That's exactly the question.*

Try to get beyond the arts section of *The Times*, and conversation can be difficult. Maybe it's because she doesn't have a television. Or because she grew up in a tiny village in Canada and doesn't share the same cultural references we do. There's just nothing to latch on to. She never saw a single episode of *Seinfeld*, for instance, and doesn't even know who Johnny Carson is. Whenever you mention something like that her eyes kind of shift upward, like there's a clue on

23

the ceiling she's trying to decipher, but she always comes up blank. *There was only one television in our entire village,* she'll say. Or, *We didn't have electricity.* It's charming the first couple of times, but eventually it just makes you feel like you're trapped in a Berlitz class, fumbling around for something to say.

Another problem is that Christie Hodgen doesn't have a car. Normally this would mean you would pick her up at her house for a date, but she won't tell you where she lives—you have to pick her up at a gas station in her neighborhood. Supposedly this is a precaution she takes because of her kid. *I just can't go giving away information like that,* she says. *You never know when someone's going to turn out to be an ax murderer. Or a pedophile. Or an arsonist.* I understood at first, but after a while it was like, Jesus.

Christie Hodgen won't let you meet her kid. She says this is because the phrase *my mom's boyfriend* strikes terror into her heart, and she never, ever wants to hear it coming out of her kid's mouth. She's the kind of person who thinks about her life strictly in terms of her kid's future memoir. Everything she does, and doesn't do, is because she's trying to inspire, or avoid inspiring, chapters in this eventual memoir. For instance, she takes her kid out to breakfast every Sunday, to set up material for this nice chapter: *Pancakes with Mom!* And the only reason she got a dog was so that later in life her kid could look back and have all these great dog memories: *Alfred and Me!* I asked her once, in addition to *My Mom's Boyfriends,* what chapters she was trying to avoid inspiring, and she had a whole list ready. *Hey, Mom, What's in That Bottle?* was one. And: *Here Comes the Sheriff, Again.* I forget the rest, but obviously she's a person who spends a lot of time imagining things that could go wrong.

There's some kind of weird history with her ex-husband. I don't know what happened, but apparently it was bad—she made a couple of jokes about being on the evening news. He's out of the picture now—*he* doesn't even know where she lives. And you've got to figure, when something goes bad like that, on that level, it can't just be one person's fault, it has to be both.

For a while I was hoping this would turn into the best-case scenario—a low-maintenance kind of thing, dinner and sex once a week—but after two months of going out to fancy restaurants—I'm talking steaks, lobsters, bottles of wine, the works—then dropping her back off at the gas station before it was even ten o'clock, I realized that this was going absolutely nowhere. Also, you could kind of tell from the way she ate that she wouldn't be very good in bed. She kept missing her mouth and spilling things onto her lap, and food was always somehow ending up in her hair.

All in all: a bunch of weird, shapeless baggage with very little payoff.

(★) Worst Date Ever by Alan R.

First off, like Nathan W. said, she won't let you pick her up at her house, she makes you pick her up at a gas station. Real classy. And it just gets worse from there.

So I pull up and she's leaning against the side of a pay phone, reading a book, which she doesn't even look up from, even when I honk the horn. I get out of the car and introduce myself and we shake hands, which she fucks up because she's struggling to get this giant book, which must have weighed five hundred pounds, back into this little canvas grocery sack she's carrying around as a purse. Then I open her door for her and she gets in the car. Then I get in. Right away I notice she's tracked oil onto the floor mat. I mean there's so much oil she must have been standing in a puddle up to her fucking ankles.

I guess I must have been staring at the floor mat with my mouth open, because suddenly she looks down and notices the stain and she's like, *Oh, did I do that?* And I'm like, *Uh, yeah?* Then she gets all embarrassed and starts apologizing like crazy. I'm like, *It's fine, it's fine. We'll just go back to my place and see if we can get it out before it sets.* And she's like, *Of course, good idea.* I think she might have been pissed about going back to my place before dinner just because of a floor mat, but I have a very nice car and pride myself on taking good care of it. I'm a realtor and take my clients around in my car, so it's important it looks good. If we have to put off dinner for an hour, well, tough shit.

So we get back to my place and I ask her to take her boots off before she comes in, which she does, and it turns out underneath the boots she only has one sock on, this ugly white tube sock I wouldn't even let my dog play with. *Sorry*, she says, all embarrassed. *I couldn't find the other sock.*

Then it takes me forever to get this stain out. I try all kinds of things—detergent, baking soda, vinegar—but nothing works. She keeps apologizing the whole time, which really gets on my nerves. Finally I'm like, *Hey, don't worry about it. I can get a new floor mat.* She offers to pay for it, and I tell her not to worry about it now. I'll get it from her later.

So then we're late to the restaurant and have to wait at the bar because we lost our reservation. I ask her what she wants, and she says a Shirley Temple. *A Shirley Temple!* I swear, every time I thought things couldn't get any worse, she'd open her mouth and come out with something like that.

By this point in the evening something had happened to her hair. It started out OK, I guess, but somewhere along the line it got all crazy. Really big and frizzy and out of control. Half the time I couldn't even see her face when we were talking. And she started doing this thing where she kept putting her elbows on the bar and rubbing her eyes with the heels of her palms, like she'd forgotten we were in public. I asked her if she had a headache and she said no, it was just something she did sometimes. She apologized, but two minutes later she was at it again. I felt like I was out to dinner with a mental patient.

Finally we get a table, and I ask her what's she's having. *I guess just French fries,* she says. Because we're at a steak house, and it turns out she's a fucking vegetarian. See what I mean? Every time she opens her fucking mouth.

On principle, I hate vegetarians. They always act like they're these big humanitarians, like they're above everyone else because they don't participate in killing animals. But half of them—including Christie Hodgen—are walking around in leather boots. So I'm like: *What about your shoes? How come you're wearing half an animal carcass, if you're so opposed to killing animals?* And she tells me her problem with meat isn't about animal cruelty. *Kill as many cows as you want,* she said. *I don't give a shit.*

While we were waiting for our meal—which took *fucking forever*—I tried to do the usual first-date thing—Where are you from, etc.—but she wouldn't play ball, she just kept giving all these vague answers. She said she was an army brat who grew up "all over the world," but when I asked which countries she lived in, she changed the subject. She asked me about my work and I told her all about real estate, how the market was worse than ever but how I was doing better than anyone else in my office, through sheer determination and probably also because of good looks. (Hey, I can't help it.) She seemed bored, except for this one point when she asked me to repeat something I said—*for all intensive purposes*—and she got this little smirk on her face. I looked it up later and it turns out it's really *for all intents and purposes.* Well, excuse fucking me. I misspoke. Big fucking deal. At least I don't walk around looking like a fucking escaped lunatic.

All through our meal my phone kept going off—like I said I'm a realtor, so I get a lot of calls and texts—and whenever I picked up she'd pull that book out from her bag and start reading at the table. When I got off the third call she just kept reading, so I asked her what the book was about and she goes: *suffering*.

So I apologized for the phone and she told me she doesn't even have a cell phone, and keeps getting in trouble at work because she never checks her e-mail. Supposedly she has some sort of technology-based social anxiety disorder, where she can't stand interacting with any kind of device that enables people to contact her. People send her e-mails—friends whom she likes and is glad to hear from—but she's afraid of opening them for some reason. She just can't open them. She feels really, really bad about it, and it weighs on her mind for weeks and weeks, but she can't seem to do anything about it. She has to wait until some kind of mood strikes. Which is pretty fucked up if you ask me.

Things were going bad at this point so I figured I'd just throw caution to the wind and try to have some fun with it. Even when you both know you're not going to hit it off, sometimes you can still go home and fuck each other's brains out, get out some aggression—I've had this happen quite a few times. So I went for it. *By any chance do you like to fuck up the ass?* I said. And she was all: *Why, do you want me to fuck you up the ass?* Like she was so clever. Ha fucking ha.

On the way out I told her not to worry about the floor mat—she could just give me whatever cash she had in her wallet and we'd call it even—because I didn't want to have to meet up with her again. So she digs around in her bag—she kept struggling to work around the Book of Suffering—and it turns out she's walking around with three dollars. *I'm sorry*, she says, *I don't usually keep a lot of cash on me*.

And I'm like: *How can you walk around with three bucks?* It just didn't seem very smart, a single woman walking around with nothing on her.

Then she got kind of pissy. *I'm sorry, but if a little oil on your floor mat is your biggest problem in life, well, then you've got more problems than you realize.* And she storms off. Normally I would have gone after her, because I try to be a gentleman, but in this case it was like, fuck it.

Then it turns out a new floor mat costs two hundred bucks. For that and the price of dinner, you're better off going to a hooker.

Christie Hodgen

(★★) SAD, REALLY by Frank K.

I went on a date with Christie Hodgen in graduate school. I guess it wasn't even a date, technically—I just invited her out after this one class, where a story she'd written was up for workshop and everyone hated it. The worst part was, it was one of those stories you could tell was true, was based on her actual life. It was about growing up in a crummy apartment building in Hackensack, with a weird mother, and how she had this old neighbor across the hall named James, who was her only salvation from the dreariness and mediocrity of life, etc., etc. The two of them would always go up to the rooftop and drink and philosophize about the world. And then one day while they were philosophizing, just like that, James jumped off the roof and killed himself. It was one of the first classes of the semester, and everyone was still trying to impress the teacher, so they went on and on about everything they hated. Christie Hodgen was just sitting there with her head in her hands, and I felt really bad for her. You could tell she was sort of hoping the teacher would step in and tell everyone that they were wrong, that the story was brilliant, but instead what happened was that when everyone had finally run out of things to complain about, the teacher held Christie Hodgen's story up by one corner and sort of dangled it in front of the class. *This*, he said, *is the kind of shit I hate.*

After class she kind of ran out of the room. Like I said, I felt really bad for her, so I caught up with her and asked her if she wanted to go out for a drink. *I don't know*, she said. She had this confused look on her face. *I guess I could, for a minute, if you want.* The funny thing was, she acted like I was putting her out, like she was doing me a favor.

We walked to the nearest bar and she ordered this drink, some kind of pink lemonade thing that was eight ounces of pure alcohol. This didn't seem like a good idea to me, because on the way to the bar she'd mentioned she wasn't much of a drinker, and she also weighed about a hundred pounds. I was worried she'd end up passing out and I'd have to carry her home, which is pretty much what happened.

For a few minutes it was just the two of us and we were having the usual grad-school conversation—which teachers we liked, what we were reading—and I felt like I was getting to know her, which was kind of exciting because absolutely nobody knew Christie Hodgen— she never came to any meetings or parties and hardly ever showed up to class. But then a group of people from our class came in and joined us, and the conversation went off in another direction. Mostly

28

people talked about our professor and how much they hated him. Christie Hodgen was quiet the whole time. She was laughing at everything everyone said, but when she laughed she covered her face with her hands, like she couldn't stand to be seen laughing.

After a while I could tell that Christie Hodgen was really drunk—her eyes were kind of glazed over and she was swaying a little in her seat—but she kept insisting she was fine. At one point I was like: *How many fingers am I holding up?* and she was like: *Somewhere between one and ten.*

Then someone asked her about her childhood, and she started going off about the crazy mother in Hackensack. She told us how her mother was an agoraphobic who made her living as a phone-sex worker. The phone would ring at all hours, and Christie Hodgen would lie in bed, listening to her mother making all these filthy noises. She said that all through her childhood, her mother used to talk to her through this ventriloquized teddy bear named Simon. The mother never talked to her directly, only through the bear, which spoke in a high, creepy voice. The bear was always criticizing Christie Hodgen, like: *Why don't you ever brush your hair, it looks like shit!* It was really her mom talking, but they both pretended it was the bear. And she'd go to the bear, *Why are you so mean to me all the time?* And the bear would be like, *Because you deserve it, you piece of shit!*

One day when her Mom was on the phone, Christie Hodgen cut the bear's head off with a steak knife. Then she didn't know what to do, so she hid the bear and its head in her closet. Later her mother went nuts looking for the bear—apparently the mother had some choice insults for Christie Hodgen that she couldn't express without the bear's help—and when she couldn't find it, all hell broke loose. Evidently there was some kind of physical violence.

The whole time Christie Hodgen was talking she was very animated and jovial, and for a while we were laughing along, but by the end it wasn't funny anymore. *That's awful*, someone said, and Christie Hodgen kind of stopped midsentence. It was seriously awkward. All of a sudden she got up and said she was going to use the bathroom, but she never came back to the table. Later, when we left the bar, we saw her a little ways down the street, passed out on the sidewalk.

So there was a debate in the group about whether to carry her home or just leave her there. It was raining, which made some people want to help her, and others not want to help her because they didn't want to get soaked. In the end we decided to help, but no one

29

had the slightest idea where she lived. We had to go through her bag. She had a wallet with three dollars in it and didn't even have a license. Luckily there was an electric bill stuffed into a book, and luckily the address wasn't far. I took her under the arms, and one of the other guys took her feet. You wouldn't believe how long it took us to carry her home. I kept thinking she'd wake up, with the rain and all the jostling we had to do, but she was out cold.

When we got to her place—she lived in a converted garage behind an old Victorian—we had to go through her bag again to get her keys. But there weren't any. So we went through her pockets and still nothing. Then one of the girls pulled on this red string around her neck, and it turns out that's where she kept her key, just like a kid. She's the only person I ever met with just a single key.

Inside the garage there was a mattress on the floor, and piles of books stacked everywhere, and a card table with folding chairs with a manual typewriter on it. While the girls were getting her settled, I snuck a look at what Christie Hodgen had been typing. It was a list of things she was working on. *Stop biting the inside of your cheek when people are talking to you. Try to look people in the eye.* Things like that.

I remember as we were leaving I had the distinct impression that something bad was going to happen to her. Like, spectacularly bad. Someday some boyfriend would cut her head off. Or she'd get roofied somewhere and wake up in a Dumpster with her kidney missing. But it looks like the worst that happened was she got old and never really accomplished as much as she hoped and started getting confused about what was real and what she'd made up, and is living kind of a sad life.

(★) SOMETHING IS SERIOUSLY WRONG HERE by Philip R.

I met Christie Hodgen in a coffee shop and asked her for her phone number, and she said she didn't have a phone. So I asked her for her e-mail address. For some reason her e-mail address is under a different name—DorotheaBrooke—which I figured was probably fake. But when I e-mailed her she wrote back and agreed to go out. Five minutes before we were supposed to meet she e-mailed me—e-mailed!—saying her kid was sick and she couldn't make it. Of course I didn't get the e-mail in time, but when I did, it was super nice and apologetic, and I really felt like it was just a little bit of bad luck. So we rescheduled for a week later, but she wrote that day and said her kid was still sick. We set another date for the following week, but supposedly her babysitter fell through. By this time I was dating someone else so could have cared less. But I just thought it was weird that she couldn't even turn down a date—she had to blame it on her kid. Grow the fuck up!

(★★★) GIVE HER A BREAK by Anonymous

I never dated Christie Hodgen, but I knew her for a while and feel like I can offer at least as good a review as the rest of you. I'm not here to dispute that she's probably not a very good person to go out with. But it seems like somebody should come forward and say a few sympathetic things about her, if not as a date then at least as a human being.

I first met Christie Hodgen when she moved into my neighborhood about a year ago, right after her divorce. It was summer when she moved in, and I kept seeing her and her kid and dog walking around, the kid on a scooter and Christie Hodgen with the dog on a leash (if you're willing to call a miniature dachshund a dog). I guess they caught my eye because Christie Hodgen and her kid look almost the exact same—they're both tall and wiry, with this crazy, messed-up hair, and they're both always wearing the same thing, all black, like they're in permanent, nineteenth-century mourning. It sort of made a funny picture, something that stuck in your mind.

Then the school year started up and I realized that our kids went to the same school—I'd always see her and her dog standing around the school parking lot waiting for the kids to be released. When the bell rang, the kids came out in droves, and Christie Hodgen's dog would start going berserk, barking like crazy at any kid who got near it. The weird thing was that Christie Hodgen never did anything to get the dog under control—she just stood there scanning the crowd for her kid, with this perfectly impassive look on her face. Again, sort of a funny picture.

Then one morning while the kids were at school, and I was out raking leaves, Christie Hodgen walked her dog past my house, and as soon as the dog saw me, he started going nuts. He practically pulled her arm off trying to get at me, and Christie Hodgen was like, *Alfred, shut the fuck up!* But he wouldn't stop barking and pulling on the leash, and she just kept yelling at him: *Shut the fuck up!* Finally, for no discernible reason, the dog just stopped and sat itself down, and she stood there covering her face with her hands. *I'm so sorry*, she said. *I don't know what to do about this dog. He keeps going crazy and I'm at my wit's fucking end.* I remember that phrase exactly. *Wit's fucking end.* That's one thing I like about her. She's always putting *fuck* where you wouldn't expect it.

You can take it to a class, I said. *Like, an obedience class.* I was just trying to be helpful, but it seemed to make things worse—she sort of started crying.

I know, she said. *But I can't be bothered.* She stood there with her face in her hands. It was probably less than a minute but it was so awkward, it felt like much longer.

Then she recovered, and introduced herself, and I told her I'd seen her in the school parking lot. We started talking, and before I knew it I was walking her dog with her. I was newly divorced too, and didn't mind telling someone about all the misery my ex and I had put each other through. The next day I sort of watched out for her and, sure enough, she was walking the dog again. So I went out and joined her. Pretty soon we had made a habit of it.

Mostly Christie Hodgen talked about her kid. She was enormously preoccupied with the fear of ruining her daughter, and was always saying things like: *My kid's future therapist is probably in med school right now. God, I hope he's paying attention.* Basically Christie Hodgen saw herself as a fuckup, someone who couldn't get her act together, and she worried that her personal flaws—her social and technological anxieties, her forgetfulness and whatnot—would end up having dangerous consequences. One day she was upset because she had forgotten to go to the grocery store, and ended up having to feed her kid potato chips for breakfast. *Potato chips!* she kept saying. *She'd be better off raised by wolves.*

On one of our walks—after her dog had gone crazy on another dog—Christie Hodgen fell into despair again about the lack of discipline and order and structure in her life, about her inability to control anything, and she blurted out that her ex-husband was in a mental facility. That one day, after they'd been fighting and miserable for years, he'd just snapped—just woken up catatonic, shuffling around like Jack Nicholson after his lobotomy in *One Flew over the Cuckoo's Nest.* It was her fault, she said, because she'd made him so miserable. *I just ruin everything*, she said. *Everything I touch turns to shit.*

That's not true! I said. Because friends say things like that.

But you don't even know me, she said. Which was also true.

Knowing her insofar as I did, I had to admit it was possible that every-thing she touched turned to shit. I mean, I didn't have a whole lot of evidence to the contrary.

So we walked like this, every morning for a couple of months, and I really felt like we had become friends, like we were building some-thing. But then we spent Thanksgiving together, and suddenly it was all over.

My wife had the kids and Christie Hodgen said she was free be-cause her ex's parents had driven up from Texas to visit him at his halfway house, and had taken the kid to visit her father for the day. *Thanksgiving at the Nuthouse, she said. I can't wait to read all about it.* It's true what Nathan W. said—she was always coming up with chapter names for her kid's eventual memoir.

We spent a nice afternoon eating Chinese food and drinking wine and watching W. C. Fields movies. But at the end of the third movie—*It's a Gift*—Christie Hodgen kind of lost it. This is a movie in which Fields plays a haberdasher who risks his family's savings to buy an orange grove in California. All through the movie, everything goes wrong for Fields—his business fails, his family hates him, his invest-ment turns out to be a sad plot as barren as the face of the moon—but at the very end, by a fantastic coincidence, he strikes it rich and lives out his dream. As Fields sat there in his white suit, at the edge of his orange grove, drinking juice that had been squeezed that very morning, Christie Hodgen blurted out: *It's bullshit like this that really kills you.* She said that the difference between life and the movies was that everything worked out in the end in movies. But in real life, things went from bad to worse, and just kept going.

Then she went on for over an hour about all the jobs she'd lost because of stupid mistakes she'd made. Like this one time when she was a waitress at this fancy restaurant in Maine, and accidentally spilled a lobster on George Bush's lap. Or this other time when she got fired from a doctor's office because every time she walked a patient back to an exam room, she'd turn out the lights on her way out and leave the patient sitting in the dark. The doctors kept com-plaining about it and she vowed to stop doing it, but she couldn't. Supposedly it was a habit having to do with her mom, who worked at an electric company and had trained Christie Hodgen to shut off every superfluous light. *I suppose everything goes back to my mom,* she said. *Which is why I'm so afraid of fucking up my kid.*

Then she told me she was about to get fired from her current job, because her students had started complaining about her. Apparently she had started throwing chalk at them in the middle of lectures, because they were texting while she was talking about Kafka, or because they'd fallen asleep while she was talking about Virginia Woolf. Recently she'd thrown a kid's cell phone out a fifth-floor window, and he'd blown up at her and they'd started yelling at each other. She told the kid to go fuck himself and threw him out, and he went home and told his mom, and his mom called the department and then the dean. Christie Hodgen said she probably would have gotten off with a slap on the wrist—the other teachers sort of regarded her as a hero, for the cell-phone bit—but then in the meeting with the dean, when the dean said she would have to take an anger-management class and cycle through other HR protocols, she told the dean to go fuck *himself*. She'd been suspended from the last few weeks of classes and was expecting a termination letter in the mail any day. She said she didn't know what happened, she'd just been on a really short fuse lately, since her divorce.

And that's just work, she said. *Don't even get me started about my personal life.* She told me about all the dates she'd gone on since her divorce, how awful they were, all the mistakes she made, her shyness and awkwardness. She told me all about the floor mat, and how it had sort of ruined things for her—how she just couldn't bring herself to go out on another date. And she told me about her problem with lying—embellishment, really, she said—how it had started out as something she did for her job, enhancing and dramatizing all kinds of things, and how it had bled over into her personal life, how in an effort to be more interesting to people, more colorful, she'd started telling stories—like she owed it to people to be more interesting than she actually was—and before she knew it, she just couldn't stop.

She was quiet for a few minutes and sat with her eyes closed. I thought she might have passed out. But then she started up again. *I didn't get into trouble at work,* she said. *I didn't throw chalk or throw a kid's cell phone out the window—I just WANT to do those things, I want to do them so badly I can see them playing out in my mind.* She started rubbing her eyes, just the way Alan R. described. *And my ex isn't even in a mental facility,* she said. *He's perfectly fine. He sees our daughter two nights a week. It was just that the divorce was so strange—it was just so strange to get to a place with someone you married, where you don't even recognize the other person anymore, where they're a stranger, when there's all this history, all this work you've done together to build your life, and the history compels you but the future, when you look at it, is just dreadful, there's nothing but dread—and it doesn't make any sense,* she said. She was kind of blubbering at this point, and hard to understand. *How you can love someone and then not. Desperately and then not. And it's like the life you lived together never happened. It's like the only person who ever knew you suddenly doesn't anymore. It just doesn't make any fucking sense. There's no other way to understand it except to tell yourself that the other person went crazy. That the other person snapped and became someone else. You just have to tell yourself that the person you married is gone, that they're locked away in some facility and you'll never be able to see them again. You can look through the barred windows all you want, you won't see them, you won't even catch a glimpse of them. They're just gone. And the worst thing is, it's your own fault. It's your own fault.*

I tried to think of something to say to console her, to tell her that it wasn't all that bad. The only problem was, I felt the same way about my divorce and couldn't really think of anything to say to the contrary. But as it turned out I didn't need to say anything, because quite suddenly she got up and ran out of the house.

After that I didn't see her for a couple of days. Finally I caught her in the school parking lot and she was very apologetic and embarrassed for having talked so much. *I was so drunk,* she said, *I don't even remember what I said. I'm so sorry I talked so much.* I told her it was OK—that we were friends and that's what friends did. But when she saw her kid she sort of slipped away, and I had a feeling she was so embarrassed she'd never talk to me again.

The last time I saw Christie Hodgen was at the kids' Christmas concert, in the school gym. She arrived late and didn't get a seat and had to sit on the floor off to the side. I was sitting pretty close to her and tried to wave to get her attention, but she didn't see me. While the younger kids were singing their songs, Christie Hodgen was flipping through a magazine, which was kind of rude. But when her kid's grade filed onto the stage, Christie Hodgen raised up on her knees, almost like she was praying. I'm hard-pressed to describe the expression on her face—I guess the word would be *rapt.* Her kid's grade was singing "O Holy Night." The kids were bad singers, of course, but something about their little voices was moving, especially toward the end when they hit the high notes. When they got to the last bit, Christie Hodgen started crying—really crying. She had her face buried in her hands and was shaking. Tears worked their way through her fingers and down her wrists and were falling to the floor—you could actually see a little puddle of tears. She kept crying even after the kids finished and the curtain fell and the lights came up and everyone got up from their seats and started bustling around. About half the audience was staring at her and she just stayed there on her knees, crying. My own personal theory was that she spent so much time worrying about fucking up her kid that when she saw something good—something beautiful—she couldn't handle it. I wanted to go up to her and say something—you could tell a few people were thinking about it—but I also knew it was the kind of thing she'd be embarrassed about later—so embarrassed that she'd probably move across town, switch schools. Which is exactly what happened. I never saw her again.

I guess what I'm trying to say here is that yes, this is a fucked-up person, someone deserving of criticism and even ridicule. But we should try our best to be kind, to be forgiving. We shouldn't forget there's a real person here, behind all of these reviews. We shouldn't forget, as we meet people and go out on dates and decide—based on their appearance and conversation and social status—whether they're right for us, and even after we find that right person and make lovers, and then spouses, and then opponents and exes of them, we shouldn't forget that there is always a real person there, behind our ideas of them, a person who's trying very hard to manage all of her failings, a person who feels our judgments and criticisms far more keenly than we might imagine. I can see Christie Hodgen right now, for instance, sitting at her computer reading all of this, these embarrassing details, I can see how she regrets them, how she winces at them, so deft they are, so intimate, so shameful, and it reminds me to try to be kind, to be gentle, to be forgiving, this picture I have of Christie Hodgen: pathetic, alone, flushing and slouching in front of her computer as she listens to all of your voices, this chorus of ridicule, hitting all the right notes in just the right order, how she nods her head to the tune of these complaints, so haunting and so familiar they are, as if she knows them all by heart, almost as if she had written them herself.

The Collected Short Stories of Freddie Prothero
Introduction by Törless Magnussen, PhD

Peter Straub

THE PRESENT VOLUME presents in chronological order every known short story written by Frederick "Freddie" Prothero. Of causes that must ever remain obscure, he died "flying solo," his expression for venturing out in search of solitude, in a field two blocks from his house in Prospect Fair, Connecticut. His death took place in January 1988, nine months before his ninth birthday. It was a Sunday. At the hour of his death, approximately four o'clock of a bright, cold, snow-occluded day, the writer was wearing a hooded tan snowsuit he had in fact technically outgrown; a red woolen scarf festooned with "pills"; an imitation Aran knit sweater, navy blue with cables; a green-and-blue plaid shirt from Sam's; dark green corduroys with cuffs beginning to grow ragged; a shapeless white Jockey T-shirt also worn the day previous; Jockey briefs, once white, now stained lemon yellow across the Y-front; white tube socks; Tru-Value Velcro sneakers, so abraded as to be nearly threadbare; and black calf-high rubber boots with six metal buckles.

The inscription on the toaster-sized tombstone in Prospect Fair's spacious Gullikson & Son Cemetery reads *Frederick Michael Prothero, 1979–1988. A New Angel in Heaven.* In that small span of years, really in a mere three of those not-yet eight and a half years, Freddie Prothero went from apprenticeship to mastery with unprecedented speed, in the process authoring ten of the most visionary short stories in the English language. It is my belief that this collection will now stand as a definitive monument to the unique merits—and difficulties!—presented by the only genuine prodigy in American literature.

That Prothero's fiction permits a multiplicity of interpretations supplies a portion, though scarcely all, of its interest to both the academic and the general reader. Beginning in 1984 with childish, nearly brutal simplicity and evolving toward the more polished (though still in fact unfinished) form of expression seen in the work of his later years, these stories were apparently presented to his mother, Varda Prothero, née Barthelmy. (*Baathy, baathy, momma sai.*) In any case, Momma Baathy Prothero preserved them (perhaps after the fact?) in individual manila files in a snug, smoothly mortised and sanded cherrywood box.

As the above example demonstrates, the earliest Prothero, the stories written from his fifth to seventh years, displays the improvised variant spelling long encouraged by American primary schools. The reader will easily decipher the childish code, although I should perhaps explain that "bood gig" stands for "bad guy."

From first to last, the stories demonstrate the writer's awareness of the constant presence of a bood gig. A threatening, indeterminate figure, invested with all the terrifying power and malignity of the monster beneath a child's bed, haunts this fiction. Prothero's "monster" figure, however, is not content to confine itself to the underside of his bed. It roams the necessarily limited map of the writer's forays both within and outside of his house: that is, across his front yard; down Gerhardie Street, which runs past his house; through the supermarket he, stroller bound, visits with his mother; and perhaps above all in the shadowy, clamorous city streets he is forced to traverse with his father on the few occasions when R(andolph) Sullivan "Sully" Prothero brought him along to the law office where "Sully" spent sixty hours a week in pursuit of the partnership attained in 1996, eight years after his son's death and two prior to his own unexplained disappearance. The commuter train from Prospect Fair to Penn Station was another location favored by the omniscient shadow figure.

Though these occasions were in fact no more than an annual event (more specifically, on the Take Your Son to Work Days of 1985–86), they had a near-traumatic—no, let us face the facts and say traumatic—effect on Prothero. He pleaded, he wept, he screamed, he cowered, gibbering in terror. One imagines the mingled disdain and distress of the fellow passengers, the unsympathetic conductor. The journey through the streets to Fifty-Fourth and Madison was a horrifying trek, actually heroic on the boy's part.

A high-functioning alcoholic chronically unfaithful to his spouse, "Sully" was an absent, at best an indifferent, father. In her role as mother, Varda, about whom one has learned so much in recent years, can be counted, alas, as no better. The Fair Haven pharmacists open to examinations of their records by a scholar of impeccable credentials have permitted us to document Varda's reliance upon the painkillers Vicodin, Percodan, and Percocet. Those seeking an explanation for her son's shabby, ill-fitting wardrobe need look no further. (One wishes almost to weep. His poor little snowsuit too tight for his growing body! And his autopsy, conducted in a completely up-to-date facility in Norwalk, Connecticut, revealed that, but for a single slice of bread lightly smeared with oleomargarine, Prothero had eaten nothing at all that day. Imagine.)

In some quarters, the four stories of 1984, his fifth year, are not thought to belong in a collection of his work, being difficult to decode from their primitive spelling and level of language. Absent any narrative sense whatsoever, these very early works perhaps ought be considered poetry rather than prose. Prothero would not be the first author of significant fiction to begin by writing poems. The earliest works do, however, present the first form of this writer's themes and perhaps offer (multiple) suggestions of their emotional and intellectual significance.

Among the small number of us dedicated Protherians, considerable disagreement exists over the meaning and identification of the "Mannotmann," sometimes "Monnuttmonn." "Man not man" is one likely decipherment of the term; "Mammoth man," another. In the first of these works, "Te Styree Uboy F-R-E-D-D-I-E," or "The Story about Freddie," Prothero writes, "Ay am nott F-R-E-D-D-I-E," and we are told that Freddie, a scaredy-cat, needs him precisely because Freddie is *not* "Mannnuttmonn." "Can you hear me, everybody?" he asks: For this is a central truth. The precocious child is self-protectively separating from himself within the doubled protection of art, the only realm available to the sane mind in which such separation is possible. In story after story, we are at first informed then reminded that this literal child, our author, had entered into an awareness of self-exile so profound and insistent, so inherent to the very act of expression, as to remind us of Fernando Pessoa. *Ol droo,* he tells us: It is all true. *Ol droo,* indeed.

It should go without saying, though unhappily it cannot, that the author's statement, in the more mature spelling and diction of his sixth year, that a man "came from the sky" does not refer to the appearance of an extraterrestrial. Some of my colleagues in Prothero studies strike one as nearly as juvenile as, though rather less savvy than, the doomed, hungry little genius who so commands us all.

*

39

1984

Te Styree Uboy F-R-E-D-D-I-E

Ay am nott F-r-e-d-d-i-e. F-R-E-D-D-I-E nott be mee
Hah hah
F-R-E-D-D-I-E iss be nyce, tooo Cin yoo her mee, evvrrie
F-r-e-d-d-i-e iss scarrdiecutt fradydiecutt, nott mee Hee neid mee.
Mannnuttmonn hah scir him hah hah
Bcayuzz Monnntmonn hee eezzz naytt
BOOOO
Ol droo

Ta Sturree Ubot Monnnuttmonn

Baathy baathy momma sai baathy mi nom mommnas sai in gd dyz
    id wuzz Baaaathy
Monnoittmoon be lissen yz hee lizzen oh ho
Tnbur wz a boi nommed F-r-e-d–d-i-e sai Monnuttmon he sai
    evvrwhy inn shaar teevee taybbull rug ayr

F-R-E-D-D-I-E un Monnuttmin

Monnuttmoon sai gud boi F-r-e-d-d-i-e god boi
En niht sai SKRREEEEAAAKKKK her wz da bood gig
SKREEEEAAAAKK mummay no heer onny F-r-e-d-d-i-e
Ta bood gig smylz smylz smilez hippi bood gig
    SKKRREEEEEAAAAAKK att niht
Hi terz mi ert appurt id hertz my ert mi ert pur erzees
Bugg flyes in skie bugg waks on gras
Whi nutt F-r-e-d-d-i-e kann bee bugg
oho ha ha F-re-d-d-i-e pur boi pour boi

Ta Struuyrie Abot Dadddi

Wee go in trauyhn sai Dudddi wee wuk striits sai Duddi noon ooh
    sai F-r-e-d-d-i-e
Bood gig lissen bood gig lisen an laff yu cribbabby cri al yu went
    sai Mannuttmon

Daddi sai sit heir siitt doon sunn and te boi satt dunn onb triyn
  wiff Mannnottmonn ryt bezyd hum te biu wuzz escayrt att nite
  nooo hee sai nooo mummma nut trayn
Hah hah
Dyddi be nutt Mannuttmon F-r-e-d-d-i-e be nott Mannuttmon
  Mummna be nott
Mannuttmon hah no Cus Mannotttmon izz mee Aruynt de Kernerr
  duywn de strittt ever evverweaur
Deddi sai Wak Faysterr Wak Fayster Whatt ur yu affraitt ovv
  WhATT
De kerner de strett F-r-e-d-d-i-e sai

1985

THE CORNOO

The boy waz standing. He waz standing in the cornoo. There waz a
man who caym from the sky. The sky was al blakk. I ate the starz
sed the man around the cornoo. The boy cloused his eyz. I ate the
stars I ate the moon and the sunn now I eat the wrld. And yu in it.
He laft. Yu go playe now he sed. If play yu can. Hah hah he laft.
Freddie waked until he ran. That waz suun. I waz in my cornoo and
I saw that, I saw him runn. Runn, Freddie. Runn, lettul boy.

WHER IZ F-R-E-D-D-I-E ??

He waz not in the bed. He was not in the kishen he was not in the
living roome. The Mumma could not find littl Freddie. The man
from the blakk sky came and tuke the boy to the ruume in the sky.
The Mumma calld the Duddah and she sed are you takng the boy???
Giv him bakk, she sed. This iz my sunn she sed and the Duddah said
cam down ar yu craazie?? Becus rembur this is my sunn to onnlee I
doin havv him. I saw from the rome in the sky. I herd. They looked
soo lidl. And small. And teenie tinee downn thur small as the bugs.
Ar you F-R-E-D-D-I-E ?? ast the man of the ruume. No he sed. I waz
nevrr him. Now I am the blakk sky and I waz alws the blakk sky.

*

41

F-R-E-D-D-I-E Is Lahst

The Mumma the Duddah they sed Were Culd Hee Bee? It waz funnee. They cri they cri OUT hiz namm Freddie Freddie you are lahst. Cann you here us?? No and yes he sed you woodunt Now. The Onne who cumms for mee sum tymes is in Feeldss somme tymes in grasse or rode or cite farr awii. He sed Boi yuu ar nott Freeddie an Freddie iz nott yuu Hee sed Boi Mannuttman iuz whutt yuu cal mee Mannuttmonn is my namm. Mannuttmonn ius for-evv-err.

The boi went dun Gurrhurrdee Streeyt and lookt for his fayce. It waz thurr on the streyt al ruff. The boi mad it smuuf wuth hiz ohn hanns. Wenm hee treyd ut onn itt futt purfuct onn hiz fayce. Hiz fayce fiutt onn hiz fayce. It waz wurm frum the sunn. Wurm Fayce is guud it is luyke Mumma Baathy and Duddah Jymm longg aggoo. I luv yuur fayce Mumma sed your swite faycce thuer is onnye wann lyke itt in the wrld. Soo I cuuyd nott staye inn mye huis. Itt waz nutt my huis anny moire. It waz Leev Freddiue leeve boi for mee. Thenn hee the boi cam bayck and sed I went Nooweehre Noowehre thads wehre. Noo he sed I dudd nott go to the Citty no I did nutt go to the wood. I went to Noowehre thats wehre. It waz all tru. Aall tru it was sed the boi whooz fayce wuz neoo. He waz Mannuttmann insydde. And Minnuttmann sed Hah Hah Hah menny timnes. His laffter shook the door and it filld up the roome.

1986

Not Long Leftt

The boy lived in this our world and in a diffrent one too. He was a boy who walked Up the staiurs twice and Down the staiurs only once. The seccondd time he went down he was not him. Mannuttmann you calld me long ago and Mannuttman I shall be. The boy saw the frendly old enymee hyding in the doorwais and in the shaddowes of the deep gutter. When he took a step, so did Mannuttman his enymee his frend. The Mumma grabbed his hand and she said too loud Sunny Boy You are still only seven years old sometimes I swear you act like a teenager. Im sorry Mumma he saiud I will never be a teenager. Whats that I hear she said Dud you get that from your preshioys Minutman? You dont know hisz name. When they got to the cornoo at the end of the block the boy smild and told to his

Mumma I have not long left. You will see. I have not long left? she said. Where do you get this stuf? He smyled and that was his anser.

WHAT HAPPENZ WEN YOU LOOK UPP

Lessay you stan at the bottum of the staires. Lessay you look upp. A Voice tellks you Look Upp Look Upp. Are you happy are you braav? You must look all the waye to the top. *All* the waye. Freddie is rite there—rite there at the topp. But you dontt see Freddie. You dont't you cant't see the top you dont't see how it goes on and on the staiures you dont't see you cant. Then the man geus out syde and agen heers the Voice. Look up look up Sullee it is the tyme you must look upp. Freddies Daddie you are,,,, so look upp and see him. Are you goud are you nise are you stronng and braav are you standing on your fruhnt lahwn and leeniung bakk to look up hiuy in the skye? Can you see him? No. No you cant't. Beecuz Freddie is not there and Freddie is not there beecuz Mistr Nothing Nowehere Nobodie is there. He laft. Mistr Nothing Nowehere Nobodie laft out lowd. The man on his frunht lahwn is not happoy and he is not braav. No. And not Sytronng. Lessay that's truoe. Yes. Lessay it. And the Mistr Nothing Nowehere Nobody he is not there exseptt he is nevvr at the top of the staires. And he nevvr leeves he nevr lefft. Hah!

THE BOY AND THE BOOK

Once there was a boy named Frank Pinncushun. That was a comicall naaym but Frank likked his naaym. He had a millyun frends at school and a thosand millyuun at home. At school his best frends were Charley Bruce Mike and Jonny. At home he was freends with Homer Momer Gomer Domer Jomer and Vomer. They never mayde fun of his naaym because it was goode like Barttelmee. Their favrote book was called THE MOUNTAIN OVER THE WALL: DOWN THE BIG RIVVER TREEMER-TRIMMER-TROUWNCE TO THE UNDERGROUND. It was a very long long book: and it was a goid storie. In the book there was a boy named Freddie. Al Frank's millyon frends wanted to be Freddie! He was their heero. Braav and strong. One day Frank Piunncushun went out to wlkk alone by himsellff. Farr he went: soo farr. Littel Frank walked out of his nayberhooid and wlked some more: he wllkd over streeits over britdches and throou canyhons. He was never affrayed. Then he cayme to the Great River Treemer-Trimmer-Trouynse and what dud he doo? Inn he jumped and divved strait down. At the bottom was a huug hall were he culd breeth and wassnt't eeven wett! The waalls were hygh redd curtuns and the seelingg ewas sooo farr awaye he culd not see it. Guldenn playtes and guldenn cupps and gulden chaines laie heept up on the flore. Heloh Heloh Freddie yeled. Helo helo helo. A doore opend. A tall man in a redd cloke and werring a crownne came in the bigg roome. He was the Kinge. The Kinge lookt anguree. Who are yoo and whi are yoo yallingg Helo Helo?? I am Frank Pinncushun he sed but I am Freddie to, and I was hear befor. And we will have a greit fyhht and I wil tryk you and ern all the guld. Lessay I tel you sumethyng sed the Kinge. Lessay you liussen. Ar we kleer?? Yes, kleer, sed Frank. The Kinge walked farwude and tutchd his chisst. The Kinge said I am not I and yoo ar not yoo. Do yuoo unnerrstan me? Yes said the boy I unnerstann. Then he tuuk his Nife and killt the Kinge and walkkt into the heeps of guld. I am not me he sed and luukt at his hanns. His hanns were bluudee and drippt over the guld. He lafft thatt boy he lafft so herd hius laffter wennt up to the seeling. Freddie he kuld see his laffter lyke smoke was hius laffter lyke a twyiste roop mayde of smuck but he kuld nott see the seelingg. He niver saw the seelingg. Not wunse.

Havana

Laura van den Berg

ELLE HAD NEVER INTENDED to become a pirate. She was a school-teacher from Tampa, fifth-grade math. Her world was chalk and rhombuses and cafeteria lunches. Now it was August and she and her husband were on vacation in Key West. They had been separated for three months. On their first night, they went to a bar in Old Town called the Pink Pony, where they drank mojitos and pretended they were strangers. Jeremy was a horror-film academic. He had just finished a paper on *Night of the Living Dead* and the one percent.

"The cannibalism is a critique of economic inequity." He was wearing a hemp bracelet. The neon bar sign, shaped like a cantering pony, glowed.

"You are making this shit up," Elle said.

"I am not making this shit up."

He paused, swirled his drink. "So what do you do?"

"I'm an architect."

"Oh yeah?" He raised his dark eyebrows. "What have you built?"

"Are you familiar with the Bacardi Building in Miami?"

"You built *that*?"

She nodded. "I built that."

"You are so lying," he said.

"You're not supposed to know me." Her mojito glass was cold and dripping. Her fingers were numb. "You're not supposed to know that I'm lying."

"Will you come back to my hotel room tonight?"

"Will you pretend that I'm really an architect?"

They had adjoining rooms at Eden House, on Fleming Street. This trip was supposed to help them decide what to do next, but it hadn't helped Elle, not at all.

"Would you like to go out on the water tomorrow?" he asked. "I've rented a boat. All you'd have to do is show up. I'll take care of the rest."

"A couple alone on the high seas? That sounds like the opening of a horror movie."

45

"Aquatic horror, a cinematic tradition unto itself," he said, then began listing examples.

She crunched an ice cube and pretended to listen.

Later Jeremy ordered another round of mojitos. The cantering pony sign glowed brighter. A man with a gray beard wandered the bar, playing a ukulele. For five dollars you could buy a song.

"What song would you buy me?" Elle fished out a piece of mint and chewed the leaf. They were still a young couple, but around him she had started to feel old. "If we had really just met, if we were really strangers. What do you think would suit me?"

"Jimmy Buffett," he said. " 'Why Don't We Get Drunk.' "

"How charming."

Jeremy added that if he was choosing something for her as his wife, he would go with "Hurricane" by Bob Dylan.

"That's a protest song," Elle pointed out.

"Exactly," her husband said.

Sometimes Elle thought that if she could just find the origin of *it*—this gnawing feeling of unclarity, which she had started calling The Thing after watching the movie with her husband—she would be able to figure out the rest. Here was one place she could start:

Last summer, her parents began forgetting. By Thanksgiving, they were in an assisted-living facility in Palmetto Beach called Marigold Manor, a name that seemed to Elle like an affront to the gravity of their circumstances. She had sat between her parents as the doctor delivered their diagnosis in his antiseptic office. Words for everyday things—can opener, driveway, rosebush—had evaporated from their vocabularies, both at the same time, as if confusion was contagious. Elle was a late-in-life child, but hadn't expected anything like this for many more years. Jeremy couldn't come to the appointment because he was at a horror-film convention in Copenhagen. She e-mailed, she left messages at his hotel, but still it took forty-eight hours to get him on the phone.

That winter, The Thing grew larger, as though fueled by cold. She couldn't concentrate. Always there was some kind of white noise in the background. She would see something through a window and become convinced that what she thought she was seeing wasn't right at all—is that really a tree, or something else in disguise? These were the kinds of questions that had gotten her into the accident.

On the highway, she'd been gazing through the windshield, trying to come to a decision about the shapes of clouds, and had rear-ended another car. No one was hurt, but the front of her Honda was busted. She needed a ride. Once again, she couldn't reach her husband. Once again, she left messages. She waited on the side of the road. He was on deadline for a paper and always worked with earplugs. An afternoon storm was rolling in. She watched the sky darken and thought of all those calls to Copenhagen.

In the end, the drama teacher at Elle's school came for her. In the past year, they'd started eating lunch together and exchanged numbers. He was in his forties, but dressed like an art student, in black T-shirts and glasses with oversized frames. He answered after the first ring.

It started when Elle suggested they forget waiting for the tow truck and go someplace for a drink. It started when she ordered a tequila shot. It started when she saw the silhouette of the motel sign in the distance. It started decades before, if she was being truthful, and by the time she reached Key West, she no longer understood her life, what it was for.

In the morning, they boarded a red motorboat and sailed into the Gulf of Mexico, bound for the Key West wildlife preserve. The water was bright. The predicted high was 102 degrees. The motor was too loud to talk over, so she sat on the floor and watched her husband work the helm. He'd done some boating in college, and he looked good in his shorts and backward baseball cap, the tails of his white button-down flapping.

Elle was wearing denim cutoffs and a T-shirt with a pink bikini underneath. She had kept her hair down. She wanted to look glamorous and windblown, though she suspected she'd end up frizzed and sunburned. Even so, she was trying to practice optimism.

An hour into their journey, he killed the engine. She stood and stretched. Already her skin was pink from the sun. The noise was still tumbling around in her ears.

Jeremy had brought along binoculars, but the view was empty: no distant ships or landmasses. Just water. She looped the binoculars around her neck. The night before, they had gone to bed separately, and in her room, she listened for his noises next door: the sink running, the floors creaking, the low buzz of the TV.

"It's hot as death out here." She reached underneath her shirt and adjusted her bikini straps. "You brought sunscreen, right? And water?"

Jeremy rummaged through the straw bag he'd carried aboard. "Sunscreen is a yes." He tossed her a plastic tube. "Water, I'm afraid, is a no."

They were another hour from the wildlife preserve. Her throat was dry.

"What a thing to forget." She had sweat marks under her arms and around her stomach. "It's only Key West in August. It's only a hundred fucking degrees outside."

Jeremy squinted behind his sunglasses. When he was annoyed, his blue eyes could go cold as stone. "You could have brought your own water."

"You said you would take care of everything."

"I meant the boat. Not everything *everything*."

Elle returned to looking through the binoculars. She tipped her head back and tracked the movement of a bird flying overhead.

When she spotted the boat in the distance, she adjusted the focus. It was much larger than their motorboat. A yacht or a catamaran, perhaps. The boat wasn't moving. Maybe there was water on board. She pictured a woman in a sarong handing her a cold glass. She could feel the liquid slipping down her throat and pooling in her stomach.

"What's that over there?" she said, handing Jeremy the binoculars.

The boat turned out to be the most beautiful thing Elle had ever seen on the water. It was a large yacht, painted a burnished shade of gold. The windows were made of black glass. Around the stern, there was a big deck with hardwood floors and a railing. Porthole windows dotted the hull. She wondered what the view was like inside.

Jeremy docked next to the yacht. They called out to the people aboard, first with regular greetings and then, after they were met with silence, ridiculous ones—*Mayday! Ahoy!* They waited for someone to reply. Sweat ran down the backs of her legs. She was getting desperate for something to drink.

When she noticed the ladder on the side of the yacht, she pointed it out to Jeremy. "Maybe we could just climb aboard."

"Wouldn't that be trespassing?"

"There could be something wrong," she said, though what she was most concerned about was getting her hands on a glass of water and holding the cold in her mouth. "They could be out of gas. They could be having an emergency."

He shrugged. "Nobody's stopping you from exercising bad judgment."

Elle hopped onto the ladder. She almost lost her grip, and when she looked down, the water was a deep blue. From the deck, she grinned and waved to her husband, leaving him no choice but to secure the motorboat to the ladder with rope and follow her.

As impossible as it seemed, the yacht appeared empty. They found the helm, which was encased in glass, and checked the engine; it was working fine. The gas tank was full. The marine radio was on. No communications were coming through. There were two different screens—a GPS and a chart plotter—and the black-leather chair facing the instrument panel looked large and comfortable. Who would leave this yacht floating in the gulf like a ghost ship?

"I guess it wouldn't hurt to see if there's any water," Elle said. "Maybe the owners are out diving."

Jeremy didn't say anything right away. She could see him eyeing the navigational equipment and the leather chair. Both their cars were leases; they had a mortgage and old student loans. She could see him imagining how different the lives of these yacht owners must be.

They followed a narrow staircase down to the lower cabin, which was padded with beige carpeting. They examined the U-shaped leather sofa and the flat-screen TV. They touched the bronze statues of kneeling, armless women. The dining area held a glass table with silver legs and a rectangular window that overlooked the gulf. The kitchen was nicer than the one in Elle's apartment: tile floors, granite countertops, cabinets made from nut-colored wood. The two bedrooms had king-sized beds and private bathrooms with Jacuzzi tubs.

In the kitchen, Elle drank glass after glass of water. She turned on the sink and rinsed her face and felt herself come back to life. They discovered a bottle of champagne in the refrigerator. They both stared at it for a moment, hunched inside the pocket of cool air. To her surprise, it was Jeremy who grabbed it by the neck and popped it open. Foam poured over his hands. They found flutes made of blown glass in a cabinet. Soon they were halfway through the bottle.

"This is crazy." Elle heard herself say this, heard herself laugh, already a little drunk. She knew they needed to finish this champagne that did not belong to them and get off this yacht that did not belong to them, that could never belong to them.

"We're out of our minds," Jeremy said, taking another sip of champagne.

*

By dark, there was still no sign of the owners. Elle wondered if it was possible to be so rich, you could just hop from one yacht to the next. She and Jeremy had emptied the first champagne bottle, plus the second one he'd found in the pantry. The bottles and flutes now sat in the sink. The least they could do was not leave a mess.

They lingered on the deck, looking at the stars. In Tampa, the sky seemed to have boundaries, but out here it was endless and glinting silver. And then he was kissing her and she was realizing how much she'd missed his mouth. She thought about her mother, who once told her the secret to a happy marriage was forgetting and remembering in exactly the right proportions. Now her parents needed flashcards to remember each other's names.

She pulled away and looked at her husband. His face was shadowed. "What do you say we go for a sail?"

"In *this*?" He squeezed her hips.

"We won't go far." She was breathless, still giddy from the champagne. "We'll bring the yacht back in the morning."

"That's piracy, Elle. I'm not even kidding. Robbery at sea."

"But don't you want to be a pirate?" She was following the impulse moving through her like a current of electricity. She wasn't considering the details. "Just for a night?"

He pulled her close and whispered something that sounded like acquiescence.

If they were caught, they could say they were sailing in search of the Coast Guard. They could say they'd gone delirious from heatstroke. This was the first time in years that she had felt free of The Thing. She would have done anything to keep moving away from that feeling.

With a pocketknife, Jeremy cut the rope that had been keeping the motorboat tethered to the yacht.

"We might live to regret this," he said.

"Fuck regrets." She imagined another couple finding their motorboat adrift. What they might think, what they might do. "Fuck yachts and fuck champagne and fuck the stars and fuck you too."

In the helm, he switched on the engine, and they sailed into the night.

Elle never told her husband about the drama teacher. She had never even planned to leave, but a week after the car accident, she found herself watching *Halloween* with Jeremy for the hundredth time, for another paper. When Laurie Strode attacked Michael Myers with a knitting needle, Elle started thinking about all the horror-movie heroines: Sally Hardesty, Wendy Torrance, Diane Freeling. These women, they got to run and scream. They got to be transformed by terror. They got to know what to do next: Dart across that street, hide behind that tree, stab the killer in the heart.

Once she was woken by a car alarm in the middle of the night. She bolted upright in bed, screaming. She didn't stop screaming when her husband touched her arm. Once, in the school gymnasium, she'd joined her students in a game of tag and pretended she was being chased by masked killers. It had felt good, all that running and screaming. In October, she and Jeremy had decorated their house with cobwebs and rubber knives. She had kept one of the rubber knives. She carried it to school in her backpack. She held it to the drama teacher's throat in bed. This was the state of her life.

In the dark of the living room, she felt damaged in ways she couldn't understand. But what had ever happened to her? Nothing, she was tempted to say, but of course that wasn't true. Things were happening to people all the time. Her parents were losing their minds and her husband couldn't be reached and the children were stealing her erasers. The happening was like breath or thought: It only stopped if you were dead.

The next afternoon, when she came home from school, she found Jeremy grading student papers in his office, the orange plugs stuffed in his ears.

She stood in the doorway and started talking, even though it took a few minutes for him to notice her, to pull out the foam. She told him that she didn't know what was happening to her. She needed to get away. She needed time to think everything through.

"Think what through?" her husband said.

She sank into the doorway. She turned up her palms. "What do I do? I don't know what to do."

Of course, the problem wasn't her husband, wasn't her marriage. The problem was her. But if she could trick herself into believing the problem *was* her marriage, there was the possibility of a solution. She had yet to find a solution for The Thing.

He stared down at the earplugs cupped in his hand. He squeezed the orange foam a few times before throwing them against the wall.

*

51

In the yacht, for the first time in months, they slept in the same bed. She had forgotten how quickly his face grew rough with stubble. She had forgotten how his hips dug into hers, which hurt a little, but not in an entirely unpleasant way. The bed felt massive compared to the futon she'd been sleeping on. The sheets were soft. His hair was soft. The boat swayed in a way that made her feel like she was being held.

In the morning, they outlined what they thought was a sensible plan. That afternoon, they would sail to the Key West Coast Guard, where they would explain about finding the abandoned yacht. They would apologize for not dialing channel sixteen on the marine radio. The radio hadn't been working; they couldn't get on the right line. Elle had been sick. The heat had made them confused. They agreed this was the best course of action.

Despite having discussed the reality of their choices, despite having come up with a plan, they made no move toward Key West. It was as though a kind of inertia had set in, as though they'd lost the ability to think beyond the offerings of the yacht. So instead they fucked in the Jacuzzi tub and baked the puff pastry hors d'oeuvres they found in the freezer and ate them standing up in the kitchen. They used the tackle Jeremy had discovered in a closet to cast fishing lines from the deck. Elle caught a small red snapper. She reeled it up and watched it flop on the wood. Jeremy wanted to kill it, to cook it, but she slipped her fingers into its mouth and pulled out the hook, the way her father, who might not even know the word for fish at this moment, had taught her. The fish pulsed in her hands; the inside of its mouth was slick and cold. When she returned it to the water, she imagined it wasn't a fish at all, but The Thing in disguise. They draped towels across the deck and sunbathed. Elle even took off her bikini top. She wondered what the parents of her students—the rumpled fathers, the harried mothers—would say if they could see her now.

This was not the first time Elle and Jeremy had stolen something together. In college, at a big state school in north Florida, their RA had an old Mustang, orange with a white convertible roof. One night, they stole the RA's car keys from the housing office while everyone was at dinner. Jeremy drove. They put down the top and roared through the dark, empty roads. It was spring; Elle's parents were on vacation in Canada, riding a train through the Rockies. Later they would show her photos of dense green forests and snow-capped mountains. Jeremy took the corners fast. Elle grabbed her knees and shut her eyes and screamed. At the time, she felt she would never age. They were smart—just a quick ride and then the Mustang was back in its parking space. She could still remember slipping the keys into the RA's desk drawer, the fast tempo of her breath, her hands tingling with nerves.

The car had been Jeremy's idea. Ten years later, the yacht was hers.

A cabinet by the flat-screen TV housed a collection of DVDs. When Jeremy approached her with *Dracula*, Elle didn't protest.

"This is the Tod Browning version." He held up the case with both hands, like a waiter presenting a bottle of fine wine. "You've probably never seen this before, have you?"

OK, she thought. *I can give him a movie.*

He turned off the lights. They sat on the couch. The movie had been shot in 1931. Elle expected it to be dated and not at all frightening, but it was somehow, considering they were alone on the water. She watched a stagecoach rattle through the Carpathian Mountains and Renfield eat flies in his asylum. She watched Dracula move like a shadow across a room.

When Jeremy paused the movie for a bathroom break, Elle tried to get comfortable on the couch. For such an expensive-looking piece of furniture, her cushion didn't feel right, didn't feel smooth. She got on her knees and turned the cushion over; it seemed far heavier than it should have been. The leather bottom was lumpy, as though someone had filled it with rocks. She pulled the zipper that ran along the perimeter and looked inside.

The cushion was stuffed with bricks of money. She picked up one of the bundles. The bills were held together with a rubber band and felt heavy in her hand. Sweat beaded on the back of her neck. Her fingers dug into the leather. She brought the brick to her nose. What did this much money smell like? She caught paper and ink and something faintly sweet.

She jammed the brick into the couch, zipped up the cushion, and pressed it back into place. She snagged her fingertip on the zipper, and the metal tore away a bit of skin. She would pretend nothing had happened. She would pretend the couch was filled with feathers. She would not think about the implications of her discovery. She listened for the flush of the toilet, the creak of the bathroom door. When her husband returned, she was sitting just as she had been, holding the remote, Dracula's face a white blur on the screen.

Dónde estás? That was the first thing the voice on the radio said. Elle was sitting in the helm. She recognized the language as Spanish, which she couldn't speak or understand.

She hadn't been able to sleep. Naturally the money was on her mind. She'd gotten up in the middle of the night and gone to the helm, where she sat in the leather chair and spun until she grew dizzy. She gazed into the screens and at the dark water surrounding them. Earlier, overcome with worry, she'd tried to tell Jeremy. She'd actually said the words, *There's money,* but couldn't get any farther. *Of course there's money,* he'd replied, ruffling her hair, a gesture that always made her feel like a child.

A crackling had drawn her attention to the marine radio. Static, she thought, but the crackling continued, followed by language. The voice belonged to a man. The cadence was precise and measured, the syllables long. She knew they couldn't keep going like this. Tomorrow they would have to take the yacht to the Coast Guard. If Jeremy resisted, she would show him what she'd found in the couch. Tomorrow they would have to go back to their regular lives.

She pressed the radio against her ear. *Dónde estás?* the voice kept saying. She did not answer him back.

From the stairwell, Elle thought the two figures were a mirage. It was morning. She and Jeremy were coming up to the deck in plush white bathrobes that did not belong to them. The couple stood by the railing. Their arms were crossed. They both wore dark sunglasses. Clearly these were the owners of the yacht, coming to claim what was theirs.

The man was tall, with sandy hair and a thin, sharp face. He was dressed in white pants and a pink polo. The woman was tan and dark haired and wore a navy-blue wrap dress. Elle considered how they might explain that they weren't real pirates, that this was all a misunderstanding. She prepared herself for accusations, threats.

"Carla, Albert," the man said instead, his English heavily accented. He clapped his hands. "We were wondering when you'd wake up."

"You weren't in the right coordinates." The woman's speech had a subtle inflection, something Elle couldn't place. "But we were still able to find you."

"Your names?" It was all Elle could think to say.

The man frowned. "They didn't tell you?"

She inched onto the deck. Jeremy stayed in the stairwell. She remembered sitting in the dark auditorium for the drama teacher's production of *Fiddler on the Roof* that spring. On stage, she barely recognized her students in their neckerchiefs and aprons; she had admired how well they were pretending. That was what she and Jeremy had to do now: Keep pretending.

"No," she said. "They didn't."

The couple was Rafa and Belén. They were under the impression that the yacht was bound for Havana. In Havana, their business would be settled and then they would go salsa dancing and eat criollo. Elle thought of the money in the couch, the thick bundles of sweet-smelling paper, and felt the muscles in her face go slack.

The woman had a thin gold chain around her wrist. The man was wearing loafers without socks; his ankles were hairless and dark. Two canvas bags sat on the deck. Elle saw no sign of another ship, of what might have brought them here. Neither she nor Jeremy was saying anything. She could see the man frowning again.

"Of course," she finally said. "Havana."

There were so many ways to stop remembering. A dip in neurotransmitters. Debris in the arteries. Sailing for so long, the starting point became a dark spot in your mind. A blow to the cortical tissue. A different set of names. Consider this equation: Rafa and Belén were no more able to recognize Elle and Jeremy than her parents were able to positively identify airplanes or lamps. Heatstroke. Infection of the heart valve. Getting blackout drunk. Subdural hematoma. Believing you were not yourself, had never been yourself, but always someone else in disguise. That you were forgetting in order to remember the person waiting beneath.

Soon the yacht was moving. Belén had disappeared into the lower cabin with the canvas bags. Elle stayed on the deck and watched what was happening in the helm. Rafa was turning the big silver wheel with one hand and pointing at the screens with the other. Her husband was nodding, his fingers pressed against his mouth.

Elle retrieved their binoculars and surveyed the water around them. She looked for a ship, a shoreline, something that could save them. The situation had spun farther away from what they could have imagined; they were ready to raise the white flag. But the horizon was the same as before: just water and sky, the surfaces deceptively calm.

On the deck, she practiced calling herself Carla. She repeated the name, breaking it into two separate sounds: *Car-la*. The yacht was moving quickly. The breeze whipped her hair. *Car-la*, she kept saying, part of a new language she was not yet ready to learn.

That evening, they decided who would make dinner by drawing knives. Blindfolded, they were expected to reach into the knife drawer and feel around until they found something they liked. Whoever picked the dullest knife had to cook. Rafa went first. Belén tied a red silk scarf around his head and he pulled out a medium-sized paring knife with a gleaming blade. Jeremy went next and kept his hand in the drawer for a long time before taking out a slender jam knife. Belén drew a knife large enough to split a melon.

When it was Elle's turn, Belén covered her eyes with the scarf. She blinked and felt her lashes brush against the silk. Carefully she slid her hand into the drawer. She felt metal on her skin and imagined the soft pads of her fingertips splitting open. She gripped a smooth handle and lifted.

She felt fingers in her hair, on the side of her neck, as Belén untied the blindfold. She was still holding the knife.

"A santoku." Rafa pointed at her knife. "Good choice."

They lined up the knives on the counter and soon Belén and Rafa were laughing. Elle watched the skin crinkle around her eyes. She spotted gold caps in the back of his mouth.

"Who could possibly tell which one is sharpest?" Belén said. Her eyes were dark and round and watered easily. "I can't tell at all."

"There are ways to find out," Rafa said.

Elle felt her husband go rigid beside her. Suddenly the lights in the kitchen were too bright.

To her relief, Rafa and Belén decided they should all just drink instead. In their luggage, they had packed bottles of fine Portuguese wine. They sat at the glass table. Elle tried to pretend these weren't the kind of people who made decisions with knives.

"In Havana," Rafa said, "we will make the right introductions."

"It's important that you listen to whatever we tell you." Belén's glass was printed with her lipstick. The more she drank, the thicker her accent became.

"But what if we decide we don't want to do business anymore?" Elle asked. "What if we just want to see Havana?"

"That must be a joke." Rafa splashed more wine into his glass. "A terrible, terrible joke."

"*Coger mango bajito,*" Belén said, making a snatching gesture. "We must grab the low-hanging mango."

Jeremy and Elle stared at each other across the table.

"So." Belén cradled her glass in both hands, swaying slightly in her seat. Her fingers were not as elegant as the rest of her. Her knuckles were knobby, her nails bitten down. "Where is the money?"

For a little while, everyone was quiet. Elle watched her husband's face darken with confusion. His glass was empty. His hands were pressed against his thighs. Meanwhile, Belén and Rafa had turned expectant. They were tipped forward, hands folded, eyebrows raised.

"To not have the money would be a very bad thing," Rafa said.

Elle stood and walked over to the couch. She unzipped the cushion. Rafa and Belén crowded around her. They started pulling out the bricks and counting. Soon stacks of paper were spread across the floor and the coffee table. Elle tried to tell herself that they were all going to sit down and play a game of Monopoly. She turned and saw her husband standing on the edge of the room, still holding his empty glass.

The bedroom closet was where they thought they had the best chance of not being overheard. Jeremy was huddled against a teak wall. Blouses grazed Elle's back. For the first time, she smelled something unpleasant on the yacht, a mix of dust and mothballs. They stood so close, she could have licked the buttons on his shirt if she'd wanted to. They kept the closet light off.

He was telling her all the predictable things: He couldn't believe she knew about the money and didn't tell him, couldn't believe she would keep a secret like that. What had she been thinking? What had they both been thinking? While he was talking, she slipped a silk blouse off a hanger and held it in her arms.

"Not thinking enough obviously," Jeremy said.

"I was in a state of shock," she said. "I didn't know what to do."

"I am so tired of hearing you say that you don't know what to do."

Maybe she needed to confess everything, right there in the closet.

57

The idea came quick and sharp, like a bee sting. Maybe there had been too many secrets. Maybe honesty would be what saved them.

"The drama teacher," she began, before she could stop herself, and the rest came rolling out. She told him about the phone call and the tequila shot and the motel. It only happened once. They didn't even sit together at lunch anymore. He was not the reason she had left.

Her husband said nothing. She squeezed the blouse to her chest.

When he finally spoke, his voice was low and hoarse. "Why did you tell me?"

"Because I'm the problem." She pinched the collar between her index and thumb and stuck the silk edge in her mouth.

"Listen." He was breathing fast. His hands were on her elbows. "It's like I said before. I just want things to go back to the way they were. Before your parents. Before the car accident. What they were like before all of that."

No, no, she kept thinking. That wasn't what they should want at all.

"Think about it." She bit down on the silk. She smelled salt and sun on his skin. "How happy were you really then?"

"Come on, Elle. We've known each other since we were teenagers."

"Yes." She pulled the silk from her mouth and felt where the collar was damp with spit. What was she saying? What was she doing? "And now we've grown up."

Jeremy swatted at the darkness. Hangers with dresses clattered to the floor. Soon there was a knock on the door. They stumbled out of the closet, their eyes adjusting to the light. They found Rafa standing in the hall in a white T-shirt and pants without a belt. Elle noticed the slim, dark points of a tattoo on his upper bicep, peeking out from underneath the cotton.

"Belén heard a noise," he said.

Earlier Elle had listened for details that might illuminate who these people were and what they wanted. She had only learned that, many years ago, Belén had shot commercials in Bulgaria—*I got to sell dish soap*, she'd laughed, her eyes damp—and that Rafa had once won a medal for long-distance swimming, the kinds of things that only made them more inscrutable.

Jeremy sighed. Elle rubbed the back of her neck.

"Everything is fine," they said.

*

Once Elle found her mother in the upstairs guest bedroom, pushing open the window and crawling out. She grabbed her soft waist. Her mother thrashed. Her hair—wild and white—got stuck in Elle's mouth.

"No," she cried. "You can't go out there."

"The deer, the deer," her mother said, grasping for the outdoors. Elle peered through the window. Across the street, in the neighbor's front yard, a small dog was playing.

Elle's father came into the room. Her mother twirled around, nearly knocking her over. Elle scrambled to lock the window. Jeremy was supposed to have picked them up fifteen minutes ago for a doctor's appointment. She felt like she was standing in quicksand.

"Clive," her mother said, pointing at her husband, whose name was Stuart.

"Not Clive," Elle said. "There is no such thing as Clive."

She would remember this moment each time she called her husband his pretend name on the yacht. *Albert, Jeremy, Clive*, she would think to herself, growing more and more confused. Which one was there no such thing as?

Fifty miles from Havana, Belén announced that she wanted to swim. Rafa agreed to stop the yacht, but for no more than an hour. After all, they had an appointment to keep. He was wearing a linen suit and a fedora. Belén emerged from the lower cabin in a black one-piece. She was barefoot, her toenails painted bloodred.

"You won't swim with me?" She pointed at Elle, who understood this was not really a question, but a command in disguise.

Soon she was in her pink bikini. Her shoulders were peeling. Her calves were speckled with mosquito bites. Rafa was at the helm. Jeremy, who was no longer speaking to her, was on the deck. She imagined her husband looking at her and then at Belén and thinking that he should never have married so young.

Belén didn't bother with the ladder. Instead she dove straight into the gulf. Elle followed her over the railing, then hesitated, clinging. What about the sharks and the sea snakes? Wouldn't it be better to use the ladder? To be gradual?

She glanced over her shoulder, wanting to meet her husband's eye, but he was staring right through her, at something off in the distance.

When she looked down, she saw Belén's glistening, seal-like head. Her skin was rough with goose bumps. She had a pain in her stomach.

Over and over, she called herself Carla.

She felt her fingers go loose around the railing. She felt herself jump.

When she opened her eyes underwater, the first thing she saw was Belén's slender legs, kicking at the darkness below.

From a distance, Havana was a sprawl of gray concrete. Rafa had packed the money in one of his canvas bags. All four of them were scrunched into the helm. It was nearly dusk. The lights dripped gold into the gulf. Belén was telling Elle about things they would see in the city: cigar factories and coco taxis and the statue of John Lennon, whose sunglasses were always being stolen, and the Tropicana cabaret. Business first, Belén said, her voice like smoke in Elle's ear. And then Havana.

Last night, after the closet, after the knock on their door, she and Jeremy had gotten into bed and made another plan. They lay on their sides, facing each other, heads tilted down. They didn't talk about the money or the drama teacher or whether they would get a divorce; they spoke only of what to do when they reached Havana. At the port, there would be a Coast Guard or a police officer. They would wave that person down and say they were being held against their will, which wasn't exactly true, but it seemed easier than telling the whole story. If that didn't work, they wouldn't be able to get into Havana without passports, without papers of some kind; that inevitable exchange with the immigration officer would be another chance to escape.

"Look." Belén tugged on Elle's arm. She pointed toward the city with her tired hands, at the gray smoke spiraling above a building.

Rafa spoke into the radio as they approached the harbor. They moved through entrance buoys and into a canal. They pulled up to the customs dock, where Rafa handed a thick envelope to a man in a white uniform. He switched on the bow thruster and the yacht eased into the marina slip. From the helm, Elle watched more men in white uniforms tie the lines.

They were allowed into the city without showing identification of any kind. No papers, no passports, not at all how it was supposed to work. Beyond the harbor a limestone seawall bordered the coast of the city. A child in red shorts stood on top of the wall, waving at distant ships. There was supposed to have been more time.

They left the yacht and climbed a staircase, the concrete steps

60

veined with green algae. Rafa carried the bag filled with money. They crossed a large square with pigeons. They turned onto a street riddled with potholes. They walked underneath old marquee signs advertising *acondicionado* and *restaurante*. Clothing hung from wrought-iron balconies. Clusters of children on bikes wove around them like schools of fish. An old woman reading on a bench looked up from her book, startled by the story unfolding before her. The sidewalk grew narrower. Elle kept looking for a policeman. Her husband's eyes were fixed on the back of Belén's head, as though he had fallen into a trance. Every step they took was one less chance to get away.

Here was one way she saw it: After the business was over, they went dancing and got drunk on mojitos. They checked into a grand old hotel, into a room with tall windows and a balcony. In the light of morning, they looked down at the street below, the soup of cars and bicycles and smoke. What if they stayed in Havana? Here there were no horror movies. No running and screaming. No drama teacher or equations written on the board. They changed in ways that eliminated the need for forgiveness; the past had been made by different people, with different lives. They started to feel young again. They used their pretend names for so long, they became real. They walked the Malecón and watched ships come and go. They ate *pastelitos* with guava. They mailed postcards—images of rumba dancers and the beaches of Jibacoa—to Elle's parents, who struggled to place the names of the senders. One night, after a few too many Cuba Libres, they stole John Lennon's sunglasses. Each time they looked at each other, they saw something new, like statues that had been chiseled away to reveal their true form.

Or: Elle stopped and shouted *La policía!* and felt the activity around her pause. How foolish she had been, to ever believe this temporary life could save them. Rafa and Belén spun around, their faces hard with danger. Jeremy grabbed her hand and they ran through the streets. Down alleys, through a café that smelled of cigars and coffee, into squares. They used the tricks they had seen in movies. They heard Rafa and Belén behind them, their furious footsteps, their shouting. A police officer with a gun slung over his shoulder radioed other officers and soon Rafa and Belén were in handcuffs, Elle and Jeremy escorted to safety. No one would know they were criminals too. On a bench in a police station, with wool blankets hanging from their shoulders, they felt the wound of the drama teacher and the lies and the inattention begin to close. They thought of all the years they had left to live together, how one day Havana would be a distant memory, like the car they had stolen in college. They looked at each other and remembered the game they had played on their first night in Key West, at the Pink Pony.

"An architect," her husband said. "What have you built?"

In the end, what came to Elle was much more ordinary. Gradually her pace would slow. People would fill the space between her and her husband and the couple who brought them to Havana. She would vanish around a corner. Maybe as Carla. Maybe as herself. What happened next, she had no idea. Jeremy was so close to Rafa and Belén, it looked like they were walking side by side. He could come if he wanted, or he could keep following them. It was his turn to decide.

A car honked. A horse and carriage rattled past. Somewhere someone was playing a trumpet. The sound settled over her like a fog. There was the rot of garbage and *Revolución* graffitied on a wall. A crumbling stone statue of a saint, votive candles, and dried red flowers laid before its cracked feet. A cat wearing a tiny straw hat. A building the color of sunset. Everything, the entire city of Havana, looked like something else in disguise. Elle took a breath. Her steps grew slower. If you were watching her from a very great distance— the San Cristóbal bell tower; the top floor of the Capitolio Nacional— you wouldn't be sure she was moving at all.

Dreamlives of Debris
Lance O*lsen*

> *Someone, I tell you, in another time will remember*
> *us, but never as who we were.*
>
> —Sappho

:::: debris

I HAVE MY DOLL and the screamings behind my eyelids. The screamings look like fluttery lights. The fluttery lights believe they live inside me, but I live inside them too.

My doll's name is Catastrophe.

:::: debris

Daddy once made his ideas purer than King Aegeus's. Now every year King Aegeus sends seven of his bravest young men and seven of his most beautiful young women from Athens to Crete to visit me. I let them wander the passages of my heart for hours—or maybe it is days, or weeks—I do not know what any of these words mean—before I step out of their frothy panic to welcome them.

:::: debris

I say *once*, I say *now*, I say *hours, days, weeks*, but I do not understand myself: Down here time is a storm-swarmed ship always breaking up.

:::: debris

The liquid architecture will not hold still. Sometimes I cannot locate the walls. I shuffle forward, hands outstretched in the grainy charcoal air, breathing mold, must, fungus, sulfur, damp dirt, wet rock, waiting for the gritty touch ushering me onto the far shore. Sometimes so many walls erupt around me I am forced to crab sideways to make any progress at all.

Sometimes the walls become a whirlwind of hands or dying alphabets.

The ceiling sinks without warning and I discover myself crawling on

63

my belly across the chalky floor, Catastrophe clutched tight to my chest.

:::: debris
Remember, angel, Mommy whispers, rocking me in her lap, *you do not need to learn to adapt to Daedalus's imagination. Survival is never mandatory.*

:::: debris
Despite my height, I should mention, my strength is not negligible.

Last month—no, last year—next—I am not sure—I am never sure—no surprises there—one always knows a sliver less than one did a flinch ago—at some point in timelessness Mommy and Daddy gave me a little sister to play with.

Our wrestling match persisted the length of one short, startled bleat.

Since then I have been an only child again.

:::: debris
Apis the Healer tells me I am thirty-three years old. I cannot remember. He tells me nobody believed I would live past thirty-three months.

This, he says, is why Mommy calls me Her Little Duration.

Why Daddy calls me the Minotaur.

I call myself Debris.

:::: debris
When I set out to greet my new guests I tuck my doll beneath my arm and carry a torch. This is not so I can see them. It is so they can see me.

The brave young men, unarmed, unnerved, usually shit or piss themselves a little when I step into the open. I think they are expecting someone else. It is not unamusing to watch their secretions trickling down their legs as they blunder into blank walls trying to unsee me.

All I have to do is stand there clearing my throat.

Matters usually take care of themselves.

I follow the women like their own shadows, torchless. They cannot hear me, have no sense of my presence, until they feel me clambering up their backs, hands searching for necks, teeth for arteries.

:::: debris
What I am telling you, I want to say, is a love story.

:::: debris
Search as I might over the years, if one may call them that, and not something else—miscalculations, for instance—I have never ferreted out the guarded portal. Surely it exists in the same way, say, future dictionaries exist.

:::: debris
Our virtuoso artificer Daedalus designed my palace.

Mommy says upon its completion he could barely find his own way out.

His brilliance lives inside the body of a pasty man-sized toad sans ass who wears the perpetual grimace of a Skeptic. I have never seen him smile. His rumpled face carries the same message wherever it goes:

Stand a little less between me and the darkness.

:::: debris
I often wake alarmed from the noise they call sleep. My world becomes all blackness and rabbit snifts. I wonder if everyone has forgotten me.

How long has it been since Mommy rocked Her Little Duration? Since the eunuch priests loosed a pig covered with sacrificial ribbons to snort its scramble through my heart?

How long has it been since my trough was refreshed? My favorite amphora—teeming with the taste of violets, hyacinths, and interesting injuries—hidden like a gift for me to root out?

When all instants fuss behind your eyelids at once they become shiny fracas.

Then they become me.

:::: debris
And then Mommy brought around Lady Tiresias.

Calling my name, listening for my response, she zeroed in on her princess.

Soon the three of us were sitting cross-legged in a chamber I had never seen before. It stank of language.

Vowels, mostly.

The blind, bony seer with wrinkled female dugs has known life as both man and woman. He had my pity. She reached for my hand. He wanted to read my palm. I hissed at her. He drew back.

Mommy stroked my scruff.

Be nice, button, she said.

Lady Tiresias tried again. She discovered my palm bloated smooth as a baboon's ass: no bumps, lumps, fissures, figures, failures, futures.

You are born, she said, of a very special race. The Minotaur belongs to a people old as the earth itself. Beneath the skin of your shoulders grow wings. Someday they will break out and carry you far away from here.

I reached back, felt nothing.

Give yourself time, she said. The number thirty-three controls your life. You are concerned not with personal ambition but with uplifting the loving energy of humankind.

Out the corner of my eye I saw Mommy shift.

Lady Tiresias's bald head reminded me of an enormous gland.

You are a born leader, he said. This is what I see. You will achieve great fame through kindness, tenderness, compassion. Remember: Whosoever is delighted in solitude is a god. Lady Tiresias has spoken.

:::: **debris**

These speech turbulences are not mine—do not seem to be mine, do and do not seem to be mine. That is, I am nearly convinced my mouth is vigorously unmoving as I ramble these branchings.

(I have just tapped it with my hoof for proof.)

:::: **debris**

That is, I sometimes have the impression I exist.

:::: **athena chorus**

:::: debris
I should mention minotaurs have nothing to do with the perpetuation of life.
The very idea of multiplication disgusts us.

:::: debris
If I am not the only numerous.

:::: debris
That afternoon Mommy led the unsuspecting blind man to the Brazen Bull. The hollow bronze beast hulked on a raised platform in our central courtyard at the edge of the shallow pool swarming with eels, each fitted with a pair of tiny gold earrings. Two Athenian slaves helped him through the hatch in its side. Lady Tiresias ordered them to be careful. They obeyed. Crouching here in the darkness I watched them light the fire. It quickly crackled into consciousness. Soon clouds of incense were shooting from the bull's nostrils. The complex system of tubes and stops inside its skull translated the soothsayer's shrieks into infuriated bovine bellows.

:::: debris
First comes pain, whispers Mommy, rocking, *then knowledge.*

:::: debris
Next day they opened the hatch and extracted what was left of Lady Tiresias. Mommy asked that the most delicate bits be fashioned into my beautiful new bracelet.
Mommy loves Her Little Duration.

:::: debris
Before that and after that I watched many wars. Or maybe it was the same war many times. Before that and after that I watched the elaborate festival at which Daddy wedded his queen, whose own daddy tainted her with the same witchery with which she tainted me. Before that and after that I watched the slow wreckage of my city bog into the earth. Before that and after that I watched Daedalus's boy attempt to scrabble

up a hidden ladder above a seascape like hammered silver, his wax wings reducing to air around him. Before that and after that I watched my sister, Ariadne, whom I have never met, hand something I could not make out to a muscular young man I could not recognize standing in front of a gate I could not place. Before that and after that I watched Daddy, whom I have never met, reclining in a silver bathtub decorated with octopi and anemones. I watched the daughter of Cocalus, King of Camicus, signal her slave to empty a pot not of warm water but of boiling oil over his head and chest and groin. Before that and after that I watched me hanging weightless in Mommy's womb, strangling my almost-brother with his own umbilical cord, preparing to bestow upon my parents my first gift, which they would in turn mummify and boon back to me, a mutual sign of our abiding affection.

(This was back when hope still helped.)

:::: debris

There are the stories that make sense. These are called lies. There are the stories that maze you. These are called the world.

I should mention your body is a haunted house you can't escape.

:::: debris

Which is to say the worst is still to come, was still to come, will still be to come, has come, had come, is coming, has been coming, might come, is going to come, will have come, would have come, but not yet, and already.

:::: j. g. ballard song

Because all clocks are labyrinths.

:::: lady tiresias chorus

When I die, it will have been inside the stomach of a bull. When I die, it will have been inside the courtyard of a doomed palace. When I die, it will have been with the understanding that the descent into Hades is the same from every point, every race, every gender, every class, every ancestry. With the recognition I will soon meet Odysseus in the infinite gray desert of the afterness and, skin ashen, eyes cloudy and blank from too much seeing, violet mouth sewn shut with black catgut, he will ask me sans voice to recollect for him what the best path of life is. Standing alone with the sacker of cities, I will advise him to forget the philosophers, ignore their metaphysics, for in the end there exists nothing save atoms and empty space—that is it, that is all, that is us, that is this. No one will arrive to save us from ourselves. When I die, it will have been wondering whether I am actually thinking these thoughts I think I am thinking or only dreaming I am thinking them as I study the glowing blue flame float out from my chest and across a black ocean, how it must at some point have ceased to be part of me and become part of something else, for it is so far away, and then farther, and th

:::: **jorge luis borges song**
Because time is a river that sweeps me along, but I am the river; it is a tiger that destroys me, but I am the tiger; it is a fire that consumes me, but I am the fire.

:::: **debris**
Because the historians chronicle how, when my brother, Androgeos, began to collect all the prizes at the Panathenaic games, King Aegeus commanded him to fight his most fearsome bull.

How brave, bewildered Androgeos was gored and died on the stadium floor within minutes of entering.

:::: **bradley manning song**
Because it was not until I was in Iraq and reading secret military reports on a daily basis that I started to question the morality of what we were doing. This is why I turned over the files to which I had access to WikiLeaks, which made them public. I understand that my actions violated the law. I regret that my actions hurt anyone or harmed the United States. It was never my intent to hurt anyone. I only wanted to help people.

:::: **debris**
Because, outraged, Daddy set off to Athens. Revenge seared his veins. On the way he invaded Megara, whose King Nisos's power derived from a single magic lock of purple hair. Nisos's daughter, Scylla, saw Daddy from the battlements, tumbled into love with him in the beat of a hurt,

and that very night sheared her own sleeping father like some feeble-minded sheep.

:::: **debris**
Networks. Weaves. Plaits. How each of us becomes hole.

:::: **debris**
Because, appalled by Scylla's lack of filial devotion, Daddy departed at once, leaving Nisos's daughter keening on the dock.
Each star in the sky a pinprick upon her skin.

:::: **debris**
Because every labyrinth is both plan and tangle.

:::: **debris**
Method and mess.

:::: **debris**
Wait. I believe I have just had a dream.

:::: **debris**
Method and

:::: **debris**
had Nisos not blurred himself into an osprey and swooped down to destroy her.

:::: **debris**
Yes: There is no other word for it.

:::: debris
Because at the last instant Nisos's daughter quivered into a tiny storm
petrel that darted away from her father over the waves.

:::: mark z. danielewski song
Because we all create stories to protect ourselves.

:::: debris
Because her father pursued.

:::: lidia yuknavitch song
Because you make up stories until you find one you can live with.

:::: debris
Yes: I can assert with some confidence I have just had a dream.

:::: debris
Because Scylla's daddy would not forget.

:::: queen elizabeth song
Because the past cannot be cured.

:::: debris
Because the screamings say I will never have heard enough.

:::: debris
They just keep on arriving.

:::: debris
They just keep rushing at me.

:::: debris

Because now and forever Nisos is one beak clip away from tattering Scylla into a burst of bloody feathers.

:::: debris

Because the historians chronicle how the Athenian courts tried and banished Daedalus.

A swineherd found him washed up on Crete's shores and led him to our palace. Impressed by his talent, Daddy took him in and designated him royal architect. Not long after his arrival, Mommy fell in lust with a giant white bull sent by Poseidon to penalize her for being herself. She ordered Daedalus to build her a wooden cow draped in cowhide to fool the bull into squalling her.

Now whenever you listen to Debris you are really listening to the echo of Mommy and that bull coupling through the night in a damp, rocky field at the edge of Knossos.

The echo's heart is sometimes referred to as the Daedalus Penance, sometimes as the Age of Loneliness.

:::: debris

Although it is equally possible to assert with some confidence I have just had a vision.

Or a memory, perhaps. Perhaps I have just had a memory.

Or perhaps one could say a dream just had me.

Whatever the case, the muscular young man I could not recognize to whom my sister, Ariadne, had handed something I could not make out now stood before the throne in a palace so sun flooded it seemed to me as if the lavish furniture itself were no longer solid but hazy diffusions of solar particles.

The muscular young man was addressing someone. I could not make out whom. I could not make out what he was saying, what land he was saying it in.

And then—all at once—I saw his mouth move and heard him speak my name and I balked awake into a rush of Mommy whispers.

:::: debris

Atmosphere greasy with my smells.

:::: **pasiphaë chorus**
and when the midwife pulled the steaming godshit from between my
legs I took one glance and commanded her *kill it kill it kill the inaccu-
racy* but my husband chuckled and said *this bounty is yours sunshine
a reward from the gods for how you have lived your life* and with that
he ordered the wet nurse to deliver my living failure into the labyrinth's
flexions deep beneath our bed and Minos strode out of the birthing
chamber and out of my love and before that day drowned itself in the
wine-dark sea the godshit had been tucked away from our citizens' eyes
and ears forever while I had discovered just how lavishly a woman can
hate a man how much you think this blistering affliction is all the white-
hot loathing you can fist inside you only to learn there can always be
more and after that more still and

:::: **debris**
Unless I am still asleep. There is always that.

:::: **bradley manning song**
Because I want to thank everybody who has supported me over the last
three years. I am forever indebted to those who wrote to me, made a
donation to my defense fund, or came to watch a portion of the trial. As
I transition into this next phase of my life, I want everyone to know the
real me. I am Chelsea Manning. I am a female. Given the way I feel, and
have felt since childhood, I want to begin hormone therapy as soon as
possible. I hope that you will support me in this transition. I also request that, starting today, you refer to me by my new name and use the
feminine pronoun.

:::: **debris**
Imagine Lady Tiresias's bracelet clicking with his bits on my wrist as I
prowl, Daedalus and his son always feeling their way along just a few
hundred paces in front of me.

:::: **debris**
Because sometimes I have the impression I exist, and then that
changes.

Lance Olsen

:::: sir arthur evans song

It was March 1900, the enamel sky a singular dry blue, the air cool, invigorating, and, having both secured the crucial land—by means of generous private donations made to me through the Cretan Exploration Fund—and ordered stores from Britain, I hired two foremen from the most capable of the generally incapable (if ever childishly cheerful and rigorously uncurious) locals, who in turn hired thirty-two diggers, and the lot of them went merrily to work on the flower-covered hill beneath which I was certain lay the inconceivable ruins.

:::: debris

And before that and after that I watched Paris steal Helen away from her husband and black flames burn through a decade. I watched beautiful broken Cassandra—pale skin, blue eyes, red hair kept in curls; raped repeatedly by Ajax the Lesser on the floor of Athena's temple where she fled in search of refuge—I watched beautiful broken Cassandra babble from the post to which she had been tied before the gates of junked Troy, disinterested pedestrians passing her by. I watched a nation suffer toward truth, believing it was sharing something important, something lasting that would unite it, even as it already knew all its beliefs had been nothing but bluffs, its politicians best at organizing human weakness. Hell to ships, hell to men, hell to cities, and Clytemnestra clawing a dagger across Cassandra's bared throat because Agamemnon had taken the disbelieved seer as war spoil. An arrow pierced swift-footed Achilles's heel and his body pitched forward into death. And before that and after that I watched him, Achilles—no trace of his own ruin shadowing his features—slit the heels of Hector's corpse, pass Ajax's belt through them, and drag the breaker of horses around the fortress walls until Hector's body effaced itself into the rocky earth. Shocked Icarus dropping through luminous blueness, hands raking sunlight, shredded wings disassembling around him.

:::: debris

Imagine death need not concern you because as long as you live death is not here and when it finally arrives you no longer live.

Now imagine you are wrong.

:::: **debris**
How there was blue sky. I won't deny it. But not mine. Not the one above me.

:::: **odysseus song**
Because I am a poor old stranger here, you see. My home is far away. There is no one known to me in countryside or city.

:::: **debris**
Or perhaps this is the dream and the other thing the other thing.

:::: **edward snowden song**
Because there is no saving me. I do not expect to see home again.

:::: **pasiphaë chorus**
despite the fact I bore the bastard Acacallis Ariadne Androgeos Catreus Deucalion Glaucus Phaedra Xenodice still Minos makes a daily art of amnesia refusing to mention the mistake barking up at us into our sleep every night or consider the boundless perplexity webbing below our feet and so it is that every day hating him I have a greater and greater sense I have how to say it have begun to approximate myself yes a greater and greater sense I am gradually becoming the how do you say it the imprecision of Pasiphaë a for example cousin yes or perhaps friend who stopped writing the lonely queen decades ago

:::: **debris**
And once I entered a chamber to rest a few millennia and when I rose to scuttle on I discovered I could not locate the door.

I assumed at first I had misplaced it, was groping the wrong wall. I made a slow survey of the room with my free hand, Catastrophe rooting me on, but encountered nothing save gritty blank surfaces and right angles.

What, I wondered, if this was another Daedalus trick? If the door was gone for good? Debris could starve in here. Debris could be forgotten.

As I stood there vexing my paws together, my brother mumbling beneath my arm, the walls exploded into a whirl of knife blades. The knife blades exploded into an applause of white hands. The white hands exploded into a mischief of mice. The mice exploded into a zeal of invisible angels. The invisible angels exploded into an ambush of orange shrieks.

And that is when I understood everything was as it should be, was as it had always been, would always be—and so I crouched in place to wait out the hot blood drizzle that had begun falling around us.

:::: **abdullah ibn umar song**
Because you must be in the world as if you were a stranger or a traveler.

:::: **debris**
Because something, in any case, is beginning.

:::: **debris**
Invariably.

:::: **debris**
Isn't it?

:::: **catastrophe chorus**
    accuse me

                  It is
true

        but it is also true

     Shall I repeat

            The sun
of a child

    gathered stones.

nothing

is communicable by the art of writing.

for the nights and days are long.

I let myself

fall until I am bloody.

But of all the games, I prefer the one about the other   .
I pretend that   comes to visit me and that I

The house is the same size as the world;

Perhaps I have created the stars

my redeemer

my redeemer

my redeemer

Song of Magsaysay
John Parras

WITH ALIPATO IMPRISONED and the rebels defeated and the nation at peace, Jejo resigned from his post at the AFP Eighteenth and returned to Lingayen, the tolerable port town in northern Luzon where his life had begun, to raise chickens. He had his army pistol (he wasn't giving that up) and fifty pesos in his pocket and ten years of war to account for, three against the Japanese and seven against himself. He would score his trespass, scrape together enough fowl to start a small business, and maybe find another Red, the gamecock who had kept his pockets full in '49 and nearly gotten him killed in 1950. He'd loved that steadfast rooster almost more than his own wife for a time, loved him for the life he enabled Jejo, those wild nights of coconut wine and outrageous bets and girls on the side and bold, furtive meetings in the jungle with men reeking of boar fat and gun oil and cash counted in the head. Back then he could reckon how many pesos in a wad by glancing at the edges of the dirty bills rolled together and tied with jute. He'd take the string off the bills and stuff them in a front pocket and use the string to tie the double-edged gaffs to Red's feet. The cock would judge Jejo with his yellow eyes, wary and fearless at once, and tense his strong wings. Beautiful, ragged, wine-black wings. Wings like those of the angels Jejo had witnessed at the Battle of Urdaneta in '43, when the Rikugun Taisa slaughtered the *sitio* of Balaoen and tossed the bodies into the Agno. Blood-black wings, hardboiled in the cauldron of war, brought now to the dirt pit of a squalid village cockfight.

Red's opponent that night was a haughty rooster by the name of Boy, a newcomer from the barrio of Bayambang, larger than Red and younger and likely quicker, with an ebony head and ocher feathers as lustrous as polished balsa and a reputation whose grass-fire spread seemed to have summoned the entire underworld of Rosales to the *sabong*. The arena bleachers creaked with feral anticipation as all those fools, hypnotized by Boy's meretricious strut, placed their hard-earned centavos into the brokers' hands. All across the islands it was a time of recklessness and seeming plenty. The new democracy had seeped like alcohol into the blood of the people, given them hopes of self-determination. As long as you weren't a tenant farmer pathetically locked up in the feudalism of the past, you had a peso or two in your pocket to wager on the future, which hovered like the prize ring on the amusement-park carousel—and here it was, brother, in Boy's gleaming feathers and brusque martial swagger, right in front of you.

Even Lamar, Jejo's second, faltered there in the back room. Jejo was annoyed at Lamar's slumped posture, at the fright in those averted eyes. It was irksome and uncalled for, and on impulse Jejo reached into his pocket and pulled out the thick roll of bills. Give this to Old Titan, he said, stretching out his arm to Lamar.

But Lamar shook his head. That one looks smart, he said. I heard he beat every cock in the Villasis *sabong*, to say nothing of Bayambang.

Well, we're not in Villasis or in Bayambang, Jejo said, we're here in Rosales. Give Titan the money before it's too late.

Lamar put out a limp hand and let the bills be placed in it. Are you sure? he said.

Jejo turned away and crouched to tighten a knot on Red's foot. He pressed his thumb softly against the gaff, sharper than a razor. He laid a warm hand on Red's warm wing.

Give him the goddamn money, Lamar.

Lamar turned and left. When he was gone, Jejo took Red in both hands and held him up to study his eyes, two roving, citrine gems with their own inner light. He was sure. And a few minutes later when he stepped out into the pit he was sure. The fellow from Bayambang was already out there in the loud, smoky air. His name was Maol and he had the look of an essentially destitute man on the string of many successes. Boy was crooked in his arm like a brand-new trophy and for just a moment Jejo doubted. He thought about the astronomical sum of money he'd put on the fight—he even turned to see if Lamar had given Old Titan the money yet, all the money Jejo possessed save for the fifty pesos buried in a jar in the ground beneath the ageless tamarind, all the money he'd risked his life for messing around in the jungle in the middle of the night selling Garands or gasoline or rice or information, then turning around and selling it back to the other side, his side—though he wasn't sure which side he was on half the time. He knew only that his veins craved what the world gave him whenever he found himself in that in-between space where people took you for what you appeared to be and what you appeared to be was what you did. And Jejo could do a lot, even more since the previous

79

ACP[1] liaison had been caught napping on duty and sacked, and he, Jejo, made regimental documenter in his place—all due to Magsaysay, a man who Jejo had by then come to recognize could do more than anybody else.

And then he wasn't doubting anymore, he was squatting in the pit dirt with Red in his hands squaring off with the fellow from Bayambang and his beautiful cock. He couldn't hear what with the betting's deafening din but saw the pit master's lips move and loosed Red into the pit with Boy, Red looking scruffy beside that golden cock and sluggish beside that cock's evident dispatch. Boy moved his head up and forth, back and down, side to side, sizing up Red's threats and weaknesses. The crowd's cacophonous cries thundered throughout the arena. Men who three hours earlier had been begging twigs at the edge of fallow fields now stretched out fistfuls of money and screamed feverishly as the cocks made zigzag feints, lifting their feet delicately, darting their delirious eyes, and with their gaffs nicking small cuts into the packed dirt of the pit, little letters of an alphabet no one could understand. The gold cock raised his head high, shot out his wings, and rushed forward like an ocean wave, Red rising at the same time not quite as high and lifting both his feet and striking out as Boy came in. Shouts surged in the smoky air. Wings flurried faster than the human eye. The two cocks were a violent knot of dust and movement at the center of the fight pit then of a sudden separate again, two roosters eyeing one another warily while a few stray feathers floated down onto the dust like discarded memories. The crowd swooned and hushed and the arena floor seemed to tilt. For Jejo it felt as though the entire island, the whole beleaguered key of Luzon had been lifted on the giant swell of a tsunami, and in that surreal and quiet weightlessness he heard his wife's voice calling to him from the kitchen, listened to her dip the bamboo spoon into the crock, hearkened to his son's small, high pleasure at the miracle of dinner. He realized it was over. The cock from Bayambang lifted one foot and, as if not wanting to step in his own blood, couldn't find a place to put it down again. He tumbled onto his side and stretched out one wing and retracted it and twitched his head three last times.

Jejo was already moving forward. He swept his rope-soled shoes across the pit dirt and scooped Red up even before Boy's eye had ceased its seeing. The bettors roared and surged, clambering from the rickety benches down onto the dirt floor of the pit and across to collect

[1]Army Civilian Personnel

or mourn their money, the fellow from Bayambang all the while waving his arms and yelling something through his rotted teeth. Jejo shoved himself rearward through the throng of men, keeping Red tucked protectively under one arm, and went out back beneath the bleachers to the coop. Old Titan would give him the money later. He patted Red as much to calm himself as the cock and quickly untied the gaffs and put them in his pocket. He placed Red in the cage and checked the water and the feed and latched the door and then Lamar, out of breath, was at the chicken wire saying, Jejo, there's something wrong. Jejo could hear a gang of men yelling and shoving their way underneath the bleachers to the coop. He hurried down an unlit corridor and out a back door and considered escaping across the dark, empty lot when Red's brave orange eye blinked as if in Jejo's own mind and stopped him. He had the money coming to him now and he could do what he wanted. He looked at the empty lot with its weeds and broken glass and at a row of battered palms in the distance and at the shards of stars overhead, and instead of fleeing he turned and walked slowly around the sagging stadium, back into the electric lights out front.

Men were streaming from the arena talking loudly and shaking their heads and grabbing each other's shirts and buying bottles of beer from a smart peasant set up outside the stadium. Jejo went over and bought a bottle himself. The bottle was green and the beer American and nothing he'd call cold. Get yourself more ice, he said to the peasant, tossing him a few centavos. The peasant took the money and put it in his pocket. Jejo moved over to a streetlight and leaned his back against the pole. Above the halo of electric light muddy shapes swooped down from the night and snapped at the flying insects. Bats. That was when Maol emerged from the stadium with some of his friends and one of them pointed at Jejo. They strode over and stood around him, one behind him to his left and one behind him to his right and another behind Maol's left shoulder. Maol was wearing a white T-shirt with a big hole in one armpit and his mouth hung open like an ugly black wound.

I know what you did, Maol said. Thin muscles rippled on his bare arms.

What did I do? Jejo said.

I know what you did, Maol said again.

What? Jejo said.

Motherfucker, Maol said, the gaff was long. No way Boy would lose to that hen of yours, not.

Take it up with the *sentensyador*, Jejo said. His name is Don Titan.
I know, Maol said. So why you rub the tracks out then? Why you
run off with your hen and untie the gaffs before anyone see?

The gaffs. Jejo had them in his pocket and he reached in and
grasped one delicately with the fingers of his right hand.

It was a fair fight, Jejo said, unlike this one, but which I won't lose
either. He took a draft of his beer, raised the bottle to Maol, and said,
Why don't you have one? And from his pocket he pulled the gaff out
into plain sight. Have a beer, Jejo said, it was a fair fight.

The tendons in Maol's neck flickered and the fraught constellation
of men with Jejo at its center seemed to quiver. It was a country
accustomed to great, unimaginable violence. Violence was a taste in
the air like the too-sweet scent of jasmine, murder a hunger gnawing
at the Philippine soul. The islanders had learned it in Bataan and
Corregidor, at Malaga and Balangiga, at Lonoy and Tupas Cebu and on
Mactan and before, in the aboriginal rites, the ghoulish ceremonies
honoring the ancient poltergeists. Jejo sensed those spirits of the other
world press in around him, greedy for another man. He felt his body
grow tight like a bow drawn back and was ready to hurl himself at
the mark.

But the world shifted and torqued. Time curved, and the spirits
withdrew as an engine rumbled into earshot and a truck pulled up.
Its brakes gave a short, loud squeal and several soldiers jumped down
from the back of the truck and headed for the beer cart. Sergeant
Castro recognized Jejo immediately. The sergeant approached in a
slumped swagger, swinging his heavy rifle low, and was about to
smile when he saw Jejo staring at Maol and read Maol's sweaty glare,
full of the hatred of a man who thinks he's been wronged or was
wronged, there was no difference. Maol's men were already gone, disappeared into the dregs of the crowd, and Maol too was about to
leave with a last look of bitter scorn when Castro called out to him.

Hey, you.

Maol turned, his face dull with hostility.

Your papers, Castro said, flicking his fingers toward him and glancing at Jejo conspiratorially.

I have none, Maol said.

Money then, Castro snapped.

Maol just shrugged.

No papers, no pesos, Castro sang in an evil voice, glancing around
to make sure he had the attention of his audience.

Jejo had seen this type of thing—one man waving a gun at another with vicious glee—too many times before, and somewhere in his mind one time was one too many. But a couple of the privates grinned at the little drama Sergeant Castro was putting on for them, pulling at their beers and happy that the universe had arbitrarily granted them power and seeming immortality.

Maol hung his arms down like two wasted puppets.

You're a sympathizer! Castro said loudly.

Maol shook his head.

You like them, don't you, Castro hissed interrogatively, prodding Maol in the ribs with the barrel of his rifle. The Communists.

No, Maol said.

Castro circled around, a hyena taking its time. Jejo could see the sweat on Maol's forehead. Maol suddenly seemed familiar, a face in the jungle dark just beyond the firelight.

No? Castro asked. You don't like Communists?

Maol shook his head.

Say they are scum.

They are scum, Maol said.

And you are scum, Castro said.

Maol shook his head.

Say it!

They are scum, Maol said.

Castro looked over at Jejo for a cue. Jejo wanted it finished. He inclined his head slightly to one side. He would, he suddenly decided, use the money he'd won to leave this abysmal place. Get off the islands altogether. Go to America and work on the railroad.

Get the fuck out of here, Castro said to Maol, waving the rifle, and Maol was gone.

Castro poked a thumb over his own shoulder. Fucking bandito, that one, he said with a grin and a shake of his head.

But Jejo was looking at the soldiers crowding around the beer peddler's cart. He said, Tell your men to pay for the beer, Castro.

Are you kidding? Castro said. We were on patrol over in Nogales all afternoon and barely had time to eat a rice ball before we were ordered over to Cubao just after sunset. You know what it's like over there? We had to bulldoze and burn. The men worked hard. We're on our way back to base.

They should pay, Jejo said.

Not on our salary, Castro said, and it was as though Magsaysay had heard him, Jejo remembered afterward, as though the secretary could eavesdrop on the multitudinous whispers coursing across the archipelago. For not two months later the law was drafted in Magsaysay's own hand on a yellow-paged legal pad and typed up by an assistant and passed on, and on 15 September 1950, word reached the Rosales garrison that soldiers' daily pay was to be raised from thirty centavos to one full peso, effective immediately, with the caveat that any soldier hereafter caught confiscating or demanding food from peasants without compensation would be punished to the full extent of the military code. But the soldiers merely smiled at one another and winked and shrugged, because who would tell on them? And they laughed like children and punched one another on the shoulder and grinned because they could finally afford some whores the likes of Niñita, the Chinese girl who worked at Madame Tin's place off the plaza and had volcano-shaped breasts and was rumored to have such a sweet spot she could squeeze the juice out of your pingo without thrusting—but pay for food? Never.

The soldiers chuckled for a few weeks, until the next order was passed, an unthinkable one declaring that from this day forth until further notice all citizens of the islands, from Luzon to Mindanao and from Palawan to Samar, including especially the destitute and the illiterate and specifically all landless peasants, migrant agricultural workers, indentured servants, and small-time merchants, were hereby empowered to send telegrams of complaint free of charge from any postal office directly to the Department of National Defense. And by November it was already clear that the telegrams didn't go straight to scissors, nor were they piled in a bin and left to fade and rot. There was an entire room in Malacañang Palace with a full-time staff scrutinizing the messages and filing each telegram and cataloging each offense, with the worst abuses passed on to the inestimable Magsaysay himself and read by him and acted on, with well-tuned army jeeps pulling up at dawn in even the remotest backwaters of the islands unloading Magsaysay's devout minions, smart young officers with ironed uniforms and heavy metal clipboards who poked around asking questions and took the peasants for their very word, swear to God Almighty.

Jejo had heard, for instance, of a farmer in Conception, half a day's walk from Rosales, who was given a hog after his own had been confiscated by a squad from the Fiftieth Regiment and slow-roasted in a shallow pit. And now that squad had been removed to Davao and was said to be clearing trees and filling swamps from sunup till midnight for forty days straight, forty days of penance for a pig. But the pig—even that paled if you believed the rumors about Davao, for whispers had been circulating among the palm fronds and rice fields of the provinces, whispers of promise and generosity, whispers that the government was giving away land on the island of Mindanao. Of course, it couldn't be true. Could anyone, could even Magsaysay care enough about the peasants to give them land? When Jejo considered the idea and found himself half believing, he scoffed for being such a gullible fool. He prided himself on being a man not easily taken in, something his father had taught him one long-gone afternoon with a stick and a coin and a bucket of water, his father who'd swept the schoolhouse every morning and gleaned the pastor's field and weeded the cemetery every Sunday for twenty years and refused to sign papers he couldn't read and so signed nothing and lost nothing, unlike the peasants who marked the church papers with a charcoal *X* legal as taxes and saw their little huts and their pitiful fields of grain and even their skinny livestock sequestered until they had nothing but rags on their backs and ten years of work to pay for what they didn't own anymore. Jejo, though he'd escaped such fate thanks to his father's strong head, didn't see that the world had changed much since then.

Still, now there were Magsaysay's free telegrams and impromptu inspections, and the peasant reimbursed a hog in Conception. Those things had happened. So, Jejo thought, why not land? Rising up inside him and gaining clarity, the idea broomed the future clean, opening up possibilities neither Jejo nor the country had ever before considered. Land for Arms—the slogan was so simple, so beautiful and elegant, and it'd been Magsaysay's idea, it was Magsaysay who'd heard the grumbling of the destitute, Magsaysay who was sending the army to the south to clear land for the peasants—or so the winds were whispering.

There were many whispers by then and, like Magsaysay, Jejo had his ear keenly trained to them. There were whispers about loads of American money trucked into the PDD[2] by night, legal tender as green as fig leaves. And it was said that in the presidential palace there existed a red Bakelite phone wired directly to Washington, DC, and that every evening at 8:00 p.m. sharp the phone rang and Elpidio Quirino picked it up and was forced to listen to President Truman's folksy but stern convictions on the politics of Pakistan and China, and now Korea, until his ear hurt. More menacingly, Truman spoke the word "atomic" often, and sometimes the adjective "hydrogen."

---

[2]Philippine Department of Defense

John Parras

Elpidio was chilled by how casually the American president uttered such words, for Truman spoke them as if he were conversing over coffee and biscuits, and Elpidio, feeling as though the moisture of the evening jungle were seeping into his bones, would motion to his aides to shut the grand palace windows.

In coming days it was noted that an unannounced military advisor, pale as a ghost but cougar strong and wily, had begun haunting the hallways of Malacañang Palace. Magsaysay's white shadow, the people called him. So pale, like a vampire. And like a vampire, capable of unspeakable acts. In the same breath came talk of something called joosmog[3] being crated off the destroyers in Subic Bay, though what it was was anyone's guess. Unmarked crates unloaded by gargantuan cranes in the early gray mornings, innumerable wooden crates the size of coffins, still reeking of pine and sticky with resin. Juice magg, someone murmured. Special feed for the horses, because a cavalry was being prepared for an assault up the plains and into the Baguio pass. Jusmag incendiary to defoliate the heavy palms and creeper vines enshrouding Mount Arayat, and they would dry up the Candaba Swamp with the sponge of the dead foliage. Jussmug: propaganda designed by Madison Avenue admen to brainwash the enemy, bullet-proof armor, undepletable energy, the ability to see at night. The seagulls careening above Subic Bay decried and laughed above the ships, the monkeys on Corregidor bayed sorrowfully from their trees, the Pasig floated rumors upstream into the artichoke heart of Luzon where the Huks around their campfires, looking up at the coconut moon, hearkened carefully, full of skepticism and cunning; hungry, idealistic men fortified and made realistic by their convictions.

Those Huks, they looked up at the same seashell moon Jejo admired walking home after Red's *sabong* and the aborted fistfight with Maol, but the rebels were in the jungle, sprawled beneath banana leaves amid swarms of mosquitoes, while Jejo retired to his grass-roofed Bontoc hut beside the river on the edge of town and drank whiskey from a bottle, just enough to give him a little push into the night, Josephine Baker at low volume on the radio. With his winnings he would leave for America, soon. He ate bread dipped in left-over adobo sauce and flipped through an old issue of *Time*, now and then lifting his eyes to gaze at the glamour shot of Lee Miller he'd clipped from a newspaper and slipped into an edge of the mirror frame, the beautiful Lee Miller sitting in her daddy's lap, her face

---

[3]JUSMAG: Joint US Military Advisory Group

86

sculpture perfect, her prim black dress boding ferocious sensuality. Right now she was in a New York skyscraper, just roused from peaceful sleep by sunlight reflecting off the East River, a long way away, Jejo mused, more than a world away from Rosales and its ignorant wooden shacks, its dark peoples, its common violences. He thought of Red crouching in his cage in the darkness behind the arena and of Maol driving back to Bayambang with Boy dead on the floorboard, how the headlights would be cutting through the darkness and edging along the blackness of the trees on either side of the road, the pine trees at the edge of the forest where the Hukbo Magpalaya ng Bayan were gathered in small bands, tending their fires and cleaning their weapons, then lying down on the ground to listen to the wind in the brush and to the spirits as ancient as darkness slipping through the trees and sleep.

Jejo too. He turned off the radio and snuffed the lamp and lay down on the mattress with his arms behind his head. July mosquitoes buzzed at the sleeping net and Jejo covered his feet tightly with the sheet to keep the *asuangs* from the scent. Those supernatural creatures were the ghosts of men and women and children murdered by the Japanese Army at Balaoen and thrown from the Santa Maria Bridge into the Agno River. After midnight on moonlit nights their busted skeletons, the bones blackened with mud and hardened by the cruelty they'd suffered, would clamber from the river seeking reprieve from their watery purgatory. Drawn to the sour redolence of human sweat, they would steal into your bedroom and grasp your ankle with a bony hand, and if you reached for a lamp there'd already be another skeletal hand on it so you were forced until morning to bear their hissed whispers telling you of gold they had buried and would you dig up the gold for them in the dead of night to pay for their passage out of purgatory? Because the afterlife was just as greedy and unfair as the Manila slums, and the murdered, though they had the sympathy of the living, were scorned by the dead and spat on and their sufferings scoffed at, for the spirits held the souls of victims and oppressors both vile. The Catholic Church was wrong and those who believed the scriptures would be miserable in the afterlife, where the spirits were more ancient than the Bible and darker and deeper than the blackest depths of the Philippine Trench.

Nearby a woman let out an eerie shriek and Jejo flinched—but it was just his neighbors bickering. He laughed at himself, and someone next door slammed down a pan and the night was quiet again. Wind whispered in the tamarind outside, a truck sighed by on the road and was gone, a night bird clucking in the brush nearby seemed to say, "Magsaysay, Magsaysay" softly. Outside the province of Zambales the name was then but a murmur, the vague promise of a future that would probably never be, like a lover's vow sworn in the innocence of youth. Jejo himself had made such vows and made them in perfect sincerity. But *Magsaysay*. Wasn't there song in the name? It wouldn't be until later, after he'd witnessed the village of Camposan razed to the ground and had himself been carried along on a river-swift current of military might, that Jejo would understand the name was no soft melody but more like the undertow in Lingayen Bay, vicious and unrelenting and vain to resist.

In the morning he arose late. He considered heading over to collect his winnings from Don Titan, but thought he should check in at the military base first. Army Civilian Personnel had some degree of autonomy, but there were limits. He'd been made regimental documenter after all. He had black coffee and cassava and walked to the center of town, making his way along the shade of the stone buildings in the old quarter to the wide, flat, sunny steps of the Spanish church. Horse traps vied with Fords and vendor carts at the circular fountain in the crowded square, and on the main pedestrian thoroughfare, flagged with tan lava cobblestones, mestizos in dark suits had their shoes shined at the newspaper stands and ladies dressed in Spanish dresses shopped for hats. A single trolley line ran from the church along the avenue to the other side of town, then more freely out past the seamstress factories and tobacco plantations toward the garrison. Jejo stood on an outer platform and hung with an arm swung round one of the poles, taking in the scenes as they passed, the urbane Castilian quarter, the shabbier shops surrounding the central marketplace, the shameful poverty of the shanties at the edge of town, then the green fields and palm trees along the farmland and haciendas just before the garrison, where the trolley looped back to town in a teardrop turnaround. At the garrison gate a food vendor had set up his empanada cart and, a bit to one side, in the shadow of a tree, a clump of beggars held out their hands and implored Jejo for a few centavos. Jejo thought again of the winnings he'd collect from Don Titan and realized he was due a pile of cash bigger than he'd ever amassed in his lifetime. He patted his pockets for spare change and handed a beggar a few coins, then showed his ID to the guard and went in through the garrison gates.

The Eighteenth Battalion grounds were jeep-busy, the soldiers marching at quick clips, the telegraphs at the comm stations clicking like castanets. Over at the arms depot, Sergeant Castro was supervising the unloading of a shipment of wooden crates.

Hey, Jejo.

What's going on?

Something big, my friend. Castro nodded at the crates being carried off the transport vehicles. Enormous shipment from Manila. And the coms are powwowing in the main office, blinds drawn. There's brass in there, and two Americans.

Americans?

White as ghosts.

Are they officers?

Uniformed but unranked, the sergeant answered.

They both knew what it meant that the Americans had shown up. The AFP was preparing a major assault into rebel territory.

That Bondoc, Castro said, did it. That mayor.

Who killed the girl? Jejo said.

I mean their stringing him up by the heels in San Luis. That can't go unpunished.

But, Jejo said, the little girl. Wasn't she American?

I don't know about that, Sergeant Castro said.

If she was American, well . . .

Don't you see, Castro said, the Communists killed Bondoc because he was sloppy, because they needed the jeeps themselves, not for murdering the girl. But it's the girl who's got the Americans all riled up. Her death.

Revenge for her death, Jejo said.

Because the Communists forced his hand, forced him to kill her. Only he got caught.

So they killed him.

Castro sighed. Something's got to be done anyway.

Yes, Jejo agreed. Luzon was fraying at the seams. In the past five days the rebels had robbed two banks near Rosales, plundered a battalion supply depot outside Asingan, and skirmished with a reconnaissance unit in the San Roque forest—and this only in the province. The Huks also moved freely throughout Tarlac, Pampanga, and Bulacan, and Jejo had overheard the term *Huklandia* murmured more than once in the bars and cafés of his stomping grounds. It was an open secret that the rebels now ruled Nueva Ecija. The mayor of San Luis, Atilio Bondoc, had been killed and strung up by his ankles in the square with his mistress, Bondoc for being a pig of a mayor and his mistress for being the whore of a pig mayor who'd ordered his Civil

Guardia to kidnap the wife of the American investigator. Only they'd taken his daughter too and now the girl was dead. So the army would strike back—but for what exactly? The army itself—the Philippine Army at the insistence of the American Army—had begun the investigation into Bondoc's reselling of surplus jeeps, and when Bondoc had tried to bind the army's hands with blackmail, the Hukbalahaps, to whom he was selling the jeeps, had stopped him. But why? The Communists were the enemies of the army and of America, and they'd been profiting from the jeeps, so the politics didn't make sense. It all spun around in Jejo's head like pebbles at the bottom of an ocean wave. Jejo remembered his former teacher, Señor Roderigo Perez, the old taskmaster at Andrés Bonifacio High School who'd taught history as a tidy storeroom of battles and treaties you could map and sequence, but now Jejo found he could hardly put things in the order in which they occurred, for who knew for sure the order in which things occurred or what caused what?

But Sergeant Castro was talking.

What was that? Jejo asked.

I said you've got a package. The sergeant unbuttoned his shirt pocket and pulled out a requisition slip.

What is it?

Something from Manila, Castro replied. Likely a carton of blank forms. More paperwork. He handed the slip to Jejo. If this army makes me fill out one more goddamn form I'll carve out my own kneecaps with a bowie knife.

But you'll have to fill out a form first, Jejo said.

Soon we'll have to fill out a form just to take a shit.

We'll have to fill out a form to fill out a form.

Sometimes I miss the good ol' constabulary, Castro said.

Don't say that too loud, Jejo said.

Another truck rumbled up to the depot. Castro turned his head, hawked, and spit. Well, the sergeant said, straightening his cap.

They shook hands and parted. Jejo walked across the dusty compound to the commissary to retrieve the package. Standing at the entrance bearing a polished rifle was a marine guard Jejo had never seen before. He showed the guard the requisition slip and was waved by. The commissary, made of corrugated tin, was sweltering inside. Two slow fans did nothing but push the heat around.

Jejo handed the attending clerk the slip of paper. The clerk went to one of the shelves, selected a box, and gave it to Jejo.

Sign, the clerk said, shoving a clipboard forward.

What is it? Jejo asked.

How should I know? the clerk answered. He pointed a finger: Sign on that line.

Jejo signed his full legal name, "Herbert Juan Dumlao," using the elegant script Señor Perez had drilled into every Bonifacio Public School cohort for the past quarter century, and the clerk handed Jejo a square box just big enough to lug under one arm.

He went out onto the veranda and opened the package. Inside, carefully pillowed in Styrofoam and corrugated cardboard, was a camera. Jejo was reading the accompanying memo when the commissary clerk stepped out onto the veranda and stood beside him.

Do I have to sign something else? Jejo asked.

No, the clerk said, I'm on my break. He glanced at the camera. What's that for?

I'll have to read the memo, Jejo said.

The clerk shrugged. His name was Eduardo and it was his lunchtime. He walked off, over to the vendor who sold empanadas from a handcart parked just outside the garrison gates. The vendor looked Mactan, with a square face and strong nose; long, straight hair black as jet and thick as fishing line; and colored loop earrings. As soon as Eduardo stepped up to the cart, the vendor handed him an empanada. It smelled delicious. Eduardo often wondered where the vendor had learned to cook such excellent Mexican food. Then again, the country was full of hybrid bastards and Eduardo didn't really care. He bit into the empanada and chewed, then spoke to the vendor.

There's a big celebration planned, Eduardo said, his mouth half full. The empanada was delicious and he took another bite. He swallowed. In Camposan and environs, Eduardo added.

The vendor looked at Eduardo with coal-black irises. When?

Maybe ten days.

How many musicians in the band? the vendor inquired.

We're looking at twenty.

The vendor's dark eyes flashed, calculating. That's four hundred pastries, he observed.

Yes, the clerk confirmed. But at least three bands will play. Probably from Calasiao, Mapandan, and Angeles, at least. In total, I'd estimate at least twelve hundred pastries.

The food vendor nodded, flipped a tortilla on the grill.

There's something else, Eduardo said. He gestured for another empanada and the vendor deftly prepared one with a few quick movements and handed it forward.

91

Gracias, Eduardo said, then continued. Extraordinary amounts of liquor are expected—American beer and whiskey, all kinds of fancy cocktails.

The vendor nodded again, his eyes moving to something behind his customer. Eduardo glanced over his shoulder and saw a soldier approaching the food cart.

One more thing, Eduardo said quickly.

Sí?

Cameras.

Cameras? What for?

Eduardo shrugged. Just mention it, it may be important.

The soldier arrived and ordered two tamales.

Eduardo wiped his mouth with a napkin and handed some coins to the vendor. *Adiós*, he said in parting.

A mañana, the vendor responded, his head down, hands preparing the food. He was indeed renowned among local workers for his Mactan-Mexican fare, and later that evening a bus driver on his way south stopped at the cart for tacos. The driver was a talkative fellow who chatted with the food vendor until the passengers grumbled, then as he drove down to Moncada seemed to be talking to himself, repeating something over and over. Early the next morning, before he forgot, the driver had some words with a man who peddled wooden kitchen implements at the market, and the day after that the peddler's brother, who was a barber, trimmed the hair of Jaime Santiago, a law student organizing peasants in Cuyapo. In a few days' time Jaime's girlfriend, an itinerant nurse, made a visit to a tenant laborer on a hacienda outside Guimba. The laborer had cut his ankle on a scythe blade and the nurse sewed the skin closed and doused the wound with disinfectant. That same afternoon the laborer's wife tied a yellow scarf on a certain fence post, and a few nights later under cover of darkness a man slipped out of the forest and onto the plantation. He whisked through the sugarcane fields, then the rows of tobacco plants, stooping low but moving swiftly toward the peasants' huts. He glanced at the scarf and for long minutes crouched motionless in the shadows of the huts. There was no danger. He stood straight and walked slowly into plain view, like a man who'd gone out to take a piss, over to the third hut on the left from the granary, where he knocked thrice. A thin woman opened the door and stepped aside with a polite bow to let him pass. Her husband was sitting cross-legged on the ground before an overturned crate with a single candle and he motioned for the visitor to sit and offered him water from a coconut-shell cup. The visitor drank and the peasant spoke. They will come in ten days, maybe sooner. Camposan, La Paz, Talavera. Big sweep. He had a bandage on one ankle that he touched lightly with the tips of his fingers as he spoke, careful to include all the details passed on by the messengers. When the peasant had finished, the visitor stood and pulled a bundle from under his shirt, a boar thigh wrapped in cloth, which he placed on the rickety table. For you and yours, he said. Then he turned and went back out into the clear night.

At the far end of the sugarcane field he cooed the night-frog call softly and upon hearing the squad's reply reentered the jungle, his brow furrowed. Alipato had never been adept at hiding his feelings, one reason he'd had to leave the senate and his Manila residence in the first place to take refuge among the trees and streams. He'd gone to the mountains to fight the Imperial Japanese Army and emerged victorious, and he'd also succeed against the traitorous AFP. Despite the long haul—he'd plucked three gray hairs from his scalp the last time he'd looked at himself in a mirror—his own People's Liberation Army was finally advancing! José Lava was already vociferating for a full-scale effort to emerge from the *sitios*, overwhelm the downtown streets, and attack every constabulary post from Baguio to the Visayas until they busted down the doors of Malacañang Palace, and Alipato was almost there himself, for the skirmishes were going their way again and again, in Burgos and Mayantoc, in Guagua and Malolos and Caloocan. Not three months ago Viernes Stalin and his men had overrun Palayan City, the provincial capital! They'd decimated the Guardia Civil, burned the constabulary, sacked the warehouses, and dragged the mayor from his home, stringing him up by his heels in the main square for the crows to peck at.

Still, despite the victories, the government pushed back each time, with newer weapons, smarter tactics, more soldiers. The revolution was not quite at hand, and Alipato frowned as he rejoined his men in the jungle. Though he loved the hills and mountains, though he loved hiking at night under a pearl moon with a group of determined men, his feet sure on the steep tracks and his ideas right and good and his followers dedicated to the teeth, the path of revolution was long and hard and the decisions harrowing. Against twelve hundred government troops with new Garands—fast on the reload and accurate at a quarter mile—his band of fighters with their outdated carbines had little chance. They had but a half dozen tommies, and the ammo for the .60-caliber mortars was running low. Alipato would have to choose the lesser evil. He'd have to break camp and shift the rebel base south to the strongholds around Mount Arayat. But it hurt him, marred him indelibly. To pull back was strategically correct, but to leave the villages unprotected wasn't right, for the AFP was indiscriminate and vile, it would torch the huts and crops, break the legs of livestock, shoot suspected collaborators—men, women, and children alike—in the basal ganglia at close range and dump the bodies in the burned fields because the besieged Huks, his very own freedom fighters, had to pull back from the overwhelming firepower and sheer numbers of the government army. He'd have to raise this crucial point yet again with Lava and Viernes and the Politburo, and he determined to go to Manila immediately, not for the revolution but because he was suddenly electrified, there on the narrow, root-strewn path twisting through the night-black forest, by a longing to be near Remedios.

Like a flashbulb in the darkness, the hot-white light of desire flashed in his groin. He became aware of a bubbling in his chest, blood lava stirring in the crater of his heart. *Remedios.* He'd betray his own father or fuck a torpedo before he'd let another night go by without seeing her. Of all the depravities of living in the jungle, its swamp filths and soft-fruit miseries, those rank odors of unwashed men, the endless belabored treks, the savage humidity, the mosquito furies, the utter fierce chairlessness of the wilds—of all the jungle's grueling deprivations, being apart from that woman was the most insufferable. He longed to lose himself in her gaze and hear her call his name, ached to enfold her in his arms. He would linger on her mouth, suckle her toes, lick her vulva like a buck preparing his doe and was already making the preparations, giving orders for his men to march south through the Candaba swamps and arranging for his own travel, alone, to the capital, though his lieutenants all advised strongly against such a move. There were checkpoints, they reminded him, roadblocks, search parties, spies. And besides, the lieutenants wanted his advice on the most minute tactical logistics of the withdrawal. What time would they set out? Where should they set camp? How would they feed the horses? But Alipato grew dark and stern and asserted his leadership. Did they want him to carry their equipment and take shits for them too? A retreat's a retreat, that's what it is, you pick up your things and head south, goddamn it. You evade the enemy, you cover your tracks, you draw straws for a rear guard. Alipato rebuked his men, then walked apart, shaking his head solemnly, his heart tinged with guilt. What did they know of love, these ragged peasants and hardened fighters? Stepping along the dark path with his squad in the midst of civil war, a thousand armed men at his command and ten times as many backing up his forces, all else paled before the image of Remedios de la Playa, her slender body and seawater eyes, her limbs tugging at him as he lay atop her on the big bed in the whitewashed Ermita boudoir dazzled with afternoon light.

For the next several days, Alipato's spirit was a stone skimmed away on water, away, away from the war. He washed and cut his hair and donned the beige shirt and black worsted trousers, slightly shiny and faded, of a pharmacist. Having insisted on traveling alone, he walked down the mountain and along the mud banks of a vast expanse of rice fields until he came to a road, where the first car he flagged down gave him a ride to Camiling. His lieutenants, of course, had him shadowed by two bodyguards—two youths with long locks and dirty fingernails whom Alipato easily spotted in the next town. But forty minutes later, in downtown Bayambang, he suddenly switched jeepneys at a busy traffic circle and left the guards behind. He needed to be alone to savor his journey. He was a nondescript man with a few pesos in his pocket traveling to Manila to visit his aunt. He loved the jeepneys, adorned with religious paraphernalia or velveted with fish imagery or luridly tricked up like whores at a discotheque.

In Malasiqui he decided to have some fun with life and boarded a Try-Tran Bus Company vehicle for the trip to Manila—the company was owned by the Magsaysay family and provided the fount of its wealth, although Alipato wasn't impressed: The seats were uncomfortable, the ride was bouncy, and the cabin reeked of diesel exhaust fumes. Still, he had a laugh with himself (Most Wanted Communist Leader Eludes Magsaysay on Try-Tran Bus Line) and hunkered down in the seat as best he could. With one half of his brain he planned what he would say to the Politburo about the revolution while the other half of him, the more encompassing part, lingered on Remedios. All his experience, the entire adventure of life, was being filtered through their mutual love. He was careful to remember every detail of his sensations in order to relate them to Remedios later on in word or simply by being near her, because time would soak into him, become part of him, and when he was with Remedios he shared every fiber and atom of his being with her, words or no words, better no words, or few. He looked about him at the other passengers on the bus, their tawny arms hanging over the armrests, the straw bags in their laps, their dull or longing countenances. He stared out the window at the expanse of Luzon plain with its tall grasses and rice fields punctuated by palms and at the brown, calm mountains in the distance. While the bus was passing through Rosales, Alipato noticed a man standing in a field with a camera pointed at the sky, and for no reason Alipato could discern the idea popped into his head that there was a difference between a shaky or out-of-focus photograph and a snapshot of clouds and fog banks. God, he must really be on a kind of vacation—Alipato smiled at himself for having such a silly, shallow thought and was pleased as the bus careened on, leaving the photographer staring up at the clouds.

Jejo had spent the better part of the week taking pictures, familiarizing himself with the specifications and quirks of the 35 mm Contax issued on Magsaysay's authorization to all regimental documenters working with the Armed Forces of the Philippines. There would be no more mutilation of corpses, the accompanying memo had stated. Dismemberment of any kind, including decapitation, was strictly forbidden. All rebel deaths were from now on to be recorded by photographs, and users were encouraged to read the camera's instruction manual carefully and train themselves to become expert with the new equipment.

Jejo began by taking photos of the boy-faced soldiers of the garrison, using the rough-box texture of a pumice wall to frame their smooth, sweaty visages. He took a snapshot of Sergeant Castro with a cigar in his mouth. He carried the camera off base and took photos of the tramline and of downtown Rosales, of his house's sagging Bontoc roof cone, of his bureau top crowded with small bottles, of the white chickens pecking the ground beneath the tamarind in the yard, their heads blurred by a slow shutter speed. He took photos of the fishermen in narrow skiffs trolling their long sticks in the muddy river. And near dusk, standing in a field beside the traffic-heavy road to Manila, he trained the lens upward at great clouds silhouetted by the last oblique rays of sunlight.

Without realizing it, Jejo was succumbing to the bewitchment of the camera, to the intimacy and seduction of its lenses, with a burgeoning wonder that resembled love. The fineness of the production of the thing—made in Germany by the same kind of men who'd set Panzer turrets 66.5 millimeters off the chassis line and lodged gyroscopic accelerometers into the throats of V-2s—the fineness and perfection of the camera's production was awesome and beautiful, stunning to conceive, as if human beings, though fraught with defects, had somehow manufactured an artificial bird wing to rival the *Troides rhadamantus*. Jejo lost himself in a concentrated reverie of the world. Viewed through a carefully crafted optic that focused and framed, the ugly town of Rosales, where Jejo had wasted the last four years of his life, became engrossing down to its last detail—the decorative crenellation along the rooftop of the Castilian statehouse, the chaotic shacks in the burgeoning shantytown, tangles of electric wires, weird reflections in greasy puddles, the livid fingernails of the beggar woman at the central marketplace. Jejo wandered about town like a man who finds what he wants everywhere he turns. Without his quite realizing it, the camera's viewfinder neutralized all that was superfluous in the enormous universe and pointed him to an examination of abstract forms, the composed or random placement of objects in dimensional space, a textured physical space that seemed to hint at the larger orders of the cosmos—the Relative Importance, the Moral Vestige, the Ultimate Indifference.

One afternoon Jejo hiked the countryside around Balungao to take photos of the brooks and knobs, of the delicate longan evergreens with their dragon's-eye pendulums, of deadwood and screes, for he'd stumbled across a trove of inspiring magazines at the garrison, the personal effects of one Stewart Travis Golding, a corporal in the US Army Press Corps who'd witnessed the liberations at Antwerp and Auschwitz before volunteering for the Pacific campaign and surviving the battle of Saipan, only to be killed by a random mortar blast out of nowhere in a Manila *sitio*. One of Golding's magazines had run a profile on an American named Ansel Adams, a photographer who refused to take snapshots of people, training his twin-lens Rollei Reflex only on the natural world, on great rocks and conifer stands, on the moon rising above Yellowstone. (In comparison, Jejo found the Philippine countryside less expansive, poorer, somehow messier.) Golding's magazines—established publications such as *Life* and *Vanity Fair*, as well as a stack of artsy affairs with names like *Little Blast* and *Dadageist*—contained reproductions of artwork Jejo could have imagined not even under the vilest torture—sailors whose eyes were portholes, portraits of society men that seemed to have been painted on shattered glass, fantastic horses with rooted saplings for legs, wondrous islands that floated not in the ocean but in a sky sea dripping with delicate green tendrils. There were photos too, of course—of perfume bottles and furnaces, of crab crockery and comfortable couches and freeway cloverleafs, of the narrow-eyed wives of Dust Bowl farmers squinting into ravaged Midwestern plains. There was a street shot of a French philosopher, his eyes dream-distorted by thick spectacles, marching at the head of a Communist parade. There was a trick exposure of an Iberian painter drawing a bull in the air with light. There were pictures of cities you couldn't see across, cars with fancy superfluous fins, buildings as complicated as chess games, and women, plenty of fair women, glamorous and slim, women in dresses more beautiful than orchid flowers. A nude with the shadow of a cello on her back. A naked girl with an artichoke placed just above her navel, the well-formed leaves with their dangerous pointed tips framed by the curve of her small breasts. Women in scarves sewed of water and light—photos of women that hypnotized Jejo, that made him hopeful and wistful and gloomy, for he knew he himself would never take such pictures.

Even so, now that he had a fine camera, Jejo often daydreamed of working with the beautiful Lee Miller on a photo assignment. He did so again days later, cradling the Contax in his lap as he rode in the front seat of a transport truck with the Eighteenth Battalion Combat Team, which was lurching down the Ecija plains and entering Gatara to hunt the Huks. From Gatara, supported by a mobile heavy-weapons unit and a battery of 105-millimeter howitzers, three rifle companies marched east across the Munoz River and turned south into Camposan. As regimental documenter, Jejo stayed in the rear with a reserve company constituted mostly of inexperienced enlisted men sweating with dread and adrenaline. The reserves would be needed only in a pinch, while Jejo would be needed only afterward, to tally death.

Two miles outside Camposan, on a wide, flat, uncultivated plain, the reserve column halted. The trucks idled for twenty minutes, the engines rumbling hotly beneath the hoods as the sun rose higher into the sky. Glaring with sunlight, the door on Jejo's side grew hot, and the truck hood shook and shimmered. Lee Miller, the *Vogue* model-photojournalist who had accompanied the US Army into Germany, would have ridden in a transport much like the one Jejo found himself in now. She might even have sat beside him had she traveled to the Philippines, perhaps to document the government's fight against the insurgents and to interview Magsaysay, and Jejo had been assigned to keep an eye on her. She was charmed by his Filipino hospitality and impressed with his dexterity with the Contax as they sat side by side in the transport awaiting word of the offensive. She was wearing short fatigues (like everything she wore, made fashionable on her slim body) and her knee was sometimes pressed against his and he smiled. It was quite tropical, very hot, was it not, Lee? Jejo turned his head as if to address Ms. Miller and suddenly became aware of a bad smell, a stench that grew awful and intense and unavoidable. He was about to complain, had already opened his mouth to speak, when he realized what smelled was the young rumpled corporal sitting next to him. Jejo swallowed, and the corporal turned to him and bared his badly stained teeth in a friendly smile reeking of putrefaction.

The heat grew baking, airless, and the soldiers unbuttoned their sweaty fatigues. After another half hour a radio squawked and the engines were cut and the men began climbing down from the transports. Jejo sought shelter in the shade of one of the trucks, but the sun climbed higher and higher until there was nothing but a thin slice of shadow barely big enough for a lizard. Some of the soldiers crawled beneath the greasy chassis. Jejo instead wandered out into one of the fields, grasshoppers and crickets popping up out of the grass away from him as he stepped. The crickets had small wings and beneath the wings blue abdomens that as the insects rose and flurried airborne seemed the winking eyes of cosmeticized girls, the eyes of Lee Miller, who had come to the Far East to document the Philippine government's battle against the Communist insurgency. Naturally, she had been intrigued by the sample photographs Jejo had shown her. . . . No, it was too hot even for daydreaming. The sun was relentless as noon approached and passed. A host of crickets buzzed evilly. The heat was savage. Jejo observed as the youthful soldiers, so excited that morning by the prospect of battle, now grew static and impotent. He walked among them, pretending to fiddle with the camera dials, and snapped a few furtive shots of the soldiers' slack, disappointed postures.

There had been no word from the advance columns for three endless hours when a roar screamed over the jungle and a mushroom-brown PAF Mustang shot across the sky at striking altitude. The soldiers jumped to their feet and whooped. Moments later the explosions came, two heavy, faraway discharges, and before long a thick stroke of blackish smoke was climbing above Camposan. The soldiers gripped their weapons tightly. A few minutes later rifle fire and howitzer blasts were heard to the south-southeast, and a great host of bats was scared from its dwelling and took to the air. Soon the sky above the village was an enormous coal smear of smoke crisscrossed by the disoriented flight of the nocturnal beasts, an awesome sight that the soldiers regarded as though reading prophecies of their own births. The spell was broken by a loud, sharp shout. An engine started and another and another and the soldiers hoisted themselves back into the transports while Jejo took a last look at the crazy sky and at the nondescript field where he'd wasted almost an entire day and which, years later, when the war was over and the united nation steamed on into the second half of the century and Jejo was walking back to his hometown to raise chickens, he would remember as the last patch of earth he'd seen before his world had tilted irreconcilably, before the truck lurched forward along the pockmarked road that led to the rest of his life.

Not far ahead, lodged in a ditch beside the lane, sat a destroyed car with two charred corpses; a picnic basket, unaccountably intact, was lashed to a rack on the trunk. Further on, the column passed several villas nicked by machine-gun fire and one house, adjacent to the bridge over the Munoz River, pounded to rubble by the howitzers. Most of Camposan's small downtown had suffered only minor damage, but the outlying barrios south of town had been ravaged. The soldiers passed stables and granaries set afire, they passed destroyed tractors and wagons, they passed felled trees with monkeys dead in the fallen branches. Wretched strings of tenant laborers stood along the roadside, the thin old men raising their hands unfathomably, the women clutching their shawls, the children wailing, the grandmothers aiming stern, hopeless stares at the passing column.

South of the village Jejo was met by a lieutenant who would take him to the bodies. The lieutenant commandeered a jeep with a shortwave radio and a driver. The lieutenant sat in the front passenger seat and went on about the engine—it was always flooding, he said, and the shocks were bad and this and that—and Jejo sat on the rear bench seat with the camera around his neck and the camera bag on the floor at his feet as they wove their way through the scarred landscape.

The first four corpses to be documented were dragged from the rubble of a granary and laid out at the side of the dirt entry road like gruesome sentries. One body was clothed in a ripped *barong tagalog* and nothing besides. Another was shirtless but wore pants and boots. The third and fourth were wrapped in dirty linen saris. Jejo stood at the splayed feet of the bodies and awkwardly tried to frame one of the faces in the camera's viewfinder, but with the foreshortening the effect was one of looking the wrong way through a telescope. He then placed himself at the heads of the corpses and bent over them from the top, but the upside-down sight of those ruined visages, bruised and frowning and pained with disfigurement, dizzied him with sickness and he had to step away and drain canteen water over the back of his neck. The lieutenant observed him, making a comment neither of dispute nor sympathy. Finally Jejo took to straddling each body, one foot planted on each side of the chest, his groin positioned vulnerably over each unbeating heart, and in this way he was able to frame the faces as in passport photos or ID cards so that they could be processed into the archives of the state, correctly dead. Throughout the next hour the lieutenant led Jejo to the other bodies: a barrel-chested gunner with a tommy strapped to his torso; a man with gray hair on his chin and a machete clutched in one hand; a boy with long hair on whose face lice crawled as Jejo framed the smooth, slack features. One fighter, a woman in a torn maroon muumuu with silver-tasseled fringe, was entangled in the branches of an acacia tree. Her neck was broken and her head hung straight down with her jaw swung open as if she wanted to say something, and when two soldiers climbed up to dislodge her she let out a terrible moan of trapped gas from her anus like a final long fuck you.

The last body lay at the edge of a field where in later decades a baseball diamond would be constructed and the children of Camposan would play Little League games. The body was lying stomach down, and when the lieutenant kicked it over, Jejo immediately recognized the face, though it was unaccountably changed since he'd last encountered it—it was slack now yet frozen in its slack. The brow seemingly thoughtful but made bovine in death. The mouth was ruined as a rotted fish. Jejo's heart stuttered but his features were stone. He raised the Contax, framed the face in the viewfinder, pressed the shutter button without checking the aperture or speed, took the picture. It was Maol, his face stupid and unbelieving, finally triumphant. The image of the dead man haunted Jejo all afternoon and into dusk, all the way back to base. It was as though the bereaved Contax had burned the image of Maol's ugly face onto a film not in the camera but inside Jejo's own head, where it loomed sullenly, menaced, cussed, and grew into an obsession that obliterated art, for there would be no more Lee Miller, there would be no more enchanting landscapes, no objects made curious by composition or shade, no more interesting portraits. There was only the image of Maol leering at him with yellow eyes, a cock on the floorboards, an open mouth rank with rot yelling in a crowded stadium.

The battalion returned to the garrison after dark. Sore and tired, Jejo had climbed from the transport, shrugged the camera bag onto his shoulder, and was heading for the exit gate when someone called out to him. It was Sergeant Castro.

Jejo, he said, did you get any good pictures?

Jejo processed the sentence, understood the sentence, but couldn't believe the sentence. He didn't answer. He shook his head and walked away. Castro called after him, Where are you going, man, where are you going? *Away*, Jejo said to himself, and walked out the gate, passing dazedly under the palm trees planted along the road and heading toward the factory zone where stray dogs and prostitutes stalked in the shadows. He walked a long time without direction, zigzagging his way through a barrio of dilapidated shacks where abject children eyed him blankly, women stood in half-open kitchens washing pots, and shirtless old men picked their teeth with fish bones while in the back rooms their eldest sons made love, sprawling afterward exhausted on the mattresses like Alipato now in Manila, supine in postcoital bliss beside the sleeping Remedios. But Alipato suddenly sat up in anxious presentiment.

Cameras! he muttered.

Remedios stirred. What did you say?

The room was palely illumed by the glow of a street lamp outside the window. Remedios tried to remember what was happening. Her lover was beside her, sitting up in the bed. Something was wrong.

Alipato put a hand to his forehead and grabbed his own hair in a tight fist. I mean, he's thought of everything, every last detail!

He threw off the sheet and hurled himself to his feet. The cameras were Magsaysay's brainchild, he recognized that immediately. He paced heavily back and forth on the planks at the foot of the big bed. The darkened corners of the room were rebuses of shadow.

Luis? Remedios said. She sat up. The cotton sheet was wet beneath her.

But Alipato said, How can we triumph over that? What are we going to do?

Darling, Remedios began, but when she saw the lamentingly distrait look on her lover's face she crumbled.

Luis Alipato Taruc, the spark that set the Communist fire, was agape at the wall as though witnessing a crucifixion. With devastating clarity he looked into the future and saw the lost skirmishes and flagging rations, he saw prisoners wasted by water cure, widows, thin orphans, he saw the eyeglasses of the man who would betray him, he saw the rickety bus, he saw the grenade in the bag of oranges, he saw the crushing of the revolution.

He raised his elbows and yanked his hair hard with both hands.

What will I do? Magsaysay's thought of everything! How are we supposed to win a war against *cameras*?

Alipato was sobbing now, and Remedios pulled herself close and wrapped him in her arms.

102

Folding Cythera
Marjorie Welish

1.

Whereabouts

would swear by

the etiquette of *the flowers were.*

Now boarding a waiting area

to entitle a swath of

complexion traipsing across the fair debris

that might have had scenographic rebus we shall have thought cemented

prospective sympathy rather than retrospective likeness

thought fair vinegar

and encounters with Ursula Oppens at the piano

Marjorie Welish

in wherewithal

exerting a glance up and damp with linen deferred to be read

as sculpture in its own right

performed on the

cavity.

Then again with Ursula Oppens at the piano

sentences will have thought plentifully

about overtaking prospective advances to avert accommodation

"What's the matter?"

a companion to warding off conclusive tragedies

and likeness wherein one couple assumed to commence to pause—

at this point the text breaks off.

Marjorie Welish

Whatsoever

now boarding a waiting area such that

atmospheric perspective at arm's length is not so

intrusive as to interfere with the matter

of conjugating the ground upon which to place bodies

as objects mindful of axonometric positions in the minuet.

At this point he breaks into a rivulet

capable of raising its armpit to a condition of alliterative waiting areas.

Retreats and advances stand oriented to each other's hour before dawn.

Let me restate that

averting a tragedy are beings are in favor of awry

105

trespass across the unlikable metrics thereupon face off and accelerating debris

for the throw of the spinet

and there are beings not going

"What's bothering you?"

will have thought plentifully

of embarkation away from whereabouts

whose sense data participate in it and how does he sustain her.

Here linen performs a fair swath of sentences

for the cavity now receiving an eventful assist from he who would get her to
her feet—

is that Paul on the harpsichord.

Appearances seem true

in an escort on his own for the eventful throw of the initiative

discernibly

of trespass and its prerogatives in a wherewithal

attaining to obscure uses

damp within an encampment of fugitives.

The etiquette of *the flowers were.*

2.

Taking leave of excerpted bodies

Folding Cythera

fro or from to and for

whereabouts

now boarding a waiting area

to entitle a swath of

complexion suggests capillaries

that might have had flowers cemented

Marjorie Welish

It is a tempest

undergoing emphasis in subconscious crease

his or her can never get can almost reach might have still

to reach have already *recapitulary*

memories to encounter undergrowth

and others' serrated edges suggestive of motives

To prospective sympathy

this is a tempest voucher

the monthly electrostatic postulate amidst

entities gathering up reluctant clothes

and others' serrated edges suggestive of motives

that can never get can almost reach might have

still to reach have already *recapitulary* his or her

skid to entitle a swath of

arm's length.

Segue to skin and its prerogatives.

Atmospheric perspective creeps up in the best-case scenario as sounds decay

to afterthought for the eventful conjugal rhetoric performed on

the figure clear and distinct likely but not likable.

"Don't mention it,"

scraped against the rim.

A bowl of

sentences folding discursive wherewithal era in her within earshot of he who

shall have scarcely thought to assuage the preexisting deposits

of likeness.

Stepping forward, head turned back

likeness

shall have scarcely thought to assuage the preexisting stencil

performed on the figure

109

a palm on her whereabouts

"What's the matter?"

ironing the other leafage

With open window to begin to fathom greenish-blue chill

companion to embarkation

in drastic posits, I am chimera clime childlike chiffon

to do today.

His askance operates a sigh

and for removing grease fremitus felt by placing

speech

on the part of a body via soft white granular variable

cycle to abet cylindrical lyric like

signs that lay a counterclockwise cygnet cyclone

from 1765, they were

ironing the harpsichord and piano together how to

how to do today conjugal infrastructure

in which becoming Paul

does embolden the dear cohort

speech of such an indictment

interspersed.

Ursula,

     face to face, personally.

Omobo
Paul West

MIDWAY BETWEEN UMKALI and Dibota, lions pause and squirt-mark the veldt, inhaling their own burly grandeur. To the human nose, the whole area reeks smoky and putrid, as of some mustard gas that drives all else away. But not to Omobo, fourteen, exiled here at the crossroads of the lions to survive for two months and kill a lion of his choosing, whose tail he must bring home with him. All he smells here is lion, no giraffe or buffalo. If he waits, a lion will come and update his quest by months, not scaring him off but picking a fight with him and his spear and shield. He is supposed to live off the land as best he can for eight weeks, then return as a hero, with a fresh lion tail; *he* can be dried out and dusty. On the other hand, after eight weeks of living off the land, he will be at his weakest, least likely to kill his lion, so he has somehow to conserve his strength until the very last day or two, for the oldest lion he can find, just to give him a better chance.

With a quick, shambling motion, a male lion approaches, rumbling and mouthing, then backs off sideways as Omobo swaggers toward it with his new-made spear. Some pride of females has pushed it out, and it is too lazy to hunt. It goes on sizing up Omobo, and then sizing him up again in perpetual prelude until, weary of the whole thing, yet roaring even louder as it backs off, the lion lumbers away to scent-mark the ground, thus guaranteeing itself a stance of partial honor while it works out what to do. Relieved that he will not be put to the test so soon, Omobo stabs his spear into the encrusted earth and starts to hum, then invents a squeal and screech to make the old lion uncomfortable. His mind is on the young white man named Douglas—whom he calls Do-Glass—who has befriended him since arriving to work at the metallurgy center. Do-Glass collects butterflies, mounting them tenderly in a big padded album or in boxes full of sawdust. These trophies he will one day ferry back to England, to his fiancée, who comes from Norway, a Ruth. Somehow, Omobo thinks he will go with Do-Glass when he returns with the butterflies, but he has no idea how unless it has something to do with the lion. Anyway,

Omobo knows the lion will decide his future for him, and idly wonders what Do-Glass would do if confronted by a lion, an unlikely event unless he were to venture out here to the lions' patch.

He makes a start by relieving his own bladder into the acrid crossroads of the lions, wondering if it would discourage them at all, while keeping a careful eye on the old lion, now ignoring him and preparing to sleep.

With good reason, Omobo has let his mind wander to find the exact essence of lion, not so much the ferocity and idleness, the jaundiced eye and dust-strewn mane, the sewn-looking line of the closed mouth and the huff and puff, as the suggestibility, the aversion to high-pitched sounds such as a woman screaming or a football whistle. They *can* be scared, he tells himself, just as we find *our* blood runs cold when a shadow falls across us at night. If you do your best, you need have no fear, but choose a lion not in its prime, or injured, though some of the jaded ones fight more savagely than others, and injured ones are never mellow. What does the tail tell? Imagine a lion not hale or hearty, but with a healthy tail, willing to slump sideways while letting out a cub's playful mew, to be read as a plea, a statement of submission. Would it not be better, over two months, to tame and train a lion that came home with you in a humble mood, ready to be patted and stroked rather than slaughtered? He realizes he isn't getting his times right, saying which act precedes which, and he cannot quite dismiss stories he has heard about youths who stared a lion down, so that the lion became like the youth and the youth became ever so gently lionlike. He has rehearsed with drawings and dreams, making hoarse roars on the point of falling asleep, only to dream of toppling from a great height into a valley of marauding lions who have not fed for days, unable to find a way out of the valley or prey inside it. The dream's contradictions occupy him not at all. A dream, he thinks, is prophetic more than it is anything, not a badge or a sequence, not a parallel or ceremony, but something that sooner or later you cannot avoid. In the end, as the first phase of sleep takes him, he sinks into contemplation of the lion in detail: its golden fleece, dung caked, but surely once upon a time used for panning gold; those bilious-looking eyes requiring, surely, soothing balm administered by some surgeon lion to them all; the pink interior of the roar, evocative of the ocean he has never seen and the coral he has had to imagine. Slow up your lion, he dreams, and it will never get you, except to nuzzle and paw clawless.

Such dreams have calmed him from time to time, but his daydreams have made him flinch, start, leap up, dreading what has just gained upon him in a final predatory leap, and Do-Glass can never save him, being from the wrong tribe, off the wrong ocean steamer. But there is this: Once you have killed your lion, you have killed them all, haven't you? This question makes him weary and awkward, slow to parry the fists of other boys, to dodge the flat, bread-kneading hand of his mother, Akira, the gobs of spit shot from his father's mouth as chewed tobacco makes its bitter slop and required escape. Talking to Do-Glass in the emphatic twang of Do-Glass had given him an alien rhythm, but only for everyday use, a small new vocabulary of words far beyond the scope of Omobo's life, more apt for cocktails on the Trongfontein terraces where bachelors of science from abroad gathered for sunset gin.

On one occasion, Omobo had fallen asleep after a recital with Do-Glass of all the creatures on the veldt, to which Do-Glass had added some butterflies and moths. In his dream, Omobo began talking above and beyond himself in a kind of bleat, communicable to Do-Glass only in the uncouthest jabber, which Do-Glass then formulated for himself. What on earth was Omobo getting at, and where had he picked up this kind of chat?

> In one kind of sleep you rest like stone. Comes near you
> has no purchase in. Current pass through me, right from.
> Don't you think I am your own true friend? How can I
> say affectionate presence without saying who?

So far as he himself is concerned, Omobo is at a crossroads belonging to lions, marked by lions. To a more educated observer, he might be said to be flanked by the Khorab Memorial and the Hoba Meteorite, Tsumeb Airport to his north, and, way to his south, some two hundred kilometers, the Waterberg Plateau Park, to none of which places he has ever been, still less to the Atlantic Coast westward (the Skeleton Coast Park Wilderness, say) or the Cape Cross Seal Reserve. All these sites might give the visitor some sense of space dominated, a tapestry of destinations worthy of a long hike or a rugged drive, most of all if you aim southward to Windhoek's recreational resorts and game parks, having skipped the petrified forest and Twyfelfontein rock engraving.

No, Omobo is oriented by scent, sogginess, gravel, and the bouncing mirage between his eyes and the far horizon. Part lion, he treasures the other part of him that still peers up at his mother's face, beyond the white shoehorn sort of thing that dangles low, then the shiny horizontal bar just above, prelude to the plaited leather rope coiled around her neck half a dozen times, even as she peers toward the sea, another Himba mother with overgrown child, photographed in Kaokoveld, northwest Namibia.

Never does she think her only son has been condemned to death by lion. The ritual with spear and shield is so deep-rooted in the community it has become almost a bastion of etiquette. It is mainly a question of *Will he do it right?* Will she be able to hold her head up in the Musika or Renkini township markets? A child should not have to figure, with leatherette skin (a dry tan) against a landscape of scrub and thorns, but such is the way of it, including that puzzled, dazzled look of theirs as they yawn at the sun, hoping it will deliver something manageable by a child instead of that huge, incandescent slab of oven pushing them, hounding them, away from where they stand akimbo, toward some indeterminate place that's cooler, but never found. The sun, she tells herself, always punches us toward evening into tolerable darkness when all the beasts come out to hunt and play. We have wizened children, old before their time. When we send them out to fight the lions, are we *really* sending them off to fight the sun? Is it lions that contribute their body heat to the sun's blaze? Without lions, would it be cooler here? She knows better than to believe in such things, but she allows herself a token credulity, to be spoken of only among women, whose notion of nobility is less fierce than that of the men.

His mother comes back often enough to the face of the lion, noting its essentially manufactured look, the way it seems all triangles, the way the features calm down into an almost set amiability: the pleased, gratified cat offering a demure repose no dog could manage. A son torn apart by those incisors and the massive paws does not enter her head. After all, the local tradition is one of the lion felled and finished off, outwitted by too much guile and an individual confidence based on communal prowess. It is almost with her and the lions as with Do-Glass and the butterflies. The hunter and the prey move into each other with calm reciprocity, and the lion and the butterfly, with little in common save vulnerability, think not about the future, but only of the few seconds after the kill—mostly wrongly. Yet there is no oral tradition among lions or butterflies actually warning them to desist, the one from tooth and claw, the other from poise on a leaf. It is an odd thought that even she, when not worrying about the outcome, as mothers will, manages to sum up, realizing that the animal-insect world functions without memory as if its creatures were there to offer themselves for better or for worse. She has never seen a teddy bear or encountered *Lord Jim*'s Stein, who asks, "Can you show me a butterfly with a weak heart?" Does she see, then, that both creatures go to do battle, passively or otherwise, for the food of their species, with perfectly intact hearts no better than those of lions and butterflies, hearts every bit as good as they get. Until there comes an improvement (the lion ravaging the man, the butterfly fending him off), the ending will almost always be the same.

Omobo, though, has thoughts apart from his rendezvous with the lion, but related to Do-Glass's butterflies: He yearns, even at so tender an age, to sail aboard the *Edinburgh Castle* to England with Do-Glass, to Ruth and the famous museums. Or to Jamaica, the land of bauxite, about which Do-Glass has told him in the tourist chat he lapses into. "The English convert it," he said, "into alumin*i*um, the Americans into alumin*u*m." He has no idea why.

"Only when you're bigger," Do-Glass said in the vague, stiff tones of his native northern heath. "Not until."

Omobo felt unsatisfied. "What must I do?"

Wishing he had not embarked on this conversation, Do-Glass said something about reading, to which Omobo answered, "I do read, I really do. If I kill my lion, can I then read until my ship sails?"

This kid will go abroad and found a colony, Do-Glass decided. I have been too lenient with him. He is going to learn to say both *minium* and *minum* so as to pass muster in both countries. At his own school he had been obliged to read in French a little play of Alfred de Musset's entitled *Il faut qu'une porte soit ouverte ou fermée* (A door must be open or closed), but why he had to read that, apart from improving his French, he had never figured out. Would he ever go to France? Could it be that so-called education entailed the unknown moving into the reader and the reader moving into the unknown, not so much because this specific reader needed that specific unknown as because the unknown called out for samples of the rest of the unknown in much the manner of certain languages, attacking one another just to see what booty they had and were unwilling to share. Such was Do-Glass's theoretical side, consecrated to unification and fusion of disparate worlds. This was how celibate gusto, such as his in Africa, Ruthless, met its opposite member, promiscuous inertia, and justified it.

Now here was this young black asking about reading.

Well, he might quit Africa before this kid met his lion.

So, it was not written that they would go together.

In any case, if the lion got Omobo, he would not need the ship.

The dreams of an increasingly light-headed Omobo included lambs from the south grown for their pelts, seals and whales from the old seafaring days, and even, as his yearning stomach unhinged his covetous brain, lead, zinc, copper, and tin, tenderized by his metallurgical ally Do-Glass. Two months of this would ill prepare him for even a weakling of a lion, but with *his* luck it would be no weakling. His dreams also included the dwarf trees of Quiver Tree Forest, little arbor tufts that gave the illusion of a landscape first planted, with nothing that shaded you, handy pushovers for the baby elephants of Etosha National Park. In truth, what he fed on, in this order if he could manage it, was peanuts (groundnuts) and corn (maize). He loved the tang of peanuts, their dry succulence, but the structure of the tiny corns on their cobs was beginning to win him over, and he fondled them between finger and thumb, having nothing else to do, appraising them and wondering if any one of them would be a perfect fit in the niche of any other. Or not: The camber and tilt of each would be different, unless the corns fitted circularly in clusters, which meant easily a dozen a quarter of an inch high would be identical. This airheaded study course among stunted trees and frolicking lions (who showed little interest in him) struck him as an ideal way to get to age fifteen, but already, in his third week, he was feeling bored, wan, and disappointed.

The next enemy, of course, was hunger, and during the ensuing days too, beginning with the familiar gnawing clutch in the pit of the stomach, then spreading throughout the trunk as a kind of incontinent brainsickness, not to be thwarted with bits of leaf or stalk, nor even tiny carcasses devoured alive and kicking or squashed with the heel of the hand, the sole of the foot. Omobo had never encountered hunger of this fashion, apart from impatient rumblings in his lower abdomen; this felt like a drooling swamp come to inflate him and bring him low, at least in the right posture to trough on insects going about their business. Perfunctorily briefed on which plants to avoid (*eschew*, said the whites when they mentioned it, and he laughed), he marveled at how many joyfully designed–looking things were dangerous (the healthy ones commonplace), and at how nature built from the inside outward, with explicit warnings delivered only to color-wise animals, birds, creepy-crawlies. It was as if, without guidance, the poor old human remained in harm's way until actually felled. It was always better, he reasoned, to hunt meat and even eat it raw (though he had matches and a lighter—but for *two months*?). In no time he had equipped himself with a stout sun-dried branch with which to belabor small rodents. His drink came from what some people called pans, and was often slimy, brackish, and speckled with midges.

And now he began to worry about the length of this imposed wandering, deeming it too much, less a preparation for a hectic hunting life than for an ocean trip with Do-Glass, that walking monster of tungsten and manganese, uranium and lithium, about which substances he had held forth at Omobo-boring length. What I needed to know, he told himself, I have picked up already, I really have. Why the extra? Is it just a device to weaken me for tackling my lion? It makes no sense. Are they hoping I will catch malaria, or is it some superclever way of teaching me how underpopulated Namibia is, with only, what was it, three of us to a square mile? I am here to acquaint myself with the vacancy of Bantu space. The South African school system has already taught me that, so is the lion stuff another attempt to teach me something else? There are more lions than people. Can that be it? What do we make? The average, they say, is about $1,400 a year, so blacks must make less than $1,000. No wonder we need to bring home the lion's tail. A stew? A fly whisk? Perhaps it was some prank of white settlers—English, German, Dutch—who seemed to spend most of their time tending crops and singing in choral groups, in devout-sounding tones alien to this bone-dry amalgam of hot Africa.

Waiting, prolonging the agony, Omobo time and again enacted the dream of doing it well, the spear snapping at the outset so that he had to thrust his arm past the lion's teeth and over its tongue, deep into the throat, losing it there, and so able only to withdraw his arm on a recoiling reflex and somehow shove his foot and calf into the lion's throat more or less choking it while the teeth sank in and in. Twisting his foot about, he managed to cause some choking effect, sapping the lion's breath and able to push with his leg only to have an open claw rake the inside of the shin and the front of his body. Was he winning or losing? The lion's roars had become bleat-like, prelude to what? A whimper or even an excruciated sob from stifled lungs. The lion tried to vomit, but choked on its own surplus, feebly waving both paws in the direction of the main offender, who felt how soggy with blood his leg had become. He was going to faint alongside this throttled beast and their outcome was to be a draw. The lion would have to recover to fight again and he, Omobo, would not fight ever again, restricted to butterflies, moths, and a white man's fishing net adapted to land games.

Then he vacated his trance, realized that the battle had not even begun. Perhaps, such was his shame at being so squeamish, he would have to fight an ostrich instead, or a baby kudu. But now he at least knew how.

Even when, back to his full senses, he had reassembled the component features of the lion's face, he could not forget how the triangles had turned into sharp chisel shapes, the mouth's trim and almost affable containment into a pink abyss. He had heard people saying how the Atlantic Ocean, which loomed on Namibia's western shore, had no memory either. To him, the veldt was more like that. Of a thousand horrific events in one day and a night, near the zone the lions marked, nothing remained save a few heaps of leftover skin and horns. The land renewed its memory with each dawn. Therefore, he judged, he would have to go on and on, wading his way through successive encounters until the day he actually took on his lion without imagining anything at all. And then? Would a vulture do instead? Was there any way of creeping up behind a lion, slicing off its tail, and vanishing without being torn limb from limb by a beast not so much injured as insulted? He knew better, and just briefly his mind shifted to cricket, a sport he aspired to excel at, as he remembered how at Lord's Cricket Ground in London if you made a high score or bowled out at least five batsmen, they at once painted your name in gold on the mahogany-lined walls inside the pavilion, for A Feat Well Done. Well, why did they not commemorate lion killers too?

Uncannily, if we probe his mind at the onset of leg choking and the next ten minutes of the process, we discover that, bit by bit, he feels incorporated into the living lion, and then the dead lion too, actually adding something alive to the waning beast. Reciprocally, he feels the élan vital of the lion has passed into him, providing an extra spurt to subdue his opponent with. In some ill-heard echo chamber of his mind, he seems to hear a familiar cry, *"Ecce homo!"* closely followed by *"Ecce leo!"* Two champs have crossed in the approaching dusk. His feeling is not morbid at all; he feels as if he has both provided *and* received, though such a view of the lion is negative, ignoring its death, yet there is precedent in his boyhood for such an imbalance. He remembers in a casual way the logo on a can of molasses (treacle) that shows a dead lion in the arena and, in its open belly, a squad of bees tending their hive. The words in the logo, perhaps treasured while he poured molasses onto his morning porridge, were "Out of the strong came forth sweetness." He has not forgotten this, but recalls it as a faint silhouette of memory, something to be fleshed out later with a dead lion's tail to show for his pains. Not that his childhood, so recent, feeds him spiritually that much; it figures only when he is dealing with beings of enormous name.

He has forgotten, or never knew, the rune about dreaming that splits one portion of the dream from another, thus disentangling the actual from the dreamed, witness to which we have embalmed in such expressions as "You're dreaming" and "Dream on." You do not have to be schizophrenic to linger in this never-never land, but you have to be stressed enough to be hosting unrelated and maybe incompatible ideas. Actually, as we comfortably say, the lion had just wandered up to spray and been distracted into aggression, the result of which was his leg down the lion's gullet, his naked foot treading on balloons and vital sponges: no help to an agitated beast. The teeth didn't quite meet, thus providing a raked effect rather than a plunge and a grasp. Not only, impromptu, was he giving as good as he got, he was giving slightly more, hands obstructing the front paws like someone remembering a bad dream enough to go through the protective motions, enough anyway to spare him the worst slashes. In other words, this was not your classic spear-thrust lion encounter, but something more outrageous, less than heroic or epical. But just about enough, provided he maintained his position of cumulative choke. That he could hardly believe what he was doing had much to do with the unfamiliar posture, not recommended for lion dispatch, but rarely tried because of unspecified attendant risks.

Now, shaken out of his useful dream, he has to cope with the next lion, real and stenchy, no doubt evicted from some other boy's dream to end Omobo's life. In went the leg, learned by heart. To remove it would mean instant death, first maimed. In a sense, to mix felines, he was riding a tiger from within, no holds barred but almost impossible to manage. Something frozen in his resolve and his demeanor kept him rigid, shoving down hard with his big hands on what was a young male, horny and inquisitive. Was there a roar? Yes, but muted, more of a phlegmy rumble as sound traffic ground to a halt in the lion's throat. Omobo had a long, invasive leg, and he shoved it for all it was worth, half expecting to see his big toe come out at the lion's other end, all blood and dung, but no, it whirred on inside, abrading and stippling while the other leg, doubled up almost beneath him, disabled the lion's foreleg, leaving only the other paw a scratching chance.

Where, you may wonder, did this access of strength come from? Surely not from the extra savvy provided by presence of mind? Had he ever thought that fast? Probably not, but because his maneuver was new, being spontaneous, it looked after itself, seeking no pattern or matrix, and was bound (we look ahead into myth) to endure in tribal memory among the ways of subduing a lion. He and who else? If it sounds preposterous it was, just the kind of event that, among other peoples, would have fitted him out with a proper name, not Omobo but thenceforth Lion Choker (*simba hunkah*), his fate and fame assured, whatever else he did with his life—cricket for South Africa, metaphysics at Princeton or Windhoek, rocket science at JPL. He did not have long to wait before the lion lost consciousness and he was able to remove the tail with his folding knife. He had not planned to do this; indeed, it was weeks ahead of schedule, but it would have to do, premature but marvelous, what you might call *leonicide praecox*. He would certainly have imitators, several of whom would lose legs in the endeavor, others of whom would equip themselves with poles that had a fudged-up wodge at one end—rags, dung, straw, sand, pebbles—to choke the lion with. It was a technique, to be sure, but all contrary to past heroics, past rite of passage lingering among the tribe much as calculus hovered somewhere above arithmetic, worth a shot, but more Ripley than Herculean.

Omobo, absent after his feat, would live on in folklore, remaining something of a mystery to others, and even to the part of himself that ached to be normal and do normal things. Another part of him, however, would relish his outrageous status and his spreading fame among other tribes, including whites, although even they hardly knew of Mucius Scaevola, who had thrust his entire arm into a bonfire, just to prove a point. Would that make him and Omobo congeners or what?

In his painful trance of lion taming by accident, Omobo had neglected to notice that one claw had managed to rip apart the tender skin at one end of his genitals, possibly qualifying him for circumcision, as required by the tribal elders of those who failed the lion test. Now, had he failed the lion test? He had blundered into it, true, but the lion was dead although too soon by almost a month; Omobo had not suffered the full course of required privation. Here he was, both conqueror and *mutilé*; if conqueror, then needlessly *mutilé*. One would wonder, and so did he, having out there nothing and no one to talk to, the belch of death hanging heavy over the otherwise much-marked area. Only some venerable synod of village elders would know what to do, but, since he had not quite fulfilled the test requirements, it was likely that, sticklers for ritual finitudes, the elders would give him a thumbs-down and he would somehow have to repeat the dose; a timely lion this time, and so by some unknown means restoration of foreskin (and a tidier job of it this time around).

This was hardly fair, considering the pain and stress he had been through, surprised by his lion, snipped by a feckless, dying claw (one slash did for it). Who is to say how long he pondered his situation, out there on the acidic veldt, with other lions keeping a prudent distance, and pounds of lion meat to cook. It would soon be the hour of the hyena and jackal, the vulture and the rat.

After butchering the lion, he set off toward his home kraal, the tail around his neck like a meat bandanna. Again, he wondered at the holy unbroken silence of Africa, really an echoic chamber for birds and moaning lions. Hardly a soul to greet him until he reached the village fringe, where willing allies took the meat from him and tugged it along behind while dogs yelped and free-running children chortled with delight. Here he came, bloodied and begrimed, the tail swinging around his neck, his loincloth saturated with blood, his killer leg twisted: hardly the image of the conquering hero, but then he was only in his early teens. It was amazing, the thought, that he had come back at all. An increasing murmur followed him, though mainly of rebuke for having returned too soon—a black mark against him, lion's tail or no. Finally, he arrived at the right doorway and threw himself on the dusty entrance, whipping the loincloth open as if to reveal a prodigy of compliance. They looked and looked away. Almost a month early, he had not needed to do it, so then he told them the lion had done it under the golden eye of heaven, not even cognizant of village law.

That did it. All he heard was agitated jabber as a gathering crowd began to shout the pros and cons of his performance while he, becoming littler and littler, shrank back to twelve, the age of ambitious helplessness.

The verdict on Omobo, who was only recently a lion-fearing boy, was not the fiat we might have expected. It said that, in accordance with tribal laws, he had misjudged the period of exile (two months of pain and penury, starvation and self-denial) and thus slighted part

of the requirement, confronting his lion in a condition of rude health
and potent strength. Not only that: He had also slighted the circumcision requirement, with or without help from the lion, by resorting
to it prematurely and, worse, unnecessarily—if one accepted his
killing of the lion as timely, never mind the means being leg instead
of spear. The upshot of all this was that, on a chosen day, he was to
repeat the entire two-month rigor, kill his lion on the very last day
by orthodox means, and bring home a second tail. It sounded like a
pedantic overdose, and it was. Omobo could hardly believe his juvenile fate had flopped into being a mere repeat, after he had done so
much the first time. In a word, he needed legal representation, like
your average thief. How swiftly this verdict of a few melted away
into the many, no one dissenting, not even the youths who had
themselves not long ago gone through the same ordeal with depriva-
tion and lion.

When Do-Glass first heard the tale, he could hardly credit it.
Surely this young man had acquitted himself nobly; he deserved the
indulgence of everyone, deep lion grass to hide in, a carbide lamp to
break the darkness with, a tethered baboon to squeal and drive the
lions mad as they lunged toward him with bass, bubbling, emetic
roar, black or yellow manes tumbling. Yet it would never be. The
elders had spoken, so it was possible that Omobo's life from fourteen
on would be a fixed nonentity of a thing. Surely he needed to edge
over into some new domain, like a cloud clinking across the face of
the sun.

And there Do-Glass left it, intent on his butterflies or on the fetch-
ing young white lasses of his senior colleagues in metallurgy, husband hunters every pretty one, heedless as he himself of the buxom
Norwegian waiting for him back home. Absorbed thus in female
company, especially after dinner when the coolness of evening really set in and the running-down world ran down even faster, he began
to notice how sweat from the heat of the day condensed in his shirts,
providing him an unnatural chill. There he sat with his brandy and
soda, arm around some girl's shoulder, distinctly beginning to shiver,
but reluctant to move or go inside. Such chaste, crisp cool was new
to him, a slice of tropical heaven unknown in the English Midlands,
where descending soot smeared all. In this way he acquired the habit
of late-night chills that soon led him into bronchitis and pneumonia,
for which M & B tablets, that period's only remedy, were too faint,
usually only making a coma worse. Bubbling in a minor key, he smothered in his own mucus, hallucinated all the terrors of lion hunting,

and began to come back to life only three months later, a thinned-out, bleached-looking scarecrow of a man, only just missing the kempt graveyard of the white settlers, who still did not know him very well. Now they would, or so they thought, but he was only his own ghost, no longer the charmer of the veranda, the eligible beau of the old-style hop.

He was the reverse of the usual formula, which demanded that those of weakened lungs head for the mountains or warmer climes. In his case, the word was that he should retreat from those chilly evenings, from the lathering heat of day, and pledge his all on the cool Pennines, mountains of medium range ascending to cloud. With him, on the *Carnarvon Castle*, one of the flagships of the Castle Line, went Omobo, the misfit, now fifteen, a kind of remittance man like the black sheep of the family, usually shipped from the UK to Australia. Around the big western bulge of Africa the *Carnarvon Castle* churned, aimed at Southampton, Do-Glass stumbling around the first-class deck with his cane, and Omobo perched on his bed, with the open boxes of butterflies beside him, siting each one at some place on his anthracite-shiny body, ever hoping for the right contrast or harmony of tones. In the open doorway Do-Glass would stand wondering what he and Ruth would do with their new-won creature, amid all the useful metals of the world in 1937, Do-Glass having found no advice at all in de Musset's little play about a door's being open or shut. As Do-Glass saw it, you did not enter through an open doorway.

Poor Belgium: The Argument

Charles Baudelaire

—Translated from French with an Introduction by Richard Sieburth

INTRODUCTION

IN EARLY 1864, FLEEING his creditors in Paris, Baudelaire boarded the train for Brussels for what he envisaged would be at most a three-week stay, during which he hoped to repair his finances by offering a series of well-paid public lectures on contemporary French literature while landing a lucrative contract for a new edition of his *Complete Works* with the Belgian publishers of Victor Hugo's recent international best seller, *Les Misérables*, banned in France. Both projects came to naught. Instead of a few weeks, Baudelaire's self-imposed exile in Belgium—a country he positively loathed—would drag on for another two years, culminating in a severe attack of apoplexy in April 1866 in the church of Namur that reduced him to a state of complete aphasia during the final year of his existence, unable to utter any words other than the sacrilegious oath *cré nom, cré nom*—a cry somewhere between the late Hölderlin's *pallaksch, pallaksch* and the Flemish *godverdomme*.

During his ill-starred residence in Brussels, living off monthly pittances doled out by his mother and residing at the Hôtel du Grand Miroir (the same hotel in which Verlaine would later shoot Rimbaud), Baudelaire worked on the unfinished mass of notes and newspaper clippings he hoped to gather together into a book called *Pauvre Belgique* (or perhaps *La Belgique déshabillé*, an ironic counterpoint to the nakedly autobiographical aphorisms of *Mon Coeur mis à nu*). First published in its entirety in 1952 (and, to my knowledge, still untranslated into English), Baudelaire's dyspeptic *sottisier* of Belgian *bêtise* invites comparisons with Flaubert's late *Bouvard et Pécuchet*, while pointing forward to Walter Benjamin's *Arcades Project*, whose montage of quotations was designed to blast "Paris, Capital of the Nineteenth Century" out of the continuum of history and into a surreal, allegorical present. Baudelaire's Brussels, by contrast, is merely *"une capitale pour rire, une capitale pour singes"*—a joke of a capital

125

whose simian inhabitants idiotically ape the worst features of contemporary bourgeois France. Baudelaire's savage satire of the recently created "counterfeit" nation of Belgium (a "diplomatic harlequin" patched together by the Great Powers in 1830 and therefore Europe's newest, and most rapidly modernizing, artificial nation-state) entails a Tocquevillian—or rather, De Maistrean—critique of the contagion of mimesis (or *singerie*) that lies at the heart of modern doctrines of democratic equality. Here perhaps is one of the reasons behind Baudelaire's failure to complete his projected *Pauvre Belgique*: the ostensible Otherness of Belgium reveals itself to be merely another instance of the Eternal Recurrence of the Same. Though he had elected residence in the Near Abroad as an economic refugee—a pathetic parody of Victor Hugo's grand political exile on Guernsey—Baudelaire comes to realize that he has really never left home. Belgium is merely "the stupidity of France cubed"—a place not unlike the America that drove his alter ego Poe to self-destruction, and that now threatens to reduce him as well to utter imbecility, utter *bêtise. Cré nom, cré nom.*

The text that follows below is the "Argument" for *Pauvre Belgique* that Baudelaire composed in January 1866 to pitch his books to various publishers in Paris—all of whom, in the event, politely turned the project down. As this synopsis suggests, Baudelaire intended his Flaubertian "book about nothing" (or more specifically, about *"le néant belge"*) as a piece of first-person gonzo journalism or mock guidebook that would combine a caricature of the manners and mores (*moeurs*) of Brussels with more specific chapters devoted to Belgium's educational system, its army, its electoral politics, its societies of Free Thinkers, its tin-pot constitutional monarch (Leopold I had just died in December 1865, which Baudelaire thought would make his book all the more topical), its fears of annexation by France (another item much in the news), and the comic peculiarities of Belgo-French. A second portion of the book was to have been devoted to a survey of the fine arts in Belgium—the paintings held in its various museums and the significant architectural features of some of its towns (Anvers, Namur, Liège, Gand, Bruges). Baudelaire was particularly impressed by what he called the "Jesuit style" of a number of Belgium's churches—a rococo *style joujou* imported from Spain into the Low Countries in the seventeenth century that he describes as follows: "hotchpotch, chessboard, chandeliers, a boudoir at once mystical and fearsome, mourning in marble, theatrical confessionals, Theater and Boudoir, rings of light and transparent glorias, angels and cupids, apotheoses and beatifications." As he waited out his death in Belgium, Baudelaire, ever the art critic, had clearly not lost his Catholic eye for the camp splendors of the Hereafter.

In addition to its "Argument," Baudelaire's Belgium Project comprises some 250 pages of additional notes (and newspaper clippings), roughly arranged under the rubrics indicated in its prepared outline. Selections from these notes will be included in my forthcoming edition of *Late Baudelaire* for Yale University Press (together with my translations of his *Fusées, Mon Coeur mis à nu,* and his late prose poems written in Brussels).

* * *

Possible titles:

The true Belgium. Belgium in the raw.
Belgium disrobed. A Joke of a Capital.
Capital of Apes.

1. PRELIMINARIES

If one goes abroad one should always "carry along a patch of one's native land on the sole of his shoes"—whatever Danton's assertions to the contrary.

France seems quite barbaric, seen up close. But go to Belgium, and you will become less critical of your own country.

Just as Joubert gave thanks to God for having made him a man and not a woman, so you too will thank him for having created you not Belgian but French.

A book on Belgium, a praiseworthy endeavor. To be amusing while speaking of boredom, instructive while speaking of *nothing.*

A sketch of Belgium offers this further advantage: it allows one by the same token to caricature the idiocies of France.

Europe has entered into a conspiracy to flatter Belgium. Craving compliments, Belgium inevitably takes them seriously.

How, some twenty years ago, we used to chant the praises of the United States in all its liberty, glory, and good fortune! Belgium inspires similar idiocies.

Why the French who have resided in Belgium won't tell the truth about this country. Because, given how French they are, they don't want to admit that they were *had*.

Voltaire's verses on Belgium.

2. BRUSSELS

Physiognomy of the Street.

Initial impressions. It is said that every city, every country has its smell. Paris, they say, smells or *used to smell* of acrid cabbage. Cape Town smells of sheep. There are tropical isles that smell of roses, musk, or coconut oil. Russia smells of leather. Lyon smells of coal. The Orient generally smells of musk and corpses. Brussels smells of black soap. The hotel rooms smell of black soap. The beds smell of black soap. The napkins smell of black soap. The sidewalks smell of black soap. The continual scrubbing of sidewalks and stoops, even in the pouring rain. A national mania.

The general *blandness* of life. Cigars, vegetables, flowers, fruits, cuisine, eyes, hair, everything *bland*, everything sad, flavorless, asleep. The human face itself, blurred, clouded, asleep. A Frenchman goes in fear of this *Soporific Contagion*.

Only the dogs are alive; they are the niggers of Belgium.

Brussels much louder than Paris; reasons for this. The cobblestones, uneven; the houses, rickety and poorly insulated; the streets, narrow; the local loudmouthed accent, atrocious; the clumsiness, widespread; the *whistling* (describe), a national trait; the dogs barking all the time.

Few sidewalks, or sidewalks suddenly ending (the result of individual liberty pushed to the extreme). Lousy paving. No life in the street. –Many balconies, nobody on the balconies. The *spy-mirrors*, signs of boredom, curiosity, inhospitality.

Gloominess of a city without a river.

Nothing spread out on display in the shops. *Flânerie*, so dear to city dwellers endowed with imaginations, impossible in Brussels. Nothing to see, and strolling out of the question.

Innumerable pince-nez. The reason for this. The remark of a local

Charles Baudelaire

optician. An amazing quantity of hunchbacks.

The Belgian, or rather the Brussels face—vague, shapeless, pasty or splotchy, bizarre build of the jaws, menacing stupidity.

The ludicrous way the Belgians lurch along. They proceed forward by looking over their shoulders, endlessly bumping into things.

3. BRUSSELS

Daily life. Tobacco, cuisine, wines.

The topic of tobacco. The drawbacks of liberty.

The topic of cuisine. No roast meats. Everything braised. Everything prepared with rancid butter (to save money or as a matter of taste). Execrable vegetables, either because of their poor quality or on account of the butter. No spicy stews. (Belgian cooks believe that highly seasoned fare means highly salted fare).

The elimination of the dessert course is also quite symptomatic. No fruits (those from Tournai—are they even decent?—are exported to England). One therefore has to import them from France or Algeria.

And to top it off, the bread is execrable, damp, soggy, charred.

Alongside the *common myth* of *Belgian liberty* and of *Belgian cleanliness*, let's place the *myth* of *how cheap it is to live* in Belgium.

Everything is *four times* more expensive than in Paris, where the only expensive thing is rent.

Here, everything is expensive, except rent.

You can, if you have the stomach for it, live *à la Belge*. Description of the Belgian diet and hygiene.

–The topic of wine. –Wine, an object of curiosity, a collector's item. Magnificent wine cellars, richly furnished, *all identical*. Expensive, heady wines. The Belgians *display* their wines. They drink wine not because they have any taste for it, but out of vanity, to validate their *Conformity*, their resemblance to the French.

Belgium, a paradise for traveling wine salesmen. What the common folk drink. Faro and gin.

Charles Baudelaire

4. CUSTOMS
Women and Love.

No *women*, no *love*.
Why.
No chivalry among the men, no sense of modesty among the women.
Modesty, something forbidden, no need felt for it. Broad portrait of the Flemish woman, or at least of the Brabant woman (setting the Walloon woman aside for the moment).
Typical physiognomy comparable to that of the sheep or ram. –Smiles impossible because of the recalcitrance of the muscles and the set of the teeth and jaws.
The complexion generally pasty, sometimes splotchy. The hair yellow. The legs, breasts, huge—tubs of lard. The feet, horrors!!!
Monstrous bosoms typically developing quite precociously, swelling like swamps owing to the humidity of the climate and the gluttony of the women.
The stench of the women. Anecdotes.
Obscenity of Belgian females. Anecdotes about latrines and street corners.
As concerns love, refer to the indecency of the old Flemish painters. Sixty-year olds having sex. This people has not changed, and the Flemish painters remain true to life.
–Belgian prostitution, high- and low-end. Counterfeit French tarts. French prostitution in Brussels.
–Excerpts from the rules and regulations governing prostitution.

5. CUSTOMS *(continued)*

Belgian coarseness (even among officers).
Back-biting comments about colleagues in the press.
The tone of Belgian critics and newspapermen.
Belgian vanity ruffled.
Mean-spiritedness and servility.
Belgian ethics. The monstrosity of its crime.
Orphans and old men put up for auction.
(The Flemish party. Victor Joly. His well-founded criticism of the Belgians' tendency to ape everything—which perhaps needs to be inserted elsewhere).

130

6. CUSTOMS *(continued)*

The Belgian Brain.
Belgian Conversation.

It is as difficult to define the Belgian character as it is to classify the Belgian on the scale of living creatures.

He is an ape, but he is also a *mollusk*.

Extraordinarily scatter-brained, amazingly thick-headed. It is easy to oppress him, as is borne out by history; it is almost impossible to eradicate him.

As we proceed to judge the Belgian, let us not stray from certain key ideas: Aping, Counterfeiting, Conformity, rancorous Impotence— these various rubrics will enable us to classify our material.

Their vices are all counterfeit.

The Belgian fop.

The Belgian patriot.

The Belgian bungler.

The Belgian free-thinker, whose most salient feature is to *believe* that *you do not believe what you are saying*, since *he* cannot grasp it. A counterfeit of French irreverence. Belgian obscenity, a counterfeit of French smut.

Presumption and fatuousness. –Familiarity. –Portrait of a Walloon *loser*.

Widespread and absolute distrust of wit. The misadventures of M. de Valbezen, the French consul in Antwerp.

Distrust of laughter. –Bursts of laughter for no apparent reason. –One tells a heartwarming story; the Belgian bursts into laughter just to prove he has gotten it. –Belgians are ruminants who digest nothing.

And yet—who would believe it?—Belgium has its own *Carpentras*, its own Boeotian. By the name of Poperinghe.

So there may well be people more *bête* than all those I have so far seen.

7. BRUSSELS

Customs.

Small town mentality. Jealousy. Calumny. Defamation.
Noses in other people's business. Pleasure in the misfortune of others.
The products of laziness and incompetence.

8. BRUSSELS

Customs.

Spirit of obedience and CONFORMITY.
Spirit of associability.
Numberless Societies (the remains of earlier Guilds).
On the individual level, laziness of thought.
By coming together into associations, individuals relieve themselves of the burden of having to think on their own.
The Pranksters Club.
A Belgian would not believe himself happy unless he saw others who had achieved happiness in the same manner. Therefore, he can not be happy *on his own.*

9. BRUSSELS

Customs.

The *Spy-mirrors.*
Belgian cordiality.
Impoliteness.
And just how coarse they are. *The "Gallic salt" of the Belgians.*
The *pisser* and the *vomiter,* national statues I find symbolic.
–Scatological jokes.

10. BRUSSELS

Customs.

Slow-wittedness and laziness of the Belgians; true of its leaders, employees, and workers.
Slow-footedness and complication of the bureaucracies.

The Postal Service, the Telegraph Service, the Customs Warehouse. Anecdotes about its bureaucracies.

11. BRUSSELS

Customs.

Belgian MORALITY. The Merchants. Nothing but success matters. Money. –The story of a painter who would have gladly handed over Jefferson Davis just to earn the reward.

Everybody mistrusting everybody else, the sign of general immorality. A Belgian will suspect the motivation behind every act, no matter how noble it be.

Unscrupulous business practices (anecdotes).

The Belgian is always quick to rejoice in the misfortunes of others. Which provides food for conversation, bored as he is.

Everybody eager to engage in slander. Of which I have been the victim on a number of occasions.

Widespread avarice. Immense fortunes. No charity. One would say that there is a conspiracy to keep the common folk in a state of dire poverty and stupefaction.

Everybody in sales, even the rich. Everybody has something they want to unload secondhand.

Hatred of beauty, to parallel the *hatred of wit*.

Not to Conform, the ultimate crime.

12. BRUSSELS

Customs.

The myth of *Belgian cleanliness*. Its basis. –Clean things and dirty things in Belgium. Profitable businesses: ceiling whitewashers. Losing businesses: bathing establishments.

Poor neighborhoods. Working-class mores. Nakedness. Drunkenness. Beggary.

13. BELGIAN ENTERTAINMENT

The atmosphere stiff and awkward.
Lugubrious silence.
The *Conformist* mentality, always. They only amuse themselves in packs.
The Vaux Hall.
The Casino.
The Théâtre Lyrique.
The Théâtre de la Monnaie.
The French Vaudeville.
Mozart at the Théâtre du Cirque.
Julius Langenbach's troupe (which flopped because of its talent).
How I managed to incite an entire hall into applauding an over-the-hill second-rate dancer.
French vaudevilles.

Neighborhood dances.
Ball games.
Archery contests.

The Brussels carnival. Drinks are never offered to one's dance partner. Everyone jumping up and down in place, in utter silence.
The barbarity of children's entertainment.

14. EDUCATION

State or City Universities. Free Universities. Athenaeums.
No Latin, no Greek. Professional studies. Hatred of poetry. Education to train engineers or bankers.
No metaphysics.
Positivism in Belgium. M. Hannon and M. Altmeyer, whom Proudhon dubbed: *this old harpy!* His portrait. His style.
General loathing of literature.

15. THE FRENCH LANGUAGE IN BELGIUM

–The style of the books (few and far between) they write here.
–Some specimens of the Belgian idiom.

They don't know French, *nobody* knows it, but everybody *affects* not to know Flemish. It shows good taste. The proof that they know how to speak it quite well: they *curse out* their servants in Flemish.

16. JOURNALISTS AND LITERATI

In general, the literati (?) here hold other jobs as well. Most often as office employees.

Moreover, no literature. At least no French literature. One or two *chansonniers*, disgusting apes of Béranger's off-color songs. One novelist, an imitator of the copiers of the apes of Champfleury. Savants, annalists or chroniclers—that is, people who collect and others who buy up stacks of paper at a low price (the financial accounts of buildings and other documents, the entries of princes, the transcripts of the sessions of municipal councils, copies of archives) and then resell all this material in a single block as a history book.

In fact, everybody here is an *annalist* (in Anvers, everybody is an art dealer; in Brussels, there are rich art collectors who also deal in secondhand curios).

The Tone of the Newspapers. Numerous Examples. Ridiculous letter columns in the *Office de publicité. –L'Indépendence belge. –L'Echo du parlement. –L'Etoile belge. –Le Journal de Bruxelles. –Le Bien public. –Le Sancho. –Le Grelot. L'Espiègle. –*Etc., etc.

Literary patriotism. A poster announcing a play.

17. BELGIAN IMPIETY

Quite a chapter, this! As is the following one.

Insults directed at the Pope. –Anti-religious propaganda. –Account of the death of the archbishop of Paris (1848). –Staging of Pixérécourt's play, *Le Jésuite*, at the *Théâtre Lyrique*. –The Jesuit-bogeyman. –A procession. –Royal subscription for burials. –Campaign against a Catholic schoolteacher. –The law regulating Cemeteries. –Civil burials. –Corpses under contention or stolen. –The burial of a *Solidarian*. –Civil burial of a woman. –Analysis of the regulations of the societies of *free thinkers*. –Rules for making out one's will. –A wager made by the Body Of Our Lord Eating Society.

18. IMPIETY AND PRIESTOPHOBIA

Again, the *free thinkers*! Again, the *Solidarians* and the *Emancipated*! Again, a last will and testament formulated in order to filch yet another corpse from the Church. An article by M. Sauvestre in *L'Opinion nationale* on *free thought*. And yet more corpses stolen. –The funeral services for a clergyman who died a *free thinker*. –Jesuitophobia. –Who exactly is *our brave De Buck*, a former criminal, persecuted by the Jesuits. –An assembly of *free thinkers* at my hotel, the *Grand Miroir*. –Belgian philosophical propositions. –Another burial of a *Solidarian* to the tune of: "*Oh damn it all! Nadar's caught a dose!*"

The clerical party and the liberal party. Equally *bêtes*. –The celebrated Boniface, or Defré (a Belgian Paul-Louis Courier) is afraid of ghosts, digs up the corpses of children who died without final sacrament in order to rebury them in sanctified ground, and thinks he will meet a tragic death like Courier and has escorts to accompany him at night for fear he be assassinated by the Jesuits. –My first interview with this imbecile. He was drunk. –Returning from the garden where he had gone to vomit, he interrupted the piano playing in order to launch into a speech in favor of *Progress* and against Rubens as a Catholic painter.

–Those who want to abolish capital punishment do so out of sheer self-interest, in Belgium as in France.

–Belgian anticlericalism is a counterfeit of French anticlericalism, but raised to the cubic power.

–The area in cemeteries reserved for dogs or reprobates.

–Belgian religious bigotry.

–Ugliness, villainy, nastiness and *bêtise* of the Flemish clergy. –See Rops's lithography of the *Burial*.

–Pious Belgians make one think of the cannibal Christians of South America.

–The only religious program that would work for the *free thinkers* of Belgium is the program of M. de Caston, a French magician.

–Curious opinion of a friend of Dumouriez on the political parties in Belgium: "There are only two parties, the drunks and the Catholics." –This country has not changed.

19. POLITICS

Electoral practices. Venality. The cost of an election in any given
locality is an open secret. Voting scandals.
Parliamentary favors. (Many illustrations of this.)
Belgian eloquence.
A grotesque discussion about campaign financing.
The republican caucus. A carbon copy of the Jacobins.
Belgium always so far behind the times.

20. POLITICS

There is, strictly speaking, no such thing as a Belgian people. There
are the Flemish and Walloon races, and there are towns that are
enemies of each other. Take Anvers. Belgium, a harlequin patched
together by diplomats.

The baroque story of the 1789 Brabant Revolution, undertaken
against a philosopher-king, and finding itself facing the French Revolution, a philosophic revolution.

A constitutional monarch is an automaton in a second-rate hotel.
–Belgium is the victim of the property qualification that determines
the right to vote. Why nobody here wants universal suffrage. The
constitution is nothing but a rag. Constitutions are made of *paper*.
Manners and morals are *everything*. –Freedom is a mere word in
Belgium. It's there on paper, but it doesn't exist, *because nobody
feels the need for it.*

At a certain moment, this comic situation in the House. The two
parties equal, minus *one* vote. –The *magnificent spectacle* of the
elections, as the French newspapers put it.

Description of an electoral assembly. –Political powows. Political
oratory. Bombast. Disproportion between speech and object.

21. ANNEXATION

Annexation is a prime topic of Belgian conversation. It was the
first word I heard when I arrived here two years ago. They have
talked of it so much that they have convinced the parrots of French
journalism to repeat the word after them. –A good portion of
Belgium is pro-annexation. But this is not reason enough. First of all,

France would have to agree to do so. Belgium is a sniveling little ragamuffin who throws himself around the neck of a fine gentleman and says to him: "Adopt me, be my father!"—but the gentleman first has to be willing to do so.

I am against annexation. There are already enough morons in France, not to mention all those we have annexed in the past, the people of Bordeaux, of Alsace, and others.

But I would not object to an invasion, to a Razzia, a raid in the ancient fashion, in the fashion of Attila. Everything beautiful could be carted off to the *Louvre*. All this belongs to us far more legitimately than it does to the Belgians, given that they no longer have a clue about it. –And the fairer Belgian sex would make the acquaintance of the Turcos, who are not very hard to please.

Belgium is the *shitty end of the stick*; this is above all what makes it so inviolable. *Hands off Belgium!*

On the tyranny of the weak. Women and animals. This is what accounts for the tyranny of Belgium over European opinion.

Belgium is safeguarded by the balance of rivalries. Yes; but what if these rivals reached an agreement among themselves! What would happen in that case?

(Place the rest in the Epilogue, among conjectures as to the future and advice to the French.)

22. THE ARMY

Is, on a comparative basis, far larger than the armies of the rest of Europe: but never engages in war. Odd allocation of governmental funds!

This army, were it to undertake a campaign, would have problems with its infantry troops because of the particular shape of the Belgian foot. But there are many men who could be quickly made battle-ready.

All these young beardless recruits (military service is quite short in duration) have the faces of children.

In this army, an officer's only hope for advancement depends on the natural death or suicide of a superior.

Many of the younger officers are quite disheartened—they are for the most part well-educated and would make excellent soldiers should the occasion arise.

Classes in Rhetoric at the military academy, studies of imaginary battles—paltry consolations for the inactivity of minds educated for the art of war.

More good manners in the army than in the rest of the nation. Which is not very surprising. The sword has always been an ennobling and civilizing force.

23. KING LEOPOLD I. HIS PORTRAIT. ANECDOTES. HIS DEATH. NATIONAL MOURNING.

Leopold, this pathetic minor German princeling, managed (as one says) *to make his brave little way*. He didn't flee into exile in a coach. Having arrived on the throne in his wooden clogs, he died with a fortune estimated at a *hundred million*, apotheosized by all of Europe. In recent days, he has been declared *immortal*. Ludicrous panegyrics. Leopold and Vapereau.

A perfect mediocrity, but with a peasant's canniness and perseverance, this young sprout of the Saxe-Cobourg family managed to hoodwink everybody, laid away a nice little *nest egg*, and in the end filched the fulsome praise usually reserved for heroes.

Napoleon I's opinion of him.

His avarice, his rapaciousness. –A German princeling's moronic ideas about court protocol. His relations with his family. –His allowances. The "pension" he received from Napoleon III.

Anecdote about the gardener.

His ideas about parks and gardens, which caused him to be taken for a lover of the *great outdoors*, but which were simply the products of his tight-fistedness.

Newspapers are censored so that King will read nothing alarming about his poor state of health.

What the Minister of the Interior said within my hearing one morning. The King's ridiculous aversion to dying. –His incredulous reaction to his demise. –He sends away his doctors. –He steals from his mistress.

Invasion of the duchess of Brabant and her children. She slaps a crucifix on his mouth and asks him whether there is anything for which he wants to repent.

Parallels between the death of the King and all other Belgian deaths. –His three chaplains quarrel over his corpse. –M. Becker wins out in the end *given his superior command of French*!

–The great comedy of Mourning begins. –Black bunting, panegyrics, apotheoses. –Public drinking, public pissing, public vomiting everywhere. –All the Belgians in the street, soused, crowded together in silence as if at some masked ball. –They find this entertaining. –Brussels had *in reality* never seen such a *party*. –After all, here was its *first king* ever to have died. –The new King makes his entry to the tune of an Offenbach air (factual). –Nobody laughs. –There are some Belgians singing: *Let's soldier on*, a fine reply to those miserable *Frenchies* who would annex them.

24. FINE ARTS

In Belgium, no Art; Art has withdrawn from the country.
No artists, except Rops.
Composition, a thing unknown. The philosophy of these brutes— a philosophy à la Courbet. Only paint what you see. Therefore *you* are not allowed to paint what *I* do not see. Specialists. –One painter for the sun, one for the moon, one for furniture, one for fabrics, one for flowers–with infinite subdivisions of these specialties, as in industry. –Collaboration becomes essential.
The national taste for vile and revolting things. The old painters are therefore the truthful historians of the Flemish mentality. –Here, bombast does not exclude *bêtise*–which explains good old Rubens, a country lout decked out in satins.
On several modern painters, all *pasticheurs*, all duplicates of French talents. –The tastes of those who follow art. –M. Prosper Crabbe. –The vulgarity of the celebrated M. Van Praet, minister of the palace. –My single interview with him. –How one puts together a collection. –Belgians measure the value of artists by the market price of their paintings. –Several pages on this despicable *self-promoter* called Wiertz, the darling of English tourists. –Analysis of the Museum of Brussels. –Contrary to received opinion, its Rubens are far inferior to those in Paris.
Sculpture, nada.

25. ARCHITECTURE. CHURCHES. WORSHIP.

Modern urban architecture. Junk. Ricketiness of the houses. No harmony. Clashing architectures. –Good materials. –Blue stone. –Pastiches of the past. –The monuments are counterfeits of France.

–As for the Churches, counterfeits of the past.

The past. –The gothic. –The 17th century..

–Description of the Grand'Place of Bruxelles (very well tended).

–In Belgium, they are always behind; the styles lag and last far longer.

–In praise of the 17th-century style, an unrecognized style, of which there are magnificent specimens in Belgium.

–The *Renaissance* in Belgium. –Transition. –The Jesuit styles. –Styles of the 17th century. –The Rubens style.

The Church of *Béguinage* in Brussels, *Saint-Pierre* in Malines, the *Church of the Jesuits* in Anvers, *Saint-Loup* in Namur, etc., etc. . . .

–V. Hugo's espousal of the Gothic has done much to damage our understanding of architecture. We have lingered too long over it.

–The philosophy of the history of architecture, *according to me.*

–Analogies with corals, madreporaria, the formation of continents, and finally with the entire life of nature. –No gaps. –A permanent state of transition. –One can say that Rococo is the final flowering of Gothic.

–Coeberger, Faid'herbe and Franquart.

–Victor Joly's opinion of Coeberger, as usual deriving from Victor Hugo.

–The immense riches of the Churches. –A bit of the curiosity shop, a bit of the junk store.

Description of this type of wealth.

Some churches, either Gothic, either 17th-century.

Polychrome statues. The confessionals highly decorated; –the confessionals at the Béguinage, at Malines, at Anvers, at Namur, etc. . . .

The Pulpits of Truth. –Extremely varied. –The true Flemish sculpture is made of wood and is at its most stunning in the churches.

–A sculpture that is not sculptural, not monumental; toy sculpture. A sculpture of patience. –Yet this art has died out as have all the others, even at Malines where it flowered so successfully.

–Description of a few processions. Traces of the past still subsisting in religious practices. –The sumptuousness of it all. –Astonishing naiveté in the dramatization of religious ideas.

Passing observations about the sheer number of Belgian festivals. Every day a feast day. A telling indication of the laziness of its people.

–Belgian piety, dim-witted. –Superstition. The Christian God is beyond the capacity of the Belgian Brain.

–The Clergy, ponderous, crude, cynical, lubricious, rapacious. In a word, Belgian. The Clergy was behind the Revolution of 1831 and therefore believes it owns the country.

–Let's get back to the Jesuits and to the Jesuit style. A style with genius. The complex and ambiguous character of this style. –(Enticing yet fearsome.) –Large openings, large bays, large light –a melange of figures, styles, ornaments, symbols. –A few examples. I have seen tiger paws functioning as volutes. –In general, the exteriors of these churches are plain, except for the façade.

26. THE COUNTRYSIDE AROUND BRUSSELS

Fat, buxom, moist, like the Flemish female—murky, like the Flemish male. –The vegetation is quite black. –The climate is humid, cold, hot and humid, four seasons in a single day. –Not much animal life. No insects, no birds. Even the beasts flee these accursèd climes.

27. A STROLL THROUGH MALINES

Malines is a nice little Beguine nun snug in her hood. –Mechanical music wafts through the air. –The *Marseillaise* on the carillon. –Everyday is a Sunday. –Crowds in Churches. Grass growing in the streets. The ancient smell of Spain. The Beguine nunnery. Several Churches. –Saint-Rombaut. Notre Dame. Saint-Pierre. –Paintings of two Jesuit brothers on the Mission. *Continuous* confessionals. The marvelous symbol of the Pulpit, promising world domination to the Jesuits—the sole sculptural piece of sculpture that I have seen. –The smell of wax and incense. –Rubens and Van Dyck. –The Botanical Garden. The stream clear, fast-flowing. –A fine Moselle wine at the *Greyhound* Inn. –Explain what a *Private Society* is.

28. A STROLL THROUGH ANVERS

Encounter with the archbishop of Malines. –Flat country, the vegetation black. –Fortifications new (!) and ancient, with English gardens. Here finally is a town that could pass for a Capital! –The Meir square. The Rubens House. The House of the King. The Flemish *Renaissance*. The Town Hall. –The Church of the Jesuits, a masterpiece. –Here again, the *Jesuit style* (hotchpotch, chessboard, chandeliers, a boudoir at once mystical and fearsome, mourning in marble, theatrical confessionals, Theater and Boudoir, rings of light and transparent glorias, angels and cupids, apotheoses and beatifications). –What I think of the celebrated Rubens, of churches that are closed, of sacristans. –Calvaries and Madonnas. –Certain houses done in modern (pompous) style. –The majesty of Anvers. The beauty of a major river. From which Anvers should be viewed. –Napoleon I's docks. –M. Leys. –The Plantin house. –The Rydeck dancehall, balls and prostitution. The Rydeck is a *joke*. It's the kind of sprawling brothel one finds on the outskirts of Paris.

29. A STROLL THROUGH NAMUR

People rarely visit Namur. A town overlooked by travelers, not surprisingly because the *Donkey-Guides* never mention it. –The town of Vauban, of Boileau, of Van der Meulen, of Bossuet, of Fénélon, of Jouvenet, of Rigaud, of Restout, etc. . . . Memories of Boileau's *Le Lutrin*. –*Saint-Loup*, the absolute masterpiece of the Jesuits. General impression. A few details. Jesuits as architects, as painters, as sculptors, as decorators. –*Les Récollets*. Saint-Aubin, a St. Peter's of Rome in miniature, an exterior of brick and blue stone, its interior white, with a convex portal. –Nicolaï, a fake Rubens. –The Street of Blind Chaffinches. (The duke of Brabant, currently Leopold II, president of a Chaffinch Academy.)

–The peculiarities of prostitution in Namur.

–Walloon population. –Better manners.

–Portraits of Félicien Rops and his father-in-law, a tough local judge and yet quite jovial, a great hunter with a talent for quotation. He has written a book on hunting and quoted me lines from Horace, from my *Fleurs du mal* and sentences by D'Aurevilly. –Struck me as charming. –The only Belgian with a knowledge of Latin and capable of carrying on in French.

–I'm heading for Luxembourg, without knowing it.

–The countryside, black. The river *Meuse*, its banks steep and misty.

–Namur wine.

Charles Baudelaire

30. A STROLL THROUGH LIEGE

The palace of the Bishop-Princes. –Cellars. –Drunkenness. –Major pretentions to Frenchness.

31. A STROLL THROUGH GAND

Saint-Bavon, a few nice things. Mausoleums. –Uncouth locals. –An ancient town made up of yokels in revolt, thinks of itself as special, and puts on the airs of a Capital. Depressing town.

32. A STROLL THROUGH BRUGES

A ghost town, a mummy of a town, more or less preserved. It smells of death, the Middle Ages, Venice in black, routine specters and tombs. –The great Beguine nunnery; carillons. A few monuments. A work attributed to Michelangelo. Yet Bruges, too, is on its way out.

33. EPILOGUE

The future. Advice to the French.

Belgium is what France might well have become had it remained in the hands of the Bourgeoisie. Belgium is without life, but not without corruption. –Hacked into pieces, divided up, invaded, defeated, beaten up, pillaged, the Belgian continues to vegetate, a pure marvel of mollusk existence. –*Noli me tangere*, a fit motto for it. –But who would want to grasp hold of this *shitty end of the stick*? –Belgium is a monster. Who would want to adopt it? And yet it contains within itself *several* elements that could contribute to its dissolution. This diplomatic harlequin could be torn apart from one moment to the next. –A portion of it could go to Prussia, the Flemish portion to Holland, the Walloon portion to France. –A great misfortune for us. –Portrait of the Walloon. –Races that are ungovernable not because of their excess of vitality but because of their total absence of ideas and feelings. Nothing there. (The quotes by Maturin and Demouriez's friend). –Commercial interests in play, with which I don't want to bother myself. –Anvers aspires to become a *free city*. –Once again, the question of annexation. –Small cities (Brussels,

144

Geneva), nasty cities. Small nations, nasty nations.

Tips to the French who are condemned to live in Belgium: how to avoid getting robbed, insulted, poisoned.

FINIS

* * *

[Alternative "Epilogue" from Baudelaire's Notes]

Epilogue

Today, Monday the 28th of August, 1865, over the course of a hot and humid evening, I followed the meanderings of a street fair (*Kermesse*), and in the streets named *Devil's Corner, Monks' Rampart, Our Lady of Sleep, Six Tokens*, as well as in several others, I discovered, to my great delight and surprise, frequent symptoms of cholera suspended in the air. Have I sufficiently invoked cholera, this monster I adore? Have I studied the advance signs of his arrival attentively enough? How long shall I have to wait for him, this horrific favorite of mine, this impartial Attila, this divine plague who strikes down his victims at whim? Haven't I sufficiently pleaded with My Lord God to speed his passage over the stinking banks of the *Senne*? And how much pleasure would I finally derive as I contemplated the grimacing agony of this hideous people caught in the coils of its fake Styx, its *Briareus-river*, whose waters carry off more excrements than the sky above provides sustenance to flies! I shall take great delight, for sure, in the terrors and tortures inflicted on this race whose traits are yellow hair, nankeen trousers, and lilac complexions!

A detail worth mentioning: after all the numerous shields dedicated to national *Unity*, to *Friendship*, to *Fidelity*, to the *Constitution*, to the *Virgin Mary*, I discover one dedicated: *To the Police*.

Five Poems
Maxine Chernoff

EVENT

An event must in some way end
before its narration can begin.
—Christian Metz

And then doves and the thrush and the late
afternoon of the swallows under the bridge
and the fathoms of sleep and then the hollows
of dialogue aspiring to contain the rich facts
of what didn't happen when it seemed to have,
and then a disquisition on the luster of windows
in the morning when a psalm is read
before lightning strikes the spire of a tall church
in the city of your birth, and then centuries
of robes of saffron or black and vespers or prayer
on cold granite or at a wall where guards
stand with AK-47s, and ghosts witness their attempts
with sorrow, unlike human sorrow, which is a stream
that evaporates when language interrupts its flow.
And the ministry of a quiet voice when what
is needed is a bell or a glass filled to a certain
level and made to vibrate with a spoon, and before
this ending another ending and after that another
and no agreement between parties as to whether
the story is over or this is a respite between
exhaustion and pleading. And the irises shallowly
covered in dirt emerge purple in spring,
world without end, as words are endless,
sending their tendrils toward the next refrain.

EMBLEM

In a film a house would be a shot of a staircase.
—Christian Metz

The chambered air
remembered—
surgical, smooth,
until location itself
seemed an invention
of will. The house,
particular to our longings,
its blue light dimming
then returning
to the story every morning.
With no name
for love's statuary
its swans or ready doves,
its trees awaiting
clarification, objects
drifted until we recovered
the ancient art
of listening as we
spoke our names
in a new language
occasioned by desire.

Maxine Chernoff

AFTERNOON

All one retains of a film is its plot and a few images.
—Christian Metz

Their shadows carved in snow,
ghosts wander in eternity,
their habit of existence
escaping our cognition
until we surrender
light and location,
dried bark and dead leaves,
decayed in their mystery
no more than summer's
cloth lowered in the garden
with its flowers behind
flowers. Lost on the screen
is the morning he said
this and you that and
the future hummed in bushes
like a slow, windowless fire.
We haunt the world looking
for ourselves, the ones
who know the soft antler buds
of deer. We forget the scene
in the room of the said,
where curtains and bed and light,
latticed as lace, made your face
unfamiliar, mine too shrouded
in layers of hope, which are,
as gauze, a semblance
of our hiding. As we opened
to the other, beyond seasons
and borders, the world,
with everything in place, held
small truths untold by any voice.

148

A vista and a ledge, custom and dust
of living, spread. Our story obscure,
the room shuttered, the lateness
of the day a tender omen. You
said a word that filled a
momentary gap, lacing the world
in tangled sound and string.

FUTURE

Forbidden flowers and herbs are history's foodstuff.
—Bei Dao

Old snow falls in this poem about the past,
our secret lives remembered
as funerals are remembered
by those who never attend
but imagine the slender coffin,
the sheen of its bright handles.
There, on the dark lawn,
you meet your former self asking
a lover to step aside as memory
impinges on an invitation
to dance. The next scene
comes unbidden as an outbreak
of disease: There he stands with his eyes
mercurial, there she weeps at her rendition
of their sorrow. Snow falls on them both,
laden with reasons and candles,
and in the corner a table is set where your
former self shares its dinner
with the one you have become.
The radiant fruit you taste has gotten
overripe, waiting for its season.

149

SEMBLANCE

A crow tends a branch
on meaning's tree, where
a single word's limit
meets trouble's dark road,
deadpan map stolid
as Keaton's face. The story
swells and grows motives,
as weeds disguise gardens
in summer's amplitude.
Nothing undoes day's dazed
grace unless it is captioned
or chiseled. No word whispered
encounters the ghost of witness
as a glass that holds water's history.

Cult

Brian Evenson

I.

IT HAD BEEN TERRIBLE from the start. He knew it was a disaster, knew from the very beginning, maybe even from the very first instant, that they were not, no matter what she claimed, *meant for each other*, that he should get away from her as fast as he could, if not faster. And yet, somehow, he couldn't. He'd always experienced a certain amount of inertia, but it was something other than that. What exactly it was, though, he wasn't sure.

After a few weeks, he knew not only that they weren't meant to be together but that he didn't even *like* her, but by then she had already moved in. The months that followed—the whole relationship if he was being honest with himself—had been like being brainwashed, if you could be brainwashed while still knowing with a painful clarity what was happening to you. It was like he was watching someone else move from humiliation to humiliation, but was powerless to do anything to stop it. The problem was that that someone else was not someone else: It was him.

No, they never should have been together in the first place. He knew that even then, but he couldn't do anything to stop it. If she hadn't stabbed him, they'd probably be together still. Even the stabbing had been just barely enough to propel him out of the relationship. Even lying there on the floor, clutching his side, waiting for her to call the ambulance, he had already begun to forgive her, to consider how her stabbing him had been, in a way, if you really thought about it, his own fault. And she hadn't been trying to really hurt him—if she'd been trying to really hurt him she would have used the butcher knife. No, she had used just a little knife, not even as long as a steak knife, a knife he didn't even know the name of. How was she to blame if the knife had been sharper than she expected?

Of course, she had said none of this to him—he had thought it all out for himself, had even said some of it to her before he passed out the first time. No, it took his friends days if not weeks to begin to convince him that even if she hadn't said it she'd made of him the kind of person who would say it for her. She had gotten into his head and rewired it, changed it. So much so that when he became conscious again and found she wasn't there, he hadn't told himself, *She's deserted me* or *She's fled because she's afraid she'll be arrested for stabbing me.* No, instead he thought, *She must have gone for help.* It took passing out twice more before he could bring himself to crawl across the floor and pull the phone off the coffee table and dial 911. Not because, he told himself even as he dialed it, he thought that she hadn't done it, but only because if both she and he called, an ambulance would be more likely to come.

It took weeks, but in the end they convinced him. She had never called 911. She had stabbed him and then fled, perhaps thinking she'd killed him. Even then, he might not have been convinced if he hadn't realized that she'd had the presence of mind to pack up her few possessions and take them with her when she left. Simply fleeing he might have been able to forgive, but fleeing with all your clothes and worldly goods was another story.

Even then, he might have forgiven her had she called, had her voice again activated what he'd come to think of as the control mechanism she had rigged in his mind that kept him in exile from himself. But his friends, his true friends, the ones who nursed him back to health, the ones who stayed in the hospital beside him day after day after the stomach wound turned septic and he nearly died, hid his cell phone. If she called, they deleted her calls, and when he asked about her they told him to fuck off. They had given him tough love, but that was what he needed to climb out of the trough that had been their relationship. And once they had given him back his phone, the few times she had called they had been there and had taken the phone bodily from him, had told her that he didn't want to talk, that she should not call again, that she should never call again, that if she called even once more he would press charges. And soon even if they weren't there, he could simply not answer the call of his own accord, could simply delete the message.

After a while she stopped calling. He felt great relief. From time to time, at greater and greater intervals, he wondered what had happened to her, but then, soon—even though a few months before he wouldn't have thought it possible—he stopped thinking about her altogether.

*

II.

He was driving and his phone was ringing, but no name was coming up above the number. *Unlisted.* It was not his local area code, but maybe was somewhere close, Pennsylvania maybe, unless he was confused and it was Ohio. Probably a telemarketer. So he didn't answer. It rang until voice mail picked up, but nobody left a message. So, a telemarketer. Or an election pollster. Or maybe some sort of robot call. He let the phone fall into the passenger seat and kept driving.

A few minutes later the phone started up again, buzzing against the fabric of the seat. He just kept driving, glancing over at its screen until the buzzing stopped. Again, no message left.

When the same number came up a third time, he considered powering the phone down, but his hand was already reaching for it, raising it to his ear.

"Hello?" he said. "I think you must have the wrong number."

But no, she did not have the wrong number: She knew exactly whom she was calling. The last thing he had considered was that it could be her. But *her* was exactly who it was.

She was calling from a convenience store, she explained. God, she said, how she had missed him, she couldn't believe she had finally gotten through, how great it was to hear his voice! Had they been keeping her from him? She really needed him.

Blood was beating in his ears. He hadn't managed to utter a word.

"I joined a cult," she told him. "I just up and joined it."

"Excuse me?" he said. His mouth was dry and the words came out sounding strange.

"Of course at the time I didn't think it was a cult, but now I see it was. They kicked me out." She laughed. "Who gets fucking exiled from a cult?" she said. "Me, I guess. I was always—"

"You must have the wrong number," he tried again.

"Wrong number?" she said, and her voice took on a hard edge. "I recognize your voice. It's me, Star."

"Star?" he said, genuinely confused.

"Oh, sorry," she said. "That's the name I took. You'll have to get used to it. I'm not going back to Tammy. I always hated that name. And Tamara's even worse. They can exile me from their fucking cult, but they can't take away my new name."

She stopped speaking. He didn't say anything, just swallowed. He

153

kept the phone pressed tight to his ear.

"Hello?" she said. "Hello? You didn't hang up, did you?"

He hung up.

Later, after the worst had happened, he told himself that if only he hadn't been alone and driving, he would have been OK. Or even if he'd been driving, if only he hadn't been on the turnpike and had had an exit or a place he could have pulled off, he would have been OK. If he was honest with himself, he didn't know if this was true, but it made him feel better to think it.

She called back less than thirty seconds later. He didn't answer it. Then she called again, and again, and again. *I should roll down the window and throw the phone out*, he thought. But it was a new phone, still under contract: He couldn't bring himself to do it. In the course of eight minutes she called fifteen times, and each time the phone rang he felt a little piece of himself weaken.

After four or five minutes he knew he'd pick up, but still tried to resist, hoping that she'd give up and stop calling. If she gave up, he could still be saved.

But no, she was persistent. He tried, as the phone kept ringing, to plan out what he was going to tell her. He would tell her that he wasn't her friend anymore, that he didn't want to talk to her. He would ask her to have the simple human decency to never call him again. He would remind her how she had stabbed him, and not only stabbed him but stabbed him and fled and left him for dead. How could she expect him to ever talk to her ever again? What was wrong with her?

And yet, when he finally did answer, he could not bring himself to say any of this. Indeed, at first he said nothing at all.

What *she* said was, "What happened, did your phone go dead? Cell phones just aren't reliable," she said. "Which carrier do you have? Do you still have the same one as when we were together? I tried to get you to change it then, do you remember? I bet you never did."

"Tammy . . . ," he started.

"Star," she said. "Who's this Tammy? There's no Tammy here. It's Star, the name is Star."

"The thing is—"

"Did I tell you I was in a cult?" she said, a sharp edge to her voice. "The Children of Light, they're called. How do you think I ended up there? Whose fault was that?"

It's your fault, a small voice in his head was already saying, a voice

154

that he'd thought had long ago been throttled out of existence. *You drove her to it.* At least the voice was still saying "you," he told himself. When it started saying "I" then he would be in real trouble.

She waited for him to answer and, when he didn't, said in a softer voice, "I need someone to come get me."

"Come get you," he repeated flatly.

"I need you to come," she said. "I need *you*."

"No," he said, ignoring the dissenting voice growing inside his head. "Absolutely not."

"I don't have anybody else," she said. "I only have you."

"You don't have me," he said.

"Look," she said, "I don't like this any better than you do, but I don't know where else to turn. If you just do this for me, I'll never ask anything else of you again."

"Never?" he asked, but he knew from how quickly she answered yes that she was lying.

"No," he said. "I'm sorry. I can't do this."

"Thank you," she said, ignoring him. Very quickly she spat out an address, a little convenience store near the Pennsylvania border. "I'm counting on you," she said, and then, before he could say anything else, she hung up the phone.

III.

He tried to call back the pay phone, but nobody answered. *Typical,* he thought, *just like her.* He tried not to go, really he did, but it was too late, the damage was done. A part of him, an admittedly infinitesimal part, thought that it was just possible that there had been a reception problem, that she did, honestly, think that he was coming. It was ridiculous, the rest of him knew, but that doubt, no matter how small it was, was not something that he could navigate smoothly past.

He kept thinking of her, alone, waiting at the convenience store, night coming, nowhere for her to go. She was a terrible person, he knew that—she had stabbed him and left him—but if he didn't go, wouldn't that make him a horrible person too?

He wasn't a horrible person, he knew it. And he could prove it. He could just go and get her, just drive her somewhere, and then his obligation would be done. Then, he told himself, he'd never have to see her again.

At the next exit he got off the turnpike and went back the other way.

*

It took four hours, each one harder on him than the one before. The farther he went, the more he felt like his mind was no longer his own, like he was once again a man driven out of his own body, like once again she, Tammy, or rather now she, Star, was in charge.

The whole drive he turned over in his head what he might say to her and what she was likely to say back, how the conversation might turn and twist and where in the end it might possibly end up. But no matter how he turned and twisted it, no matter how generously he slathered it with luck, no matter how willfully he tried to squint away what she really was and the control she had over him, he could not see any way in which things would turn out well for him. At best, at absolute best, he would see her and it would devastate him. Even if it did turn out that she really was asking just one more thing, that after this she would be willing to walk away and let him go, it would still take him weeks, if not months, to recover.

And that was only the best possibility. Chances were he'd be back in a relationship with her, suffering for months, if not years, until the time when she once again stabbed him and, probably, this time killed him.

For a while he tried not to think about it, but how could he help it? He turned on the radio as loud as he could, tried even for a few miles to sing along to drown out his thoughts, but all the songs were about mending shattered relationships. They were giving the wrong part of his subconscious ammunition.

When he stopped for gas at the service area just shy of Buffalo, he got out and stretched his legs. He used the bathroom and then sat in the food court for a while. On a whim, he looked up "Children of Light" on his phone. Nothing listed as a cult, but there was a collective on the edge of Pennsylvania. Nonreligious hippies, it seemed, running a farm and a craft store. Hardly a cult. Idealistic anarchists at best. Not the kind of people to kick anybody out unless they absolutely had to. But knowing Tammy, knowing Star, they had probably had to.

He tried again the phone number she had called from, but still got nobody. He climbed back into the car, kept driving.

It was dark by the time he reached the convenience store. It was at the corner of a two-lane state highway and one of the long roads dividing one set of farms from another that came in these parts only about every mile or so. There wasn't much else to be seen beyond farmland. The lot of the convenience store was lit by a single sickly floodlight rigged on one corner of the roof.

She was sitting there on the edge of the curb just below the pay phone, her arms wrapped around her knees, her back against the building wall, staring straight ahead. Next to her was a well-worn paper bag, clothes spilling out of the top of it. When he pulled in, she put a hand up to her face to block the light. She looked, he thought, harmless. Deceptively so.

Watching her, he suddenly remembered the strange way when they first kissed she had drawn her hands over and around his body, her fingers whispering just over his clothes, touching but not touching, like she was making a cage around him that was only just barely larger than his body.

He put the car in park and turned off the lights. He waited, but she didn't move. *Maybe she's dead*, he thought hopefully.

But she was not dead. From time to time she moved a little. Maybe she was asleep? But no, he could see the gleam of her eyes; they were open.

She wants me to get out and come to her, he thought. A dull anger began to grow within him. He would just wait her out, he told himself, he was not her slave.

But a moment later, he could not stop his hand from opening the door. He watched his body climb out and move toward her.

She did not respond when he spoke her name. She waited until she felt his hand on her shoulder and then immediately she was up and holding onto his arm.

"I knew you would come," she said in a voice that he wanted to describe as breathy. He couldn't tell if she was genuinely out of breath or if it was simulated. "I was waiting for you and you came. You still love me after all."

I will take her where she wants to go, he told himself. *I will drop her off. I will never see her again*. But there was more to it. They weren't on the road, not yet. No, she had to go back to the cult and get the rest of her things.

"They're not a cult," he said. "I looked them up."

"Who would know better, me or you?" she asked. They would go back to the *cult* and they would get her things. It wasn't far, she claimed, probably not more than a few minutes by car.

But it was more than a few minutes. It was, maybe, twenty, and it felt much longer. She talked nonstop, about him, about them, their relationship, which she didn't seem to realize was over and done. She was there beside him, leaning over the center console, stroking his arm. He kept flinching away, but she either didn't notice or didn't care. Now that she was in the car with him, she would have her way.

He felt worse than he had in years, worse, in fact, than when she had stabbed him. She was talking, talking. He just tried to ignore her. They would get a little house together, she was saying, unless, of course, he already had a little house, did he? Somewhere where they could be together, separate from the world and safe, living in exile from everybody else, just the two of them together, nobody but the two of them.

Oh God, no, he thought, though somewhere within him, his heart leapt like a stag.

They would have a baby, she went on, they owed it to the world to have a baby, but please God make it look like her rather than him. Sure, he had his good qualities, but after all, they could both agree that she was the one with the looks. She would stay at home with the baby and with the baby's nanny and he would support them and watch the baby at night.

Yes, that small and more insistent part of him was beginning to assert. *She has a good point.* He shook his head, tried to stay himself.

Look at him now, she said. Who had chosen that shirt? Had he stolen it from a homeless man? Didn't he know he needed someone to take care of him, to keep him from humiliating himself?

And then, mercifully, they were there. He was out of the car and heading toward what he guessed to be the main building of the so-called cult, waving her back, no, he would get her things, no, they had kicked her out, she couldn't come in, he would do it, it wasn't any bother.

She was still calling something after him through the open driver's-side door of the car when he started knocking on the door. He tried not to hear what she was saying. The door opened and a thin woman with a windburned face revealed herself.

"Yes?" the woman said.

He introduced himself, awkwardly shook the woman's hand. "I'm here to gather Star's things," he told her.

"Star?" said the woman. "You mean Tammy, right?"

"Didn't you rename her Star?"

"Us? She started calling herself Star, all right," said the woman. "We went along with it for a while. I mean, why not?" The woman craned her neck. "Is that her in the car?"

"That's her," he said.

The woman nodded. "Come on in," she said. "I'll close the door behind you."

He was led down a central hall and through some sort of dining area, containing five big tables and eight stacks of chairs. Past that, the hallway began again, doors punctuating it. The woman led him down near the back of the building and opened the door on the left.

"There you go," the woman said. There were two black garbage bags balanced on a narrow cot. Each looked half full, the tops knotted closed.

"What's in them?" he asked.

The woman shrugged. "Nothing much," she said. "Worldly goods. So-called chattel. The millstone round the neck. Nothing anybody needs, least of all her."

Puzzled, he just nodded, then moved forward to gather the sacks.

"She's bad news. Still, we would have sent them to her," the woman said from behind him. "We would have paid her bus ticket too. You didn't have to come fetch her."

"I didn't want to," he said.

She gave him a sharp look. "Then why did you?"

Why had he? It seemed so far away now, days in the past. But no, it had only been a few hours. Already he was back at the bottom of the trough and there was no getting out.

He sat heavily on the bed. He didn't realize that he had until the woman was beside him, asking if he was OK.

"I just . . . ," he said, "maybe just a moment to catch my breath."

The woman nodded. She watched him incuriously for a little bit and then went out.

IV.

How long can I stay here? he wondered, a garbage bag on either side of him. How much time had actually gone by? Ten minutes? Fifteen? When would she have had enough and come after him?

*

Wouldn't they stop her from coming after him at all? She was, after all, exiled, was not allowed to come back. The front door was closed and locked. Even if she wanted to, she wouldn't be able to get in. Maybe he could claim sanctuary with the Children of Light. He could fall on his knees and beg them to save him from himself. As long as he was here, he would be safe.

He took a deep breath. Yes, he would stay here. He wouldn't move from this spot. Here he was safe. There was no reason for him to ever leave, no reason to ever see her again. Losing the car was a small price to pay. Losing his connection with the outside world a small price to pay, as long as he could stay himself, as long as he never had to see her again.

Yes, he would stay, he told himself again.

He took another deep breath and then, gathering the two bags, went outside to his own destruction.

Celebrating Russian Federation Day with Immanuel Kant
Robin Hemley

FIRST MAXIM:
Embrace Change
(Do you have a choice?)

THE RIVER PREGOLYA, KNOWN in Immanuel Kant's day as the Pregel, its waters calm and lily padded, flows past tourists, Russians mostly, but also Polish, Lithuanian, and the occasional German, lounging at a café near an imposing red church, Königsberg Cathedral. The only survivor in this immediate vicinity from Kant's day, the church puts on a show merely by existing. In August of 1944, English bombers carried out two nights of raids on Königsberg. The buildings of the small island of Kneiphof on which the cathedral sits, once a warren of twisting medieval streets, were nearly leveled on the second night, the cathedral demolished, the hundred small children seeking refuge in its basement . . . *kaput*. What survived that night—the shell of the building and Immanuel Kant's tomb.

The cathedral's new spire, lowered by helicopter into place in 1994, exactly resembles the old spire, except for the molecules of which it was made, the hands that crafted it, and the crucible of history between the cathedral's 1335 dedication and the late twentieth century. Though the buildings that surrounded it have long ago vanished, the scene is pleasant if you restrict your gaze to the river, the cathedral, and the other businesses along the Pregolya done up like actors at a Renaissance fair, and ignore the massive supermarket across the street, the sex shop with its flashing lights and dark windows, the apartment blocks of the same variety found all over the former Soviet empire, lined up like spectators in the cheap seats at a pageant.

Today is Russian Federation Day. I've come to what is now the Russian city of Kaliningrad for this and for Immanuel Kant, specifically because of his treatise "Toward Perpetual Peace: A Philosophical Project," in which he attempted to convince the world of the late eighteenth century that we should replace classical law with "cosmopolitan law," and consider ourselves citizens of the world. Even at that time, the notion seemed a tad unrealistic, and none of his friends thought he would get far, but some admired his bravery for trying. Kant argues that all nations should be republics (though not necessarily democracies, of which he was skeptical) founded on three ideals: the freedom of all people as individuals, the equal application of laws to all citizens, and the equality of all citizens. He likewise proposed "universal hospitality," the right to move freely between states.

Kant loved travel books, but he loathed change, and so it's a safe supposition that while he thought people should be able to move freely between states, he wouldn't have approved of what's transpired in his hometown, a case of states moving freely through people.

But I haven't ventured here to engage in pointless nostalgia for a dead philosopher's city that was destroyed before I was born. I *am* here for the irony of the place, that the author of a treatise on perpetual peace should have hailed from a realm of total and merciless war. After World War II, the Soviets made Kant's city into a military zone forbidden to outsiders. When the Soviet Union's borders receded, Kaliningrad, renamed after one of Stalin's cronies, was retained by Russia. A region a little bigger than Connecticut, Kaliningrad never was Russian before (except for four years during Kant's lifetime when the Russians occupied Königsberg), and is now Russia's westernmost territory, surrounded by Poland and Lithuania. An extraterritorial part of a country, like Hawaii or Alaska, Kaliningrad is an exclave of Russia and I've come here because I'm intrigued by exclaves and perplexed by notions of nationhood, patriotism, and nationalism, which only seem to lead to trouble. I'm here for Russian Federation Day, in a Kantian spirit, as a cosmopolitan, a citizen of the world.

The Russians do not see me that way. The Russian Consulate in Chicago gave me exactly a week's visa, no more, no less, and when I discovered two days before my trip that they had shortchanged me by one day, it wasn't the visa that needed to change, but my plans. Consequently, I spent a dismal afternoon in an Aeroflot office in Hong Kong, proffering a Visa of a different sort, one that extends universal hospitality in its own special way, erasing almost all borders between nations.

SECOND MAXIM:
Be Skeptical of Everything You Read
(except for this)

"Happy holiday," the ticket taker says at the entrance to the Kalinin-grad Zoo (formerly the Königsberg Zoo). The people of Kaliningrad "kind of inherited the zoo," in the words of a young guide at the town's tourist-information center. The inheritance took place on April 8, 1945, when the Russians launched a surprise attack from two sides, led by "hero of the Soviet Union" Lieutenant Lopshin, who with his troops killed thirty and took 185 "Hitlerites" prisoner. If they were lucky, those prisoners survived the war and spent the next five years or so at hard labor, rebuilding the city they had helped destroy in the name of their leader. The animals fared no better than the Hitlerites. Only a deer, a badger, a donkey, and a wounded hip-popotamus named Hans survived. Hans lived many years beyond the war and became the zoo's symbol.

Today the zoo is filled with animals again, though the only cries are those of the peacocks and small children as they run in front of their parents. Spiderman encourages passersby to have their photos taken with him. A child has her face painted. A small tram ferries families around the wooded zoo, and amidst all this gaiety, of a variety found in small municipal zoos everywhere, few signs of trauma persist. But they are not ignored. Suitcase-sized placards dot the grounds, depicting the zoo as it was before the "inheritance," or directly afterward. One placard shows the main hall and restaurant of the zoo, the Gesellschafthaus from 1911, a group of women wearing hats the size of sombreros sitting on park benches beside conical hedges, and the same building in various stages of ruin and reconstruction, devoid of hedges and people after the war.

An enlarged photo of a woodcut from 1927 shows a couple viewing animals inside a barnlike structure, now rickety but still extant, its blue paint nearly stripped from its wooden sides. Its cages hold a macaque and vultures, the macaque staring at visitors as though engaged in a chess match, and it's their move. Some visitors have pushed bananas through the bars of his cage, but he disdains these, and I remind myself that this is the zoo for the people of Kaliningrad, not me, and I need to leave my American objections out of this.

Two jagged slabs jutting out the ground, the height of a person, have been repurposed as art, artifact, stone tablets bearing not commandments but subtle cautions, Kantian values written in Russian on one slab, German on the other:

Logic, Freedom, "The thing in itself," Metaphysics,
Reason, Worthiness, Self-Respect.

In his old age, Kant thrived on routine and lived his life by maxims he formulated after much thought and logical consideration, and from which he never wavered. As his maxims became more ossified, he and his friend, the learned English merchant Joseph Green, who also lived his life in this way, tried almost to outdo one another in how unwavering they could be with their maxims. When Kant missed an early-morning meeting time for a country jaunt, Green took off in the carriage without him. Kant caught up with Green down the road and waved his arms wildly to get Green's attention, but Green never slowed down. Slowing down would have gone against one of his maxims. Kant was perhaps a little less rigid than Green, but not much. Every morning at five, his servant, Martin Lampe, a former soldier, would shake him awake roughly. Kant hated getting up early. So his day would begin. He'd drink a cup of weak tea, follow it with a bowl of tobacco, the preparations for his lectures, and/or writing until seven. He lectured in his home lecture theater from seven until eleven, after which he'd write some more until taking a modest lunch at Zornig's coffee house on the Prinzessineplatz, preferring the company of ignorant soldiers to that of the many people who wanted to curry his favor or "hammer his head full" with their ideas and disputations. After lunch, he took a stroll and then visited Green. As he grew older, he still only smoked one pipe of tobacco a day, but the bowls of the pipes reputedly grew larger over time.

All inhabited landscapes, and some that are not, are constantly being read and translated in new editions. Kant's city, translated from German to Russian, has a complex beauty that you might not expect, certainly not if you read an article written in 2010 by Ben Judah for the UK journal *Standpoint*, in which Judah decries Kaliningrad as "one of the world's ugliest cities." Places change, but what Judah describes is a kind of stereotypical midnineties post-Soviet nightmare:

> The factories have mostly closed. The jobs will not come back. Humiliated men without work turn to the bottle. Women talk about being abused. Their sons are not remotely equipped for the e-age.

The Kaliningrad I visit, just three years after Judah's visit, is only in a vestigial sense like the city he disdains as "full of crumbling communist estates, with glinting neon hoardings. Maintenance is unheard of and faulty wiring hangs across dank, filthy socialist avenues, each wide enough for three tanks abreast." The crumbling communist estates, in any event, are not unique to Kaliningrad. Judah's new Russian Orthodox church in Victory Square is a "white slab of golden domes," the malls are empty, and with hardly anything bought, women tart themselves up for sex tourists or advertise themselves as "your Russian bride." There is a pall of pollution in the air that tastes to him like toast.

No polluted mist hangs in the air now, no buttered-toast smell. Young couples, not drunks, lounge on the benches near the cosmonaut statue. The electric lines that carry the current to the city's trams seem in good repair. To scan the boulevard across from Victory Square, full of men and women, some dressed fashionably, some not so, and imagine anything even vaguely "socialist" in the Soviet sense, or tanks three abreast, would require the dementia my mother suffered from when she imagined the Iraqi army unloading bodies on the pleasant avenues of the town in which she spent her dotage. Victory Square is alive with fountains—a toddler evades capture as his mother pursues him with his carriage. The Russian Orthodox church and its bell towers that dominate the square, along with a red obelisk, a memorial to the war, gleam indeed, but no more tastelessly than any gleaming dome.

In Jerusalem, an occasional pilgrim suffers from Jerusalem Syndrome, a psychotic break in which the sufferer believes he or she is Jesus or Mary or Joseph. Luckily for me and Judah, neither of us thinks we are Kant. Kaliningrad is not Königsberg. It hasn't been for over seventy years. Those people are gone. That town is gone. In Judah's England, in the Rust Belt of the United States, there are countless examples of cities in worse shape than Kaliningrad. But it's not what it once was, indisputably.

Königsberg Castle was dismantled by the Soviets after World War II, and in its spot was erected a white building of Lego-like angles, known around Kaliningrad as "the Monster." You can go to town on the "What-Was-Then-Known-As" game, and also the "On-This-Spot-Once-Stood" game, in former Königsberg, then East Prussia, now Kaliningrad, Russia.

Following the path of Kant's daily walk today is mostly a depressing business with little that would have left him less than horrified.

And you know you're in the right area because a neglected plaque along the way memorializes his famous quote, in German and in Russian: "Two things awe me most: the starry sky above and the moral law within me." If there's anything that produces awe here now, it's the fact of change itself—you won't find anything vaguely Kantian in the vicinity of his walk until you reach the reimagined faux-historic buildings that make up Fish Village.

Two tramlines now intersect the spot where Kant once gave his lectures to packed audiences of students who sat in awe and terror. Many didn't understand him but wanted to say they had attended one of the great man's lectures. They lived in dread of his metaphysics and logic, but his lectures on anthropology were more entertaining. Now an electronic sign blinks dozens of advertisements a minute at the intersection: a lecture of economics, not reason.

THIRD MAXIM:

Better to Be a Fool in Fashion
Than a Fool out of Fashion

Before the Black Hills were sacred to the Lakota Sioux, the tribe lived in what's now known as Minnesota. Before a Jewish homeland was established in what's now known as Israel, other candidates for the homeland included Uganda and the western desert of Australia. Facts mean little when it comes to a people's attachment to the land, but the identity of a place is mutable, not constant, though most of us want it to be so.

Before Kaliningrad became an exclave of Russia, it became an exclave of Germany. The Treaty of Versailles formally ending World War I ceded to Poland a large corridor to the Baltic that cut off East Prussia, including Königsberg, from the rest of Germany. When Germany invaded Poland in 1939, the first troops landed on this corridor, conquered it, and for the next six years, Königsberg became an ex-exclave before changing its identity yet again.

In Kant's day, the Russians occupied Königsberg after Frederick the Great's troops were defeated at the battle of Gross-Jägersdorf. Königsberg was ceded to Russia. For the next five years, Russian holidays were observed and Russian currency used. All public officials including university professors had to swear an oath to Empress Elizabeth. Kant had no problem with this. He didn't fawn over the Russians as did Watson, the poetry instructor at the university. Neither did he

166

keep his distance. He got along well enough with the Russians, especially as the Russians favored the university and nothing much changed for the worse, only the better. The Russians acted more cultured than the Prussians, introducing French cuisine to the city. Königsberg had been a provincial town with ultraconservative mores, and the religious leaders frowned upon the scandalous things the Russians introduced: dinner parties, masked balls, and the drinking of punch! But Kant and his crowd felt liberated. The Russian officers liked to attend his lectures. Enacting a kind of social mobility he had never experienced before the Russians, he was often invited to fancy dinners at the homes of nobles, Russian officers, bankers, merchants. Kant, a handsome man with blond hair, became a bit of a dandy during this part of his life, the color of his clothes following the color of the flowers in season, even wearing a ceremonial sword, though he never could have brandished one, due to his weak constitution, his hypochondriac nature. His guiding maxim of the time: Better to be a fool in fashion than a fool out of fashion.

If the Russians had stayed forever that time, or at least the forever of Kant's lifetime, he might never have taken off that ceremonial sword and stopped the chitchat over punch. But the Russians eventually left and Kant stayed put. He had chances to leave as well, better opportunities at other universities than the ones afforded to him in Königsberg, but Königsberg defined him, and without his city, he felt lost. For quite a while, he had his eye on the professorship of logic and metaphysics at the university, and he waited for the position to open. When a professor of mathematics dropped dead, Kant sent a letter the next day to Berlin suggesting that Professor Buck, who held the position Kant wanted, should be moved to the vacated mathematics position and he should be installed as professor of logic and metaphysics. After all, Professor Buck had obtained his position at the behest of the Russian government.

Fifteen days after he made his request, Kant was appointed to the position of professor of logic and metaphysics. Buck was flummoxed. Why hadn't he even been consulted? Kant had said nothing to him. Buck had never once entertained a desire to be a professor of mathematics. But it hardly mattered. Kant didn't care what Buck wanted. Kant had pitted the wounded pride of the Prussians against the Russians with whom he, like Buck, had been on the friendliest of terms. Ever thus it was in the world of academe.

It's fitting then that his grave was the sole survivor of the bombing of Kneiphof in 1945, and that the university that rose from the ashes of the one at which he taught moral law now bears his name.

The Origin of Suffering Is Attachment

Within a few years after the end of World War II, few Germans remained in Königsberg, a dozen or so women who married Russians at the end of the war. The surviving Germans were deported by the Russians, and the German POWs remained only as long as they could help rebuild Kaliningrad. The region or Oblast of Kaliningrad became for the Soviets Terra Nullius, a place devoid of people, needing to be resettled with Soviet pioneers.

In Kant's view of the perfect world, visitors were always welcome, but they weren't supposed to stay. They were supposed to treat their hosts well, unlike those people of "civilized" nations who, by way of visiting other lands, conquered them, considered them "lands without owners, for they counted the inhabitants as nothing." But the situation after World War II wasn't as clear-cut as white settlers displacing Native Americans in North American or aboriginals in Australia. The Prussians themselves hadn't been exemplars of good manners on their four-year-long sojourn in Russia.

The Soviets' propaganda campaign promised the new Russian settlers land, a cow, a German house! Most of the thousands who flocked to the Oblast received none of this, but by then this blasted land was their new home, with no return to where they'd come from.

The strong feeling persisted among the settlers that this was *not* their home, their uncertainty evident in the postwar architecture of Kaliningrad, in what's absent. In Kaliningrad, Brezhnev- and Khrushchev-era apartment blocks dominate, but little in the way of Stalinist architecture. For the first twenty years or so, life in Kaliningrad felt temporary. Whatever German structure seemed salvageable was restored, and not simply out of frugality but also from timidity. Any month, any week, any day, the rightful owners might come knocking.

They didn't. They couldn't. The Soviets installed in Kaliningrad a huge military installation of a hundred thousand men. Two-thirds of the Soviet Baltic fleet was stationed there. For all outsiders, including those who had been born in one-time Königsberg, especially them, the Oblast was off-limits.

A Russian joke: An adventurous young tapeworm emerges from someone's ass so that he can explore the world. He travels and sees snow-capped mountains, jungles, the great oceans, birds flying through the sky. Upon his return, he reenters the rectum where he was born, and he immediately asks his mother, "Why do we have to live in all this shit, Mom?" His mother answers, "Just stay put, Son. This is your motherland."

Kaliningrad was indeed a version of the shithole that Ben Judah describes. Certainly after the war that destroyed it, but people, unlike tapeworms, are sometimes able to transform where they live into something better than a shithole, even if what the place once was is forever out of reach. For authenticity's sake and the tourist ruble, people try all the same, hence the Epcot Centers of the world, the Williamsburgs, the small Fish Village (across from the supermarket, sex shop, and Brezhnevian apartment-block sentinels) of Kaliningrad along the Pregolya River, with its wan imitations of nineteenth- and eighteenth-century cafés.

Here, no place is simply itself, and that's what lends Kaliningrad its complexity, making it one of the sad, beautiful places of the world. Every building a combination of what it was once and what it is now; the people of Kaliningrad can never forget this completely, not that they want to forget. The complexity of a city such as this transcends the usual tourist experience.

FIFTH MAXIM:
No Matter What the Holiday, Celebrate It!
(and ignore the contradictions)

Russian Federation Day is in full swing at the Central Park of Culture and Leisure, formerly Luisenwahl Park, by midafternoon. Instituted by Boris Yeltsin in the 1990s for a newly created country, the Russian Federation, the holiday is not marked by the fervent strain of nationalism you might find on May Day, or Victory Day, or even Victory over Japan Day. Russian Federation Day! Such a banal and unthreatening ring it has—though a pleasant sort of banality, more the sort of thing you'd find in America as a greeting-card company's ploy. National Secretaries Day. Or some kind of civic-minded festival. Taste of Poughkeepsie.

"Happy Russia Day!" a banner proclaims at the entrance to the park, amid a mattress of red, white, and blue balloons. The flag on the banner isn't exactly the simple red, white, and blue stripes of the Russian flag, but a somewhat nostalgic, if not conflicted, hearkening back to history, displaying both the Russian eagles of the old monarchy and an emblem of St. George slaying the dragon. Not an actual Russian flag in sight, which seems charming and a little odd.

Amid the leafy grounds of the park, stalls line the paths, vendors hawking cheap earrings, weavers weaving, babushkas on green park benches watching the action, children being led on ponies, kebabs called *shaslik* for sale, and a pilaf-like dish called *plov*. But no beer tent, alas, though you can probably score a cold cup of kvass, the mildly fermented drink popular throughout Russia.

For now, a red-bearded man in his thirties wearing a traditional cassock and holding a microphone teaches a group of bystanders Russian square dances, belting out instructions and berating a boy for being too shy with his partner. Carnival rides swirl in one quadrant of the park and people take photos sitting in the lap of a brooding statue in the enormous likeness of Vladimir Vysotsky, a national music icon the likes of Bob Dylan or John Lennon. Three folklore choirs, made up largely of children and young adults, serenade one another with traditional Russian songs while nearby men dressed as Teutonic knights engage in swordplay.

Hold on. Teutonic knights? At the large bandstand in the park, a group of Ukrainian men and women dance and sing. Isn't that sort of like having Canadians at a Fourth of July celebration? They're followed by a belly dancer gyrating to Arabic music while smoke billows around her. A troupe of eleven young women from Armenia, long braids draped over their flowing white robes, dance to balalaikas and autoharps. A Belorussian group of five stout women play the accordion and belt out folksy music. Does this celebration feel less Russian than Soviet, the move of an empire displaying the diverse cultural riches of its farthest reaches? That's one way of reading it. You can also read this as a simple display of cultural diversity— though when was cultural diversity ever simple?

Stalin liked moving people around, to put it mildly. For the Jews, he fabricated an ersatz homeland in Siberia called Birobidzhan. Koreans he moved to Kazakhstan. Even ethnic Germans he put in their place, though not the place they wanted. Stalin deported them by the thousands to the Volga region and Kazakhstan during the war. When the Soviet Union collapsed, several thousand of these ethnic Germans and their progeny moved to the Kaliningrad Oblast "as a compromise," according to Evgeny Vinokurov, an economist and one of the world's leading experts on enclaves and exclaves. They wanted to be close to relatives in both Germany and Russia. A somewhat odd choice of places to settle, such an unsettled place of liminal identity, especially, you'd think, for a German. But perhaps they're the perfect settlers precisely because of that mixed identity.

At a stand selling homemade dolls in ethnic garb, the only dolls left to purchase are those representing the former Soviet republics. All the purely Russian dolls have been snatched up, the closest sentiment of Russian nationalism in view all day.

SIXTH MAXIM:

You Can Be Loyal to an Institution, but Don't Expect the Institution to Be Loyal to You

In Moscow, ten thousand protesters have gathered today for the "March against Executioners." Here in Kaliningrad, however, those who do not see this as a day of celebration but as a day of outrage and rebellion have only mustered a dozen participants. They've chosen one of the main theaters of patriotism for their protest, a central plaza of Kaliningrad, beneath a Soviet-era statue of Mother Russia bearing the grief of her war dead with grim pride, symbol of another era. The protesters hold their signs dutifully, but not as grimly as Mother Russia, some milling about as if at a cocktail party, chatting and laughing, both protesters and an equal number of bored police in silent agreement, it seems. Perhaps the protesters actually outnumber the police if you count the baby in its carriage, beside its banner-wielding mother.

One of the protesters, a skinny woman in her thirties named Anna, says there have been more protesters in the past. On their banners are fighting words: "Oligarchy is the mother of disorder," "In battle is where you acquire your rights," "Hierarchal power demands victims." But there's no fighting in Kaliningrad, not now, not today at least. In the Central Park of Culture and Leisure, Spiderman has cajoled a young boy to pose for a photo. In the Skipper Hotel in Fish Village, a young hotel clerk chats with the restaurant manager about his recent trip to Berlin while the Red Army Chorus belts out patriotic songs on the lobby TV. In the Kaliningrad Zoo, a woman in her forties and her teenage daughter explore the slabs jutting from the earth with Kant's words on them, the mother's eyes slipping over the text before hurrying on to the lion exhibit, the thing they came to see. Her shoes are too tight and she wants an ice cream cone and a cigarette, but besides that, she feels content to spend this holiday with her daughter, whose pretty face has been marred too often by sullenness lately. Maybe after the zoo, she'll treat her daughter to a meal at McDonald's. That's always been something they've bonded over, their shared love of fries.

SEVENTH MAXIM:

Those Who Cross the Sea, Change the Sky, but Not Their Souls

Evgeny Vinokurov grew up in a formerly German house in Kaliningrad that lay in ruin until 1957. Both of his grandfathers fought in the war and in 1946 ended up in Austria, where they met their future wives, one a nurse, the other worked in a supply office. Today, he favors changing the city's name back to Königsberg, though that name isn't the only option. It could be renamed something like Baltisk. But the majority of Kaliningraders don't agree with him, nor does Moscow, made nervous by any change that hearkens back to what the city once was. Any country's main directive is to maintain its sovereignty, the foundation of patriotism and nationalism. If you can name a place, you can lay a claim to it, hence China's current foreign policy claiming virtually all of the South China Sea. Place names can cause wars and often do. In the early 2000s, populist national candidates often played the Kaliningrad card, issuing dire warnings that the Oblast wanted to break away to become part of Germany, Lithuania, or even Sweden.

That's about as likely as the city being renamed Putingrad. Sociologists have been taking polls for over a decade and have found Kaliningraders' sense of identity fairly stable. Only 2 percent say they want to be part of Germany and another 5 percent want to form a fourth Baltic Republic. At least as many Alaskans and Hawaiians would leave the United States if they had the chance. Probably twice as many Texans.

Kaliningrad is Russian because Russians live there. If Kaliningrad had mostly Germans living in it, then the Kremlin would have reason to worry. The difference is akin to that between the Falklands and Hong Kong. The Falkland Island inhabitants are largely Brits, not Argentines, and so they have no desire to be Argentinian. But Hong Kong is largely Chinese, and while the identity of the Hong Kong

172

Chinese is always an issue and consequently fragile, threatened by their sense of political difference from Beijing, they nonetheless do not wish to be British. Few tears were shed by the Chinese citizens of Hong Kong when the British lowered the Union Jack for the last time in 1997.

From an economic view, it would be useful for Kaliningrad if EU members could visit the Oblast visa free, in Vinokurov's view. The local *Duma* lobbied Moscow on that point twice and both times the proposals were rejected "quite rudely." Emissaries from Moscow were dispatched to Kaliningrad with the message "No, this will never happen."

Everyone except Moscow seems to understand that the page has turned irrevocably for Königsberg. Even the old-guard Prussians have given up. In 1990, the Homeland Association of East Prussia counted a hundred thousand members, and was an influential conservative force in German politics, but no more. The East Prussians of old have mostly died off and their children and grandchildren have largely ceased to care. Or perhaps the yearning has simply been subsumed by other day-to-day considerations and will manifest itself again in a thousand years.

In the meantime, the nostalgia from the old Germans who visited Kaliningrad and wept in the nineties has, like their zoo, been inherited by Kaliningraders, partially a commercial nostalgia but not entirely. Photos of German street scenes from the turn of the twentieth century abound in restaurants and offices around the city, and the city takes pride in the old German castles, ruins, and nineteenth-century fortifications outside of the city proper. In Krakow, Poland, a group of Roman Catholics started a Jewish Festival, the world's largest, running strong now in its third decade, because they wanted to know who these Jews were who had made up half their population before the war. Should it be any different for Russians living in a formerly German city?

As a university student in 1998, Evgeny Vinokurov studied German at the University of Marburg, and there he met a retired professor of religious history born in the East Prussian town of Trakehnen in 1926. Wounded in the war in April 1945, the man was transported from the front on a hospital ship to West Germany afterward.

Despite the age difference and the clash of their personal histories and places of birth, they got along well and Evgeny invited the man to visit him in Kaliningrad, which he did the following summer, taking the train from Berlin and spending ten days with Evgeny's family.

The city was uglier than it is today, but the old man seemed unfazed, saying that he well understood this was Russia now, not Germany.

Trakehnen had been renowned for the powerful horses that were bred there from the early 1700s at the behest of Frederick the First of Prussia. Kant would have admired such horses, famous in his day as warhorses, a favorite of the Russian Imperial Army. Perhaps some of the Russian officers who listened to Kant's lectures bought their horses from Trakehnen. And he would have seen them working in the fields when he took his occasional carriage rides in the country with Joseph Green.

Between the world wars, Trakehners became the most famous sports breed in the world, but by the end of World War II, only a few hundred of the horses survived, led on a legendary trek by some brave souls across a partly frozen sea to escape to the west. Along the way, the Russian air force further thinned the ranks of the fleeing Prussians and their horses by shredding the ice with their machine guns during the day, scores of horses and people drowning in the churning sea. The kind of sport young men perverted by war can only play at such times. And the town from which they fled, "the City of Horses," fared no better, laid waste to and renamed ironically by the Russians Yasnaya Polyana, the name of Tolstoy's estate.

The religious-history professor from Marburg, wounded and evacuated, had not been back since. The drive to Yasnaya Polyana took several hours, and by the time Evgeny and his family arrived, the normally chatty professor received the vision of this devastated place in silence. The horse farms gone, the drunks falling down the streets of the ruined village, the streets leading to the shattered school he had once attended.

For the rest of the return trip, the entire three hours, he was silent, except for muttering one word that Evgeny, sharing in his friend's disappointment, heard. After that trip, predictably, they lost touch.

If anything of old Prussia survives, you can see it most authentically in the dressage event at the Olympics: Trakehner horses prancing and strutting, their elegant bearing, their name intact.

EIGHTH MAXIM:

We're All World Citizens in the Boneyard

It's delusional to think that land, indifferent nature, could yearn for a people the way a people yearn for the land. And yet, there's a case for just that, even if it's a kind of collective delusion. Visit some of the other sad, beautiful places of the world, where a people have been decimated and/or displaced, Tasmania or the Cathar country of Southern France, which once held populations of aboriginals and Albigensians, respectively, and try to see the land as similar to any other land. Even if you didn't know the land's history . . . but let's stop there. It's ridiculous. You *do* know its history and that's the point. And so you can't help but think that the land's emptied castles, its very hills and streams, yearn for someone else. Perhaps it would have been better if you'd never read Chief Seattle's famous speech:

> Every part of this soil is sacred in the estimation of my people. Every hillside, every valley, every plain and grove, has been hallowed by some sad or happy event in days long vanished. Even the rocks, which seem to be dumb and dead as they swelter in the sun along the silent shore, thrill with memories of stirring events connected with the lives of my people, and the very dust upon which you now stand responds more lovingly to their footsteps than yours, because it is rich with the blood of our ancestors, and our bare feet are conscious of the sympathetic touch . . . And when the last Red Man shall have perished, and the memory of my tribe shall have become a myth among the White Men, these shores will swarm with the invisible dead of my tribe, and when your children's children think themselves alone in the field, the store, the shop, upon the highway, or in the silence of the pathless woods, they will not be alone. In all the earth there is no place dedicated to solitude. At night when the streets of your cities and villages are silent and you think them deserted, they will throng with the returning hosts that once filled them and still love this beautiful land.

On the day Kant died in 1804, the frozen earth of Königsberg didn't want to accept him, but since then Kant could not be moved from Königsberg, not even in death. Not even bombs could dislodge him. The stars have not changed much in the sky and the moral law hasn't changed much either, but everything else, from the walk he took each day to the name of the city in which he spent his life and its people, has changed. What then is this piece of land? Is it really any more Kaliningrad than it is Königsberg? What makes it any place at all and its people any people? Who belongs here? The only person who seems to belong here indisputably is Kant.

Perhaps Kant was simply a more dramatic example of the way

most human beings feel about their homes, that their homes define them, when really, it's the other way around. Kant and Chief Seattle aside, all our homes were something else once before and will be something entirely different in the future. Kant never had to confront this problem in his lifetime, as did the Prussian professor of religious history from Trakehnen. He must have understood finally on the silent journey home that his sense of belonging to a land had simply been a collective but necessary delusion. The thing that made him Prussian. Necessary because without this delusion there's nothing except for the perilous passage across the nearly frozen seas through which we trek in our own solitudes. And what is laid waste is what we lead forward invisibly, the collective herd, our fragile inheritances.

So let's not forget it's Russian Federation Day, a day of recalibration, if not celebration. Little in the Central Park of Culture and Leisure recalls Prussia, though this ground has been hallowed by sad and happy events, and soaked with Prussian blood. It's true, there are no places on earth dedicated to solitude, not even Antarctica—one tribe or another has experienced them all, and, when possible, claimed them. Today, any lingering Prussian ghosts might feel especially forlorn. If Kant's ghost sits on a bench among the babushkas, he must be waiting for nightfall, when the last of the fireworks have tailed away, the park has emptied of cultural and leisurely Russians, and, looking up, he might still hope to detect immutable laws.

Dog's Journey
Edie Meidav

I.

WAVES LACK SURFACE when you are weak, nothing risen quickly enough to keep you up. Keep pulling toward midpoint between both islands where you could be lost but must keep going like a brute force of nature despite the dwindled sap in your arms. If you never had faith you find enough to say if this is what you have in store for me, either kill me this next moment or I will be your humble servant for the rest of my life. Strike me down now and let us not wait for jellyfish or sharks or else please stick by me and let me get there.

II.

Other barefoot kids call you Bones because you are long and ropy and you were with them pressing your nose to the grille of the gym in your neighborhood after school. One day you ask the coach what it takes to train since you have seen him wrapping big kids' hands or ambling about to spray water into their mouths from a tumbler. The strangeness of such motherly gestures makes you think he may be that odd adult who doesn't bite, Jimenez with brows raised in the center as if the worst he has seen shocked him into generous surprise. When he asks how old you are and you say seven, he says your height qualifies you as eight and you get to start the next day.

No reason needed. All you did was ask. On the way to the gym, you kick a can because this is something you always do but then two days later no longer need because you will not walk but instead rehearse positions that burn once you get there, the backstep and combinations while your mind stays sharp, this time one-two-two and the next one-shuffle-one, the bob and weave but also just the sheer joy of battering an object that could be anyone, you controlling the bag that loves you back, making you shine with focus. What Jimenez lends you is heart, your eyes fixed below the chin where his pulse throbs. The trick is to make your gaze a tabletop no matter if he tests you by walking circles around, barking, *the periphery!* a word that at first you think means throat, his a kinder growl than those you've known, your knees bent, stance wide. For one second no one can stop you even if on your first time trying a roundhouse, you knock yourself off center. The next lands square on his pad. When he is pleased, the corners of the mouth lift despite an invisible bulk tugging them down, the heaviness saying someone like you comes once in a lifetime. Don't fall asleep looking at my face, he roars, the periphery! One day you stop hitting with your fourth and fifth knuckles, though to use the second and third takes trust. These will not wear out so quickly, he promises, dancing back then lunging over, holding the pads. Don't breathe not yet but slide forward, remember the sequence, double jab and cross, under, under, knees bent, click click clack, duck and slide back, block, chin to chest, shoulders hunched the way they should have been back when your father used to come at you. To punch Jimenez's pad is to swallow confusion. Sometimes he says, jab through, give it more, but then says, what, you want to kill me? That middle ground dances away, hard to find the balance of warning alive in his eyes. Don't look, he says, but can you help it? You make sure not to hurt the first man who shows caring by holding up pads for you to thump but who then takes a surprise jab. You must learn his way. Duck and learn. And the great curve of pleasure through your gut when the footwork falls and the pattern bursts, less about remembering to turn on this toe, no, the other, knee bent, and just about socking through like one of the old revolutionary songs they hammered into you back in school.

At home your mother watches as if you have grown tentacles. Don't care. Slop meals into your gut before heading back to the gym. One, two, side, then curl, three, five, then block.You've known the other kids in the place forever but if they used to be able to hurl the casual insult about your stringy legs, inside these walls you predict their moves three paces ahead. This one will throw an undercut, no, four, you disgrace no one but your vision sharpens. No need to wear a helmet like the older kids since a knowing pulses at the base of your palm, the one you stretch out after practice, unfurling what could be your future, the way out, bending your fingertips back toward your shoulders, making the intention of your mind and fist one. Less distance, get close, make it your game, Jimenez whispers, play it. After hours in that light slanted down late, you and the bag study the day. Punch back what you missed. Until you stop Jimenez will not either but there comes a point where his face thins and he sprays water into your mouth from the angled straw, making a step

in jest as if to spray the little kids loyal covering your old spot outside, noses against the grille, shadowboxing and spitting the way you
never did since once you were too awed to move, something big still-
ing you into being the last bird to land on the pole, the one waiting
its turn to leave who then outlasts the rest. Back then you knew
Jimenez would never chase you off. Only now does he tell you to
quit for the day, Jimenez seated on an overturned oil can to unwrap
your hands while offering stories chewed out the corner of his
mouth. Tactics of the greats. Hunger, he always says, quoting Dempsí.
Sure, hunger, but no one gets fat on dreams, he says, confusing you.
Which do you need, hunger or dreams? He talks about aim and you
cannot help wanting to look at his nose, fallen with its massive
sewn-up gorge on one side as if someone slid a machete out from
putty. The nose and then the bloated knuckles, the first and second
of his right hand puffed like a girl's breasts. My trophies, he calls
them, one day you, he says, half cuffing the side of your head. One
day you will be his trophy. One day you study him the way you did
back at the grille, the way he spits a pellet chaw of tobacco into the
milk can nailed to the wall and he says, terrible habit, follow my
words, not my deeds. Once the kids leave, behind them the yellow
dogs clump at angles, those who love the stink of the place the way
you do, a history of fluid soaked into split-rubber mats and gloves but
still what does Everlast mean? Jimenez also knows little English
but he knows the one pair of Everlast in the gym goes to you, and you
hang them on their rusted hook with dedication, in love like maybe
the dogs who might think the stink of the gloves and mats make one
eternal, sweaty dog mother body. It must be Jimenez who names the
children and dogs your first fans but after that whenever you see
them, crouched or prone, you can't help some inner nod at their loyal
powers of recognition.

    When your history teacher calls you to the head of your class, it is
not to rap your raw knuckles because you can't recall which white
man had come to rape and plunder the virgin territory of the island
nation but because at nine you are getting selected for some tourna-
ment not in your hometown but in the largest city near you. When
you have barely traveled beyond your town's own mountains, your
pueblito not known for being a spectacular example of the famous
system yet strangely producing a coach like Jimenez whose athletes
stream from their homes to haul glory to the nation. Apart from
Jimenez your town is mostly dust stretched short next to mountains
from which the cowboys ride out into the main street. Families'

tobacco farms here were surrendered to the government. Once they got sliced up, sometimes they were given back in pieces but most farms just got swallowed. Your town known for guavas and tobacco, not trophies and gloves, the warmth of these a secret deep enough you wear your love openly. Probably you love it too much, Jimenez tells you one day, a smack blasting onto your shoulders. Nothing wrong with love, he says, helping you up.

Then you cannot help but continue since most things make sense in the gym, a place your mother calls the cathedral. In the cathedral, you take what life cloaks. Outside, Sundays at four you go to the queue for the fresh bread that will emerge from the government bakery, palming ten pesitos, and when you first approach the people sitting in all sorts of combinations, no one's idea of a straight line, you say the words—the last? And the last person signals so you know you are now the last the way you will also signal to the next person who arrives, the same way people try to leave the island, waiting for their Boca uncle or Tampa aunt to send for their escape, hoping to one day tell others they can fret behind them. Waiting, you pace, flipping coins in line for two hours, talking in the heat with kids whose mothers have sent them or watching grownups who lose any friendly shine whenever they enter this waiting in which life stops. And no matter how long everyone has postponed anything else, once the bakery opens its door, always there arrive the adults who show up on magic gliding feet, free to cut to the head without waiting for anything, just picking up their bread. Perhaps in the breadline the idea of abroad and escape begins biting hardest, because when the gliders skim off, some small murder clots in the face of those who stand and wait, a murder you understand since you've also seen it settling into your mother whenever your father hates the scent of her cooking, he can't help it, gas flame and onions do him wrong, all her damn ritual irritates, but when home and joyless, he bolts down her moros and cristianos. One day your older brothers and sisters are nowhere, leaving you and your mother plunged into the rites you like, she accepting your slump on the sofa. Your father gobbles behind you at the table before shoving his chair back, ready to head out after eating because he hates the stench of her cooking oil but instead of complaining and disappearing, he falls to his knees and then his face. You think he is joking, papi, you call, and then your mother slaps him, calmer than you would think, all of this two minutes? Three? He opens his eyes and comes back with a roar, cranky, telling you tranquila already, he has come back, he's fine, what's the fuss? Once he is back, your mother flutters, suggesting possibilities, but your father says he needs no doctor since he trusts no one outside the family. He has seen the excellent doctors the revolution produced: no one has supplies and they improvise with cheap Chinese equipment they can't operate. His bad joke: this was just a knockout! In the run-up to this moment these last few months he has rued your new habits, forever reminding you he used to box so that you know he once did something more than be a ruined shell in the government system. He wants you to know he is someone with a vein back to the man he once was, entering a ring of equals, bare-chested and ready to swing. Later your mother will regret having listened to him. I should've called for an ambulance, she will say, leaning into your shoulder a little too hard.

The moment after returning to life, your father draws the drapes before collapsing into the sofa to watch a government man intone about the exciting new drilling the government's doing off the Havana shore, television light playing off his face, making him a statue, his strangeness compelling you to jump rope in the apartment, part of your training, legs crisscrossed and tricky, what your mother usually forbids indoors but the rhythmic slap soothes, your stomach up in your throat from the effort, and then you almost don't notice your father screwing his head around to look at you so you pause and hear him apologize for the first time ever, saying, sorry, mijo, sorry, I am not going to make it. Then he passes out for good.

He didn't make it. Sorry. But your discipline manages to cleanse you of some of that sorriness. Advantages flock. Your coach Jimenez fills you with new stories. He tells you to stop eating bread so that only two weeks after the funeral where your father lay waxy, you are free, no longer waiting in the Sunday breadline because your mother and Jimenez had talked. She'd finally made her way to the gym, wearing the mourning kerchief that made her look even tinier while Jimenez spoke his condolences and then with slow patience recited the litany: fish-head soup, beef nearly raw, root vegetables and greens, avoid our staples, rice, sweets, bread and butter. We'll try, your mother says, our boy's skinny. But fast, Jimenez tells her, and a southpaw, which surprises everyone. Plus he's long but strong, like iron, we should call him Hierro. She takes this in enough that she will never again send you out for bread, you for the first time one of the men of the house. Only occasionally do you hear the ghostly heavy tread of your father's feet on the broken linoleum. Two weeks in, your future already tastes better. If your mother had never seemed happy

181

around your father, after he is gone she sinks deep into herself so you start to feel Jimenez, who calls you Hierro, is the mother you might have had if only seven kids and a dead husband hadn't tired her out. Your father, anyway, was hardly your mother's first death. You may be the seventh child but the sixth died before you were born. Into that sadness you grew, the last but no one's runt, taller than even your oldest brother, taller than your father was, and maybe this tallness you half-overhear whenever your tired mother and pretty lipsticked aunt discuss matters in the kitchen as they do now more frequently, half whiffs of bits, nothing you can locate. Far more understandable to spend hours in the gym, far more understandable the first time you fight a real opponent and hear a roar not because of a crowd but because you are going up against someone the coach from the capital has brought in, a rising star, a boy named Franco who has agreed to fight. The two older trainers watch you say hello to Franco as if watching their youth or a meteor shower: nothing for them to do at this point. Franco shows his toughness by not staring you down the way others from your town do, the cheapest tactic of fighting dogs, instead focusing only on his coach who ignores him, too busy trading stories with Jimenez about their time in the national training camp, all this camaraderie sickening as if you're meant to kill your cousin, one so sturdy as he watches his coach wrap his hand with gauze, treating it like a sacrament while ordinary boxers, or at least ones you've sparred with, glance around as if the second someone starts wrapping their hands they become bureaucrats or movie stars. This kid instead glowering as if the smallest zone of his knuckles matters, the winding of the gauze as important as the fight to come, its first round starting so radically with the cousin coming at you that you forget everything your coach has ever said though somewhere in the back you hear him bellowing from the ropes something about the candle, a series you know but the candle makes no sense, not when your opponent heaves in, left hooks and cross-jabs out of nowhere, eyes tricky and hot, this boy from a world different from others, you cannot see his moves, but you bear down to find the opening, you almost see why the candle would make sense, and you lure him into what Jimenez calls the house, becoming the candle with the flickering head who can then land the one-two that gets this tricky fighter to his knees with the sting in your fists making you hungry for more, not wanting him to go so quickly. Happy when he gets up for a new round though that gloved fist comes to buzz your jaw, your southpaw a pop and snap. You trying to remember that

182

control comes if you breathe out when you retract, no one else ever having told you this secret about the breath, most people only complaining when someone toward the end of a match starts mouth-breathing, losing his guard, and though you end up learning all eight stages of mastery, you keep the breath your own, all of this spelling first freedom, that you could have chosen to let the roar that started defeat you but instead you bore down and absorbed. Those first punches hadn't hurt enough. It could have gone otherwise but you end up leveling your first real challenger. Dignity is the first choice, your schoolteachers had said, quoting the great man, and this dignity becomes what you still think is your choice, even though the great man said it first.

Because here is the alternative: digging. Digging anywhere. In garbage cans next to piles of blond sleeping dogs to see if you can scrabble up metal to bring to the repair shop so they can patch cars and bikes. Or digging for favors like your neighbor on one of the government plantations where blistering sprays leave a person sick but still able to see a doctor at the hospital for free. Or digging for shelter like your father in a government job where people argue all day, sharks snipping bits, complaining about how tiny rations have become while trying to bribe you on the side. Or digging to bury yourself, to forget, becoming one of the men betting on dominoes on the street while drinking cheap *aguardiente*. Or forget digging and instead take a bus to the city to see what makes the city happen. Your brother Felipe did it and became one of the smartest drug dealers near the hotel with the best Internet, the one luring the neckless Italians and Swiss men looking for a place that doesn't mind them living it up with their mulattas before they escape the island to send home packets of money. He told you about it and didn't have to leave the island to send home those packets. Then in an islandwide raid at dawn your brother got nabbed and spent seven years in prison boxing mousetraps. At this point your tired mother lacks guidance, trusting Jimenez because he is the first man to take such interest in her brood. While you trust Jimenez because he is the first to find the god you never knew lived in your fists.

He must not be wholly wrong. Others find it too. Consider that first lunch, you already fourteen. A lady, the wife of an official who oversees one of the later tournaments, in the capital where maybe the great man will also one day watch you fight. She asks what you would like to eat, her voice from bowed lips under a cloud of hair, her shiver visible inside a shirt so pale her cat's shoulder bones could puncture the cloth. You realize she must not be that much older than you and shift in your seat at her perfume as she orders for you. The plates start coming: beans and rice, bread and custard. Forget fish-head soup, you want to swallow three times more quickly than she nibbles, your hunger massive, capable of gobbling the golden life of her voice. In a week you will go live with boys at the camp to train for the elite team and this lady is the welcome sent your way by the government. Other than the mayor of your dusty town, she is the first government person you have ever met so you too shiver, your hands shaking while her speech sings forth, so gentle you have to strain to hear it. Knowing that if you could just understand that voice, you might find your future made up of more lunches. All will open.

What would you—and her cheeks flame the way faces on white people do, making your own cheeks blaze as if you are midmatch and she has just landed an impossible hook in two places. What would you—

—and whatever she has to say matters less than the flame ripping inside you. A silent roar. Whether the roar is what Jimenez always called hunger or your understanding of what might be granted you solely because of the hunger, you cannot say, but you know the hollowness that steals your insides a week later when you leave for the national training camp and Jimenez gets sick. Rather, and maybe it's not because you're leaving, his kidneys fail and you must go through a front door where no one stops you since it is a hospital accustomed to shocked people entering. You cannot be anything but numb all the way down a corridor of bad cases, their luck hard and your peeks horrified into rooms where all you see is yellowed feet and sagged flesh. Walking this corridor means sparring the nightmare of Jimenez in this place and the choice of whether to turn back before seeing him so fallen not two days before you are meant to take the bus to the sports commissioner in the capital and from there to the national camp. In the last room Jimenez lies, dirtbox of a room holding a man who looks as if some viper has sucked all life spirit out. Because the room is tiny, you can't touch him. His cheeks fallen, he is out of reach, too close and nodding, and only a version of the smile you remember travels with difficulty across the mouth.

You know about his family only that the revolution broke them into shards, his family one of the biggest plantation holders near your village, a few of his brothers imprisoned for treason and bad capitalist thinking. One of them got shot, one spoke a false confession for the radio, one fled for Miami, the last came back never the same. In this way, Jimenez learned all revolutionary lessons. He like you was a younger sibling who knew how to hide his power and had been good at counseling you in the same strategies but to look upon him so broken you need all he ever taught.

He'd be the first to say he taught you to hold back your capital. Even if you were never supposed to use the word capital too loudly in public, except as a curse, Jimenez had been no stranger to using the obscenity, capital going through your head as you stand in the hospital, smelling the butter acid of urine. Which part of him are you supposed to touch when you want to run away and his right trophy hand bulges in your hands, nubs of those knuckles his last capital. No one speaks, your gut tight for the punch, this man more than ropes and mat, trophies and everything else. As usual he can read your mind and cracks out the truth in a dry voice.

Seven years? meaning those seven he trained you and knew you best.

And then with the same tone tells you not to worry, there is nothing you have to say since once he had this exact thing, sick kidneys, back in Angola while working as Fidel's chauffeur, did you know that, he was the one driving the national jeep. He survived working for Fidel and so it follows he will survive this and at this point there could be no more useful lie, both of you nodding, but now he can't stop, telling you stuff that will not help you, how he hadn't believed in that war, the one where they had pressed him to play foot soldier for Fidel. Imagine what a number that does on a man's head, he says, as if this is meant to be a joke like the breadline but the only thing you see is the coughing, spittle condensed in the corner of the same mouth that used to make you move like one happy puppet.

No one has equipped you. You'll be okay, you say, imitating his lead and lying, knowing Jimenez won't batter this sickness down. Your gut has dropped seven floors. Already you know that this is one of your hardest goodbyes. Jimenez tells you as much in his thin, splintered voice. You are good at holding back, he says, don't let them know what you're made of. Hold something back so it stays your own. Maybe you'll get to America, he says, another dim joke.

Blinded, you tell him he will be fine.

He reaches up, finger sliding along your stinging jaw. Don't think too much about me. Or if you do, remember—

The breath? you say. Your code. He smiles and falls into his version of sleep, rattling out his own so that staying means invading a face gone slack with only the slit breath in and out that crushed monument of a nose. Do you dare stay? You do, dabbing at the drool coming out the mouth with your shirt and then leave backward as if from a king toward the bus line outside where you say the phrase with the greatest energy you can muster, the last? and then freeze thinking about the other thing he had said in the hospital room, which is that if you hadn't been so set to leave the town and head toward whatever the national camp will give you, maybe even an escape, he would've asked you to be the one to run the gym. He had said this and you had wanted to say, yes, that's right, I am staying, let me be the one to carry on what you gave me. In his hospital bed he had thought this along with you and then said no and for the first time called you his son. Go, mijo, another old friend, the tobacconist, will run the gym, but also had motioned for you to take an envelope. Once you stand in the bus line you finger the spare key inside that envelope. And cannot go straight home so instead you try the key at the gym, one hard tap at the door all it takes to make you realize all these years you've never entered the gym without Jimenez. Whatever had given you its welcome now looks injured, even the peeled-paint grille where you began. What sucks your heart out is you don't even have it in you to spar with the body bag, all of it like one mad game, a belly filled with scuffed appendages and so you pace, your step echoing on the unlucky mats. This becomes then the first place you have your own first crack, because your feet, which up until then were clad in shoes you'd found the month before in a rummage bin at the government market, navy shoes with only one hole in the toe, become no feet, only shins: you have lost your feet.

And on these stumps (the ones you find again the day you try getting one dry foot onto American soil) you run all the way home to find yourself tumbling like a heavyweight onto the couch where your mother flaps over you. Afterward you have rice and beans and her sugared coffee as a going-away treat, all of it a stirring betrayal against Jimenez and his own disloyalties, all that hope swallowed just like that, and if it is true that after the meal you are sated and your feet are back, or enough to take you to the capital, one day you will land sputtering salt water into the way the future will ignore you, the one you were bitten by back in the breadline, the one no has ever equipped you to imagine. The future in which Dempsí will seem to have gotten it all wrong. Not hunger. Rage.

III.

Ten years of tile-laying. The good homes are the ones where the owners bother offering you a glass of water. The bad ones barely nod. To them you're just another dark head speaking broken English and they're paying illegally so better be quick with the transaction. In the ring we used to call it the quick slide, as in the quick slide off the ring. Try knocking out someone in round one and you take the gamble you're losing your energy but it can still work.

At least I work with friends, standing outside in the morning at La Floridita while the cars rush by but we are happy to linger over our coffee and croquetas and maybe it was for these friends and this over-sugared coffee that I came, or for my little eight-year-old girl and her mother but I can't explain why I always make excuses and don't bring them whenever I go to dinner at an American's house, but mainly I don't want Americans to know how bad off we are since Americans lack basic capacities for understanding certain truths. Instead I iron my best shirt whenever I go over to eat their unsalty food because I take care of myself, not blaming anyone for anything that happened and so I'm the clean one they always invite. One of my bosses loves to show me his Florida room with its low ceiling and three dark walls looking out at the one that opens up to the covered swimming pool but the Florida room confuses me, making it impossible to suss out how any American goes from where I am, a citizen, to where my boss is with his Florida room but maybe the Cuban in me rips my pockets.

Sometimes at the bar too, people raise a glass to me, people I don't know who remember when Fidel was on a rampage, who believed when he said I was the greatest amateur boxer in all Cuban history and that I chose to leave the island and became a traitor, the day he called in all the papers the day Iron Lost Its Strength and because he was on such a public rampage I changed my name back from Hierro to Icaro, my birth name, just another story, my mother in pain calling me the name of a dead son, just another story like the match that never happened between our homegrown Stevenson before he became a drunk and the great Ali, the one they always rehearse like the flowery words in Che's goodbye letter to Fidel among all the other stories we had to memorize in school, all of it a story I want to tell everyone on the island who thinks my name means the great young boxer who swam away to become a Judas and traitor, a shame to the nation. For a few months I was Fidel's sport, my case getting its coverage, with no way to spit anything back while my mother was watched by the police day in and out, her punishment for my escape, what she never guessed I would do. People liked calling me back then the crown jewel of Fidel's system and say I had thrown away my mestizo royalty by going toward the imperialists.

Here in Miami no one knows these stories. As one promoter said right before he dumped me, back in my Hierro days after I lost that one crucial fight, Florida is white, boxers are black, in New York they support their Puerto Ricans and in California they support the Mexicans, but here you have the American nightmare, the way it is, sorry, son, which could make a person start to feel foolish after a while. Too much sorry son starts to go below the belt.

At lunchtime I go to a little hole of a place on Eighth Street where we have one riqueño who joins us Cubans, the food islands of grease waiting all day for some drunkard to think it decent and making it always the superior choice to stick with the bread and butter, but none of this matters since a long time ago I gave up the training, not eating fish-head soup and running three miles before six in the morning. Now coffee and sugar melt into the kind of buzz I would have just before a fight and the bread into the calm of right after, the cigars we share the buzz of the crowd that make me like everyone around me even as they laugh too hard, snaggletoothed at their own jokes and what else does a new citizen need?

When I was eight I used to help my father haul bags of sugarcane, his one near joke being his strength was why the company liked him, that he was good for the national company because slave traders in West Africa must have chosen his great-grandpa for his strength. In his time, my father was The Ox, which was why he didn't like my skinniness and all the kids calling me Bones before the system discovered me and I jumped above the slavery my father had to live through, my reflexes the best part of me. Maybe Jimenez was right in calling me born to box, but tell me any greater camaraderie exists on this earth than about eight day laborers in a hole-in-the-wall on Calle Ocho in Miami, drinking and smoking at around one o'clock in the afternoon, most with at least one beer inside, the television blaring nonstop videos of Latinas with the kind of face evangelists love to recruit dancing half naked with ribbons and the place has a name we know if the sign went missing a long time ago: the Miami Dream.

*

What happened during the fight I lost? people sometimes ask. I was fighting an Irish guy from Chicago, the reigning champion, and so what if people later criticized me and said I was boring, like a spider in the web, I had my reasons, come out of Cuba and you can't help being a technical boxer and an outside puncher while here, in the pros, they want you to throw inside, get your whole weight pushing through. My trainer had me fighting like a Cuban, parallelograms on the mat until round six when I turned American and knocked him out, American even more in how I strolled the ring with my fists up before the last count was struck. As a person I like to act as if my triumph is inevitable, some of the American stuff I learned early, the way I used to beat my chest like no dog but a happy ape—and then the guy gets up in the last seconds. This throws me and he knocks me out. Did I make a mistake thinking I had a sure bet? When the contract the banker had me sign was that if I lost even one fight, he could cut me. Though if I had started getting big, the banker would have had first option. So here I am, cut, a few years past when any promoter could take me seriously, laying tile and having coffee, my name Icaro on my American passport. Things could be worse.

There is a joke that people like to tell around here and it goes like this: the Cuban dog swims over and lands in Miami where the American dog greets him with a big lick. The Cuban dog complains to the American dog: I am so hungry.

The American dog says, well, hombre, you got to get a job so you get money to eat.

The Cuban dog says, fine, but I am too sick from all the bad water I drank coming over.

The American dog smiles. Here you got to pay the doctor, you got to get a job.

The Cuban doesn't understand. But how can I if I'm sick?

The American dog gets fed up. Look, if you want to complain, why'd you bother leaving Cuba?

The Cuban: Because at least here I can bark.

And that much is true, at least I'm here, barking, Bones with dreams once so big on a map none of us have the gut to pinpoint them anymore.

The Zip
Stephen O'Connor

ROGER IS THIRTY-SIX, but earns his living in the manner of a twelve-year-old boy, by mowing lawns, pulling weeds, shoveling snow, and vacuuming swimming pools. Apart from a solitary semester at college, he has lived with his parents his entire life. One morning, troubled by an unnatural silence, he knocks on his parents' door, and when they do not respond, he opens the door to find them lying on their bed, candle white and smelling faintly of raw hamburger. There are half a dozen capless pill bottles and two empty glasses by his father's side of the bed, but no note. Roger spends days looking for a note.

His father had an inoperable brain tumor and could only speak in grunts—so, OK, he kills himself; no mystery. But his mother: She sang every morning as she made breakfast. She played tennis with women half her age (sixty-seven) and beat them. And, when speaking about her husband's illness, she would shrug and say, "You take it as it comes." No note. Why didn't she leave a note? Her death is a black pit into which Roger falls and falls.

His sisters both live abroad, one in Argentina, the other in Thailand, and neither has any interest in returning permanently to the United States. The night of their parents' funeral, the three siblings are sitting around the kitchen table. The younger sister looks at the older and nods. The older sister draws a deep breath, picks up a salt-shaker, and puts it down. Then she tells Roger that she and the younger sister have decided to relinquish all claim on the house in return for his handling of the estate. Roger is profoundly embarrassed by this offer, as are his sisters.

The reason for their embarrassment is what they all know but cannot say: that Roger's best hope for staying off welfare and off the street is to sell or rent the family home—a well-kept Victorian in a neighborhood of well-kept Victorians—and find someplace cheap to live.

*

Roger suffers from what he calls "images." At uneven intervals—twice a week, a dozen times in a single day—an image will flash into his brain, and he will become transfixed, rocking back and forth, making a buzzy uh-uh-uh noise low in his throat, and staring into space. Almost all of these images are grotesque: a girl having her arm amputated in a tent hospital without the benefit of anesthetic; a dog with a slit-open belly floating motionlessly in coffee-brown swamp water. Sometimes, though, images seize hold of his attention through their sheer impossibility. One of the most common is of a crumpled wad of gray—like a piece of used chewing gum—that is simultaneously enormous and microscopic. Roger can't stop trying to see the wad as either one size or the other, and so his mind cycles from extreme to extreme like a computer stuck in an infinite loop.

His images have gotten him fired from every job he has ever had. They disturb customers and fellow employees, and leave him nauseated and exhausted for hours. They also prevent him from driving anything faster than a sit-down mower. He spends almost all of his time alone, and his isolation has made him odd. He has no real friends.

Roger handles the estate with perfect efficiency, never letting a document rest on his desk as long as twenty-four hours, and usually returning all e-mails and phone calls from his parents' lawyer and accountant within minutes. He learns the names of all six nieces of the notary at the Scott Street Stationers, and gives the secretary at his parents' bank a box of chocolates on her birthday. He and his sisters figure out via Skype conferences what they each want of the family belongings, and Roger ships off his sisters' shares (jewelry mainly, some china, photographs) immediately. He moves his share into the apartment he builds for himself in the garage, then auctions or junks everything else. Exactly a year to the day from his parents' death, he walks across the bare floors of the echoey, paint-fragrant house with the first people to answer his rental ad.

Bill and Marie are moving to town from Chicago for Bill's new job at NML Industries. Bill is middle sized, balding, and cube headed. His nose is the shape of a radiator steam vent, and his five o'clock shadow is so dense, his jaw seems hammered from coal. Marie is slight and long limbed, with hair the color of winter grass. If Bill is a rock, Marie is a breeze, and so retiring that Roger doesn't notice—neither while leading the couple around the house nor when they

191

sign the lease at his lawyer's office—that her left hand, fingers rigid and slightly bent, is made out of plastic.

The morning after Bill and Marie move in, Roger looks out his kitchen window onto a small metropolis of cardboard boxes while waiting for his coffee to brew. There is a banging on the door. When he opens it, Marie is sweeping away a lock of her pale hair with her left hand, and Roger notices for the first time that the hand—faintly textured with skin-like crinkles—fits over the end of her arm like a glove. It looks so like one of his images that he can't speak.

"Hi," says Marie.

Roger's voice takes a couple of seconds to make it all the way up his throat. "Hi."

Seeing that he has noticed her hand, Marie makes a smile-like expression, and swings the hand around behind her left thigh. She is wearing jeans and a Radiohead T-shirt.

"Sorry to bother you," she says, slinking her head down between her shoulders. She looks like a baby vulture when she does that, maybe because her neck is so slender and long, and her eyes are so big and round and summer-sky blue.

Roger feels bad for having stared at her hand. "Would you like some coffee?" He lifts a fist as if clutching the handle of a full mug. "It's brewing now."

"Oh, no." Marie slinks her head again and winces. "Thank you. . . . It's just—" She looks back toward the house. "We have no heat. No hot water. . . . I was wondering . . ."

Roger makes a jabbing motion with his index finger. "Have you hit the reset button?"

The center of Marie's forehead darkens.

"On the furnace?" he says. "One second." He retreats from the door and returns a moment later, wriggling his toes into his flip-flops as he walks.

"Every now and then the furnace shuts off all by itself," he explains as he leads Marie along the cracked cement walkway between his kitchen door and hers. "I don't know why, but it's easy to take care of."

He opens the white wooden door, still gouged from when he was eleven and used it as a knife-throwing target. To the left: Three steps lead up to the kitchen, where he remembers sitting at the table eating a peanut-butter-and-jelly sandwich—the smell of peanut butter actually makes a sweet itch in the space just behind his eyes. And to the right: Six steps lead down to the basement. As he walks through the musty dimness, he passes his father's old workbench, void of tools now, except for the built-in vise. At the base of the furnace there is a quarter-size hole, into which Roger sticks his finger. The furnace sighs, gasps. A hoarse roar fills its fiery heart.

"Simple!" He smiles and lays his hand flat on the side of the water heater. "You'll have enough water for a shower in twenty minutes."

Now Roger is back on the cracked sidewalk, and Marie is standing just inside the kitchen door. She sweeps another lock of her hair away from her eyes. Noticing Roger's glance, she holds her plastic hand vertically between their faces.

"I was in a car accident. When I was a little girl."

"Oh." Roger can't think of anything else to say.

"The last thing I remember is lying down in the backseat so I could sleep. I put my hand like this." She places the back of her wrist—exactly where her plastic hand joins her arm—against her forehead and closes her eyes. For a moment she seems actually to have fallen asleep. All the tension drains from her lips and the faintly freckled skin around her eyes.

A few minutes later, as Roger crouches at the end of the driveway to pick up the morning paper, he notices a very small man walking toward him along the root-heaved sidewalk slates. The man is shaped like a beer keg and has a red buzz cut. Just exactly as he passes Roger, he mutters in a baritone duck voice, "Bet that girl's got one slick pussy!"

Roger stands. The man continues down the sidewalk. After two or three steps, he glances over his shoulder and laughs derisively. "You heard me!" He walks down to the end of the block without looking around, then turns left on Abigail Street.

Two days after Roger resets the furnace, he parks his sit-down mower in the new shedlike garage that he has built onto the side of the original garage, then walks around to his kitchen door, grass flecks clinging to his nose and neck, the fragrant steam of his body wafting against his cheeks. It is late May and eighty-six degrees—the first truly summery day of spring.

Marie is kneeling in the backyard, her shoulders heaving over a stack of collapsed cardboard boxes. As Roger watches, she lifts a taut length of twine high into the air. Something about the sight of her laboring all alone so touches him that he can't help but call out hello.

She reels around and grabs something pink out of the grass: her hand. Her shoulders jerk up and down as she holds it between her knees and slips her left arm into it. Only then does she turn, wave (with her right hand), and call out, "Hi!" She is wearing her Radiohead T-shirt again.

"Sorry to disturb you," Roger says.

"Oh no! That's all right." She pulls her hair off her face (also with her right hand). "I'm not really doing anything." She twists her hair up behind her head, holds it in place with her plastic hand, then tucks it into a sort of bun.

"Getting ready for recycling?"

She sticks out her tongue. "Yeah!"

Roger hesitates a moment. "Want some help?

"That's OK." She remains motionless.

"You sure?"

"Well . . ." She smiles wearily, then slinks her head down between her shoulders.

Roger crouches on the opposite side of the heaped cardboard and she asks him to hold it flat while she ties it. She has to jut her left elbow straight out from her shoulder so that she can press the bent plastic fingers down on the twine with sufficient force to keep it in place while the fingers of her right hand twist and yank with an almost magical fluidity and produce perfect square knots. It would clearly be easier for Marie to hold the twine with her unencumbered stump, and Roger finds it both sweet and sad that she should feel she needs to keep her plastic hand on for his benefit.

Marie is in the process of tying the final knot when Roger's brain is seized by an image. He starts to rock back and forth. Buzzy moans escape his throat. His lips open and close like the lips of a fish drowning in air.

"What's the matter?" Marie says. "Roger! Are you OK?"

He tries to nod, but she doesn't understand. "Oh my God! Can you breathe? Do you want some water? Can you breathe?!" She crawls around behind him and pounds his back. He lets her because he hopes it will keep her occupied until the image has passed.

It is a new image, unlike any he has ever experienced before. He can hardly believe it is happening with her right there beside him.

"Lift your hands in the air!" she shouts. "Lift your hands in the air!" She tries to force up his arms. When he is unresponsive, she reaches into her pocket. "I better call 911."

"No!" he gasps, shaking his head. He grabs her hand and crushes it in spasms, while the vision in his mind pulsates with such electrical vividness that it all but erases the world.

What he is seeing is Marie's naked pelvis and Bill's thick-fingered hand clutching an antique gold-plated safety razor as he shaves off her pubic hair. Roger watches the hairs mounting in webby clumps along the forward edge of the razor. But what makes the image so magnetically horrifying is that, with every stroke, the razor comes closer to Marie's clitoris, which Roger imagines a pink twig stump. He has never actually seen a clitoris, at least not apart from representations in pixels or ink. He is terrified about what might happen with every next razor stroke, and the one after.

Once he has grabbed her hand, Marie seems to understand he is OK and that there is nothing to do but wait. It is possible that squeezing her warm, soft fingers actually helps override the image, because, in what seems less time than normal, a neuronic crackle passes through his brain, and the image fades into the sight of his driveway, lawn, and garage home.

He lets go of Marie's hand, a hard pain pulsing in his temples, nausea twisting up from his gut to the root of his tongue.

"I'm sorry," he says.

"That's OK." Her brow puckers with concern, but her mouth looks relieved.

"I get these . . ." He decides not to tell her. ". . . These petit mal seizures. They're not very serious. I'm sorry."

"Don't be. I understand."

She seems to be reaching for his hand again, but he pulls away. He is too embarrassed. He can't even look at her face.

"Are you on medication?" she asks.

"Yeah. But it doesn't work very well. These aren't really normal seizures."

"But you're OK now?"

"Yeah. I better go. I just need to sleep."

"Is there anything I can do to help?"

"No. Thanks. No."

He gets stiffly to his feet and walks toward his kitchen door, never once looking at her.

He sleeps in all his clothes until the need to urinate drives him from bed—at 4:26 a.m., according to the luminous numerals on his clock radio.

Drinking a glass of water in his dark kitchen, Roger looks out the window toward his house, ink shadowed and deep gray in the light of a gibbous moon. Six bundles of cardboard lean against the wall beside the basement door. When he has finished drinking, he lingers at the window a moment longer, singing so softly his voice cracks in and out of whisper: "*I want a perfect bod-dee-ee-a-ee. I want a perfect soul.*"

He puts the glass in the sink and returns to bed.

Roger rides his roaring mower down East Meadowlark Avenue to Abigail Street and turns left. The previous day he got a phone call from a Mr. Hart, who said he was new to the neighborhood and needed someone to mow his lawn. Roger knows the house in question, a pink, asbestos-shingled split-level that has been deteriorating for years, ever since the old woman who lived in it went into a nursing home. He has seen no indication of the house even being on the market, let alone that someone has moved in. Indeed, as he pulls up to it on his mower, the house looks as if it is stuck in dank winter, while all the others on the block are radiant in spring sunshine.

Roger shuts off his engine. The grass—tufty, shin high—will need several mowings and some reseeding before it's a proper lawn again. There is no car in the driveway, no lights on in the house. Bits of faded construction paper taped to the inside of a dust-hazed window over the garage look as if they have been there for forty years.

He has only just started up the walk when the front door opens with a suction wheeze and the keg-shaped little man with the red buzz cut steps out onto the doormat.

"Bisco?" he says. Roger nods—Bisco being his last name. The little man extends his right hand. "Hart."

"Hi," says Roger, shaking the man's hand.

"Come on inside." The little man turns and walks into the dark house. "I need to talk to you."

The house is airless and vault silent. The electricity seems to be off, and the old woman's furniture is scattered about the dim living room like cattle in moonlight. The smells of mice, rotten orange, roach spray, and urine are so dense in the stagnant atmosphere that Roger feels them coalesce on his cheeks and inside his lungs.

The little man stops at the center of the room and turns about-face. "Listen," he says, "I'm going to fuck with your head a bit." He holds up both hands as if Roger has protested. "So bear with me, OK? You'll get my drift."

Roger takes a step backward, but after that is paralyzed.

"OK," says Hart. "Your breakfast this morning was honey yogurt with a piece of toast, smeared with bitter marmalade. No butter. You have that every morning, though sometimes the yogurt is vanilla flavored. Your second-grade teacher was Mrs. Lowendorf, and you couldn't pay attention in class because you were too distracted by her clicking dentures. You took guitar lessons at twelve, but quit before you even learned the chords for "All Together Now," and you underreported your income by a third last year, even though you wouldn't have paid taxes anyway. You had the first of your image fits in the middle of a school assembly when you were eleven, and all the way through high school Brad Mehlman could humiliate you just by opening and closing his mouth. And you're wrong about your mother. She tried to kill herself three times before finally getting it right. You yourself saw the red water in the bathtub that night your father drove her to the hospital with her arms wrapped in towels."

"What are you talking about?"

Hart holds up both hands again. "Let me finish! I'm getting to the most important part—which is that we know everything about you. We know that you had a goldfish named Goldy, and a hamster named Hammy . . ." So far, Hart has been speaking in an expressionless staccato, but now he pauses and smiles. ". . . And we know you finally got to see Marie's lovely little pussy. Too bad about the razor, but that's not the worst thing he's done. Believe me! You don't even want to know. That guy's evil on two legs."

Roger's brow is convoluted, his mouth fixed in that warped oval thought to signify extreme stupidity. He is not breathing.

"Here." Hart pulls a silver case from his pocket, opens it, and holds out a business card between his index and middle fingers.

The card has no name on it, and no telephone number, e-mail, or street address, only the words "Central Command for Crime Prevention," and, directly below them, in big red letters: "CCCP."

"CCCP?"

"Stop!" Hart grimaces and shakes his head. "That's the first thing *everybody* says! That is so fucking *ignorant*! *Ancient* history!" He snaps his silver case shut and slips it back into his pocket. "Anyhow, nobody calls it the See-See-See-Pee. We call it 'the Zip.' We're working for the Zip. And we need your help."

"Help?" says Roger.

"We just want you to keep your eyes open. Marie's husband—Bill—he says he's here to work for NML Industries, but don't you believe one word of it. That's just a cover-up for some seriously evil shit."

Hart puts the back of his hand up in front of his mouth and burps before continuing.

"But I can't tell you about that. Don't want to spoil your objectivity. Just keep your eyes on him, OK? I'll check in with you every now and then, and you can tell me what you see."

The smell of garlic and sausage drifts across Roger's face. His brow is still convoluted, but the oval of his mouth has narrowed to the point that it expresses something on the skeptical side of astonishment.

"And look after Marie. That's the main thing. She's completely innocent. We don't want anything untoward to happen to her."

Roger shakes his head and is about to say, "This doesn't make any sense," when Hart walks toward the front door. "OK—time for you to go!"

The door is open. Sunlight pours into the fetid dimness, along with a blast of car noise and bird squeak.

Roger steps out onto the front porch and sees his mower. "What about the lawn?" he says.

Hart smiles as if Roger has confessed a nasty secret. "Here." Clipped between his index and middle fingers is a crisp, unwrinkled one-hundred-dollar bill. "For your trouble."

Roger stares at the bill, not quite able to make sense of it. Hart stuffs it into Roger's pocket and gives him a shove: "Go!"

Only when Roger is sitting at his kitchen table, listening to bubbles scintillate the surface of a glass of Coke Zero, does he remember the bill. He reaches into his pocket, but it is empty.

"What are you looking at?" asks Marie.

"Nothing." In fact, Roger was watching her tamp down the soil around a quartet of red and orange tulips that she has planted at the base of the porch steps. "Just trying to figure out when the lawn's going to need mowing."

"Didn't you mow it yesterday?"

"Day before," he says, though in fact it was yesterday. He pretends to survey the lawn. "Looks fine. It can wait."

She glances into his eyes, then smiles before picking up the galvanized watering can beside her.

Roger blushes. She knows he has lied. He has already turned to go back to his apartment when he hears her voice: "I hope you don't mind."

He turns back. "Mind what?"

"That I'm doing all this stuff."

He glances at the window boxes of pansies she has attached to the porch railing. "It looks wonderful. Why would I mind?"

"I just thought it might be hard—you know, seeing other people living in the house where you grew up."

Her words touch on a deep sadness, but all he says is, "Ah, well." He feels as if he should leave, but his feet won't budge.

"I'm sorry," she says, looking up at him with her summer-sky-blue eyes, her lips pursed sympathetically.

"No," he says. "I really love what you're doing. I think it's beautiful. It's just—" He kicks a hummock of crabgrass. "It's just that it makes me realize my family never actually *lived* in this house. Not like you do. We never did anything to make it beautiful. We just occupied it—like all we were doing here was waiting."

"For what?"

"I don't know." He kicks the crabgrass again. "Nothing really. I think that's why my sisters got out as soon as they were old enough. They couldn't stand it."

"What about you?"

Roger laughs. "Where would I go? Anyway, I'm happy here. This town's—you know!" He laughs again. "And now you're making the house look beautiful and everything. I think that's great!"

Marie looks at him as if there is something she can't say.

Roger's mouth goes dry, and a chilly sweat springs up along his hairline. "Oh, well. Better be going. Work to do."

He turns and goes to the garage, where he starts his mower, then heads off down the block. In fact, he's got no work to do, and nowhere to go, but he can't let Marie know that. His plan is to ride over to Seabell Park, wait there for an hour, then ride back. But no sooner does he turn the corner than a huge red sun burgeons before his eyes and he is lying on the deck of the Starship Enterprise, looking up at Captain Kirk, Scotty, and Mr. Spock. All of them have orange faces, like an old-fashioned television picture when the color is off—except for Spock, whose face is a deep red, and seems blood covered. His mouth opens slowly. He is about to speak, and Roger knows that when he does, what he says will be impossible to bear.

The image dissipates in the sonic blast of a truck horn.

Roger and his mower are stopped in the middle of an intersection, the truck's towering grille roaring an arm's length to his right, a Subaru Outback, horn tooting impatiently, directly in front of him. So queasy and weak that he can hardly keep upright in his seat, he puts his foot on the gas, turns the mower around, and heads home.

When he pulls into the driveway, Marie is no longer outside. He is able to hurry into his apartment without having to speak to her.

May becomes June. Moths blizzard the porch light above Marie and Bill's front door. Crickets jingle in the darkness amid a sparse galaxy of street and window lights. The hum of the world is sometimes intensified by the long, sad moan of a distant train, or the crunching whisper of rubber against asphalt as a car rumbles behind two advancing cones of illuminated roadway.

Several times a night Roger tells himself that he is just restless, or that he needs a breath of air, or that it is simply too gorgeous outside to surf the web or watch TV. But whatever direction he goes, his walk invariably leads him in front of his old home, where he lingers five, ten, or more minutes, just thinking, absorbing the night, taking deep, head-clearing breaths.

He learns things. He learns that the lights in the master bedroom—the two rightmost windows facing the street—often go on a little after nine, while, directly below, blue light flickers against the living-room curtains until eleven, at which time all the lights on the first floor go off, one after the other. Then the upstairs bathroom light—back, side—goes on for a few minutes, then off, and the bedroom light turns off some ten minutes later.

The only room that Roger can see into from his own apartment is the kitchen, and the light there often goes on for an hour or so at three thirty in the morning. Over the half curtains on the kitchen window, he can see the top of Marie's head as she stands beside the stove, and then the dark shadow of her shoulder touching the curtain as she sits at the kitchen table. From the way the shadow periodically shifts forward and back, he imagines that she is turning the pages of a newspaper or magazine as she sips a cup of tea.

He learns that Bill's voice is like another room inside the rooms of the house, and that Marie's is like a bread box. He hears Bill pronounce the words "circumstance," "waiting," "asshole," and "hockey puck," and cannot understand a single word that Marie says. But around four o'clock one morning, he is woken by a ragged, toneless moaning. As he leans his head against the screen inside his kitchen window, the moaning seems like the cycling of cat mews into off-key whale groans and back again. From the cracked cement walkway outside, it is clear that Marie is lost to grief. Now Roger is standing with his hand flat against the clapboards directly under the kitchen window; inside, Marie, sitting at the table, is sobbing helplessly. He imagines her right hand cupped over her right eye and . . . her stump? What would she do with that? Would it comfort her to touch it to her tear-wet cheek? To rub it over her brow?

Roger wants to speak her name softly. He wants her to know that he is near, that he yearns to help, that her sorrow so affects him that he has to swallow to hold back his own sobs. But he is silent, of course. She would be horrified to learn that he is standing so close, intruding on her private suffering. "Oh God, oh God, oh God," she says, and a little later: "Oh fuck, oh fuck." But apart from that, she says nothing that Roger can comprehend.

After a while, sniffles begin to interrupt her sobs. Then she blows her nose: two, three, four times. Roger estimates that his hand on the clapboard is no more than thirteen inches from the gap between her pelvis and rib cage. As the chair screeches against the linoleum and her head appears then disappears over the curtains, he can feel her receding through his fingertips and palm. Her heel thumps hum faintly through the layers of plaster, insulation, and wood. The light goes off. Ever so softly, he hears her mutter, "Fucking idiot." And then she is no longer in the kitchen and, from where he is standing, barefoot on the dew-chilly lawn, her progress though the dark house is undetectable.

"That is fucking useless information!" says Hart. He and Roger are sitting at Roger's kitchen table, sharing a liter bottle of Coke Zero. "Don't you understand how serious this is? Crime *prevention*! That's what the Zip is all about. *Prevention!* We're on the verge of fucking Armageddon, and all you can tell me is that this light went off and that one went on! Are you actually as useless as you look? Get with the program here! We're talking End of Days! Final Reckoning!"

Roger goes to the refrigerator for a new bottle of Coke Zero, but when he returns to the table, Hart is gone. A little later, Roger enters his dark bathroom and finds Hart, orange tinged in a diffuse illumination, looking back at him from the mirror. As Roger darts right to turn on the bathroom light, Hart darts left, and when Roger looks again at the mirror, he sees only his own face, blinking and befuddled, as if he has just been roused from a nap. He turns off the light again and nothing happens except that most of his face goes dark while the planes facing the curtained window turn waxy white. Roger can only conclude that Hart's apparition is just another of his images, but he will never be sure.

What Marie sees is the bad haircut of a thirteen-year-old who wants to look like a rock star. And under that unruly helmet of hair, she sees dog-brown eyes and lips exactly the dusky red of raspberries. She sees a long jaw just slightly uplifted by hope, and a long, slender torso hollowed by an extreme lack of confidence. She sees an odd-looking young man who could just possibly be handsome if he weren't so heartbreakingly lonely and afraid.

"They're just out of the oven!" She is holding a platter heaped with brownies.

"They look great!" he tells her. When she moves the platter in his direction, he takes it and says, "Thank you."

She waits for him to say something else, and when she sees his face go crimson and worried, she says, "Uh."

"These are so nice!"

She slinks her head between her shoulders, takes one step backward, and makes something like a smile. "Well, guess I—" As she sees the worry deepening in his eyes and on his lips, she feels ever more helpless.

One more step back. Another.

"Bye," she says, turns, and hurries toward her door.

Roger signs for a large box that arrives when Marie and Bill are out. As they don't get home until after eleven that night, he waits until ten the following morning to bring it over. The box is from an office-supply store, and is the size of a small filing cabinet, but so heavy that Roger arrives on the front porch panting, the bridge of his nose glittery with sweat. He wipes his face with the belly of his T-shirt and rings the doorbell.

"Coming!" Marie calls from upstairs. Then a little later, "Right there!" After close to a minute, he hears chaotic foot thumps on the stairs. "Sorry!" Marie says, even before the door flies inward. Her hair is soaking wet and uncombed; her features are in disarray.

"Oh!" she says, as soon as she sees it is Roger. For a moment she seems disconcerted, then she smiles weakly. "Sorry. I was in the shower."

"No, please. I should have waited." Roger's apology is deeply earnest. He feels he has committed a grave transgression by having intruded on her morning like this. Marie's green T-shirt is stippled darker green all down the front. Water seeps along her cheeks and neck from her wet hair. But what most disconcerts Roger is that she clearly is not wearing a bra. The material of her T-shirt is stretched in such a way that he can see the full convexity of her left breast's outer edge, right up to the point of her chilled nipple.

"Don't worry about it!" Marie smiles as if she is about to laugh.

"I'm really sorry. I shouldn't have interrupted you."

"No!" she says. "I was already out. Really." The incipient laugh has faded from her smile. There is a glittery restlessness in her eyes.

The reason her T-shirt is so tight is that she has tucked her left arm way up behind her back. Roger pretends not to notice. He tries not to look below her water-darkened neckline as he tells her about signing for the package.

"Thank you," she says. "Thank you so much!"

"What do you want me to do with it?" He can't imagine how Marie could carry such a heavy and unwieldy package, especially since she could only grip it with one hand.

She gives the bottom of her T-shirt a couple of fidgety tugs, then shoves open the door. "Why don't you bring it inside?" She steps back. "It goes in Bill's office. You can just leave it there, and he'll take care of it."

Once she sees how Roger strains to lift the box, she tries to help, but since she can only use one hand—the left is still behind her back—her effort only throws Roger off balance, and the corner of the box collides with the door frame.

"That's all right," he says.

"Sorry." Her brow is dimpled with concentration while her mouth is a seam of uncertainty. Then she is smiling again.

She retreats as he comes into the house and presses her back against the wall, telling him Bill's office is upstairs, her arm concealed the whole time.

Roger thinks it sad and wrong that she should be so embarrassed about her arm, and he wonders if he should tell her.

"Heavy!" he grunts, as he struggles up the stairs.

"I'm sorry." She is climbing behind him. "I should have just had you leave it inside the door. Bill can carry it upstairs."

"No problem."

He places the box on the floor of Bill's office and shifts his head from side to side to loosen his back muscles. "This used to be my room," he tells Marie.

"Really?" She is standing with her back to the wall. Perhaps her arm is actually touching it.

"See this?" He points at a gouge the width of a pencil in the edge of the windowsill. "I used to have a kind of winch in here, so that I could raise and lower stuff out the window." He touches the gouge. "This is where the cable used to rub."

"Wow! What sort of stuff?"

"Nothing really. Just toys. Rocks." He shrugs. "I made the winch myself, so I just had to use it on something. It never actually served any purpose."

"Amazing!" She looks self-conscious, standing with her back against the wall.

Roger points at the box. "So what is this thing? A filing cabinet?"

"A shredder."

"A shredder! Whoa! That's a big shredder!"

"Well, Bill's a big shredder." She laughs, and puts her hand over her mouth. "I mean he's always shredding things."

Roger meets her eye, then blushes and looks at his feet. "Guess I better be going."

She backs out the door, then up the hall a bit so he can get to the stairs. As Roger steps past her, he says, almost angrily, without looking around, "You know you don't have to do that."

"What?"

He turns to face her, and gestures toward her concealed arm. "That. You don't have to be embarrassed about it."

Embarrassment floods her freckly cheeks. Her summer-sky-blue eyes go a shade lighter. "Oh," she says, giving her shoulders a writhing shrug. Then she doesn't seem to know what to do.

"It's really OK," he says.

More embarrassment. Another writhing shrug. "It's just . . . Most people—"

"Not me."

She looks him straight in the eyes.

"Really," he says.

She keeps looking at him even as she lowers her arm behind her back. She only looks down as the arm comes around in front of her.

Roger is amazed that her arm should seem so perfectly the arm of an attractive young woman all the way down to that point where her wrist ovals off into empty air. He blinks. It is hard not to feel there is something wrong with his eyes.

Roger and Marie are both silent a moment.

"You see," he says. "Everything's OK."

She looks as if she is going to cry, but then she smiles broadly.

Roger asks if he can use the bathroom before he leaves. On the soap-clouded glass shelf under the mirror, he sees a gold-plated safety razor.

Roger continues to learn. He learns that Bill leaves for work at 7:15 in the morning and never gets home before seven at night. He learns that Bill has only one suit, and it is dark blue, and only one tie, which is shimmery and yellow. But the suit never looks rumpled, and the tie remains spotless and radiant day after day after day.

June becomes July, and July sets heat records. Bill wears his suit jacket when he trots down the porch steps in the morning, but it is always off when he comes home, and there is a splattery inverted triangle darkening his pale blue shirt from his neck down between his shoulder blades. Every time Bill gets out of his car, he pulls a toolbox-size brushed-aluminum briefcase out of the backseat and carries his jacket over his arm. His shoes always make a sort of horse clop when he descends the porch steps in the morning, but they resound like funeral drums when, head lowered, he climbs back up in the evenings.

Days, Marie is like a ghost haunting Roger's childhood home. He sees her as a deeper dimness in the dimness of the downstairs rooms, or as a brilliant flash crossing the oblongs and trapezoids of sunlight spilling through the windows, or as a winter grass moon rising and setting over the half curtain on the kitchen window. She plants marigolds around the screen porch at the rear of the house and a vegetable garden in a corner of the backyard. It turns out she has no trouble using a shovel, but only when she takes off her plastic hand. Sometimes she puts the hand in the grass beside her, and sometimes it sticks up out of her back pocket as if it is reaching for something. Every time Roger sees Marie, he tells himself he should stop, make neighborly conversation, but all he can ever manage is a wave.

There is a knock on his door. When he opens it, Marie is standing there with a smile like a squashed laugh. She is holding out a greenish-yellowish pie, its surface faintly burnt a buttery brown. "It's a zucchini pie," she tells him. "From my garden."

"Wow," he says. "Thanks."

When he takes the pie, he sees that she had been supporting it with her stump. He pretends that what he has seen is insignificant, and—except for the faint wariness in her smile—so does she.

He thanks her again.

She says, "You'll have to tell me what you think."

"I'll have some right now!" He takes half a step back into his kitchen. "I was just getting hungry."

"Great!" she says. When he doesn't say anything else, wisps of worry begin to accumulate around the edges of her smile. Her head slinks down between her shoulders, which means she is about to say good-bye—a prospect that is suddenly more than Roger can bear.

"Would you like to have some?" he asks.

"Oh, no," she says, worry all but obscuring her smile. But then her shoulders twitch up and her smile emerges like the sun out of a fog bank. "Well, maybe just a little taste, so I know I haven't given you a bum pie."

They sit at his kitchen table and she keeps her stump in her lap as she eats—except once, when she uses it to stop a bit of crust from toppling over the edge of the plate in front of her fork.

At first Roger only thinks, "You don't even need a hand," and then he decides to say it.

"Well, I get by," she says. "But . . . you know."

Roger blushes, now thinking his remark entirely stupid, and possibly hurtful. "Is it hard for you?"

Marie smiles sadly. "I'm used to it." She picks up her glass and takes a swallow of Coke Zero. "When it first happened, though, I was always '*Why me!*' Like everybody else, I guess. But now I think the worst thing is that it proved to me that I'm just an object. You know? Just a thing among things, and I can be damaged." She looked at him intently under her crumpled brow. "Does that make any sense?"

"Sure." In fact, Roger doesn't have a clue what she means.

"I really used to believe that there was this way in which the world existed *for* me. Like it was a show I could enjoy and even participate in, but that I wasn't really a part of. Sort of like when you're in a dream."

Roger makes an expression that he hopes is sympathetic, but he still doesn't understand.

Marie tilts her head to one side and looks at him for a long time.

206

He thinks she is about to reach across the table and take his hand, but instead she leans back and lowers her hand to her lap.

"Life mostly sucks," she says.

"No, it doesn't."

"Yes, it does. Good things almost never happen, and everything that does happen is just mediocre—when it's not terrible, that is." She pushes her plate away. "Like this pie. The zucchini was bitter. I tried to compensate by adding honey, but I added too much. It's disgusting."

Roger wants to tell her that the pie is delicious, that he loves it, but it *is* disgusting, in fact, and he could hardly bring himself to put each forkful into his mouth, let alone swallow. He is silent. Marie's eyes redden and go glossy.

"Sorry," she says. A tear breaches the rim of her eye and hesitantly descends her cheek.

Roger wants to lean forward, place his forearms along hers, and take hold of both her elbows. He wants to bring his face close to hers and tell her that she is beautiful. He wants to tell her that she is the most beautiful woman he has ever seen. And then he wants her to cry some more so that he can kiss away her tears, and, while his mouth is still salty, he wants to kiss her lips. He wants all of this with such fierce intensity that he can neither move nor speak. And after a while he becomes so filled with self-loathing that he only wants her to leave—which is what she finally does.

"Look, I can't tell you everything," says Hart, "but I can show you. True evil is beyond words, which is exactly as it should be. I mean, if evil could be put into words, it would be comprehensible, and if it was comprehensible, it wouldn't be true evil." Hart is removing the milk and juice cartons and the bottles of Coke Zero from Roger's refrigerator. He never once looks at Roger as he speaks. "I mean, think about it: What *is* true evil? It's pointless. Right? Cruelty when there's no reason to be cruel." Having cleared the top rack of the refrigerator, Hart yanks it out and places it—wire bars clanging—against the cabinet under the sink. He sets to work on the lower rack. "It's not even sadism, because sadism gives the sadist pleasure, and so it makes a kind of sense. Evil's like sadism without the pleasure. Cruelty for cruelty's sake. You see what I'm saying? It's like the evil twin of God's will." The second rack finished, Hart sets it clanging against the first. "Except, of course, there's no logical difference between true evil and God's will. God tortures innocent babies to death with boils and bleeding sores—right? He sends psychos into school cafeterias with AK-47s and grants barbaric dictators long and bliss-filled lives. Does any of that make sense? Of course not! And that's the point. If God had to have a reason for doing things, then he wouldn't be all-powerful, right? That's just elementary logic. But the main thing is: If what God did made sense, we'd have no use for him. We'd just be like, 'Ho hum, another perfect day.' It's only because so much crazy shit happens that we think, 'Somebody out there must be *doing* this! There *has* to be a *reason!*'" The bottom shelf clear, Hart removes it, and the two drawers underneath. "What I mean is: Of course nothing out there makes sense, but that doesn't mean we can't resist it. Right? And that's what the Zip is all about."

Hart gives the thermostat knob at the back of the refrigerator a violent turn to the right, forcing it, with a loud clack, way past its coldest setting, and the rear wall of the refrigerator swings back as if it were a door. All that is visible beyond the refrigerator bulb is swirling darkness and a dull gleam, but Roger can distinctly make out the athletic-sock odor of a high-school corridor. "Follow me," says Hart, flinging himself headfirst into the refrigerator.

As Roger's refrigerator is a "Bachelor Special," Hart has to wriggle his stout middle through, but after that his legs bounce like logs in a rapid, and his scuffed leather soles flip skyward, then vanish. Roger hears the hissy whisper of shoes on linoleum, then the thwats of pant legs being smacked. "Come on!" Hart shouts from an echoey space beyond the refrigerator bulb. "What the fuck's the matter with you?"

Less out of volition than a vacuum effect, such as causes road litter to spiral after a hurtling truck, Roger flings himself into the refrigerator and is soon standing beside Hart.

The truth is that there is a gap between the back of the refrigerator and the wall of the kitchen, and behind that wall there are three plastic garbage cans and a quarter acre of lawn that ends at a neighbor's fence. But, even so, it is also true that the high-school corridor in which Roger is standing stretches straight back from the refrigerator and diminishes, according to the laws of one-point perspective, for a possibly infinite distance.

"I almost never do this," says Hart, "but you don't leave me any choice." He flicks his knuckles against Roger's shoulder. "Come on! We don't have much time."

There are windows along the corridor, like the windows in museum displays or like the transparent side of one-way glass mirrors, and even though Roger's apartment should be behind him, he can look though a window on his left into his kitchen, its floor strewn with bottles, cans, chicken bones, and shreds of plastic, paper, and Styrofoam. The refrigerator door is closed, however, and the wire racks aren't leaning against the cabinets. The next window shows his living room, also garbage strewn: coffee grounds heaped on a throw rug, a brown banana peel dangling off the corner of a family portrait. And the next window shows his bedroom, the sheets twisted and trailing onto the floor, his open laptop balanced on a pillow and surrounded by a small mountain range of crumpled Kleenex. "You know that eighteen-plus website you like so much?" says Hart. "I got news for you: The average age of those girls is sixteen. Maybe a quarter of them are fourteen or under. I'd destroy that computer if I were you. There's enough evidence on there to send you up the river for life. The only reason you're not in jail right now is that I'm being nice to you."

Roger, mouth open, brow vertically corrugated, makes a noise like a hand-cranked generator, but he can't speak. He staggers after Hart.

Now the windows are on the right side of the corridor. The first looks into an entirely dark room in which an old-fashioned television is flickering, a fireball burgeoning famously out of the striped flank of a massive skyscraper. Hart jerks a thumb in the direction of the television: "You see what I'm saying?" In the next window, Bill, in a black graduation gown, sits at a wooden desk, his right hand tapping a metal stapler as if it were a telegraph key. There is an expression of fierce concentration on his brow as, with his left hand, he scribbles on a white legal pad. In the next window, Bill, in the same black gown, is soldering a coiled yellow wire into a metal device about the size of a shoe box.

"How is that possible?" says Roger.

"What?" says Hart.

Roger glances back at the previous window, where Bill is still staring and scribbling. "How can he be in two places at once?"

"That's exactly what we're trying to figure out. One theory is that he and his coconspirators are trying to make Schrödinger's cat a law of nature. You know about Schrödinger's cat, right?"

"I think so," says Roger.

"That's the cat in the box that's alive and dead at the same time."

"Oh," says Roger, who maybe doesn't know anything about Schrödinger's cat after all.

"Do you understand how catastrophic that would be?" says Hart.

"It would be the end of factuality! If that were a law of nature, dunderheads would know as much as the certified geniuses! Murderers would be exactly as innocent as they are guilty! And neither you nor I nor anyone else would be what we actually are! It would be the end of civilization!"

"I don't see how that could be possible," says Roger.

"It's not possible yet, but it will be if we don't stop him." Hart jabs Roger's sternum with his chunky index finger, then jerks his thumb over his shoulder. "Follow me. There's one more thing you should see."

Hart hurries past a couple of windows with heavy curtains drawn over them, and stops in front of one that, as he waits for Roger to catch up, bathes the side of his face in a pinkish light.

A steady hiss comes through this window, and a high voice singing sadly, slowly: "*I want a perfect bod-dee-ee-a-ee. I want a perfect soul. . . .*" Roger looks into the steam-filled bathroom of his childhood home through what would seem to be the mirror over the sink. A gold-plated razor, enormous from this perspective, rests on a glass shelf along the bottom edge of the window. Clouds of sandy pink waver behind the wobble-textured glass of the shower.

Hart slaps Roger's shoulder with his knuckle. "Two more minutes!" He winks. "See: She's just rinsing her hair. Soon as she's done, she's coming out!"

"No!" Roger is sidling away.

"What's the matter?"

"We can't do this!"

"What are you talking about?" Hart laughs. "We *are* doing it!"

Roger turns and runs back down the dim corridor toward the distant white rectangle of his illuminated refrigerator.

The streetlights buzz pinkly. There is no moon, so the ragged gleams cast between the fat leaves of the century-old plane trees make the shadows so black they seem interruptions in the continuity of things. Roger has gone for another of those walks that are only excuses to come back home and observe the lit windows of the house where he grew up. He is standing within the shadow of a tree trunk, and so is utterly invisible except as a black silhouette against a collage of blacks.

He is just about to return to his apartment when he sees Hart tiptoeing from shadow to shadow down the driveway, holding a metal shoe box spewing coils of yellow wire. When he reaches Bill's car, Hart gets down on his knees and stretches the arm carrying the box under the car, directly beneath the driver's seat. There is a resonant clack, then Hart stands and tiptoes empty-handed back up the driveway.

Light-headed and short of breath, Roger remains motionless until Hart has gone. Then he is the one tiptoeing down the driveway. Then he too kneels beside the car. He can't see anything in the blackness, but he can distinctly hear a faint fizz of spring-driven gears and an insistent ticking. He starts to reach under the car, but then stops.

No. Not a good idea.

All evening long Roger has been wondering if he should tell Marie and Bill about Hart's spying; now he decides that he has no choice. He has come to believe that if anyone is the embodiment of true evil, it is far more likely to be Hart than Bill. From the beginning, Roger was embarrassed about spying on Bill and Marie, but now he feels like a criminal.

Taking a deep breath, he rubs the palms of his hands against the sides of his pants, and walks toward the house, faintly aware of multiple sirens—all far, far away, in another town. Marie is sitting inside the kitchen window, reading a magazine. The shadow of her shoulder on the half curtain shifts forward as she turns a page, then shifts back. Roger has just raised his hand to knock at the door when the once-distant sirens grow suddenly so loud he has to clap his hands over his ears.

Tires screech. Glossy black cars with strobing blue parking lights surge up the driveway. Two of them. Four of them. More. They surround Bill's car. They tear up the lawn. Once they stop, the volume of their sirens descends through something like wavery human singing to an enduring chicken moan. Their doors bark, and shadowy men leap out, their stiff arms forming isosceles triangles aimed directly at Roger. They are shouting but he can't understand a word and doesn't know if they are shouting at him or to each other.

Marie is looking at him over the half curtain, her eyes wide, and her mouth asymmetrically open in a way that sends a jolt of sorrow through Roger's chest. Her face is orange in an undulant, uneven illumination, and her corneas gleam sharply. An enormous roar, like a rocket taking off, is shaking the ground. Roger turns. Where his apartment once stood, a tower of flame rises straight into the sky.

Someone throws him to the pavement. Someone else puts a knee on his spine. His arms are yanked behind his back. Cool metal encircles his wrists. The knee lifts, and he is hoisted to his feet, driveway grit embedded in his cheek.

It is morning, and Roger is lying in his bed in his apartment—except that it is not his apartment. He is surrounded by objects so familiar he cannot remember when they entered his life: the bureau that had once been in his parents' bedroom, the dozen framed photographs that had once hung on the staircase wall, the brown Naugahyde chair from which his father used to watch television. All of these objects are exactly as Roger arranged them when he first moved in, but, still, this is not his apartment. He gets out of bed and puts his hand against the wall. It is cold and coated with a layer of condensation, like the walls of a cave. Roger built the walls of his apartment himself, but these are not the walls he built. Those had been made of Sheetrock and wood studs; these are made of stone.

There is no sound except for the whisper of his feet on the floor, his heartbeat in the center of his skull, and that needle of high-pitched noise that pings and recedes in his right ear. The cold air does not move, except as he displaces it by moving himself. But there is no reason to move. Nothing to do. He cannot go anywhere but back to bed.

But wait—there *is* a sound: a rock slamming the bottom of an empty Dumpster, perhaps, or a gun going off in a tunnel. Roger doesn't hear it so much as know that he has heard it. He must have been asleep.

He sits up in bed, listens, swings his feet to the floor, and wriggles them into flip-flops. The sound seemed to come from the kitchen, which is no longer a mess; which is, in fact, unusually orderly, but not so much his kitchen as the kitchen in a house that has been abandoned. Here too: the cave coldness and still air. No natural light. He sweeps back the yellow curtains over the sink, and finds a rectangle of cinder block, imperfectly cemented, where the window used to be. He opens the kitchen door and finds another door behind it, made of greased steel, bolt studded, with a slot-shaped hatch at its center.

The hatch does not budge when he presses it. And the door resists his strength so implacably, it is as if it were implacability itself made into physical object. But as he turns away, he hears a loud clank. He looks again and sees the door has fallen open half an inch. He pushes and the door swings beneath his fingertips with a sound like a donkey groan on a PA system.

Fresh air wafts against his cheeks and tousles his hair. It is night, and he can hear the clinks, dings, and electric burbles of thousands of birds, near and far. The moon is brilliant and full, and, in its blue light, his house seems made entirely of coal. Its clapboards and roof shingles have exactly that mineral sheen. And the trees have the rainbow sheen of crow feathers, as do the bent grass blades of the unmowed lawn.

And now he is on the cement walkway, breezes stirring the hair on his neck, jetting coolness up his T-shirt, sliding across the tops of his feet and toes. Someone else is standing in the driveway, where Bill's car is normally parked. She is motionless. Waiting. Her pale hair waves in the gentle turbulence like arcs of electricity around a Van de Graaff generator.

He is standing beside her. "Feel like a walk?" she asks.

"Sure," he says. "It's such a beautiful night."

They cross the yard and enter a field of waist-high grass—tufted and silvery in the moonlight—then descend a small bluff into a railroad cut. Smell of creosote. Crunch of gravel underfoot. They each walk along a blue-gleaming rail.

"Amazing that I should see you in the driveway," Roger says, "because I was just thinking about you."

"Really?" She smiles. Her smile is closed lipped, tender. Her eyes are moon colored in the moonlight.

"I was thinking about what you said."

"Oh?" she says.

Not just creosote, but the pungency of methane. And a coppery tang.

"About when you said life sucks." He stops walking and faces her. She stops too. "That made me sad," he says.

She steps down off the rail. So does he. They are standing on the same railroad tie, so close that heat begins to accumulate between their bodies. "You're sweet," she says.

"I just don't like the idea of your feeling that way."

"I didn't really mean it," she says.

Somewhere amid the shadows and moonlight an animal cries, and then, a moment later, there is a softer cry, like an echo.

"Then why did you say it?"

She shrugs. "I don't know. I guess it's just my way of guarding against false hope."

213

"What do you mean by false hope?"

"I just don't want to be hurt." She slinks her head down between her shoulders and looks away. Only now does he realize that she is not wearing her plastic hand. In the moonlight, her arm is like a sandy path through beach grass that stops for no reason.

"But if you're afraid to hope," he says, "you're afraid to live. How are you going to do anything if you don't have any hopes?"

She looks up at him again. "I have hopes."

"Good," he says.

"I just worry that they're for the wrong things."

"What do you hope for?" he says.

A bird passes just overhead, feathers hissing. A humming pump pulses in the field above the cut.

"Oh, God!" she says so softly he almost can't hear. "Oh, God! Oh, God! I don't know. I just don't know. What do you want me to say?"

Preparing One's Consciousness for the Avatar
Gillian Conoley

Was a rare sun   its sudden mouths,   shrugs and voices.

A birth   a sleep   a forgetting   a God

or scientist   or brain.   Or when in   mind or on a freeway   a red/orange sign

drops down   says

do not   neglect, nor demonize   the demons.   The lice are feasting.

Drafts,   computations,   clean for more   space, rid unnecessary surfaces

bottled water   Agua pura, sabor perfecto.

Avatar, atavistic   just a brief, lettristic shuffle   *avatar* chiefly Hindi,

manifestation   of a deity   or released soul   in bodily form

on earth   (*are you? maybe, don't flatter me*)   from the Sanskrit

ava "down" + tar "to cross,"

and atavistic   origin nineteenth century (*in your dreams*) from the Latin

atavus "forefather"   via French

atavisme. Frankenstein bewildered   at his limp or rising member

still a little angry   re parlor game   his cheek   tingles   nuzzles and buries

215

itself   in verdant marl.   World welcomes more   world   in sun

the young muscled   amputee in basketball shorts   heading cheerfully,

quickly to the ferry.   *Don't stir*

                                                  the trash,

                                                  writes Sappho.

                          *

                      It's you and I   in pursuit   counter pursuit,

in the long epiphany   of having a face.   Was it sixteenth century—

to simulate rain—water spray   was released over   mechanical dolls

sent flying near the masterpieces—Or was that you   who were tired

                            of not being

                            and so began   calling for help?

                            If I   were a mothering belly

                            would I

heave or contract   out your   tangled, wired tissues   a silkworm

cocoon,   put your head at my feet   and we'll pretend.

                          *

You would not think it is this young Russian

who wants us all to live forever. Walking earth down

to basalt, shale, slate.

Sea roaring is the blood

in sparrows of the Holy Ghost

a ting, ting in bell tower.

Maritime, lorikeet, sleet. Dmitry Itskov

(pale yellow Borelli blazer,

rose-gold watch, thirty-two, a mild-mannered, Internet billionaire)

is nonplussed, sweet of face

which someone

(David Hanson, of Hanson Robotics) in Plano, Texas,

is duplicating, carefully,

paused above a tiny-haired brush   for the eyelids   in the *Times*.

Thirty-six motors to reproduce facial expressions and voice.

"No more world hunger," says Dmitry Itskov. At least for you. While others
  are always

hungry. So some refrigerators   will have to stay, some sent to dump

in silver or white array—look in, look away.

*

Gillian Conoley

How to figure   when to leave the body

summer's blue jay   calling   caw caw caw   quick-diving down to peck

the calico/tortoise mix,   who is   so calmly taking it. Only

to pounce later. Do you play   cat or bird?   Blue jays lift and spin,

graze the sheet on the line,   turn

into a tumescent   subgroup, the organs of our fancy . . .

                                  Felonies and phantoms

                        of DNA   like sharp notes

                              cleared   of choir

                  while floats a

yellow Post-it,   postage size,   cropped fabric/memory   of my dead

father's blue/gray   wet plaid swim trunks—   a flash—

The burled handrest   at the end   of the burnt stairway—

                        Time to clean, to clean and polish, the figures and friends

are coming over, the ones   who read, command   and trail us,

hello canary,   hello reptile,

parrot   brother   sister   and oh wow,   is that you celebrity?   and child.

218

If you don't see them now you

will soon—no turning back—

they are mostly atavistic,   powerful in what

they get us to look like, do and say.   At least you—still in production—don't

have to sleep next to them,   or wake up and wing it—

The wind bellows and rattles the house.

Ice, ice drops another cube.   Tiny tinny birdsong.

Wild red fox   purple zinnia   stone pelican   raven.

The celebrities scrub themselves down to the shine.

My mother who is now speaking

in sentences of no more than four words

reclines on the armchair

to watch

like a bony glamorous cheetah,   an unwrinkled sleeve   stilled

in the complementary then analogous

Gillian Conoley

color theory of the room, the

debris box they are taking away

a week from Friday.   One of the figures

has died.   And jumped into the debris box.

One of the figures   trailing the friends.   Delete, clean.

Old sound of empty chimney when wind dips down

into sudden clang.   Is that you again—uniting, hiding, expansive in

the silence   after sound?   OK,   I will give you my childhood

neighbor who sat in the backyard painting her china plates,

her dyed black hair   done up in a knot—

Breasts loose in a housedress.   Her wondrous teats

fallen over her waist   above the astonishingly small petals

she is painting on the plates   with tiny-haired brushes.

The rotting garage behind her.   And what's this?

Cloudy afterimage of myself and cousin   in her upstairs bed her

funeral night? Cool, old, dark, empty house.

Fooling around in riverbank's low grasses

the day before? The same

cousin, at least.

Blue palette extending

beyond sky over windless   sidewalks that tilt and buckle

at most tree-rooted spots. I know this way

like I have trudged it all along

every new street.   Immortality,   if you are coming,   you are

the last figure off the boat.   I am the one   who gently pushes the boat

away, and wishes you well,   the friends and figures slowly extinguishing

then enlivening   the word love,   and the love in gone and ever.

*

And the boarded-up window

in the rotting garage,   and still no relief.   The palm tree that rises

through years then molts in windstorm   its deeply crevassed

bark canoes.   Black crow bringing in the wake,

soul made   to deflate, inflate

to transfer   like breath   to a summer hammock.   The neighbors dragging

chaise lounges in   thick smears of sun.   Red nail polish fades

off the key used most.   Windows

preferably high, clear

so puppet theaters of day

bring   cloud, tree   car, fence.   Some stranger

is getting in the front seat.   First one spindly leg and then the other.   Plump,
    liquefy,

reconstitute. Hot light-rinsed light   where the celebrities

stand for   our smoothing of the images,

the labor of the evening out

    of the images which works   to heal

the celebrities'   carved faces

    and bodies,   the frayed hoodies

they retreat to, the scraped-out images

    of the cloaks and rags and rugs—

In imitation of prayer, palm meets palm,   our hands designed

    to make a folio. The start of childhood is one folio

in which the family gathers to stand

as before a window, each individual so rarely pictured with the entire group,

    unless it is a storm where one can point and pass,

evaporate as ghosts to sea. Oh optometry,

hazel, mauve, ocher   low field of burning barn across which one can holler

a centering "amen" and "we shall live again" a species

of rock and trace mineral,

of many marks and laughter.   These formations you will inherit just by

staring us back in the face.

Canary, parrot, brother, sister, celebrity, child. Expenditure, skeins,

who is Your Excellency?

Who your dissimulated author? I am sad under my sheets

if you are amped tireless soldier.

[I am going to dissolve/suture all this back inside me

while in storm light drops the lantern.]

*

And why

is your Dmitry Itskov face painted so blue, so boy blue

if only to make us think death, or Thomas

Gainsborough's blue-velveted boy,   boy on the brink

of childhood's end,

when so many imagine their deaths red,   or colorless, somehow more free—

Gillian Conoley

antiphonal,

if you want to lift the blood that way . . .

Of all my friends and figures

I prefer the woman who walks   in the loosest way

down the conveyor belt, along the metronomes and mechanical dolls,

like one who prefers to not be there—had nothing to do with it—

does not want to   command or suggest,   only to go one's own way

through the   discordant   collective sweep.

Most brains are not quite done,

and have regions

disturbed or blank, this area

without wire shooting away

from itself—She's in one, looking for a place to stand

and wish for elsewhere and harmony,

the slow dangling of the branch   into black water that is a part

of how we, being 'round thee, forget to die?

And can drop anchor

into knowing   one another

through projecting expressions,   timbres, tones of voice

    and even   clothing's   pale importance   then loud colors   though all this

dies down   when one is alone,   bearable days on end for some,

        only a few hours for most—

Leagues of contagion   residual beauty   recorded, battered candlelight.

She's the kind   no one is the single file of.

You will come to see

these figures and join their ranks

perhaps? Eventually though later than we? Given your fuel,

your ability to last   be last.   I'll just stand

and wait in snow's   meandering   lost call, called back.

    If we go down these stairs, the besotted government

of each continent,   village, and hut.

    If we go up, the beginning

crevices of the infinity,   each step disappearing beneath the

blooms and ducts   of a repatterning,

Gillian Conoley

sun-struck sky. Gone this thing

of having two feet on the ground   unless they are

curled up in a chair   or tucked or

splayed out elsewhere. Gone the floors of polished jasper. We'll fly,

   imaginary, expenditure, skeins,   through gates of

           rust-stained bougainvillea   heartbreaking over the

   ringing in our ears   in the long division

      of our end's negation   and its annihilation

shadow shadow shadow   follow follow—

Coal

Can Xue

—Translated from Chinese by Annelise Finegan Wasmoen

YIN XIU WAS A YOUNG MAN of twenty-one who looked like his name, *xiu*—he was elegant, refined, fair, and wore a pair of rimless glasses. Yin Xiu worked at the coal-supply station where his job was to sell coal to the other residents. In our little town, coal was one of the major necessities of life, second only to food and clothing.

Yin Xiu sat behind the counter of the coal-supply station and every time he signed a customer in and finished collecting payment, he stood to shovel the customer's coal. His method of shoveling coal was very practiced, tidy, efficient, and in peculiar harmony with his slight, thin frame.

When Yin Xiu was not selling coal, those who noticed his pitiful boniness and his melancholy air often had the impulse to protect him. He was an only child. His entire family consisted of his mother, who had been ill for many years.

In fact, it was not only the people of the small town who tried to protect him. Yin Xiu paid close attention to protecting himself as well. He had never played soccer, for example. When the other children his age asked him to play he always declined. He did, however, install a set of parallel bars at the entrance to his house and every day after work he hung upside down on them like a bat. He believed this to be the safest method of exercise. The other boys all sneered with contempt at his way of exercising.

It may have been due to the importance of Yin Xiu's work that he had a certain status in the eyes of other residents. He was not the kind of person who could easily be ignored.

Yin Xiu had only been working for three years. Three years earlier, his father, who had worked at the coal-supply station, got drunk, was run over by a car, and killed on the street, so Yin Xiu had replaced him. Yin Xiu soon grew passionate about his work at the coal-supply station, where his serious approach earned him the high regard of the customers and his superiors. As for Yin Xiu himself, he found, without knowing exactly why, that he enjoyed being in contact with the coal, especially the goods that were of higher quality, raven black and shiny. He gently swung the iron shovel into the coal as if he were playing with it. He could even hear the coal's quiet laughs of protest at this disruption. Yin Xiu was completely different from his father, who was so disgusted by his job and being in constant contact with the coal that he often drank to excess. Yin Xiu remembered how his father would sometimes point at the coal and say to him, "It's the transformed bones of the dead." At home his father always had a stern expression too. When he couldn't fall asleep at night, he complained to Yin Xiu, "All this black coal pressing down on you, covering the earth and the sky . . . how do you dare shut your eyes? You have to hold them open, like this." Yin Xiu knew that for his father, coal was the most loathsome thing in the world. And that was why his father had never once smiled at him. After his father died, his mother lay down in bed. From then on she seldom rose again. She lay propped up among the quilts and pillows, watching with hollow eyes as Yin Xiu moved busily back and forth across the room. She could hardly get enough breath to speak half a sentence.

Yin Xiu lived a five-minute walk from the coal-supply station. He only had to cross one street and he was home. So at night Yin Xiu often ran over to the station and spent a little time there.

With his shovel he would make the already neat coal even neater, piling it into a tidy, symmetrical little hill. If it was summer or fall, he would stand, leaning on the shovel abstractedly, recalling what things were like in the winter. In the winter, when it grew cold and the ground of the small town froze, the coal-supply station became a naturally advantageous workplace, because he was permitted to burn a small coal fire in the stove when he arrived at work. Yin Xiu gathered the gleaming, flickering lumps of coal (he called it "black gold") and placed them in a wooden bucket. When the bucket was half filled they went into the stove. Lump coal is durable and can last from morning until afternoon. The reddish-yellow coal flames made his heart leap merrily inside of him. At such times the thought of his father always mystified Yin Xiu: Why hadn't he loved this "black gold"? Coal was valuable, it was needed to prepare food or boil water. The people of the small town were not allowed to warm themselves by the fire. Yin Xiu's little coal stove stood behind the counter and the customers would stand on tiptoe to look at it enviously. Sometimes they said, "Yin Xiu, you share your father's good fortune! How could he give this up and leave?"

When they said this, Yin Xiu lowered his eyes, his whole face reddening. He thought it was a reproach directed at him.

Silent coal, beautiful coal, how did it refine itself into treasure in the deep reaches of the earth? Maybe it wasn't true that his father couldn't stand the coal. Maybe its short life made him depressed, and because this sadness was difficult to bear he pretended to hate it? Yin Xiu knew it was unreasonable to think this, but he could not help it if his thoughts turned toward dark places.

Every day when he left work Yin Xiu emptied out the coal ash. To him even the coal dust was beautiful, especially the lumps of coal that had turned into corpses that collapsed, ever so calmly, when tapped lightly. Father had said coal was transformed skeletons, but then he said unconventional, illogical things.

One day Yin Xiu had very few customers. Snowflakes were flying outside as he sat behind the counter leafing through an old family photograph album. Only a small opening remained in the stove through which the coal fire shot out blue stems of flame. It was a measure Yin Xiu had taken to save coal.

A vagrant named Zeng Hu, or Zeng the Tiger, entered the coal-supply station making such a racket that Yin Xiu stood to look at him.

He leaned on a walking stick, his left foot swollen into a pillow-like shape too big to fit a shoe over and wrapped in a dirty towel instead. Yin Xiu knew that ordinarily Zeng Hu lived at the garbage-dump building.

"Are you cold, Brother Zeng?" Yin Xiu asked him.

"How could I be cold? Once I enter this coal station I feel warm and dry inside! You ought to know that this is real coal. Look at it. If you grab a handful you can squeeze out the oil! You can't compare this to those pieces of scrap wood and old newspapers at the garbage dump."

He murmured in admiration and jabbed at the tiny mountain of coal with his walking stick until one side of the pile collapsed, but then he laughed heartily.

Yin Xiu laughed along with him, hoping the laughter would dispel the tramp's coldness.

"Brother Zeng, where are you from originally?"

"A coal-mining area in Shanxi. I ran away."

"Coal mining? What was it like?"

"How can I even describe it? It was warm there, but it's my nature to prefer the cold. That's why I ran away. I'd rather live above the garbage dump than there. But when I see all this coal I get homesick."

"How deep were the coal mines?"

"Too deep to see to the bottom! It's a busy atmosphere down there, with coal as a companion. Have you seen anything like it before in a dream? All alone by yourself in the dark and on all sides of you, everywhere, is coal." His voice was elated.

"No." Yin Xiu reflected for a moment, then spoke again hesitatingly. "I'm trying my best to think about practical things, but this coal, this coal . . ." All at once he wanted to cry.

"It's silent, is that it? Young man, believe me, this is my favorite place to visit. You understand coal, and that's no small matter."

Zeng Hu scrutinized Yin Xiu carefully, wanting to see his tears, but Yin Xiu did not cry.

"I think," Yin Xiu said, struggling to regain his composure, "that since you've seen and experienced so much, you must have known my father. What did you talk about with him?"

"Of course!" Zeng Hu raised his voice. "Your father was a courageous man. When there was a snowstorm, he and I would talk the whole night through, up above the garbage dump. I really miss him."

"Talk the whole night? But he slept at home every night."

"It was a secret. He slipped out so quietly no one noticed."

Yin Xiu suddenly felt tired of Zeng Hu. He was homeless and had wandered here from the north more than a decade ago. He'd lived above the garbage dump ever since, collecting scrap material to survive, passing his days in poverty, without dignity and without involvement with the world. Maybe he was like Yin Xiu's father. Had Zeng Hu run away because he hated the coal? Yet from his way of speaking it sounded as if he was full of love for coal. When his father was alive Yin Xiu could not understand him; now he could not understand this vagrant either. He began to panic from the strain.

"When I lived in the mining district I went back and forth between all the different counties because I can sniff out the location of coal. Don't you believe me?"

Zeng Hu had not detected Yin Xiu's change in mood and was still sunk in reverie.

"Really? You're amazing!" Yin Xiu managed to answer unconvincingly.

Then a customer came in and Zeng Hu limped away in a hurry. Yin Xiu saw the dirty towel that had been wrapped around his foot left behind at the door of the coal-supply station, making him think how cold Zeng Hu would be.

The customer who had come to buy coal was Uncle Ying, a competent, experienced man of middle age.

"Do you know why Zeng Hu stays here instead of leaving?"

Uncle Ying scowled in the direction in which Zeng Hu had left. Not waiting for an answer, he burst out, "Because of his unique skill! It's too dangerous for a man like him to stay in his own village."

"Like my father?"

As Yin Xiu spoke, he stared straight ahead, dazed, the shovel in his hand refusing to follow his orders.

"Oh, you misunderstood me. I wasn't talking about your father!" Uncle Ying quickly apologized. "What I meant to say was, he's as good as ten or even twenty prospecting teams! In those days back in Shanxi, wherever he pointed, they would uncover layers of coal. Oh, Yin Xiu, what are you doing? Did you splash coal dust in your eyes? Let me see."

Uncle Ying snatched the shovel from Yin Xiu's hands and shoveled the coal into the basket himself.

Yin Xiu was hardly ever inattentive to customers, so he stood off to the side in shame.

"We can't do without coal. If you let the flames die down after you finish boiling water in the evening and don't add more coal, you can start a new fire the next day. Who dares look down on coal?"

Uncle Ying spoke cautiously as he shook a small scoop of coal into the basket, staring at the weigh bar of the platform scale as it shifted up and down. His expression grew gentler.

Before shouldering the two baskets of coal on the carrying pole, he turned his head and said to Yin Xiu in a serious voice, "Such an abundant natural resource wore down Zeng Hu's willpower. I know what he is."

After Uncle Ying's silhouette disappeared from the doorway, Yin Xiu felt a few small sparks scatter through his own dark heart as a faint hope came into focus there. He thought of his mother. Did she hold on to hope, like he did? He had seen with his own eyes how she did everything in her power to resist the demon of her disease. If it hadn't been for that car, his father probably wouldn't have gone away. Hadn't he and the vagrant been meeting above the garbage dump? As for the coal, which of the two men had a deeper understanding of it?

A scene appeared in Yin Xiu's mind: a young, handsome Zeng Hu working his way through a mountain forest, an enormous crowd of people following behind him. . . . He rushed to a spot where there was a shortage of coal, and everything his glance fell on turned into coal. That's what it must have been like. Yin Xiu began to piece together the conversations Zeng Hu and his father must have had above the garbage dump.

The sorrow in his heart lifted all at once. He walked to the doorway and saw that the snow already had stopped falling; the pale sun shone without even a thread of warmth; the small town was still, as if it had decided to muse in silence under the cover of snow. A child appeared, walking closer and closer. His name was Baby Niu.

"I'm cold," he told Yin Xiu. "Cold everywhere."

"You're a child, you should run around and then you won't be cold."

"I tried that already, but I'm still cold. You can keep warm by the fire. There's no fire at my house." He looked accusingly at Yin Xiu.

"What can I do about it?" Yin Xiu said sadly.

"I want to get a job at the coal station too, later on. But no one in my family works there. What should I do? You are really lucky to take over your father's work. I'm about to die of cold."

He stamped his feet resentfully. Yin Xiu saw his toes showing through his broken rubber shoes, as well as the tears in his eyes. He drummed up the courage to say, "Baby Niu, aren't you only twelve years old? A child so young cannot die. If you want to work at the coal-supply station later on, then from now on you should start thinking about it every single day, even in your dreams. If you keep dreaming of something, then you will make it come true someday, no matter what it is. Have you noticed Mr. Zeng Hu? That's how he got here."

Baby Niu's whole face burst into a smile when he heard Zeng Hu's name.

"Yes, that's right! I'm so happy you brought up Mr. Zeng Hu! I'm going to go find him, he'll burn those wood chips so I can get warm by the fire, and while I warm up he'll tell me stories about coal! The last time he told me there is coal five meters underneath our feet."

After Baby Niu left, Yin Xiu went back behind the counter, sat down, and continued trying to piece together those conversations above the garbage dump.

After work, Yin Xiu exercised for a while on the horizontal bar until he was panting and out of breath.

His mother had gotten out of bed and sat in the armchair looking at her fingernails.

"Mama, you must be cold. It's snowing outside again."

"Don't be silly, how could I be cold? You work at the coal-supply station warming yourself at the stove. There's so much coal there that once I think of it I'm warm all over."

"Isn't coal the most valuable thing in town?"

"Of course it is, Yin Xiu," his mother answered proudly.

Yin Xiu observed that once he brought up the subject of coal his mother's illness seemed to improve to a surprising extent, and her cheeks even flushed a pale red. She must be thinking about some happy memories. Yin Xiu grew more cheerful.

"Mama, think about it a little more. Won't my thoughts become wild if I spend all day with such valuable objects? What I mean to say is, will I be like Zeng Hu and full of crazy ideas?"

His mother's face overflowed with a kindly smile. Yin Xiu had very seldom seen her like this.

"No," she said confidently. "People like Zeng Hu are extremely rare. You're a good son."

Yin Xiu felt that his mother could see to the bottom of his heart.

He went outside to chop firewood and build a fire. He was not at all handy when it came to household duties, and the weather was so cold that his hands were frozen numb. He managed to fill the whole area around the stove with billowing clouds of smoke. At last, the fire was finally lit. He quickly washed the rice and rinsed the vegetables. When the meal was almost ready, he heard a muffled thump from somewhere inside the house. Terrified, he rushed from the kitchen to the other room.

His mother had fallen out of the armchair. She lay on the floor calmly, her eyes revolving as she tracked some invisible flying object in the air.

"Mama, did you hurt yourself falling?"

Yin Xiu bent over and took his mother in his arms, carrying her to the armchair because it was time to eat.

He carried the food in, set it down, and helped his mother to spoon the rice into her bowl and pick up the vegetables with the chopsticks.

His mother quietly began to eat. Her eyes returned to their customary vacancy. The expression in them before had appeared like an ephemeral night flower. Yin Xiu suspected that his mother's mind held a lump of coal inside of it that only burned at suitable moments. Ordinarily it was ice-cold.

After his mother finished eating, Yin Xiu ate too. Holding her arm, he helped her wash her face and her feet. After washing, she went to bed quite early. A short while later she began to snore. Yin Xiu stared at his mother's round, unlined face in the dim light of the lamp. He felt that there was a look of profound meaning on her face. Yin Xiu said to himself quietly, "This is someone who lives in the world of coal too." There was a silent agreement between his mother and father that Yin Xiu had never understood. Ever since his father had died, Yin Xiu no longer remembered things from the past.

"Yin Xiu, Yin Xiu!" Someone was knocking at the window of the house.

"Come inside!" Yin Xiu said in a lowered voice.

"I won't come inside, I have something to give you."

Yin Xiu could tell that it was Zeng Hu who threw an object wrapped in newspaper into the room.

"Yin Xiu, pick it up and hide it." It was his mother speaking.

Yin Xiu went over and picked up the paper bundle, opened it, and found a lump of shining, raven-black coal.

"Why did he give me this?" Yin Xiu asked his mother.

"Your father wanted him to. Wherever this man points there will be coal. He has never lacked for money, even though he's homeless."

Yin Xiu listened to his mother as she lay in bed, amazed at how clear her sequence of thought was. He had realized some time ago that even though his mother lay in bed most of the time, she was actually living in another place, a place known to her and his father, and also to Zeng Hu. Yin Xiu called it the birthplace of coal. Now Yin Xiu understood that his attachment to coal was not without cause. But why did this foreign, ghostly, heavy lump of coal shining in the lamplight feel like such a great burden to him?

Faintly he could hear Baby Niu's tearful complaint from across the street: "I'm cold, I'm cold . . . I want to come inside. . . ."

His mother had fallen asleep again and was sleeping soundly, probably having entered the warm realm of dreams. Yin Xiu took the lump of coal and hid it inside a clay jar on top of the closet, placing it next to his father's ashes. He stood in front of the closet for a while, a net appearing in his mind with the face of Zeng Hu at its center. He remembered how Zeng Hu had come into the coal-supply station and gradually he straightened out a few of the main threads from an accumulated mass of questions. So, had Zeng Hu come to their small town to deliver a kindling spark? The former hero had chosen this place to start a new undertaking. Thinking up to this point,

Yin Xiu felt a warm heat glowing in the pit of his stomach, just like his mother's. What was the pattern of the distribution of the coal mines in that coal country of Shanxi Province? Yin Xiu turned off the light in his mother's room and returned to his own, preoccupied by his thoughts.

He sat at the desk feeling a kind of gratification in his mind and a comfortableness in his body that was difficult to describe. His father had never actually left him then. That tangle of flesh and blood three years ago was not his father. He wrote a few words on a piece of paper with his father's old fountain pen: "One falls, another follows." He heard Baby Niu run past his window shouting something as he headed toward the garbage dump. What a persistent child.

Yin Xiu could not sit still. According to the alarm clock on the desk, it was already 11:00 p.m.

He went outside stealthily, slowly shutting the door to the house.

A layer of soft pellets had fallen on the surface of the road, but it wasn't all that slippery.

"Yin Xiu, is that you?" the tramp asked.

Zeng Hu surprised him outside the garbage dump. The small figure of Baby Niu stood by Zeng Hu's side.

"Were you waiting for me?"

"Yes. Let's go upstairs. I'll walk ahead, then you and Baby Niu follow behind."

Yin Xiu saw that his legs were miraculously healed and he walked like an ordinary man.

Smelling an intense odor of trash, they climbed the staircase running up the side of the garbage dump. In the dark Yin Xiu heard Baby Niu breathing loudly with excitement.

Up above there was a narrow walkway with Zeng Hu's spring cot in the middle of it. He beckoned Yin Xiu and Baby Niu to sit down on his bed. Waiting until the two of them were seated, he announced, "There is top-grade coal 350 meters underground."

A gust of cold wind blew into the walkway. Yin Xiu was covered in goose bumps. He heard Baby Niu saying, "It's nice and warm here."

Yin Xiu's face flushed red, but fortunately no one could see it. He was waiting for Zeng Hu to begin telling stories about the coal-mining district, but Zeng Hu remained silent. What made Yin Xiu angry, though, was that Baby Niu also remained silent. What was happening here?

235

Gradually, the stench of the trash grew lighter until finally he could not smell it at all. The frozen tips of Yin Xiu's toes, which had grown numb, began to burn, and slowly his entire body started burning, growing hot enough that he broke into a sweat.

"Brother Zeng, say something," Yin Xiu pleaded.

"What should I say?"

"Talk about anything. Talk about when you went on expeditions to explore the forest, or something like that."

"But there's nothing good to say about that. What did that adventure count for? I only started exploring once I arrived here."

"So, what do you think of our town?"

"This is a city of hope. Everyone here works diligently."

Yin Xiu stretched out a hand to feel around him. It was empty to his right. Had Baby Niu slipped away?

"Baby Niu is asleep," Zeng Hu said with a laugh. "He goes to sleep all at once. This is the second time he's slept there, the clever little fellow. You should head downstairs first. I'll be down in a little while to talk with you about something."

As Yin Xiu walked down the stairs he had a very strange sensation: On every step it felt as if he were stepping on the body of an infant. The crying of the infants was weak and feeble. He finally reached the ground, where he stood at the side of a road covered in gritty snow.

He waited and waited but Zeng Hu did not descend.

He waited until he grew impatient and was about to return home when he heard Zeng Hu say from overhead, "You should go ahead. Baby Niu and I have things to do during the night."

When Yin Xiu had first come down the stairs he had felt a bone-piercing cold and by now he was nearly frozen stiff. He began to run. Then something happened as he raced along through the snowy night: He saw his own shadow running out in front of him. He had no strength left to take note of what was happening. He was in an exceptional amount of pain from the frigid cold. He ran back home heedless of anything else. By the time he reached the house, even his thoughts were numb.

He poured some hot water from the thermos, soaked his feet, and went to bed. He wrapped himself tightly in the blankets and was about to go to sleep when he heard Baby Niu's mother wailing from across the street, "Baby Niu, come back—Baby Niu! Come—back—now!"

Yin Xiu wondered why this lively middle-aged woman would be grieving. It made no sense. He remembered how she looked when she carried the shoulder pole with buckets of coal, letting her long, thick braids swing in front of her chest. Normally she was both optimistic and cheerful. Why did she have such a melancholy son?

Early the next morning Yin Xiu moved the lit coal stove into the kitchen.

His mother had already been awake for a while and lay in bed with her eyes wide open.

"Yin Xiu, was there a battle last night? I heard the entire thing."

"What?" Yin Xiu answered her back.

"Don't be a coward. Your father was never a coward."

"Did my father . . . did he like that vagrant or not?"

"Of course he did. You stupid child. They were partners."

"But you, Mama, are you their partner too?"

"I suppose so. Today you seem a little distracted. Will it keep you from going to work?"

"No, it won't. I'm not like Father. He threw his body and soul into everything, but I'm halfhearted and always stay on the outside thinking about things. But . . . but . . ."

Yin Xiu's face reddened and he said nothing further. Through the window he saw Baby Niu flying through the door of his family's house across the street.

The holidays were about to arrive so the coal reserves in the supply station were piled almost to the rafters. For several days Yin Xiu had been in charge of the workers who transported the coal. He saw someone who looked like his father among the men at work moving the coal, but it turned out to be someone he didn't know. Yin Xiu knew almost all of the workers who made deliveries to the coal-supply station.

"Sir, are you local?" Yin Xiu asked him.

"No. I'm from Shanxi originally."

As the fellow looked at Yin Xiu with kindly eyes, Yin Xiu's hands shook the coal shovel he held. He heard the man say something quietly: "This really is a town where heroes come from."

After the man left, Yin Xiu put down his shovel and sat behind the counter. The room filled with coal was silent. The workers who'd brought the coal said it was transported from Shanxi. But could it have come from the secret mine 350 meters below the ground instead? Did that mine exist? He was always terrified when he thought about questions like these that had no answers. He asked himself: Why couldn't he figure it out the same way Baby Niu did? Was it already too late?

A customer came in. It was Baby Niu's father, a thin man with a dark complexion.

"Why are you only buying fourteen kilos? It's almost New Year, buy a little more," Yin Xiu said after taking his coal notebook.

"There's no quota. Baby Niu, the demanding little brat, complains all day long that the house is too cold."

"It's always like that. Children are afraid of the cold."

"You're wrong!" He said the two words so sternly that it startled Yin Xiu.

He saw Yin Xiu's alarmed appearance and became immediately embarrassed.

"Yin Xiu, your mother is fortunate. If Baby Niu was like you, everything would be all right. But it makes no difference. Baby Niu's mother and I grit our teeth and bear it."

He shouldered that tiny little bit of coal and left. Yin Xiu stared blankly at his receding back, remembering how he looked fishing beside the river. There were practically no fish in the river yet he always sat there calmly, holding the fishing pole in his hand, entirely still. Yin Xiu knew that there were a few people in the town like him, the firm believers. Baby Niu had found somewhere warm to go, so why were his parents unwilling him to let him go there every day? Did they actually admire Baby Niu's behavior and only obstruct him in order to temper his spirit? There were no customers that morning and the coal filling the room made the atmosphere very solemn. The lumps of coal in the stove burned with particular vigor, the flames roaring up high. Yin Xiu had a great desire to sleep, so he leaned over on the counter. But he did not fall asleep because the coal was making chattering sounds, as if it wanted to tell him something. Later he simply stood up and used the shovel to pack the coal in more tightly. Every time he tapped the coal to pack it in, his chest tightened a bit with the worry that something was about to happen. What were Zeng Hu and Baby Niu doing during the night in that warm place at the top of the garbage-dump building? Yin Xiu felt a certain regret. He should have stayed longer at Zeng Hu's that night. But given his shy nature, he lacked the courage to stick around anywhere. For that reason, his failure to see the truth of the situation was also inevitable.

A burst of confused noises came from the corner of the room where one side of the pile of coal had collapsed. It was piled up in an orderly way. What could have made it fall? Nothing like this had ever happened before. Yin Xiu grew nervous, his hands began to tremble. He felt that, in his little world, energy was coming into focus. Perhaps, long ago, this barren, impoverished town had been the birthplace of coal. Wasn't this often revealed today in people's faces and their movements? He stood there waiting, thinking the entire heap of coal would fall.

Yet it didn't. The coal silently guarded its history.

Waiting in the quiet, Yin Xiu suddenly gained entry into what his father had been thinking that year in the past. His mind rose and fell, half in the dark, half in clarity. He had figured it out: Father left for that place out of greed.

Just at that moment, a large number of people swarmed into the coal-supply station. Some were shouldering large wicker baskets, others were carrying smaller bamboo ones. All of them were saying, "It's almost New Year, almost New Year. . . ."

Yin Xiu helped them one after another, signing them into the register, taking payment, weighing the coal.

When it was Young Wei's turn, Yin Xiu was about to shovel the loose coal from where the pile had collapsed, but Young Wei dragged him to a stop.

"I don't want that coal. Give me some from the other side!" he said.

"Why? This is good coal."

"It smells like a corpse."

Yin Xiu turned around, shoveling the coal from a different angle.

He finished weighing Young Wei's coal, took off his glasses, and wiped them on his sleeve, since both lenses had tears on them.

Once Young Wei left the coal-supply station, everyone closed in around Yin Xiu.

"Yin Xiu, Yin Xiu, don't mind him, he's a fool." All of them reassured him.

"No, he was right in what he said. It's just that he doesn't like corpses. Some people don't like dead people. But coal is just the opposite, isn't it? People die because of coal, and it loves the dead too."

"Right! That's it!" Everyone spoke at the same time.

With a red face, Yin Xiu helped the next person sign into the register, took the payment, weighed the coal. He felt a gust of flame rush upward from underground. In the blink of an eye the room became even warmer than the night at the garbage dump. What was happening 350 meters below?

The coal was carried away continuously by the customers, until by afternoon only half a room remained. He could finally leave work.

Yin Xiu measured the tiny half mountain of coal with his eyes, his mind unusually at peace.

On the way back to his house, many people greeted him, shouting, "Yin Xiu, Yin Xiu, it's almost New Year!"

"Yes, all right," Yin Xiu responded vaguely.

In the distance he saw his mother standing in the doorway of the house, looking full of life.

Samuel Johnson's Eternal Return
Martin Riker

THE SUSQUEHANNA IS A PLEASANT, avuncular river that winds down through Pennsylvania toward the Chesapeake, past airy forest and farmland, and these days, of course, past those endless suburban expanses. But if you drive north along the edge of it, under Harrisburg's small-city skyline, then purple mountains sliced away at the ends by the highway administration, past the last Amish fruit stand and tiny beleaguered college town, you will eventually arrive at what is left of Mr. Penn's once-illustrious woods: a sylvan paradise, empty of humans, thus of human concerns. Continue on, along a narrowing road beneath a sky of leaves and branches, and soon you begin to imagine, or half imagine, that this place, these woods, are everything that exists in this world. Whatever you'd meant to accomplish, whoever you'd hoped to become, all you'd previously called reality seems suddenly a distant memory. . . . And as the last thought of human society extinguishes itself, as your last worldly expectation slips away, if at that point you turn right and continue for about twenty more miles, you will come to the town where I was born, called Unityville.

It is a utopian name, Unityville, and well earned, in my opinion. There is great, near-total unity in Unityville. There are also only about thirty people, all of them religious zealots, or rather there were thirty at the time my parents first moved there, that time being very long ago now. Today the number is probably closer to forty-five.

My parents, who were also religious zealots, arrived in the town eight months pregnant, having lived full lives in the world of society and come to see that world as nonsensical if not pernicious, and certainly no place to raise a son. I've often tried to imagine how they felt that first day, driving up our single dirt street, passing our houses, stopping before our church. Were they pleased or disappointed by its smallness? Disheartened or emboldened by its shabbiness? Its isolation, at least, they'd signed on for, and I imagine them awed by it, and by their own resolve, convinced they'd accomplished something existentially profound by finding such a crummy place to live.

241

They were not long in town, however, before my father discovered that a stockpile of righteous indignation is no substitute for a job. And so it came to pass that every morning of my childhood, my father climbed into a blue Studebaker station wagon to depart for the impossibly distant-seeming city of Williamsport, where he worked for the phone company, doing what I don't know. Each night he'd return, visibly crumpled. Far from escaping society, it seemed, he'd only increased his commute. My mother, faced with shouldering both halves of our family's churchly burden, immersed herself in religious activities, to which I was invariably dragged along. My childhood, then, was spent largely alone, waiting out activities that did not personally involve me, loitering in the church foyer or hiding among the pews, where I proved to have as little aptitude for religious belief as for any other sort. Days were blank and formless. Weekends filled with church and chores. Year followed year, and if I was never particularly oppressed by feelings of discontent or dissatisfaction, it also never occurred to me that there existed a reality either better or worse than the one I'd been born to, or a person more vibrantly alive than the dullard I seemed destined to become.

I should clarify that when I say I was alone, I don't mean that there were no other children in Unityville. There were several, but they held no interest for me, or no more interest than anything else. There was one girl in particular, Emily, who was close to my age and fond of me. She was an imaginative, enthusiastic young woman, always trying to engage me in one activity or another, and the perfect indifference I showed her is as good an illustration as any of my personality at that time. A loner. A mope. Whether I'd brought it into the world with me or picked it up along the way, mine was a magnificent vapidity, an unprecedented nullity of spirit. I was a compulsive nonengager, a natural-born audience member, a couch potato who'd only to discover his couch.

The event that brought an end to this mortal stupor and determined forever my fate was the arrival, one autumn morning in my twelfth year, of a television set. By what star-crossed circumstance a television came to be in Unityville is a story I will tell in a moment, but suffice it to say that at a time when television was still new, when programming was scarce and sets were not yet ahead of sofas in the hierarchy of family furniture, the arrival of a television in Unityville was less likely than a stigmata, and considerably less welcome. What interest had these people, who sought nothing so much as escape from society, in watching an idealized version of it?

No interest at all. In fact, the argument that arose among the towns-people—the first argument I'd ever witnessed in that town—was never about whether the television should be *used*, since all agreed it should not be. It was simply whether the set should be disposed of outright or stowed away and forgotten. Why the latter course was deemed more prudent is what I'll now attempt to explain.

Although citizens of Unityville were sometimes forced to venture outside our small community, the only people who ever visited *us* were from a large Amish colony some miles south. These people, having lived apart from society far longer than we had, were considerably better at it. They lived without electricity, for example, something the people of Unityville would never even attempt. They were also quite handy, so conveniently so, in fact, that Unityville had become grossly reliant upon them, even for basics of survival. They built our houses, planted and cultivated our crops. We paid them, of course, and thus a relationship had grown up between our two communities. It was strictly a business relationship, but courteous and respectful, and beneficial for everyone involved.

But there was one among these Amish called Brother Abram, a huge muscular boy-man of perhaps twenty at the time I'm recounting, whom the people of Unityville secretly referred to as "the bad one." He was not bad in the sense of being angry or devious, but he fit poorly into our understanding of what an Amish person should be. He was not a bad *man*, in other words, but simply a man who was not good, we thought, at being Amish. He was very outgoing, for one thing, even gregarious, and took a somewhat aggressive personal interest in our community and way of life. Generous with his time, always offering to help in one way or another, often for no payment, always teaching and advising, and more than once he had been the solution to one great crisis or another. In short, "the bad one" was quite good to us. And while there were certainly those suspicious of the interest he took in our lives, and particularly his interest in the period lived *prior to* Unityville, the lives our citizens had left behind them, and while these suspicions occasionally led one or another townsperson to suggest that Brother Abram had questionable intentions and distinctly un-Amish ambitions and would for these reasons be best kept at arm's length, nonetheless, at the end of the day, even the most cautious among us had to acknowledge how greatly we benefited from his particular combination of enthusiasm and expertise. Dubious, there seemed no doubt, but the people of Unityville were beholden to him.

243

Thus when "the bad one" arrived one brisk autumn morning, after the leaves had already turned their fiery colors but before they'd all fallen to the ground, with a television weighing down the back of his buggy, the citizens of Unityville were not sure what to do. It was a light, crisp morning, in my memory it still is, a morning both chilly and bright, with both breath clouds and birdsong, and we watched him ride up toward the church steps as all of us were wandering out. He pulled up and parked and stood on the driver's bench, arms spread wide. He never said where he'd found the television, but he said a great deal else. And if I remember his speech distinctly, with perhaps here and there those slight embellishments that memory inevitably tacks on, this is because it was the largest number of words I'd ever heard spoken by an Amish person, and because it was the first truly memorable thing that ever happened to me.

"Prethren," he began, in his Amish way of speaking, "I haf ridden me all ofer craetion, o'er hill and dale, tru holepots and downwet to gift to you onest this haethen lichtbox. Yay, well nuff know I vhat you'd say! Put, Prother, you say, ve left us long-go the crotch of vorldlitude, what naed us this daemon's fernhoodle? Whereforhowever I say unto you, in naet but gutvill and frien'-veeling, that the low-chance of use in yourn Crustian hands outwroughts the nochance of use in mine own! For tho ve Aemish uset no 'lectrical 'vices, yet you gut Crustians do kip a stiddy 'lectric s'ply, vhich maketh this costly paece of mudren 'lectrical funiture saemwhat fruitfillier in yourn than in mine own kippin! An since I haf bin a gut frien to you, and gut and hand-lendin nibor, I truss you vill receivedeth that vhich I haf ridden me o'er hill and dale, tru holepots and downwet at no small cost an confenience, an kip it vell an grossie saf, that even twould you maketh no use upon it yourn ownselfs, nonelesso twould you saf it up for coompn'y, and"—actually, I will summarize what he said.

In summary, then, what Abram said to the people of Unityville was that he wished his "gift" to be housed there, in our electrically wired town, where he himself might make use of it, regardless of what the rest of us did. He never explained or justified his interest in the television, but pummeled away instead at the question of why we should house it, or rather how we should, in what manner. *This* was the question he had ostensibly brought to us, and he proceeded to offer, as solution, that he would build a special dwelling, at his own expense, and by his own hand, a "gut nibor haus." Set far off in the woods, this "haus" would be near enough to receive electrical current, but far enough to remain out of the town's way. Opened to all, visited by none—what did we say? He stopped short of enumerating the consequences were his proposal to be poorly received.

His speech over, Abram at last lifted the television—an enormous wooden console; truly he was a mountain—placed it upon the ground, and rode off in his buggy, leaving at our feet both the television's fate and, in some unspoken yet clearly understood sense, our own.

For a moment, those who'd warned of Brother Abram's dubious intentions allowed themselves to bask in the self-satisfaction of having their suspicions confirmed; yet their glory was short-lived, and soon they, like the rest, became morose with the moral perplexity before us. How did the necessary good of Abram's labor weigh against the relatively ignorable bad of his television set? What constituted a compromise of our values, versus a Christian respect for values not our own? Does the Bible address directly the question of *proximity*? Of where lines get drawn? Or does the need to draw a line at all mean the battle is already over, that goodness and righteousness have already lost, and that all of us were doomed to some horrific fate, simply for entertaining this topic? The next day Brother Abram returned and, finding the television still among us, smiled warmly, but not too warmly—he did not overperform "warmth"— attempted to lay hands upon shying-away shoulders, then cheerfully took to the woods, scouting locations for his "haus."

This is the point at which I at last enter this story, for among the very few pieces of useful information to be found in my head at that time was an extensive explorative knowledge of the town's surrounding geography, and Abram, who knew the area poorly, or at any rate claimed to, very pleasantly asked me along. Thus began what quickly became a sort of apprenticeship, for after the site was chosen, Abram continued to involve me, throughout the planning, the building—he showed me things, taught me things. He claimed to enjoy my company, although I can't imagine what part of my company he could have meant. Nor can I explain even now why my parents agreed to this arrangement, although I have a few theories: 1) that they felt they had so skillfully raised me that nothing untoward could come of Abram's influence; 2) that they were happy I'd finally found something to occupy me (meaning the acquisition of useful work skills, not the television); 3) that they were simply too busy to bother about it.

Whatever the case, in a very short time Abram had erected, with my help, about a hundred yards from town but surrounded entirely by forest, a two-room "haus" with a large antenna. The outside, being windowless, was a bit forbidding, but the inside included a main room with a small kitchen area and a comfortable sofa and chair, as well as a back room whose purpose was not at all clear to me. At the center of the main room stood the television, always off while I worked there, and which Abram, to my ongoing surprise, never once suggested I might watch. It simply stood there as we worked around it, this wood-and-glass object, the first true "object" of my imagination—it seemed I had an imagination, after all—curious to me both for its exoticism, having come from the world outside, and for what I understood it to do. Part magic, part invention, a box that opened with light and exhaled infinity, through which a fantastic pageant of voices and images beamed into the room, a vision of life through a window from another world.

As construction neared an end, Abram's visits to Unityville became more frequent. Daily, in fact, and never with his Amish brethren, but always alone. He would appear in the morning and work through the day—for food, on various projects—then in the evening retire to his "haus," where I now know, but at the time did not know, or perhaps simply did not bother to acknowledge for myself that I knew, he almost certainly spent his nights. I, at any rate, would see him only during the day, as I continued to work alongside him, and in fact took on an increasingly useful role. For whereas previously I had done mostly lifting and hauling, by now I'd acquired such abilities as to handle more skilled work, which Abram happily relinquished to me, even while failing to take upon himself any of my own menial labor, so that increasingly I found myself doing *all* the work, while Abram sat by, talking about television. Not that I minded! On the contrary, I was always encouraging and prompting him for descriptions of the various programs he'd watched. There was a grown man named "Miltie" and a puppet named "Howdy." There was a dog named "Lassie" and a singer named "Perry." There were things called "game shows" in which people answered questions for money, and there were dance programs and news programs. I tried to imagine them, those living pictures, those fantastical scenarios, but my field of reference lacked acreage, and there was not enough varied material in my head to create for myself a vision even half as stimulating as Abram's descriptions themselves.

By now the reader will have assumed that I eventually made my way to Abram's "haus" to insinuate myself on the sofa there—and of course, yes, I did. But what you may be surprised to learn, as indeed

I was very surprised to find when I arrived late one summer night of my thirteenth year, having squeezed out a back window an hour past my parents' bedtime—the figure I was surprised to find perched upon the couch, beyond Abram's doorway silhouette, her face washed gray in the television's flicker, was Emily, the girl who always tried to get my attention, the one I'd largely ignored. I'd never seen her with Abram, nor even imagined her with him—yet now the sight made such an impression upon me that it would remain in my head forevermore. Before I first laid eyes upon a living screen, I saw the glow of that screen on a human face. There was Emily, whom I barely knew. There was Emily, watching television.

"Emily?" I said.

She looked back, broke away from that television to smile at me. She said: "It's you!"

Meanwhile Abram was turning from one to the other of us, caught in a rather ugly scowl, as if his face had momentarily forgotten it was visible to those around him. Finally he shrugged: "Vell, in you coom."

It seems they had been expecting me for months—Emily explained, much later, that this was what Abram had told her—and had been often disappointed that I continually failed to arrive. Now I was there, however, and the next stage of my life began.

Tuesday was Uncle Miltie with Martha Raye; Thursday, the Lone Ranger; Friday, Rin Tin Tin. Lawrence Welk, whom I never cottoned to, was Saturday at nine, while Lucy, whom everyone loved and whom I loved more than I loved any actual person, was at nine on Monday, later moving to Wednesday at seven thirty. By that time there was *Wagon Train* and *Father Knows Best*. There was *Perry Mason, Dick and the Duchess*, and *Gunsmoke*. Next there was the Beaver—how I loved the Beaver! There was Zorro and Pat Boone. When I think about them chronologically, one thing I've noticed about those early years of my television viewing is that the programs seemed to mature in subject matter at more or less the same time I did, from childish pie-in-the-face variety programs to the antics of bowl-cut young men to the adolescent romance of Western adventures. The culmination of this trajectory was a season sometime in the late fifties that saw an unbelievable concentration of *Bonanza, The Rebel, Lawman, The Alaskans, Maverick,* and *The Life and Legend of Wyatt Earp*, with the Beaver—whose brother, Wally, was so close to my age that I was able to imagine him aging right alongside me—having moved by then to eight thirty Saturday from his previous Thursday spot. One tends to think of watching television as a solitary activity, if not downright isolating, the opposite of wholesome social interaction. In reality, though, television is often the very site of such interaction, connecting direly inhibited humans across impossible social voids. And when you consider the sort of person *I* was, or rather the nonperson I just barely personified, you can see why my residence on Abram's sofa represented a great upward turn in my development as a social being.

It was not that Abram and Emily and I discussed what we watched or held other conversations of any length or depth. Rarely was that the case, and never to compelling result. In fact, if either Emily or I presumed to talk during a program, Abram was quick to shush it away. No, what we shared, instead, was a time and a place and participation in an unsanctioned activity. Passive activity, it's true, but we shared it. And not for a night or a week or a month or even a year, but for the several years that we met this way, on our regularly scheduled evenings. And this was how I came to have what might properly be called a life. A life with people and a life with television. A life with people and television.

Here is perhaps the moment for a logistical note: The reader might be surprised to learn that signal reception in Unityville was quite strong, even in those early years. This was due to the coincidence that Williamsport, where my father worked, housed the regional television-relay antenna serving central Pennsylvania and large parts of New York. I know this because in the 1970s, the entirety of which I spent entombed in a trailer home some thirty miles down Route 11, doing little but watching television surrounded by a truly horrifying number of cats—during those years, that is, all of the programs began or ended with a short station announcement, "You are watching" whatever station it was, followed by "with Williamsport translator." This announcement was repeated four times per hour, per some bureaucratic broadcasting regulation, and served as a chilling and constant reminder of my past, of the Sisyphean circumstances that had led to that torturous present, and of the incredibly poor prospects my future at that time seemed to hold.

We now come to the spring of 1960. It was the year CBS's Sunday lineup ran *Lassie*, *Dennis the Menace*, *The Ed Sullivan Show*, *General Electric Theater*, *The Jack Benny Program*, *Candid Camera*, and *What's My Line*, and the year my fate took its next definitive turn. I was eighteen, was now well into my life with television, and had little sense of, much less ambition for, my life beyond—when one night Emily and I arrived to find that Abram was gone. It was a vibrant, fresh-scented evening, the sort that fortifies the blood in the exhilaration of springtime thaw. I'd met Emily along the path to the "haus" and we'd been talking a bit about the programs for that evening—in fact, we'd been speaking more and more lately, not just about television but other topics as well, and not just along the nighttime path but during chance meetings throughout the day, or when Emily, not at all by chance, would stop by my workplace to chat, until Abram would grumblingly remind us all of the work that needed to be done. But there was a pleasantness there, is all I mean to say, and it was a lovely, spirited evening, and so we were quite unprepared, emotionally, to arrive and find Abram gone. Of course, each of us had been sick or otherwise absent on various occasions over the years, but this was something else. He was gone. The television was on, as was usual when we arrived, yet set atop the console were several pieces of yellowish paper that turned out to be a rather long note.

I apologize in advance for its wordiness, but as it has always been an important document for me, I include the entirety of this letter below.

Yungins,
Many a nite-an-day haf I pourt myself a hedful of thinkins visavis this telefussin, and vhy gut Crustian maems an daeds get acheybelly and knickertwist ofer a thing so entratainin an gut-joyable an plessur-makin an faen. I doubtnot you haf vundered after such yourselfs. Yay, tis tru that vatchin you much telefussin can bit-tarnish normalif an make normaday appaer saemwhat dullish by the counterast. I disputeth no part nor paece a this claem. Putanyet, to unterstant full this awe-filt Gott-lik power telefussin holdeth to sow into souls many insatsfaxons visavis normaday lif, we naed us fursht consitereth how a mudren peeples mostdays are lift. An this is vhy I haf preparet me this note of thinkins my own for yourn considerin.
In truth, the vorld as we lif it is mostpart filler, like a Viener schnitzel, scrappl, or an uttervise low-graed vurst. This VURST VORLD containeth mostly scraps an feddyparts, with oft whol yaers pasht tween meat-filt goins-on. Nay, yout not belif yourselfs to see it, put even hi-aventuring pipples out in this mudren vorld knoweth ownly the teenymost chunk of tru liffiness, happed in there amongst the scrappl fat of the eferdays. The mudren vorld is just this and thaers no uttervise posbil.

Now, if telefussin shown naet but the fanciedest mudren lifs put *shown the full bits* of them, there then twould be naet for Crustian maems and daeds to spaek boo ofer. Off unto that vorld a smartish yoongin could set and could maek that of themselfs, could maek of themselfs that, or much alik it. Put the awe-filt Gott-lik power of telefussin lieth naet in the parts it showeteth, put ruther in the parts it lefteth off.

Spaken plaen, telefussin taketh away lifs dullish parts, the scraps and feddyparts, and maketh any lif atall saem intrustin. Yay, vere it posbil to lif a telefussin lif, could you be any soul atall an twould not matter, insomuchus how intrustin yout be. Vere it possbil to lif a telefussin lif, all yourn moments twould be momentious, all yourn thinkin twould be perfown, all yourn chooses twould be of grossie an eferlastin import. Nay, put none can lif a telefussin lif, and the raeson isht a thing I stall myself from tellin. Long haf I stallt an kippeth me from discusin vith you this matter heretofor. Put now I do feel me in my hart and hed that you haf grewn old nuff vhere you isht bitter off hearin than not hearin it.

Isht Gott. Yay, I spake it plaen. For Gott writ the Book of Lif, an Gott writeth it still, an He doth naet removeth from out His Vorks noneparts vhatsoefer, naet the feddy nor the meat-filt parts naether, nay, nor doth He stand for uttersome to removeth such parts, as do chestion the purfiction of His Vorks. Putanyet the shows you vatcheth on the telefussin, by *naet* showin the full bits, do *naet* gift full Grandur to Gott's Vurks, His VURST VURLD in all its allness, put ruther moldeth and shapeth mostdays lif to fit pipple's self-maginin. It craeteth from tru lif meer idols of self-delisation. It melteth down the mettle of Gott's VURST VORLD an maketh instet a goltin calf to vurship! Vhich isht HERESY plaen simpl. Nor naet doth it matter if the telefussin pergram be tru or falsht. It mattereth only that ve *selectet* from His Vurks. Ve stareth us in the mouth Gott's Gift Hass. Biggers tho we be, we Choost!

Such isht the sin foranvhich ve are punsht with impetual insatsfaxons—yet asto the faerness of it, I do atimes vunder. If Gott Himself did removeth from out His Vorks some bits of the feddy, mudren lif twould be a faer bit more entratainin, naet to say gut-joyable and plessur-makin and faen.

Yoongins, the raeson I haf writ me this note of thinkins my own for yourn considernin isht that you are now grewn an changt much, and our cowch hasht becum alast overcrowtert. Tis time I ventur into this VURST VURLD in serch me of a bitter. Much as any mudren man, I feel insatsfaxon visavis my lot, yet I knoweth too a truth: that there isht naet so much choosin in this vurld as He vould haf you belif. Theretofor, if you can lif in Gotts VURST VORLD and be

gut-happy here, vhy, you most surly shoult. They naem that "graes," and pipple can only haft it long as they know naet vhat it is. Oncet you know, then try as you vould, normaday lif vill forefermorafter insatsfie, and youll forefermorafter prifer yourself the telefussin sort. Mibbe I just ruint it for you by tellin.
    Vell, gut luk!
    Abram

In the coming years, I would read this letter many times, on many a doubt-stricken evening. On this particular evening, however, in the understandable intensity of having a great surprise suddenly thrust upon me, I failed to take in much of Abram's letter at all. I was pre-occupied instead with the sheer fact of it, the shock of the sudden absence that had occasioned it, and also with something else, quite unrelated—an even more pressing development, which I'll now do my best to explain.

We were sitting on the sofa holding the letter, sitting in our normal spots but without Abram's body between us, and Emily had turned off the television, our attentions more occupied, for once, with the reality at hand. As the smoke of the situation began to clear, how-ever, and as we ourselves settled, she now got up and switched the set back on. I did not make much of this gesture, assuming she meant simply not to miss any more of our program, or at most to divert us from the various worries we'd been discussing. Only later did I realize there was more to the gesture; a diversion, yes, but not from worries. Rather, it was her effort at dissipating the uncomfortable emotional situation that was already developing, at that point, in the room. A shift in the air, the social dynamic. For it was not simply Abram's ab-sence that hung heavily in the air that day; it was also the newfound presence of our aloneness together, a before-then-unheeded tension between Emily and me, which I tried to attribute, as we settled into the program, to Abram's absence, the shock of it. Impossible to dis-cuss or outwardly acknowledge—yet this tension continued to grow stronger, even as the television's characters paraded past. It swelled in the space where Abram would have been sitting, and was soon so oppressive that I began to feel nauseated by it, as if by the onset of a sudden inexplicable illness. No longer able to follow the program, utterly oblivious to the television's images and sounds even as my brain passively received them, I watched my body shiver as if cold, my pulse elevate, I sensed the onset of a vomit deep down and would have hastily excused myself to the woods had Emily's body not appeared to me, in that moment, to be suffering the same condition. Eyes met, and rather than vomit, we gave ourselves over to a wave of passion that carried us far out to sea, to a place we had never gone, had barely imagined, and from which there was—one instantly knows—no returning. It was a churning, disorienting wave that twisted our bodies into brilliant, reckless contortions, a calamitous journey outside of time and bereft of perspective, and when at last it subsided, I felt as if ages had passed. We found ourselves floating, still clinging to one another, surrounded in all directions by a new placidity, a transcendental calm, with a great, dark emptiness beneath us, a thrilling and terrifying depth, and with the muffled voices of our favorite television characters just barely reaching out to us from some distant, long-forgotten shore. It was my first experience of being inside of life, of attending life's essential performance not as spectator but as fully engaged participant. I knew then that my childhood was over, although I hadn't the slightest idea what came next.

Nine months later, when Samuel Jr. was born and when my dear Emily died giving birth to him, I experienced again this extraordinary feeling, not a "bad" or "good" feeling but a powerful, participatory one. After that, I felt it quite regularly, in the daily up and down surges of life with my son, until the day when I lost it forever, which we are getting to soon enough.

It will seem all too befitting Unityville's biblical pretensions that the first major event of my adulthood was banishment. In fact, it was a rather mild banishment, as banishments go. Nor was it Emily's pregnancy that earned us this sentence—that was reconciled with a quick wedding that we both agreed to happily enough. But it was the inevitable revelation of our longtime clandestine affair with the television that led several in the town to suggest that Unityville might not be the ideal location to start our new life together. There is a generous interpretation to this suggestion and a less generous one, but I will not bother with either, since other circumstances made the question largely moot. There was a child on the way, after all, a child who was heartily welcomed by Emily's parents, perhaps slightly less by my own, a tiny human still innocent of the world and deserving every sort of stability and care. And so, to balance these various considerations, it was decided that Emily and I would move together into the now-abandoned "haus," whose location would once more prove providential, being near enough for grandparents but far enough for lives of our own.

Thus began the most pleasant, carefree months of my life, spending

252

mornings and evenings with Emily and during the day providing semiskilled handiwork for the town, where Abram's sudden departure had left more than enough opportunities for his "apprentice" to regain (or more likely gain in the first place) the gratitude and approval of the citizenry. And outside of town, Emily and I were left to grow our relationship in whatever manner made sense to us, whether that meant watching television or discussing television or, as was increasingly the case, spending hardly any time at all with television, and instead taking walks, and making love, and holding long conversations about our future, the seemingly wide-open possibilities of our new life together.

And when my son was born, and was placed naked and tiny onto my trembling chest, and when, holding my son, I watched my wife watch us both, even as she herself bled out onto the table, and when I saw her face fill with horror at what I assumed was the same thought I was having, that she would die, that she would not be around for him, that she would not be around for me, that we would be abandoned and this beautiful child would be deprived of the one thing no child should ever be deprived of, his lovely mother, his mother who loved him more already in that instant than most people are loved in a lifetime, and when she spoke no words but only watched us until the pain was too great and she succumbed—in that moment I was filled with the pure light of life. I personally contained more life, in that moment, than any person should ever be asked to.

Emily, my wife, I wish we had had more time. Who knows what would have happened, the people we might have become. I wish everything had had more time. I am writing this for Samuel, our son, but also for you, of course, in a way. I mean to say that there is the bond of husband and wife, and the bond of parent and child, but there is also a bond between parents, the unspoken bond that says that everything you do for your child you also do for each other, that all the love you give to your child you also give to each other. And I think it also says that anything you *would have* done, any love you *would have* given, that too is for each other.

And then we were alone, my son and me. Emily was gone, she'd been taken from us, and I was instantly filled with the most powerful need to protect him. I whose life had never known anything like "ambition" or "direction" was suddenly more charged with purpose than I would ever have thought possible. Where before I had let whole years slip unheeded through my fingers, now I would seize the day so firmly I'd need to take care not to choke it. This was life, this child in my arms. I would never leave his side, never fail in my attention to him. So great was my protective impulse, in fact, that for the first few days I would not even let his grandparents near. I carried him with me at all moments, slept with him on my chest, although in truth I did not sleep for fear I might roll over and harm him. But I was determined we would live this way, two hermits in isolation even from that isolated town, my love lording over us to the end of our days.

Understand that if I take pains to emphasize the severity of my love, its unhealthy possessive nature, my purpose in doing so is not to glorify it, nor to extract pity for the real duress I was clearly suffering. Rather, I underscore my emotion and conviction during this time so that you might comprehend how deeply perplexed I felt, not many days later, when anxiousness and boredom reentered me.

To understand what I am about to describe, you must accept that a human being is a vessel with many compartments. One's heart never holds just a single feeling, no matter how strongly that feeling is felt. I had learned this lesson at the moment of my son's birth and my wife's death, yet in the days and weeks that followed, I discovered that in fact my body could maintain over very long periods the most profound contradictions, watching and loving this beautiful child, unable to imagine a more perfect being or a place I would rather be, and at the same time exasperated by his cries, overwhelmed by his constant care, and wondering, with increasing frequency, how I might manage to take a break from him. At such times I began bringing Samuel to his grandparents (Emily's parents), who were extremely understanding if not outright joyful to see what they assumed was the natural fading of my (perfectly understandable, they said) irrational possessiveness and the burgeoning of a healthier, more responsible, more sharing sort of fatherly love. For my part, I allowed them to hold on to this hopeful interpretation of my mental state, although I knew it to be false. I knew that my love had not been tempered either in type or degree; it still raged in my heart with all its surety and power; it simply contended, now, with this other force—I thought of it as fatigue rather than laziness—a force that did not lessen my love but simply interfered with and frustrated it. Every time I left Samuel's side, no matter for what duration, I would swoon with guilt at the inconsistency of my actions, the inconstancy of my resolve. But while relinquishing neither my passion nor my guilt, I would explain to myself—I thought of it as being reasonable rather than making excuses—that it was a matter of exhaustion. My brain could only provide so much attention at one time, I told myself. I could sustain that level of engagement for only so long, and the speed with which I found myself going from profound immersive joy to direly needing a recess was in reality a testament to the profundity of the joy, since the more profound the joy, the faster it would consume my mental resources, as a more intense flame burns more quickly through its wick. Mine was not a peculiar combination of laziness and obsession, I told myself; rather I was too loving, my emotions too raw and burdening. And I would need to learn, for the sake of my son, to temper this affection, to parcel it out, so that I would not be so often forced to take a break from it.

Yet I was not able to temper my affection (the fatal flaw of a too-loving father, I told myself, although I'm afraid this was as much a self-compliment as a criticism), and as my need for distraction and "downtime" increased, along with the explosiveness of my caring, I found myself edging back toward the television.

The television, which Emily and I had been slowly growing away from. The television, which in fact had been pushed back into a corner months earlier to clear a play space for Samuel, and at one point had even had a tablecloth draped over it. The television, which now made its way back to the middle of the room, where it shared Samuel's space in such a way that I could watch both simultaneously. It demanded my attention just as my son did, but unlike my son, it demanded precisely nothing else. No emotion, no real consideration, no responsibility whatsoever. It was an escape from life, from my son, from everything that mattered. And the more I watched, the more I felt compelled to watch, swooning all the while with self-loathing.

How had I become this way? I sometimes wondered. Actually I wondered this all the time. Had television done this to me? Had it sewn into my soul a restlessness so pervasive that even the most profound wonders of real life were to be ruined by it? I thought often of Abram's letter, and reread it many times. When I looked at myself now, I saw a man who expected every instant of his life to be compelling, who, when faced with a moment that was not immediately compelling, felt desperate to replace his own life with someone else's, with the life of some character on television.

As Samuel grew, my weakness only worsened, and when he began to walk, and talk, and run, the situation got quite out of hand. I would spend an entire afternoon playing with my son, and would to the outside observer appear to be a generous and loving father, attentive

255

to my son's wants and needs. Yet at the end of the day, I would realize, with something like shock, that I had not *enjoyed* a moment of
it (well, moments, of course), but had spent the entire time counting
down the minutes until it was over, until I could escape again to the
thoughtless engagement of my television. As if my son were some
horrible torture I was being subjected to rather than the joy of my life
and the only living thing I loved! To be fair, the games he came up
with were extremely boring (the game "neighbor" in particular was
torturously dull, with "school" and "family" tied for a very close
second); yet when you consider that the very sight of this child was
enough to fill me with a sense of euphoria (and yes, I would often
flash with euphoria throughout these incredibly boring days of playing, when I looked into that handsome little face and saw there
the embodiment of beauty and wonder, and it would be extremely
strange, this mixture of boredom and euphoria, this simultaneous
living in the moment and wanting only to escape it)—all of this was,
I've said it already but I have no other word for it, exhausting.

My love was exhausting; my boredom, presumably caused by my
exhaustion, was exhausting; my exhaustion was boring and guilt inspiring, yet never did this accumulation of frustrated feeling lessen
any part of the profound enormity of my love.

I think I have now sufficiently described the peculiar circumstances of my early existence on this planet so that we may at last
proceed to that period's defining event, the moment I have been both
hurrying toward and steering away from since first setting words to
these pages.

It was 1965. It was winter. It was just a few days before his fourth
birthday.

I could probably list for you the complete programming from each
night of the week for that season, but the night that will forever be
scheduled to air on the Guilt-and-Despair channel of my conscience
is Monday's mixed-bag lineup of local news, *To Tell the Truth*,
I've Got a Secret, *I Love Lucy*, *The Andy Griffith Show*, *Hazel*,
and *The Steve Lawrence Show*, although I never got past Mayberry
that night, for halfway through the 9:00 p.m. slot is when tragedy
struck.

My son was, as usual, not watching with me. For some reason, he
hated television. He always had—I'd never been able to convince
him to watch even the kiddie programs. This night I'd put him to bed,
or at least I'd taken him to the bedroom an hour earlier and assumed
he was either sleeping, now, or else playing, but quiet in either case.

On *Andy Griffith*, the episode was about television, of all things, although I have never thought of that as anything other than an odd coincidence. In fact, the greater coincidence might be all the guns. After a national law-enforcement magazine publishes a profile of Andy titled "The Sheriff without a Gun," a group of television producers come to Mayberry saying they'd like to create a program based on his life. There is a lot of talk about guns, the virtues of having or not having them, and I remember sitting there wondering whether anyone in Unityville kept a gun, since I was sure I'd never seen one. In fact, I had never set eyes on a real gun in my life, only guns on television, where there were an awful lot of them. In the show, the "producers" turned out to be con men hoping to rob the local bank by staging a "robbery scene," but I had not reached the point in the episode where Andy foils their plot (one assumes Andy ultimately foiled their plot) when I heard an unfamiliar voice shouting out in the woods, "Samuel Johnson! Samuel Johnson!" and, startled out of my television daze, rushed out to see what it was.

No parent could be prepared for the sight that met me. If any parent could have been prepared for it, it would've been me, who over the years had created in my mind every sort of terrifying paranoid scenario that could possibly befall my child. But those were mere nightmares, tricks of the parental imagination, and when reality struck, they'd not prepared me in the least.

Here was my son, out in the cold night wearing only his pajamas. (I later wondered how he'd left the house without my notice. Was I truly that oblivious? And how might things have gone differently if I'd been more attentive? If I'd not favored the television, that night, to the company of my own son?) Here was Samuel Jr., though, being physically restrained by a lunatic, a crazed long-haired man with my boy in one hand and an actual gun held over his head with the other. There was no time for thinking, there was not even a "me" to think, for nothing existed, now, except this man and the two things he was holding: All of life in one hand, and in the other, nothing but death. The one I lunged for was the gun, and there was a struggle, and the sound of it going off. Then there was more struggle, and noises in the dark, and then even greater darkness, and suddenly my son was standing next to me screaming as I looked down upon—myself! There I lay, shot through the chest, my eyes wide, my body quite obviously dead. What was happening? Was my death happening? Could it be? Was my son, whom I tried but failed to reach out to, for I no longer had control of my movements—was it possible that my beautiful, motherless son was now without a father as well? How had this happened? How had I failed him? What could I do? Until at last my soul turned and flew away from there—I could not even look back at him—and I was lost forever to despair.

What happened next happened quickly, and in the midst of my shock and emotional confusion, I took for granted that everything passing before my eyes was part of the standard procedure for a soul departing this world. I failed to wonder, for example, as I sailed over the forest floor, why my flight was horizontal rather than vertical, or why I seemed to be headed into town, rather than in a more heavenly direction. Not until later did I recall a noise like hyperventilating, or notice that the voice in my mind shouting "Samuel Johnson!" did not actually sound like my own. Even when I tripped and fell on the path, even then I was in no state to ponder why a soul would trip and fall, and only when that same soul fumbled with its keys to start a rusty truck parked by the trailhead was I at last struck by the odd turns my path to the afterlife was taking. In fact, the thought that finally broke through to me was simply that I did not know how to drive. "Samuel Johnson!" cried the voice meanwhile, and I noticed then how strange it was, a voice unlike my own, yet familiar. And the hands, the grungy hands scrambling, the heavy, wheezy breathing, the truck's unmuffled revving that brought lights on in the houses and *Thank goodness*, I thought, they will see that something's happened, they will check on Samuel, he will not be alone. . . . And when the truck then plunged into darkness, it was not the darkness of death, but a darkness with headlights, unless death also had headlights, perhaps it did, how would I know, who'd never before died, who'd barely even lived, and *Oh God*, I thought, *I'm dead. . . .* "Samuel Johnson!" cried the voice, while the night's black vacuum sucked me ever deeper in the only direction that road traveled—away—my soul ferried ever farther from my son, until at last the terrible Charonic truck pulled out onto a much larger road, a highway bright with moonlight, then south—away—the moonlight flittering, on my left, off the great, wide river, already farther than I'd ever been from home, now farther and farther still. . . . Until at some point my soul's grubby hand grabbed and twisted the rearview mirror and I found myself facing not my own ghostly visage but rather the very much living visage of my lunatic killer, the man who'd orphaned my boy. . . . "Samuel Johnson!" cried my mind's voice, and in that moment the truck veered, flew through the left-side guardrail off a cliff, and down into the moon-shimmering waters below. Then blackness, and blackness, and finally silence and stop.

When I next "came to," I was looking down upon the black earth from far above, at the tiny dots of light that mark the larger roads and scattered houses of rural Pennsylvania at night, and at the blacker black of the Susquehanna cutting south over the land. My movement was gentle, like oozing. There were no sounds but a comforting hum, no feeling but stillness and peace. I had just died again, it occurred to me, two deaths in quick succession, which was bewildering, yes, but this time it seemed to have stuck. And as I floated over the sleeping planet, trying to pinpoint which patch of forested darkness might contain my son, I told myself that things would be OK for him, after all, that his grandparents would care for him, and that the lunatic, whoever he'd been and whatever he'd wanted, was now gone. Samuel would be safe, I thought, with a good life, a warm and loving home. He would not be "better off"—how could my boy be "better off" without his father?—but there was nothing to be done about that now. His future was out of my hands. . . . Yet no sooner had I begun to make peace with my fate than my entire field of vision was once more interrupted, my soul suddenly turned, tilted, and I saw that I was not floating heavenward at all, but rather was sitting in a long, dark compartment surrounded by seats and sleeping bodies. I'd not departed this mortal coil, but had simply been looking down out the window of what I now recognized—having seen them on television and as specks of metal overhead—as a commercial airplane in flight, speeding me away from my son with near-sonic velocity. I'd not made peace with my fate; I was, if anything, more lost than ever.

Alone there in the darkness, with no sound but the plane's low rumble and the soft snores and rustling about the cabin, I eventually forced myself to calm down. So abruptly had I been yanked from life to death, then from one death to another, then from what I believed was a heavenly trajectory back to this mundane sphere, that I felt wholly overwhelmed. Why was I here? What happens next? A man's balding head rested inches from my shoulder, yet I have never felt so alone. I told myself this was clearly a dream, and I should simply wait patiently to wake up from it. But as my own eyelids soon closed, and remained closed, and were quickly joined by a slower, heavier breathing that seemed also to belong to me . . . and since, despite my body's having apparently fallen asleep, my mind remained perfectly awake, there in the darkness, with nothing to see or to do . . . and since I remained in this wakeful state for what felt like days and was in reality perhaps two or three hours, I eventually did begin to take stock of my situation.

Upon death—I surmised for myself—my soul had flown into the killer's body, and upon *its* death, I'd flown again, presumably into the body closest by. That body, this one, belonged to someone seated in an airplane flying overhead—and here I was. As to my condition, I could see and could hear, but not, as far as I could tell, taste, smell, or touch. Was I a ghost? If so, I seemed unlikely to haunt anyone, having neither a voice of my own nor any other corporeal presence. Unseen, unheeded, that appeared to be the state of things. Trapped, in fact, in the darkness of another person's head, a person being carried in a metal cylinder through the emptiness of night, night itself being nothing but the default state of a planet floating meaninglessly through space—and I began to suffer something like vertigo, my consciousness in danger of spiraling into pure chaos, when fortunately my eyes again opened, and my body rose from its seat, squeezed past my sleeping neighbor, and made its way by the tiny floor lights—everything about this environment was entirely new to me, bear in mind—to a cramped metal closet that was apparently the bathroom.

My first look at the face of the human being I was trapped inside— there, in the bathroom mirror—was a little surprising, and caused my mind's eye a hard blink, because the young man looked so much like me, my living self. He had finer features and was better groomed, but in height and weight, skin tone and hair color, he might easily have been my twin. As he proceeded to use the toilet, I saw that his penis was larger than mine, and his waist slimmer—and of course in time I became aware of so many differences in his behavior and physique that I no longer saw any resemblance at all—but for a moment I could not escape the déjà vu–like feeling that I had somehow been trapped inside myself.

That turned out to be purely coincidence, I later decided, but at the time this déjà vu feeling fueled my imagination (although clearly reality had already out-imagined me by a considerable margin, and I was merely catching up), and I began to consider that there might be a purposeful Design at work. Perhaps the events transpiring were not random, I thought, but rather shaped by Reason, or by particular reasons, by an intention of some sort.

A punishment from God—it must be, what else?—a punishment for my negligence toward Samuel, or for having sex out of wedlock, or for watching too much television, one or all three, since these were the only sins I'd committed that seemed at all worthy of God's attention. And yes, they were serious sins, or seemed so at the time, and deserving of punishment, perhaps even a punishment like this— were it not for my son. For although some time earlier, while floating over the earth, I had told myself Samuel would be safe without me, that was only because I'd assumed I would be gone. Whereas now that my fate had proven otherwise, I was again convinced that he desperately needed me, if only because I was still here for him to need. To remain in this world, to continue to exist on the same mortal coil as my boy and yet have no means of protecting him—the situation struck me as indefensibly sadistic. And I determined in that moment that I would never accept this fate, but would do everything in my power for as long as it took to return to him.

And why couldn't I return to him? I went on, my body by now back in its seat and sleeping, so that I was once again speaking to my-self in the dark. Was the world so large (at that time I did not actually know how large the world was) that fortune would not eventually land me back with him? True, this airplane was taking me away, but airplanes, I knew, also return, and the same people who take them in one direction tend to take them back in the other. Surely, I thought, I will soon be returning to my son with as much haste as I now speed away?

For the remainder of the flight I went on this way, and by the time the pilot came on the loudspeaker to announce the plane's descent, I had fully deluded myself with hope for a swift and sympathetic con-clusion to these profoundly unsettling events. The cabin lights had come on, and now my body awoke, as did the other bodies around it. The plane then landed, followed by a long period of taxiing around the runway, during which my neighbor, the one who had been sleep-ing by my head, spoke to me as if we were already familiar, as if per-haps we had spoken at the start of the flight as well. Thus I learned that his name was Burt ("by the way") and my name—my body's name—was Christopher. I learned that he had come to California (this was how I learned we were in California) to join his wife and daughters, who'd moved here some months earlier while he looked for a job. I learned many other things about Burt, who spoke contin-uously throughout what ended up being an incredibly long tour of the tarmac, until at last Christopher was asked what brought him to California, and the voice that was not mine said: "Oh, I . . . That's a very long story. I was involved in . . . Actually, it doesn't matter. Only that my parents, for various reasons . . . It seemed prudent that . . .

Martin Riker

You see, they offered to send me, out of the 'kindness of their hearts,' so to speak . . . or perhaps, to be fair, out of the actual kindness of their actual hearts . . . This morning, that is, I'm to set off on a yearlong cruise. To 'see the world,' they said . . . I told them I've no intention of seeing any such thing, ha ha . . . At any rate, there you have it."

I'd been anxious to learn about this young man's plans and what they augured for my swift return to Samuel, but at the words "yearlong cruise" and "see the world," my mind's heart collapsed. I spent what remained of the journey—from the tarmac through the airport, from the airport to the ship—in a kind of hate-filled daze. The situation was too ripe for mere coincidence, of course, and it struck me that Fate, if not God, was in fact viciously ironic. If there was Design, clearly its intentions were set against me, and rather than help me return to my son, it was steering me as far away as possible. Whatever was to be done, therefore, I would need to find a way to do it myself. That this ended up being insurmountably difficult, but not technically impossible, is the story of my exile, and of my eventual return.

The Gujjar at the River
Wil Weitzel

> The night of destiny is better than a thousand
> months.
>
> —Qur'an, Surah 97 (Al-Qadr)

PELAL WAS A GUJJAR, a kind of Gypsy, a nomadic seasonal herder who did not settle in a single place or have holdings beyond cattle and goats, oxen used in winter for heavy portage or as investments to be mated and sold, and donkeys for lighter burdens. She had silken dark hair and knew animals, could touch them and soothe them. Her body appeared long and mobile beneath thin robes of wool and her quiet was stirring, less than silent. When she ran, a whir occupied her gaze.

"Run with me, Pelal," Khalid said to her now, in the midst of her second winter marooned in his house, and Pelal, who seemed to love to run, ran out with him into the snow. This was something that Khalid's mother frowned upon but still allowed. Though Khalid, at sixteen, was no longer young enough for such outings, as long as they stayed in the village they were permitted to stretch their legs and he to accompany her.

Pelal had come to the family as recompense and lived far from her own people. Her father had killed Khalid's cousin when the two had feuded in the highlands. Rarely did it come to violence in such cases. Yet since goats and cattle grew fat in high summer pastures and sustained families in the valleys below over long winters, parcels greened to emerald by glacial melts were prized within the steep watershed south of the spine of peaks thrust upward toward Shandur.

Though Pelal's father fairly won the bidding for the acreage at the auction in Mingora, Khalid's cousin, Abbas, who had leased the parcel for many summers running, stole three goats from him to counter what he perceived as disruptive greed. Pelal, out herding in a ravine far above their camp, witnessed the theft. She told her father, who, along with his dogs, pursued Abbas through the night across the Jan Shai Plain. He found and slew him in self-defense when Abbas shot forth first with his mouth and then with an old hunting rifle he carried more for show than for use, as it hadn't felled a markhor or an urial ram in years. Pelal's father buried the corpse on rare flat ground above pine steeps dropping toward a stream and was silent.

But his silence spread. Shepherds and cheese makers, talking as they churned in mountain pastures where Pelal's family was herding goats, spoke of the slaying and wind took reports to the south into the lower Desan Valley, to the villages perched on the precipitous slopes of the river, and at last to the bazaar in Kalam. In the end, Pelal, walking behind her tall, silent father, came by the path along the river to Khalid's family with eight she-goats, five more than were stolen, to betoken the fingered hand of a man who'd struck another, and there was no further blood.

Now it was late January. The days were short and burned with frost and the smoke from chir pine and spruce fires. All through that autumn, Khalid had climbed above the steep western ridge into the upper Desan Valley and collected felled fir and spruce boughs. On occasion, wind had taken the boughs and sent them crashing. At other times, though the government forbade it, he or his father cut the trees at their bases, walking around the boles before they began, and Khalid would drag the slash and heavy branches down the slopes.

Pelal, because she was a girl, did not normally join him on these ascents. But that autumn, as his father was often ill, and because Khalid had long since grown heavy enough in the shoulders to wield an axe but still needed help with haulage, she had occasionally climbed with him. Once, beneath fir branches, well above the cliffs overlooking the village, he'd thrown her down while they were jesting with each other, as Pelal was taller than most girls of his village and she was lithe, hard to lay hands on for long. Just for a moment she hadn't defended herself when he fell upon her with his full weight to roll her and rough her, to make her tumble. She'd paused and in a kind of startled awareness his body had moved wrong, come toward her.

Khalid was lagging behind all of it, unsure. Yet his body had known. Pelal, he'd been thinking through the length of that autumn grown steadily to winter, had paused beneath him like a furred cat, a snow leopard, an animal that held a taut stillness in its limbs. Ever since the snows had come, as they were cooped up inside, he yearned more than ever to reach forward and touch, to return to that moment so he might close her in a privacy he'd never sought before.

It was shameful, he knew, to see in one's sister anything beyond what deserved protection until the day of her wedding, for the sake of one's own honor in addition to hers. Even so, Khalid looked upon this girl differently. How differently he didn't know. In winter, when families huddled together in their homes made of the spruce forest above them and sank into knowledge they could only reach in silence, such things slowed down long enough to become puzzles and then, in a belated sense, threatened to grow into action.

Ordinarily, as she was fourteen years old, Pelal would have been assimilated immediately into the family as a bride. Yet Khalid was young, unmarried, and Pashtun from a landowning class and would be expected to take a Gujjar bride only as a second or third wife. Moreover, he had no brothers and two of his uncles were already dead, the third deeply lamed by a truck in the Madyan bazaar. As Khalid's father, the sole male eligible for an additional marriage, was himself unwell, with malaria dating back to his stint in the employ of the government, building roads north of Karachi during the 2010 monsoon, he had opted to take Pelal as a daughter to work in his household and to bring him, in time, a bride price.

Now Khalid ran with her in what was nearly twilight away from the road where they were supposed to remain and, at his bidding, toward buried terraces of potato and buckwheat fields. He was always surprised that she followed him toward these places, that she never questioned his direction, his motives. Covered with snow, these fields were ponds of fullness where you could step beyond yourself, suddenly, into the midst of great depth. Here was unevenness in the growing darkness, and chance falls, and the need to help one another if snowbanks, particularly after a fresh storm, formed giant catchments. Here too were stone walls that divided fields and, in July and August, held apricots picked to dry in the sun. But now these walls were hidden step-offs. Now, Khalid could imagine, you might bring aid, in all earnestness, when someone had tumbled. And then fall in on that someone into a deep body cave of snow.

Pelal soon passed him and ran ahead but she did not tumble. She was an expert runner. She could run in all seasons. She was not only tall but terribly thin and swift, a wisp, and her waist grew still when she ran, unlike the other girls, whose thicker middles swirled in their *shalwars* as they moved, water in high tin canisters sloshing on their shoulders. Khalid had invited her to run—rather than walk, which he feared suggested to others a controlled intimacy that lurked near courtship—for almost a month now, and only once had

265

she demurred, holding her belly after eating rotten winter-sown wheat the family had stored, wrapped in thatch and plastic sheets, for nearly a year.

"You're running like an ibex," he called, his voice hushed. Ever since his desire had slunk down out of the mountains and dropped into the village and climbed inside him, he feared everyone, Pelal most of all, then his family, and lastly the villagers of Jalban, which was a small hamlet perched among terraced fields on the sloping western shore of the Swat River that ran turquoise and wild through the Kalam bazaar.

They rested in snowbanks beneath apricot trees nearly covered in drifts, the trees planted along walls now submerged. Some of the villagers purchased poplar in the valleys to the south, where it grew abundantly and quickly, and stacked it here in sheds along the walls. Khalid and Pelal at other times crouched on the roofs of these sheds when the snow was high and watched the light striking the western aspect of giant Falaksair, the mountain across the valley that began an eastward spur of the Hindu Raj and loomed above Kalam. But today they swung themselves into the banks beneath the trees and made chairs by curving their backs and pressing until the snow was firm and stiff.

More and more, the two of them came to such moments. Running led to sitting, never far apart and out of view, with Khalid looking brazenly over at Pelal and Pelal gazing off in the distance toward the river.

"God willing, I'll be taking you with me in the spring," he said to her softly. It wrenched his courage to blurt out such a thing to her. All in a tight bundle.

"Taking me where?"

"Down to Mingora. And Mardan. Then straight for Islamabad, past Lahore. If God wills it, even to Karachi."

"My father will be in Mardan in the spring," she mused, as though to this girl far from her people such movement hardly mattered, or she'd scarcely heard his words.

Before the Pakistani army came through Mingora in March of 2009, the Swat Valley had largely emptied ahead of the offensive, with Kohistani villagers and Gujjar herders alike descending the long, snaking route from the Malakand Pass and turning south to find refuge from the fighting. Slow lines for dole had sprung up with refugee aid coming from NGOs repackaged and sold by villagers, first in stands and shacks, then in piles by the side of the road. The

Taliban themselves came down from the mountains to collect food and supplies in this dole market and sell them for funds to purchase guns and munitions in the towns to the south, below Peshawar, along the Afghan border. Khalid, traveling with his parents, already had been as far as these dole lines in Mardan. He knew the time it took to get there and the place in Saidu Sharif where trucks picked up travelers who sat atop their loads and paid in small coins.

"By now my father will have sold his *dzos* in Mardan for goat and cattle feed," murmured Pelal, as though only half present. "Then, in spring, he'll buy back his *dzos* for pasture." She sighed, turning briefly to Khalid. "How he has betrayed me."

Dzos were crosses between yaks and cows and these hybrids carried burdens and pulled plows. Khalid knew from his father that Gujjars could fatten them on roadside grasses deemed public lands as a means of storing money between seasons, since the animals were hardy. But could she not understand the gravity of what he was saying?

"Or we'll head northwest toward Tal," he continued, ignoring her remarks, pointing with his whole hand in the other direction from her father and Mardan, seeking her eyes, which were again turned away from him toward the river, and, so it seemed, could not be steered to the west. "Past Gabral town. After Dir, *Al-hamdu lillah*, we'll cross the pass to Chitral, where my father has said there are now mostly Afghans."

He paused, then added more softly, gently, staring at her for some sign of comprehension, "So no one will know us."

In the end it was like talking to a child or the river itself. Indeed, throughout the cold, white month of January, Khalid had frequently said things to Pelal he believed were increasingly daring, anxiously awaiting her reaction, and it was as though they had never been said.

At last, staring outward from his seat in the snow, he felt the familiar rush of significance begin to shout inside him. It had been nearly two years since the village *jirga*, which included two of his great-uncles, had decreed Pelal a blood prize. As all along she'd been old enough to wed, and as her beauty had only grown until now it was obvious, a thing accepted among them like the snows, surely in the coming spring she would be presented to a man for suitable compensation. His own father, ailing, desperately needed this money to support their household. Yet betraying that need and hot with desire, he lingered, tarnishing her with words.

Khalid rose suddenly, his head swimming, and swervingly reached out his hands to Pelal. To his surprise, she raised her own hands gently to his, the palms downturned and knuckles all but disappearing. Her fingers were long and thin, and when she extended them they bent upward to form a backward bowl. The hands themselves were warm, slender, and once he'd lifted her, the two of them pulling against one another and she rising lightly to her feet, he loosed his hold in a kind of shock. It was the first time he had touched her skin at rest, when he wasn't pushing or shoving, attempting to upset her balance. Now, without his saying a word, she began to run, not toward their home, where she was living in a house full of strangers, but toward the pine and fir forests in the steeps, and, more precisely, toward a stand of tall deodar cedars poised in a dell beyond the fields, rising in a shroud of snow that lay draped across their heavy branches.

Pelal didn't seem to get cold. Khalid had noticed that she could sit or run, as though from long practice, for hours in the snow. Her skin was amber, a brightened liquid brown. In winter, when Khalid's nose and chin and ears stung until he took two thick scarves and wove them around his head in opposing directions, Pelal wore only her thin sky-blue cloth *dupatta* covering her hair and brow while her face shone naked and evenly, sheltering light, providing a kind of molten quality to her eyes. As far as he knew, she had but one *dupatta*, the one she'd worn when she arrived, and she refused those offered by his mother. Yet it looked always the same, free of the henna he'd seen on her father's beard on the day she was delivered, free of the lampblack she wore from time to time beneath her eyes against the sun. It was clean.

It was a long run to the cedar dell and Khalid's lungs were bursting in the cold to keep pace. In the end he was unable. Pelal was too swift. She was indeed a kind of antelope, or the mix of an ibex and a plush snow hare. When she ran, even a fool unaware of such things could see the wildness in her hidden legs that stung the eyes with their motion, and, he'd no doubt, were wholly Gujjar, uncontrolled and unordinary.

Now Khalid decided, much as he'd like to settle himself on top of Pelal and still her, he would not have that pleasure, whatever that pleasure was. He slowed, ceased to waste himself, allowed his lungs to heave and gather the crashing air. Pelal was not in sight when he descended into the dell. Willows spread farther on, settling near the stream that in summer was many streams, the land riven and stained brown in the murk then gray in the shallows and at last a deep cerulean blue in the center deeps of the great alluvial fan of the Utror River. This river ran bright blue from snowmelt, unlike the rivers higher up the valley and to the east, near Kohistan, that brought glacial till with their courses and crossed high scree fields carrying turbid runoff and alpine slurry and gray silt to the flow of their waters.

"Where are you, ibex?" called Khalid. But he could see her tracks, far apart and cased in spray, and he climbed into the great Himalayan cedar she'd chosen and began, once again, to pursue her.

In the spring there would be terrible mudslides, he knew, engulfing whole sections of the high jeep track into Tal from the east and delaying his pursuers. But no one he'd known had ever stolen a bride from his own hearth. Others had buried themselves in potatoes or thatch in the flat beds of harvest trucks headed south for Mingora. That was done. But they were lovers fleeing feuds and honor killings wherein women bore the brunt of the violence. Or escaping *watta satta* in which female exchanges brought pairings between village families seeking to consolidate ownership of tillable land for seeded potatoes, or between warring factions whose hostility was reduced, in this manner, to a kind of shrugging peace. Such flights were staged by desperate people from separate houses who'd succumbed to their passions and were fleeing not only for love but for their lives. And they were few.

Pelal was a high climber and now, at this height, in this tangle of strong arms of deodar, she was far from the bole and her *dupatta* had shifted, then fallen, revealing her long hair, a pallid sheen resting on its blackness, with the light slung low and swiftly sinking farther, gathering on the crown of her head and in the single, tucked fold of her tresses that curved out from where the nape of her neck lay concealed.

Khalid could see all of this from below, as Pelal had a way of climbing that permitted her to hammock herself and hang from branches to shimmy beneath them. Then she'd swing her body up and enfold those branches, her narrow belly pressed on them quickly from above. He'd seen these maneuvers before and they were hard to imitate; there was a strength required and, more than that, a length of muscle, a supple flexibility, he did not quite possess.

Nonetheless, he could climb well enough and rose to her, now and again glancing upward, craning his neck to sight her where the light remained. The broad limbs of the deodar were giant and slimmed only gradually, the bark notched to a rough grid and coated with snow except where it ran nearly vertical. At last, he pulled even with Pelal and she smiled, her lips full and bright and slow as they came open.

"You must miss your father very much," he said after resting a moment, hoping she might reveal something that would bring them closer.

"Miss him, no. I feel nothing for my father. I cannot forgive him for what he has done."

Khalid looked quickly over at her and he thought he could detect the sadness, what must have been a terrible loneliness sweeping through her for nearly two years and then, each night when she grew empty, turning around and sweeping through her again.

"He's killed a man," he said soberly, looking away. "This is difficult to forgive."

"Not for that," answered Pelal. "That was in defense of his own life. No—for abandoning me."

She began to descend the broad Himalayan cedar, just for a moment pausing to set her hand at the base of her neck and then, as though exhausted, allowing her head to rest upon her wrist.

"For never telling me a word. For bringing me here and saying nothing. For lacking the courage to look at me, one of his daughters, and explain himself."

From the heights of the tree, looking south along the valley, you could see squares of thinned snow where winter-sown buckwheat lay in the dusk beneath drifts only recently cleared and now beginning to deepen. Blue pines, cloaked in snow, were seated in notches amidst the steeps, while junipers and tamarisk trees with branches that piled the snow into thin vertical slabs clung to the river far below. Always, it seemed to Khalid, when he watched Pelal, her gaze drifted toward the river that flowed even now when the world was frozen.

"Think how hard for me," she continued, shifting downward, her body moving fluidly through the cold structure of the tree, "to give him back his honor. When *I* am given, one of his own, for the honor of other men."

Her voice was scuttled and strange, full of the river. Having never before heard her anger, or even her voice at such length, Khalid said nothing. It was a rough voice, not gentle, roiled with passion. He pictured the tall, gaunt figure of her father, who had said nothing to any of them when he'd brought his daughter, who had towered above them all, and whose face, like Pelal's, was vacant and inscrutable. Now Khalid watched her angling, bringing snow from the branches onto her neck, shaking out her hands and placing them quickly, shifting, and always moving down.

"He's as lost to me now as I am to him." She sounded close, as though whispering, but in fact she was moving below her voice down through the tree in the dim light.

He too began his descent through the cedar, more careful than Pelal, trusting grooves but not slick snow, flatness and two feet rather than one foot or a hand, his mind on her but his eyes on himself, on what he could see, now feel, of the tree. Suddenly Khalid stepped down onto what must have been her shoulder. He tested for a moment, to determine stability, and felt a kind of softness firming. She reached up to take his foot and place it on a bough.

"*You*," he blurted, startled.

"Yes," answered Pelal, whispering upward. She reached and brought his second ankle, then his foot, to another bough, strong and broad and steplike. Her clasp was powerful, almost fierce.

"I'm without anything here," she went on, still whispering, perhaps beginning to weep. "He has saved himself by leaving me nothing."

And the language that seeped into Pashto carried the strange roots of Gojiri, as though she was laboriously translating herself and her people, slowly and purposefully, and again, to Khalid, the sound was gravelly, of mountains and rivers. He was silent.

"You climb well," Pelal murmured after a long time had passed, her voice morphing back to her household voice, even-timbred and quiet. Now he rocked in the tree, standing and rocking with his eyes shut while the cedar held still. He waited for the world to settle and cool, but it did not. When he opened his eyes, the snow was blue, more visible at some length, out toward the fringes of the cedar, than at its center.

Finally, having said nothing at all through the course of her avowals then lowering himself to sit on a branch she'd chosen for his feet, Khalid took his own hands and reached down toward her head. It was the color, just then, of unlit coals. He did nothing but reach to where the dark below his knees tensed to a denser, fuller darkness. They remained there, the hands, suspended. Then with nothing but a wild light in his mind, he leaned down and gently touched her hair. When there was no sound, no movement, he softly cradled her head, the hair invisible, the same color now as the pitch of the air. He held the small bowl of her skull in his hands and began to move them slowly, in slow circles upward, seeking the firmness beneath her scalp, navigating by the feel of the crown, which he stayed under, polishing softly until his fingers, all of them, were curled beneath the weight of her hair and he was touching gently down to the bone, brushing the shape of her while this girl who filled him with awe stayed throughout perfectly silent and still.

At the back of the skull was a knot in the smooth curve of the bone, a node of intensity he returned to, playing over it with the tips of his fingers then reluctantly moving off and away. At last it was over; he'd brought his hands down. He could see neither her eyes nor the contour of her face beneath him. He could scarcely make out the dim-bright limbs of the cedar holding them aloft. After a while she told him to help her find her *dupatta* or they would be lost. Even this "lost," coming from the unseen curves of her mouth, made him again begin to rock, his legs now dangling in the cedar, unharnessed. The thought that the two of them had something to be exposed, far from terrifying him, brought back a fire from beyond where he could see in the darkness to burn inside him above the level of his eyes.

In the end, she herself found her *dupatta* and they traipsed back through the covered potato fields. The snow had begun again, building force. It plunged down from the heights, dropping swiftly below the tree line as far as the blue pines on Desan Mountain, then into silver firs hunched in narrow swathes on the exposed slopes to the sunken cedar dell at the base of the steeps, settling finally upon the willows bending beneath their freighted boughs along the river.

But Khalid saw none of this. There were a few smudged lights far down to their left at the floor of the valley where the bazaar crept along the road, but in the fields he glimpsed only Pelal's movement ahead and felt the broad slip of snow striking his face and sensed her haste, for it seemed she was in a great hurry after so much stillness, until finally, the snow grown so thick as to blind him, he could no longer see her at all and she was running.

In subsequent days, then weeks, Khalid noticed nothing in the demeanor of Pelal to suggest she thought of him differently or that their paths had veered together and now were indissolubly fused. He waited patiently, at first, for signs he was now her lover. But they did not come. She smiled as always when she caught him gazing from across the room or when, escorting Pelal and his mother to the bazaar, he glanced furtively to admire the sharp tips of her lashes and, feeling no doubt the heat of his eyes or the closeness of his chin, Pelal turned her own face blandly toward him. Yet there was nothing here that seemed out of the ordinary. So he hoped for greater and greater snows, for the season to intensify beyond all measure, for snow to fall so deeply around them as to fill the whole dell of Himalayan cedars then creep up into their branches, until at last, in such dreams, he and Pelal were engulfed in the center, staring outward.

In February, the school for girls was closed. The old schoolteacher was home in her gardens in the southwestern outskirts of Karachi, near the sea and the old hill graves of her ancestors. She was fed through a charity pool in which each household contributed to her meals, and it was little to pay since she lived easily on potatoes, dried apricots, and chapatis and, on occasion, salt trout with *daal* or walnut paste and dried onions and thin buckwheat pies. Yet despite the protestations of Khalid's mother, Pelal, as a Gujjar, had not been allowed to pursue her education with the other girls, so it was a relief to the family that this Sindhi woman had been trucked out of the valley before the roads had closed. Now, as there was a way into the building beneath the eaves in the back, Khalid would dare Pelal to accompany him there, to climb inside and sit across from him in the dark so he could detail his plans. She would shrug and consent to these pleas as if they meant nothing to her or as if her life, no longer her own, rested entirely in the hands of others.

Often, as the schoolhouse was well above the village and some ways apart from the uppermost houses and fields, he would suggest afterward to Pelal that they run across the top of the ridge rather than descend directly down the valley, cutting into the line of the forest for cover and tracing with their prints a long, curving blade through the snow. All of it entailed risk but, with desperation brewing in his heart that he could not explain, Khalid increasingly embraced the danger of being discovered in his passion by onlookers whose scrutiny this snow running invited. Ultimately, he would throw himself down and call to Pelal from the ground. She'd return laughing soundlessly, her face lit up by exertion, and fling down her hands to help him rise, as he'd done for her in the potato fields below. Then they'd pull against one another until Khalid regained his feet. He'd run off while she silently pursued him, veering into glades and swerving through stands of spruce and fir, with the tightly laid branches carrying walls of snow that struck them in the neck and face and ribs and spilled coldly against their bodies.

In the deepness of these places, he would often stop, choosing them for their walled-in fervor, then pivot suddenly to face Pelal. She'd in turn come rushing into such tight mosques to find him straight up and standing, arms at his sides, and nearly crash into him, thrusting out her hands to break her speed, even touching him on the chest for a fraction of a moment before skidding and swerving, stopping and backing away. Then Khalid would laugh as she turned her head away from him until, fearful she'd cease to follow altogether if he allowed these privacies to swallow them, he'd run off again, having stolen a moment to admire her, still laughing and calling out her name.

Once, in the midst of all this, Pelal did not return to him when he fell, collapsing into deep snow at the base of the long, curving slopes beneath Desan Mountain. He called to her, but in vain. It had grown late. Khalid rose and followed for what seemed a long time, threshing through glades of blue pine in nearly a straight line and seeing only her tracks, far apart, as she herself was invisible, gone too far ahead. At last, trying for greater speed, he rounded a tight corner between laden branches in a thick belt of pine, and there was Pelal, facing him and standing firm with her arms crossed over her chest. Taken by surprise, he crashed directly into her, sending them both tumbling into the drifts.

It was early April. The snows had not relented. But the days were longer, the skies brighter at the edges. Khalid landed directly on top of Pelal, the bone of his shoulder on her head, and hastened to roll off her. She was motionless. He had struck her very hard in the temple. Her eyes were closed. From what he could see, looking quickly, she was not breathing.

"Pelal," he blurted, a tightness clasping his throat and making his voice compete with his lungs for air. The word "Pelal" came out shrill and watery.

She did not respond.

"Pelal," he shouted, bringing his face in close to hers, examining her, beginning to feel her neck. She was warm and soft and damp.

"Pelal, are you breathing?" he asked more quietly, seeing that she was not, seeking her life. Moving his hands now freely upon her neck. Reaching down for her wrist, which was limp but still pulsing.

"You must speak, Pelal," he said to her. But she was utterly still. No air was coming when he brought his cheek to her mouth. Her face remained empty, hollowed out.

"Pelal, Pelal." Now he was shouting loudly, lifting his voice high into the trees, seized by panic.

At last, when for another few moments nothing had changed, when she was motionless beneath him, he began howling, his head thrown back, his eyes shut and a new pain filling his ears with blankness and turning him dark and cold.

"Breathe, Pelal!" he hurled in long, rattling agony against the sky.

Only then did she reach silently upward and cover his mouth with her hand. Indeed, her eyes, he realized, had been open the whole time, watching him. They'd even moved when he moved, and followed his own eyes.

She smiled and took several shallow, clipped breaths, then spread her shoulders and inhaled fully so her whole chest rose toward him. She began to laugh the way she laughed, deeply and soundlessly.

He collapsed beside her into the snow.

"Pelal," he whispered, exasperated.

"Yes," she said softly, as though she now knew something beyond worry or question.

He watched as she stood, turning toward him to smile, then disappearing out of the glade. And looking back later when he was warm in the house, he thought they'd shown nothing, those eyes, that there was no way to know that the dark brown in them was ever alive.

There was money his father kept in the larder, or what functioned as a larder in the back shed attached to the house. It would be sufficient, he hoped, to buy transport from Mingora or, alternatively, from Dir town once they'd crossed the Badwai Pass below Tal. From that point, as he told Pelal in the schoolhouse in mid-April, they'd head south toward Peshawar and, if it pleased God, go on, via the Grand Trunk Road, which admittedly he himself had never traveled, to Rawalpindi, where there was work in the bazaar. It was a thin plan, he knew, but Pelal did not turn him down, or correct him, or appear openly pensive. So it seemed it would suffice. Clearly, he told himself, she was deeply afraid and, set among strangers, had lost her way, was struggling to know her own mind. So now, as he thought it through, it had fallen to him to protect her.

Indeed, during those few occasions in early spring when they sat in the schoolhouse and Khalid described the future, Pelal was conspicuously silent. She nodded from time to time and pleaded halfheartedly for delay but ultimately agreed to the necessity of departure and submitted to the fact that they could not wait forever, certainly not beyond the end of May, because the villagers, his family above all, would notice their habits. Only once did she break into his monologues to suggest a route, which surprised Khalid, but the logic of which he could not contest. She suggested they stay close to the river in case they were tracked and needed to cross or double back and conceal their direction. The southward road to Mingora would likely be open by early May, as in other years, and that, she suggested, would be the obvious path for fugitives. As his father would pursue him first down out of the valley rather than up into its steeps, they should aim for the high road first north then west to Tal. It would depend, Pelal finished, her voice grown quiet and serious, on snowfall and mudslides, which, so long as they found a way to navigate them, would likely delay pursuit.

So when the twenty-ninth of May arrived, in accordance with the count of days in Mingora, Khalid made cryptic preparations. After he'd gathered supplies sufficient to cross the pass, and found his father's money and taken it from its place, then stared meaningfully at Pelal who only that morning had shrugged and consented to his choice of nights, he filled himself with the thought of her, a thought that was still rough-edged, unclear, and difficult to embody in a single person. He covered himself with blankets. At two in the morning, he rose and slipped out the door and stood waiting beneath the walnut trees behind the house. A storm was due, judging by sharp winds from the northeast and clouds, earlier that evening, banking against the upper face of Falaksair. They were planning to walk up through fields past the schoolhouse rather than down to the bazaar, then cut across the heights to the north where they'd run in the past. The hope was that snows would come and blur their tracks, even bury them. Pelal had suggested they walk in single file with Khalid behind to obscure her prints with his own larger feet and in places where there was tree fall to drag a branch. Then it would appear only that a hunter or woodsman had passed through, caught unawares by the swiftness of the storm.

To Khalid's surprise, she emerged from the house with almost nothing, leaving most of what her father had left her behind and carrying only a tiny burlap sack that appeared to hold a few belongings, he knew not what. They set off moving swiftly up the slope in the darkness. Meanwhile, there did indeed seem to be a brewing storm, as it smelled of coming snow and the stars were shrouded while the moon rose young and listless.

In just under an hour, snow was falling thickly, in large swooning flakes. Having walked out the night, they sheltered for several hours in a den they carved together beneath a fallen tree in the long kilometers of blue pine stretching above Kalam, separating the two great tributaries of the Swat River. Late the next morning, the thirtieth of the month, they continued, resting near dusk east of the Utror River in a dense forest, risking the smoke of a pine fire because even Pelal claimed to have grown cold. Khalid assumed by now they had pursuers, though he hoped they would believe that he and Pelal were far to the south or dead. Perhaps it was conjectured in the village that the two of them had been overtaken by the storm. In any case, the campsite they'd chosen was an ideal one, in a dense thicket overhung with sheesham and juniper, and he gathered a ring of stones and sought to contain his fire, having piled snow against the wind to shelter it, all the while admiring Pelal, who was skillfully gathering boughs, shaking them, drying them as she could upon her faded *shalwar kameez*.

From time to time, she even smiled at him, as she always smiled, a slow, mysterious smile full of promise, and her presence, made richer by the prospect, the knowledge, that she was his, was nearly overwhelming. His legs were angry for travel, for distance to safeguard the surety of her. At the same time, despite this haste, Khalid was reluctant to leave such moments and allow them to pass evenly away when each one carried the depth of this silent industry, the two of them making fire, building camp, seeking shelter together against the darkness and the cold.

Though he wanted very much to sleep beside her, in fact to enter her garments and warm her belly with his own so they'd leave only one imprint in the snow, a great, thick swathe that might belong to a bear, Khalid watched as Pelal set out her things on the far side of the fire. After they'd eaten sparingly, each taking a potato wrapped in a chapati with dried ginger and onion, Pelal reached across, smiling, to hand him what she'd saved of her own potato. He rose and approached her, leaning far over and waiting for her silently to brush his cheek, or his mouth, or the nape of his neck with her lips. Instead he felt only her moist breath. After a moment, she reached out to touch his hand in the snow and covered it for an instant with her warmth before releasing it. As there was nothing more, he pulled away, standing above her in the flickering dark, thinking it had been a rare enough thing already, already enough.

*

When Khalid awoke, the night was old and purple. It was very cold. The fire he'd built was no longer smoking. Pelal was no longer lying on the far side of the ring of stones. The tight burlap sack she'd carried and never opened was gone. There was, of course, the imprint of her body, made larger by blankets and capes she'd left behind. But the smell of her, which was something he knew even outdoors, had departed. At that very moment, she was gathering firewood for a new fire, no doubt, slim boughs of silver fir higher up the valley, so he would have something to wake to. She'd work silently, so as not to rouse him prematurely, to nourish his strength. She'd return with the gift of herself, laying down the wood so quietly it would be as though she'd never left to gather it, as though it had come to them by the workings of the forest, and soon the two of them, huddled together, would gaze at the growing flames and warm themselves. Khalid lay back to rest.

Snow began to fall, lightly, a faint change in the air toward moisture, then steadily, filling the tracks leading from his spent fire not westward toward Tal but toward the other tributary off to the east. First dusting then filling them to half before, in just over an hour, they lay dimpling. In under two hours, the tracks, splayed wide to suggest a runner's gait, were stuccoed, nearly clean.

By the time he awoke again it was nearly light. Khalid followed what remained of those tracks for most of a kilometer, all the while calling out her name, telling himself that perhaps she was waiting around a corner so he would again come crashing in on her in a tight circle of trees and she'd lie there beneath him, her remote eyes gleaming in the snow. He couldn't know that Pelal, moving swiftly since he'd first dropped off to sleep, was now only seven kilometers from the western bank of the Ushu River, which feeds the boiling blue holes of the Swat River above Kalam. Or that she'd promised a thousand times to return on or near the first of June, two springs from her arrival in Jalban, to the cleft between two rocks, reachable each year via a spit of glacial moraine before the snowmelt grows to torrents in the center of the river. From there, one of many donkey paths leads eastward into the mountains toward Karang and ultimately down to the Indus River and the Karakoram Highway before, via an offshoot, past Skardu and on at last to Kashmir.

Indeed, her father, who had taught all of his children how to run and be silent and to conceal both themselves and their intentions, had taken her to that shaded cleft on many occasions when she was still very young, and it was a great adventure to cross the bright shallows into dark hiding and feel the cold current of the river rise past them into the air. Just under two years before this night, they'd gone over it a final time. She'd quietly rehearsed the details of their arrangement, repeating the same words back to him over and over until her father was satisfied. He'd at last convinced her, for his own peace of mind, to take among her things his precious, small-shafted shearing knife secured in burlap, which she assured him she would never need to use. Only then had he consented to bring her north to the village of Jalban, filled with misgivings, traveling without his herds, to deposit her in the house himself and warily inspect its precincts.

But Khalid knew nothing of the Gujjar at the river. He was unaware that the old man had been waiting for his youngest daughter for most of a month for fear she'd be forced to come early by circumstances or weather. Nor would he have guessed the sufferings this entailed, the two years of ransacked sleep, or the fact that often it is those left behind who bear the weight of such loss and the men whose daughters are taken who wear this damage on their faces. He did not imagine, moreover, the shame and mastery of the tall, old Gujjar who had instructed his daughter to lie about all things but most importantly to lie about her father, to conceal from the people of Jalban his love for her, which was ruinous and total, so they would not divine her intentions. He had urged her, instead, to speak only of his indifference, of her lasting estrangement, and to join their world just enough to find an opening in its fabric without compromising her dignity.

Khalid, as he lay beside the fire he had rebuilt in the juniper break and allowed his mind to return to the cold, dark cedar where he had touched her, knew only that, after everything that had occurred, it was impossible now to give up the chance of her return while it still existed. Having lost her tracks to the snow then called her name for hours, telling himself that surely she was adrift or had grown confused, he put off the long trudge west toward Tal. There at his fire, in that closed world of sheesham and snow, in the late heart of winter where nothing could penetrate, where his pursuers, he was certain, would not find him, and where his thoughts revolved around the few words of Pelal, spoken with such sincerity despite the vagueness of her eyes, he could not see out from the laden trees and across the kilometers down to the blue glint of the current where the Gujjar at the river had already welcomed his daughter and, having sold his

279

herds and prepared a new course for his family far to the east, broken down in her presence, coming at last to his knees in the falling snow beside that rushing tumult and, after so many months, lifting her above him into the air.

—For Rufran, who is gentle

A Damn Sight
Matthew Pitt

PHONE WENT OFF around three, maybe four; an hour, anyway, only here for sleep and fever. Its peal pinched my airflow. And my brain—logical but Southern—asked in reply to its ring: *What is that sound, starting gun for the rapture?* Of course I was a boy when I ceased believing in any rapture but rapture of the deep, a muddle that accosts me during my scuba dives, which this moment felt cousin to. Third thought (second ring): *Maybe it's Allie; Allie may not be as chafed at you as you thought.* Followed by, *Last night you said before passing out, Allie was a prison in flesh, now you hope it's her?* My mind had flashed to its ninth notion by the phone's fifth ring, the way thunderclaps lag behind the light that invents them.

I straightened my undershirt, my hello aiming for irritation.

"Asa," the caller replied, in an epicene rasp I couldn't quite place. Or had taken prior pains to *displace*. "Asa. Asa. Asa." A sound like babble patients repeat for doctors assessing lung quality. But I knew whom the caller meant.

"This isn't he. This is Perry."

"Yas I know '*This isn't he.*' You can answer me. Asa can't no more. He gone."

To this news, I had no reply. Just silent, naked regret. Sweet sweat vapors rose off my blue sheets.

In his heyday, Asa wrote some of Mississippi's milkiest blues tunes. Though these songs spoiled more than spilled. Gone unheard by so many. If he'd ever once set foot in a recording studio, his sound would be living on in homes across the nation. His name, graduated into one of those you know you should know.

Before I could lug up enough words to build a crisp question, the line died.

Three days later I took a plane to a plane to another plane, winging me from DC to Memphis to Jackson to, finally, Baldesta, Miss.: delta town of tin shacks, flaccid roofs. Asa's boyhood town, and mine. Asa's final resting place, and nearly mine. I disembarked from an MD-88 into nerveless refrains of heat, forgetting this was a commuter airport, with no baggage claim. Nearly walked off without my soft-shell suitcase until a tarmac worker thumped my arm. *Was this mine?* He wore a hunter's orange earmuffs; if they could block propeller grunts, no way would my reply break through. I nodded and left. In a hurry to make my tour as in and out as possible.

Ever since the current budget passed both houses, Baldesta has been Congress's concern. My Corps of Engineers division targeted the town as a "Green Phoenix" site, a municipality of moribund means, dwindling populace, decades past its best, but still shy of ghost-town status. Less a dwelling than a relation hooked to a ventilator. We'd advised shuttering handfuls of such flailing towns. Baldesta was set to enter Phase II. Field agents were to inspect the town soon. If its heartbeat was as pale as surmised, its land deemed by surveyors to be sound, all inhabitants would be relocated. Existing homes and retail dismantled, then transformed into a hydroelectric plant.

Best thing, I claimed to colleagues, that could happen to Baldesta.

A team of grunts three rungs beneath my pay grade was supposed to be here. But after my late-night Asa call, I'd arranged to make the tour myself. This tripped some departmental quibble. But this passed once my team saw pictures of the unsightly hole I'd spared them from. By early afternoon I'd hit Baldesta's main drag, shedding a skin of hot sweat. Strolling in ill-chosen footwear, shoes hard as skulls. Each time I planted down, the ground beneath me squished like sediment in a jug.

Little grocery said it was open. So did our barber. And the catfish counter. But at 2:00 p.m. on a Tuesday, nothing was. A bug of neon coursed through a broadcast tower sign claiming WOEB as *Voice of Baldesta, Shiver by the River.* But the only life in sight was windblown dust. On this anecdotal evidence alone, I could've signed my hometown's death warrant. Nine hundred sixty-one: This is what the latest census made of Baldesta. My division calculated a −19 percent postcensus pop-drop, in a town made of fertile land people got paid not to seed. Median income was hardly half the nation's, meaning folks here didn't see dentists when stings shot through their mouths: They purchased 80-proof Novocain from package stores.

Asa had lived downtown. Near, but not too near, Mother. He liked being one flight up from the juke joint he played, and a safe distance from the woman's grasp.

As I walked, a low moan rose up near my old high school, still named after the Jim Crow cracker who toiled for years in courts to keep us out of decent classrooms. He had died; he had won. His school housed petrified books, filled with fossilized falsities or long-dismissed claims. One hundred and eight elements. Pluto as a planet. I couldn't make sense of the glyphs of graffiti on our handball court: PHELSHEPLEHASEPLA. The only art consisted of smeary stick figures, striking dirt with swords or canes. Asterisks covering the eyes.

As I closed in on the moan, patches of clouds briefly covered the sun's glint, the way a bandage soothes wounded skin from raw air. When I tried to rap the door of the house holding the moan, it peeled back like a can lid. A heavyset man stood in its frame, wearing a wide grin. Only a few teeth remained in his mouth. The rest hung, like hunting trophies, on a length of wire looped around his neck. He chuckled; they jittered in turn. When he gazed past me into that blade of a sun without wincing, I knew he was stone blind.

I offer his greeting here as a complete sentence, though truth is it took me hours to decode: "You, ah, out here offering your hand or your hello? I'm obliged either way."

Before me was Rutabaga Rollins, one of Baldesta's baddest and most versatile bluesmen. Player in any area gig of merit for four decades. Usually he just slunk onstage whenever he got an urge. No one chased him off. No one could. He was budge proof, wide like a tuber. With eyes now, apparently, as useless. It occurred to me he'd pawned his vision on cakes and candies. The sugars he was soft on had softened his belly and gumline, uprooting teeth, defeating him in a way no Greco-Roman warrior ever could.

Unsure what my host had asked, I didn't know how to reply. Not that it mattered. Rutabaga struck my ear trying to wave me in. Grinning, he sank his bulky butt on a sofa. Stuffing from its threadbare armrests had settled like flab into the mushrooming cushions. His hand swept through a tin tub, scooping a beer from a watery basin filled, I suppose, at one time with ice. Amazing the ice in that baking room hadn't sublimated to mist. When he popped the can, its contents smelled of melted crayon. Tepid thing tasted as if I'd opened my mouth inside an active carwash, during the hot-wax cycle. I was so used to a Rutabaga with working retinas, it never hit me to just dump the beer and pretend to drink it down.

I let him do the talking. He and Asa had been musical rivals, and I didn't want to step out of my role of invisible stranger yet, rupture any truce they'd made since I left. Strapping on a guitar, Rutabaga garbled an intro to his first song, then began.

She scrambled my eggs
Bout half past ten.
Now they sitting so long,
They done hatched they own hen.
Got six little children
Livin here in the shack.
Trippin over they toys,
When they mom coming back?

Flies swooped at Rutabaga's chin, nuzzling beads of perspiration. In the course of shooing them, he dropped his pick. While flailing for it in his massive lap, the moan surged. It hadn't come from him. And it wasn't one moan, but several. I tensed. Crept to the kitchen, bumping a crumpled baby-doll stroller. When I did, the moan shifted into a whimper.

It was Rutabaga's brood. I didn't see them straight off, spotting the skillet before the spawn. Antediluvian eggs, stiff and saffron, sat inside that skillet. Then I saw the kids—none older than five—all twisting up some object. For a dim instant I thought it was the wrung neck of a live rabbit. But as they edged into the light, I saw it was only a stuffed toy they'd torn apart, hoping nuts or candy might spill from the cavity.

Won't you tell me now, mister
Do they all look like me?
Way my woman ran round
I'd be happy for three.

After crunching my can and leaving Rutabaga's hutch, I found a coffee shop one town over with semis in the lot. I wanted a brawn-flaunting brew. Wanted to sort out what I'd seen between bites of peach pie.

Air from a fan's blades tickled my sweat-soaked ribs. The coolness first brought comfort, then nostalgia: for the town women I'd once had here. Like that one who'd claw my kneecaps as we built to gratification. Or that one over whose bed hung a mirror, warning us when her man's car lights gleamed up the drive. I could finish and shimmy up her chimney within a minute of seeing that beam.

"You fixed, baby?"

I checked my mug—half full, still steaming. "I'm fixed. You my new waitress?"

"Yas, just starting my shift." I promised I'd be on my way soon, promised not to loiter. "Naw, your ticket's paid. Fill up slow as you like."

"I thank you, Miss . . . why, Miss *Embry*, isn't it?"

"Perry?" She switched one pair of glasses for another. "Boy, you done grow. Up *and* out. Must be twenty-five years." Her hissing laugh reminded me of an iron primed to steam cotton. "You know I still get chuckles ever so often, thinking how Asa'd bring you by, in a porkpie hat, singing his music. You were such a fine little sawed-off version of him."

I filed crumbs off my fingertips. "That time's far gone."

"Only far as the tide, baby. Ain't you come here for him now?"

My shoulders rolled, but she didn't catch the shrug. "I'm here for all of you."

"Yas, Asa said you a DC man. I *was* Miss Embry, by the way. Then Mrs. Laird, next Mrs. Pine. Now I'm Embry again. Slipping off names like so many sundresses."

I told her I'd just heard about Asa a few days before.

"Shame," she said, "he can't lay eyes on me no more. Least the Lord's watching him." She wanted something, my consent or comment, and squirted a fresh whipped cream rosette on my pie while waiting. But I sipped the coffee slow instead, to avoid getting into hereafter hypotheses about the man who sired me.

"Shame I missed his service," I muttered, fluffing my whipped rosette.

"Service? He ain't have no service." Embry's lungs wheezed then. She poured her pot's dregs into a mug of her own, so the coffee might carve her rasp. I asked if she'd gone to a clinic. "It don't usually sound bad, 'cept at night. Anyway. Been curious to see how you turned. I coulda turned to him to learn. Yas, you'd be brothers, if you weren't father and son."

"Crossed Rutabaga's path just now," I said, switching topics. "First I've seen him since he went blind. Guess diabetes bested him."

Now Embry's laugh was a cottonmouth working up venom. "His sight didn't get strick from chasing *that* kind of sugar. Rutabaga started slinking around—doing to others the acts he was sure his woman was doing to him. When his lady got sick of it, she lashed him with lye."

"Lye?"

"They *saul* blinded now, baby. Pretty near each Baldesta man, who knows how many, got his sight stole. Women did it a while ago, in a

285

kind of spree, then peeled out of town. The church bring by food for them men. They can't much help themselves. Fact is, it's my turn to make drop-offs. Sacks are in our dry-good closet. Would you want to minister in my place tonight . . . ?" She eyed me carefully, killing her coffee with a slurping flourish. "Since you say you've come back here for all of us?"

The wind had whipped up; warm, acrobatic. Cradling groceries, I studied Embry's map of Baldesta's blind bluesmen. First on her list was a man I'd never met. When I poked in his shack, he was locked in a twelve-bar tune, cigarette bouncing on his lip like a diver at a board.

He'd vary verses for hacking, stuff coming out the tint of poultice. Each time his ash splashed the carpet, I'd kneel to put out the embers. Once he stopped midsong to say, in his combustive voice, "Think you saving Blind Dwight. Don't you? Snuff some flames? Well, you dint save shit. Ever since my sight flamed out, my other senses been ablaze. I hear that wind. I can open my door and let it rush in, if some spark get ideas." He patted his coat. "And if *you* get ideas, I keep cutlery on my person. Now, you really like to help, drop a dollar in my guitar case."

I dropped down five. Or tried—folding Lincoln's face, but Dwight flicked his tongue against the currency before I could let go. Bragging he could tell any bill by taste. "Mmm, a ten. They got tang. That rate rates accompaniment." He dragged out a wooden pallet and foot-operated double cymbal, punctuating his performance with pallet kicks every second beat. Cymbal pedal stomps every fourth.

Dwight sang a three-song cycle, yardstick of his torment: His woman Lizette needed his love; her skin blistered when she lacked for it too long. She in turn made him feel like a man so well, the bed in the country home they bought new in November was all busted up by June. They had to move to this shack, since structural harm caused by fierce love wasn't covered in their homeowner's policy. The moment Dwight arrived at his new downtown digs, neighbor men sealed windows so wives couldn't pick up his scent.

Lizette didn't scar Dwight with lye for his lapses. She hauled him to church, to get set right by a right-hearted preacher. Man tried to cure Dwight of his straying, and "It almost worked, that preacher's toil, he nearly torn my roots out the Devil's soil." But then during a session, preacher's wife paid a visit. *Shoulda seen these hips on her, man. Wanting nothing but to be clutched. Broad as salvation. A temptation too much.* For emphasis, Dwight dug his uncut nails into my hip. *What could I do but heed the call?* When he did, Lizette took up a copper paperweight of Noah's Ark and clubbed his skull. Then the preacher wrested it from Lizette and took a shot of his own. Dwight saw the arc of one last rainbow in his head, then had seen nothing more since.

An anguished buzz filled Dwight's hall. "You keep a pet in back?" I asked. He said nothing. I repeated.

"That's mine and Lizette's child."

Unplugging his lead, Dwight steered me to the back. I heard feverish lowing. Stepping inside, I saw a bed by the window, quaking, humming. Its posts chattering against a wall, *luk-aluk, luk-aluk, luk*. A canary sheet atop the mattress twisted into a braid, then shook free again. Now. Will you roll your eyes when I tell you this all happened of its own accord? That there was no body atop the bed to incite it? Or that Dwight's windows were closed, shut off from any groping gusts?

"Jest look," implored Dwight. "Still carries our impressions on her. Shakes its sheets the same way Lizette and me used to make her. Thinking of all them times we worked out our love on her springs. It wants us to lie back on it. How you tell a bed you won't be using it?

"Can't sleep on her no more," he added, removing his hat. "Bed's too sad. Quiets more each month Lizette don't return. A year more of disuse, she'll go completely still. And if I don't soon find some steady vein of money, I won't be long to follow. Hell, you know how it is, Asa. I heard you tried to split Baldesta last week."

"There's been, uh, a mistake here," I told him. "I'm not . . ."

"I told them church folk Asa wouldn't leave us long. Baldesta is your cradle and cross, man. You could get buried in another town, you'd still find a way to tunnel back. I'm honored you chose my house as a rest stop on your return journey."

Maybe Dwight *did* have a taste for charity. Stepping over his guitar case on my way out, I threw in another five.

Again on the streets: The gusts had gone frigid and mean, and were dashing open my excuse of a jacket. Asa was alive. The bitter air paired with my thoughts over this "good news." I dwelt on how he never cut the record that could've launched him out of here. How he never made my mother an honest woman. I thought of Asa's body, drunk, snoring, maybe in one of these shacks, draped on some sucker's borrowed sheets. Hours before, when he'd been dead, he had a lost legacy. Now that he was alive again, so were his failures. I didn't want to face that again. Didn't think if I even found him that I could stand to look. At that wasted life, wasted gift; wasted manhood. Still wasting yet.

Hard winds thrummed the shack windows like angry interlocutors. Each house I came to was occupied with hapless males singing refrains, plinking Jew's harps, hands cupping hidden harmonicas. Because the men were performing before but not for me, with no interest in what I thought, or if I left, I found myself listening to their playing sumptuously, the way I'd eat a dish in solitude, differently from how I would in front of guests, letting all the tones strike me without distraction, the savory and sour and the sweet alike. Each time gusts snapped screen doors shut, the bluesmen would rise, head to their windows, and play louder. Sightless but watchful. Sure the wind was their women coming back.

As a boy, I looked through windows for a woman too. Only I hoped not to see whom I squinted for. If I did see her, it meant Mother was wearing her wares at work, spending hours in some stranger's home, larded in lipstick or jewelry that shone like candied apples, that she let men bid to bite off, long as they paid a light bill, or her boy's braces. In clothes worn to be torn, stitches made for slashing.

Men she never should've put herself on consignment for. River rabble, except, at times, Asa. Who at least tried to treat me as a son, not just what came of his coming.

And on evenings as a teen, I would look through windows of Hash & Burn, the local diner on 61 where I worked. For the arrival of Sharna. Sharna was cheery, chunky. And, better blurt it now, white and blonde. Will you believe, though, I didn't seduce her to incite the town? It was her voice, a sweet ether, that doped and decked me.

I'd pull full shifts at the diner after school. She'd work dinner rush with me. After closing time, we convened again in secret. Making love in soybean rows, or near catfish ponds, spreading our acts around like crop rotation so as not to get caught. We did that sort of slow-burn sex you don't think much of while making it, but later you can't shake it, believe you're still living its exploits long after the fact: *Perry*, I'd have to tell myself during my next shift, *stop grinning. Come to. You aren't stroking her sternum, you're shaking salt on an old man's order of grits.*

Sharna and I were Hash & Burn's open secret. Patrons saw how we shuffled figure eights around tables. Caught me tapping her tummy, which expanded when she sang as if with gestating child. Whenever she dueted with the jukebox, my indifference to her singing had to seem too stiff to be true.

"Cut! Shit, it cut me again."

I looked up. I was no longer with Sharna at our diner, thumb dragging discreetly over her silk blouse. I was instead tracing lines on a woman's glove I'd picked off the next blind bluesman's dirty floor, making one last stop on Miss Embry's circuit.

Beside me, the latest player had just slashed his hand on a tin of cashews. Dawn winked clumsy light on the fresh wound . . . and several more closed cuts just like it. Scores of pink and beige lacerations scored his chicory palms. Scars like snakes slipping through a farmer's soil, to claim a foolish pullet waddling outside her henhouse.

The smoking queen reserved in my name was in a motel one county over, smack between the airport and Baldesta. My plan had been to do my tour, throw flowers on Asa's grave—if I could find it, and find a florist—squirrel a half pint of gin in my motel room, sleep off said gin, and then flee back to DC.

Instead I'd learned there was no grave for Asa. He was alive. Maybe even here for the finding. Instead, I'd put my dress shoes through tours of duty they weren't built for, straggling all night, shack to shack, in a blind blues parade that never moved. What braced these men through the filth and helpless stretches, the brushes with botulism? Kept them howling and half starved in their ragged clothes?

I entered my motel. Courtesy continental breakfasts lounged in wicker baskets, waiting to be snatched. My suitcase's rumbling wheels trailed me inside, a hanging bag was bowed double over my forearm, but the desk clerk was too engrossed in solitaire to notice. "Checking out, sir? Room number?"

"Checking in."

He frowned, scanning the lobby for escorts or harlots. Hesitating to run my card.

"Lost track of time reuniting with friends in town," I offered, as alibi. "Start gulping old stories, I forget to come up for air. You won't be seventeen someday, son. See how it is."

His maddeningly warm grin was proof he considered me no threat, and irrelevant, besides. I turned to a kiosk by the stairwell, stocked with tourist pamphlets and placards. Flipping through rows of fliers, I asked the young clerk how it could be that not one sheet so much as cited a bit of Baldesta.

"Why would they? Bit's more than there is to see."

"Yeah, it may seem that way now. But the string of blues songs crafted there was once this region's main cash crop."

"Man . . . what you want for? Rhubarb pie? Then go here." Shaking his head, he spread out a brochure. "Want to see folks quilt, this place has it covered. Water sports, outlet malls, lunch counters, fishing lures, got it all, within an hour's drive. What they got in common? None are Baldesta. You could go to your room, dunk your head in your bathroom sink right now, then hold it down until checkout, you'd still be doing a damn sight better than Baldesta."

In my room I stripped quickly. Asked the shower to unbind ropes in my back, an unfair task for plain water. Stroked medicinal ointment over my feet. Applied lotion, bunion creams, gels, bay rum, green tea, and eucalyptus. Kneaded myself. Aired out.

Then I returned to the lobby to turn in my key. "This has got to be a record," said the clerk, helping himself to a mint dish he'd replenished in my absence. "But for future reference? We got a truck stop folks can clean up just as nice in. Would've cost you six quarters instead of sixty dollars."

Before my flight back, there was one more visit I needed to pay. Motel clerk was on to something: I'd been holding my breath ever since learning Asa was still in the world. I needed to go by, pay my respects to a living man. Setup of his shack was the same as the others—tossed clothes, spilt beer. Only here, a Bunsen burner stood upright on a remote shelf.

Ah-uhm (beat), feeling out my feelings
Oh yeah, uh, ah-uhm (beat), feeling out my feelings
Ahm rock bottom with you, we ain't nothing but through,
Ah-uhv (beat), hit the wall with ceilings.

Asa noticed my presence . . . the sight of his blind eyes winking bent my mind. "Morning. Didn't see you standing there." He chuckled. "Reckon I still don't. You part of the church mission, yes. Bringing along canned goods and unchained gospel?"

"No, sir. Well, yes to the can part."

His head, quivering before, shook arduously once I answered. "Only the church ever showed up before. After what I did to my woman—and I did do it, I ain't here to claim otherwise—no one's come by but them. That's been it, for's company goes."

"You think they're"—I stocked his pantry and pulled out a different pronoun—"we're . . . this whole town is shunning you?"

"For's I know."

He had no idea others like him were scattered throughout Baldesta, that all his neighbors were stricken the same way. Not one of the men here knew he wasn't alone in his affliction.

"Well, I'm here for you now. Here to see you through anything you can't. How long's it been for you since you lost your sight?"

"Lost count. But my back porch hasn't. Go grab a look."

Piles of weekly newspapers, three years' worth, lay on Asa's steps, bound in rubber bands, ruined by rain. Vines shot between the tri-folded pages, a kind of vine I had never laid eyes on before. I gently pulled one back, pinching a purple flower for my pocket. Headline on top of the stack of papers read: BALDOXTA BLINCNESS STREtCHWS INTO THIRC YEAR. Thanks to muscle memory and hunt-and-peck luck, that typed story was legible enough. All the other column inches, though, were filled with random letters, alphabet soup strung on a placemat: gYfbjv eljIok lochnister manlexty. Framed by ink-blotched ads, staggered and light-bled photos: giant thumbs. Blurry birds.

"Don't mind my not minding you," Asa yelled, launching into his next number. "I tried leaving this town on my own a bit ago. Tried to go after her." Go after whom? I hoped he meant Mother—I'd have liked knowing she was out there too—but didn't dare ask. "But I barely could stumble for's the depot. And there hasn't been a train to catch here in years. So I turned back home, picked my playing up again. And I got to *keep* playing . . . until her return. Until she sees I see her better since she washed my eyes out with soap. Follow? I heard her rustling last night. Rattling my window. For's I know, she testing my faith, doving between towns until I prove worthy of her again."

Dove, I thought, as a verb. Yeah. To exist, without striving, in a state of grace. Mother had had her moments of this. Sharna had too, when she sang. Sharna, who I'd heard had flourished since Hash & Burn. Atlanta, three kids, mortgage-loan officer.

Less than a dot on a map, but all of Georgia for me.

I punctured his can-opener's tooth into a tin of soup, but my host interrupted me.

"No, no, I don't want those," said Asa. "Church dishes that shit out all the time, frying Vienna sausages, cooking pork and beans. Fixing without asking. You want to make something, you know what I'm hungry for. Same thing me and you always liked to eat together. Right there. Purple-top turnips cooked in neckbone. Scoop me a mess of that, I'll be good to play to you for two hours."

His finger was pointing into a bare pantry, but I knew where those turnips got kept, and so I nodded, and didn't quibble.

Walking back to my car, I had to lean on a porch within ten steps. Ten more, wipe my brow. Another ten, dab the eyes. The ridiculous heat here ridicules: Once the sun sears you to a spot, it's true toil to wiggle away. While resting, I spotted a scorched victim that hadn't found shade in time: a petrifying lizard. Glossy as slate, it'd mistook a dark stone stoop for refuge, a fatal error I understood. If during my walk I had spotted a dendrite, I'd have hoisted it over my head, hoping to unleash leafy shade. Just as even after three years, these men shot useless glances through windows, playing madly anytime they heard a flutter, hoping to lure back the women who'd impaired them.

Of the hazards facing a black boy who pairs outside his race, one is rarely mentioned: when the boy dares to end the romance. Those in Baldesta who simmered silently over my coupling with Sharna did not hold in check their havoc when I severed ties. Whites who had thought her tawdry for mixing with me rushed to her defense. Up to that point I'd been as respected as a man with my skin and mother's rep could be: apex of a low temple. To spurn that . . .

Why *did* I spurn that?

I made it through my youth on low-grade craftiness. My mind ever enthralled by experiments and a drive to possess knowledge before happening upon it in a book. Or at least not accept what limits those books discharged. But in order to avoid the charge of *uppity*, I also hid in convention's quiet shell. Partnering in the chemistry lab with respected but dull white boys. Winning team-based Young Orbiter Prizes in Science, never solo trophies. Pretending to piggyback on the diligence of others. Whites say they want you bettering yourself. But that means you're supposed to grab for what they've already attained. Show of hands: Who thinks *that* can end well?

It was assumed I'd stay in Baldesta, modest credit to my race, my acumen whittled to serve the rank-and-file smug. I could remain at Hash & Burn, whistling, mopping, counting receipts like a whiz. On my way to first black manager of the white diner. This is always how they rewarded our silent striving: allowing the brightest of us entry into the dimmest of their domains: night watchman, sharecropper, ibid., ibid., ibid. Because they despised me, they wanted me staying put.

Still, I might've not minded fastening down. With Sharna. Only it was expected she'd soar away the instant she got her diploma: *That honeyed soprano of yours gonna float you all the way to Hollywood.* Her life was tacit, breathy promise.

As for me? "Your pal Perry can count your royalties. You can trust that boy to balance a ledger." I was supposed to grin. Hunger for the tilted compliments like greasy potato chips. I didn't grin, but didn't object either. I did know about accounting.

What made me spurn her? A disposable-as-shit dialogue, at the tail end of a shift.

"Hey, Perry," she asked, totaling someone at the register. I was on the line, scuffing beef grease off our grill. "Do chop steak come smothered?"

"Just on request. And it's seventy-five cents extra."

"How do I . . . ?"

"Ring up #11, then punch clear twice. Not there. Under 'Special Merch.'"

She did this, then my instruction flew from her mind. If a customer ordered the dish an hour later, I'd have to repeat the steps. I can't say it any different: Knowing this measly truth clawed at me. I darted out for a cig—had to run off. Light up my lungs—with tar and tobacco, sure, but at least some sort of taste. Sharna and I worked side by side. But she didn't know how to ring chop steak, or set the thermostat four degrees warmer with the place only half full. Didn't have the plumber's number committed like catechism to memory. Didn't know the first thing about locking up.

I knew all these things and more. I had to. We both had escape on our minds, but her escaping was inescapable; foregone conclusion. I had to hope she'd follow through, and then take me with her. I couldn't afford being casual about even the breaths I took. She could exhale any damn time she wanted.

Approaching the airport that afternoon, fluffing a travel pillow's gossamer innards, I considered what I could import. Bury Baldesta's shacks and crops, replace them with a grand dynamo. Drown this town, so it might flood others with power: a vernal frontier. The ache and aim of public works. With my signature, I could discharge the refugees, arrange for them all to be given a pile of government larder. But how much cash would it come to? Enough to keep the men going? Cover burial costs? I wanted them *seen* . . . paying them into exile would be an insult to love and loyalty. I should know: A month after the chop-steak flap, Sharna's stepdad angrily offered me a cashier's check to flee, wash my hands of her and the town for good. Slipped it atop a booth I hadn't bused—grease spots quickly came to light—so that one way or another, I'd have to touch it. Studying it, I thought of the anonymous johns laying bills on end tables after lying with Mother.

Yes, his check was an insult. But an insult I took. Took and fled: first traveling to the Caribbean, to spearfish. It is so alien and lucid there, that deep down. So you dive, again and again, loose yourself from the surface for as far and long as you can.

Later I fled to DC, making my deposit on a place in Columbia Heights.

Pushing ahead with Phase II of my division's study meant meeting many specific criteria. The main standard at this point was my verdict. That the town no longer functioned. Agreed. But it also contained, in this assessor's professional and neutral view, an endangered natural habitat.

One that must be protected under corps' auspices.

I put in a call to a man on the Heritage and Preservation subpanel. He owed me his career, for splashing bureaucratic Wite-Out over an egregious decision he'd made long ago. I explained how, during my Baldesta tour, I'd stumbled upon a species of Faboideae on a porch. Its purple-flowered vine prevents soil erosion and is remarkably hearty—makes kudzu seem like tender lettuce. But unlike kudzu, it enjoys isolation; its vines grow slowly and tend not to spread. A crucial plant, I assured my man.

I sensed grave nodding on his end—what makes us nod when we can't be seen?

This vegetation, I pressed, demands study, years worth, before we can even consider cleaving the residents from their town. *Yes. Oh yes.* Still making a show of gravity for those strolling by his office, but relieved to have me finally call in my favor.

Like that, Baldesta was designated a Conservation Landmark, given immunity from Phase II's tendrils. Judged well enough to be left alone.

All we needed was a nearby town to swap it with. I told my con-spirator I knew just the one. Other than an all-night truck stop and dinky motel, I explained, the town due north of Baldesta has little to recommend it.

Within days of the Hash & Burn incident, I'd turned cruel on Sharna. Humiliating her with flagrant indiscretions, done not for joy but to frighten her view of our future. Think of the monster I'd have built if we'd wed. Prowling our town regular as police patrols. Sharna would've spent days chasing me out of foreign beds, engaging in wars of speculation each time I was absent or the wind kicked up strange perfume embedded in my collar. I would have punished her with no fist, no knife but doubt. And who can say how long she'd have al-lowed my eye to stray without striking back?

No man's fate is a replica of another's. But these musicians' yearn-ing strums, their lashed fingers scrabbling for beans on tin-can bot-toms? I know them. To toil in pursuit of your promise, in a town that refuses to recognize you until you get out of or out of joint with it? Of course, that puts you in a reckless state when you enter your own home. With a hundred ways to crack and only a few chords to patch you up.

More than I can play, or could have counted on to comfort me in a juke joint. Sharna, I couldn't heal here. To wash demons, I needed to take deep dives, not rely on cold-water-shack showerheads. Needed, to rinse away insults that scorched like sun, more than lye.

Water Calligraphy
Arthur Sze

1.

A green turtle in broth is brought to the table—
I stare at an irregular formation of rocks

above a pond and spot, on the water's
surface, a moon. As I move back and forth,

the moon slides from partial to full back
to partial and then into emptiness; but no

moon's in the sky, just slanting sunlight,
leafing willows along Slender West Lake,

parked cars outside an apartment complex,
where, against a background of chirping birds

and car horns, two women bicker. Now
it's midnight at noon; I hear an electric saw

and the occasional sound of lumber striking
pavement. Glancing into a teacup, I notice

leaves at the bottom form the character
individual and, after sipping, the number *eight*.

Snipped into pieces, a green turtle is returned
to the table; while everyone eats, I feel

strands of thrown silk tighten, tighten
in my gut. I blink, and a woodblock carver

peels off pear shavings, stroke by stroke,
and foregrounds characters against empty space.

2.

Begging in a subway, a blind teen and his mother stagger through the swaying
     car—

a woman lights a bundle of incense and bows at a cauldron—

people raise their palms around a nine-dragon juniper—

who knows the mind of a watermelon vendor picking his teeth?

you stare up through layers of walnut leaves in a courtyard—

biting into marinated lotus stems—

in a drum tower, hours were measured
as water rising then spilling from one kettle into another—

pomegranate trees flowering along a highway—

climbing to the top of a pagoda, you look down at rebuilt city walls—

a peacock cries—

always the clatter of mah-jongg tiles behind a door—

at a tower loom, a man and woman weave brocade silk—

squashing a cigarette above a urinal, a bus driver hurries back—

a musician strikes sticks, faster and faster—

cars honk along a street approaching a traffic circle—

when he lowers his fan, the actor's face has changed from black to white—

a child squats and shits in a palace courtyard—

yellow construction cranes pivot over the tops of high-rise apartments—

a woman throws a shuttle with green silk through the shed—

where are we headed, you wonder, as you pick a lychee and start to peel it—

3.

Lightning ignites a fire in the wilderness: in hours,
200 then 2,000 acres are aflame; when a hotshot
crew hikes in to clear lines, a windstorm
kicks up and veers the blaze back, traps them,
and their fire shelters become their body bags.
Piñons in the hills have red and yellow needles—
in a bamboo park, a woman dribbles liquefied sugar
onto a plate, and it cools, on a stick, in the form
of a butterfly; a man in red pants stills
then moves through the crane position.
A droplet hangs at the tip of a fern—water
spills into another kettle; you can only guess
at how flames engulfed them at 50 miles per hour.
In the West, wildfires scar each summer—
water beads on beer cans at a lunch counter—
you do not want to see exploding propane tanks;
you try to root in the world, but events sizzle
along razor wire, along a snapping end of a power line.

4.

Two fawns graze on leaves in a yard—
as we go up the Pearl Tower, I gaze
through smog at freighters along the river.
A thunderstorm gathers: It rains and hails
on two hikers in the Barrancas; the arroyo
becomes a torrent, and they crouch for an hour.
After a pelting storm, you spark into flame
and draw the wax of the world into light—
ostrich and emu eggs in a basket by the door,

the aroma of cumin and pepper in the air.
In my mouth, a blister forms then disappears.
At a teak table, with family and friends,
we eat Dungeness crab, but, as I break
apart shell and claws, I hear a wounded elk
shot in the bosque. Canoers ask and receive
permission to land; they beach a canoe
with a yellow cedar wreath on the bow
then catch a bus to the fairgrounds powwow.

5.

—Sunrise: I fill my rubber bucket with water
    and come to this patch of blue-gray sidewalk—
I've made a sponge-tipped brush at the end
    of a waist-high plastic stick, and, as I dip it,
I know water is my ink, memory my blood—

the tips of purple bamboo arch over the park—
    I see a pitched battle at the entrance to a palace
and rooftops issuing smoke and flames—
    today, there's a white statue of a human figure,
buses and cars drive across the blank square—

at that time, I researched carp in captivity
    and how they might reproduce and feed
people in communes— I might have made
    a breakthrough, but Red Guards knocked at the door—
they beat me, woke me up at all hours

until I didn't know if it was midnight or noon—
    I saw slaughtered pigs piled up on wooden racks,
snow in the spring sunshine—the confessions
    they handed me I signed—I just wanted it all
to end—and herded pigs on a farm—wait—

I hear a masseur striking someone's back,
    his hands clatter like wooden blocks—
now I block the past by writing the present—

as I write the strokes of *moon,* I let the brush
~~swerve~~ rest for a moment before I lift it

and make the one ~~stroke~~ hook—ah, it's all
    in that hook—there, I levitate: No mistakes
will last, even regret is lovely—my hand
    trembles; but if I find the ~~gaps~~ resting places,
I cut the sinews of an ox, even as the ~~sun~~

moon waxes—the bones drop, my brush is sharp,
    sharper than ever—and though people murmur
at the evaporating characters, I smile, ~~frown~~,
    fidget, let go—I draw the white, not the black—
oh, my asthmatic niece will be released today—

6.

Tea leaves in the cup spell *above* then *below*—
glancing out the kitchen window, I catch

a spray of wisteria blossoming by the porch.
What unfolds inside us? We sit at a tabletop

that was once a wheel in Thailand: An iron hoop
runs along the rim. On a fireplace mantel,

a flame flickers at the bottom of a metal cup.
As spokes to a hub, a chef cleans blowfish;

turtles beach on white sand; a monk rakes
gravel into scalloped wave patterns in a garden;

moans issue from an alley where men stir
from last night's binge. If all time converges

as light from stars, all situations reside here.
In red-edged heat, I irrigate the peach trees;

you bake a zucchini frittata. Water buffalo
browse in a field. Hail has shredded lettuces,

and, as a farmer paces and surveys damage,
a coyote slips across a road, under barbed wire.

7.

The letter *A* was once an inverted cow's head,
but now, as I write, it resembles feet
planted on the earth rising to a point.

Once is glimpsing the Perseid meteor shower—
and, as emotion curves space, I find
a constellation that arcs beyond the visible.

A neighbor brings cucumbers and basil;
when I open the bag and inhale, the world
inside is fire in a night courtyard

at summer solstice; we have so loved living here
and will miss the bamboo arcing along
the fence behind our bedroom, the peonies

leaning to earth. A mayordomo retrenches
the opening to the ditch; water runs near
the top of the juniper poles that line our length—

in the bosque, the elk carcass decomposes
into a stench of antlers and bones. Soon
ducks will nest on the pond island, and as

a retired violinist who fed skunks left a legacy—
the one she least expected—we fold this
in our pocket and carry it wherever we go.

The Invention of an Island
Gabriel Blackwell

AT THREE OR THREE THIRTY or, I don't know, sometime in the very
early morning around then, my wife woke me up to tell me that we
needed a change (or maybe she said *she* needed a change? I don't remember). She had decided to install mirrors on all of our walls, ceilings, and floors. She didn't put it in quite this way, I think—it doesn't
sound like her—but that's as close as I'll get now. Not quite awake,
I told her that we would have to be extra careful. Extra careful? When
she asked why, what did I mean, extra careful, I couldn't answer.
Why exactly did we need to be extra careful? I had no idea. I didn't
even remember the conversation the next morning. Why did I feel so
sleepy? What was it that had kept me up the night before? I must
have been napping when she ordered the mirrors. I remember thinking, just before I lay down on the sofa, I hope I wasn't supposed to
pick up the boy at school.

Often he asked questions, the boy. It was one way I could tell that
he was my son. To be perfectly honest, buddy, I would tell him, I don't
know what happened to the creatures on Dr. Moreau's island at the
end. (This is something that my wife would have handled better,
telling him that the story isn't really about the creatures, and I'm not
saying she wouldn't be right.) He can be a bad influence on me. I'd lose
a day's work wondering, What did happen to them? Were they destroyed? Prendick just leaves them there, I think. Were they sterile or
maybe sexually incompatible (a conversation I'm not yet willing to
have with my son)? (Was that something that Wells put in the book,
or is it something I've invented, this issue of sterility?) If they weren't
destroyed and weren't sterile, could they—or their descendants—still
be there, on that island? My wife, I think, would say that this is nothing to waste time over; she is, so often, the voice of reason. (I tend to
get wrapped up in my son's games and inventions.) It's just a story,
she would say. It's a book. Real life gives us enough to worry about
already. But think about the second- and third-generation hybrids,
honey, the sloth-vixen-wolf-women and the puma-hawk-monkey-
men—in the book, the animal men return to their original states, sort

of, but would their descendants? Would their descendants even be able to, or would they be so far removed from both their ancestors and from what Moreau had wanted them to become that there would be no dry land to swim for, metaphorically speaking? Can that be how the first *Homo sapiens* felt? It's worth thinking about, I think. No, it isn't, she would tell me if she were here. I have a million other things to do. Don't you?

And now I think I remember that Moreau's creatures did produce offspring (For some reason I'm remembering them as maybe resembling newborn rats? Kind of unformed and pinkish and slimy and gross?), but that maybe *they* were sterile? Like mules are sterile? A lot of the reason I have trouble remembering certain things is that my books are gone and I have no way of getting to them. I say this so that you—as though there were a you!—understand that if I get something very basic wrong, something that would be a matter of just opening a book and checking a few words, it's not because I'm lazy. Besides, as I see it, it's always a question of my story versus "the story." Really. I've had some time to think this over. See, the story isn't as important as what we remember of the story. Claiming otherwise is kind of like claiming that the fact that an orange has this much vitamin C means that the person who eats it will experience the benefits of exactly that much vitamin C. That isn't the case. Each person absorbs as much as he or she can at that moment in time, and that's what stays with them. It's Plato's cave, I think. (It is, right? Plato's cave?) Again, I don't have the book here in front of me to check, but I'm pretty sure that what Plato is saying is that there *is* a figure behind the shadow thrown on the cave wall, it's just that we never see that figure, we only see the shadow.

I tried out a version of this argument on my wife a few days ago (she didn't buy it, but I hadn't completely thought it through then, so it's understandable that she didn't). We had been discussing the boy— I think; we usually were, although lately she had wanted to talk about the book instead—and she brought up something I had once said that she thought contradicted what I was saying then and accused me of playing devil's advocate. (Actually, I think what she said was something more like: You always think I'm wrong. Which isn't true, but for me to have said so would have contradicted what I was trying to say. She's so smart!) I told her that if I couldn't remember what I'd said that I probably didn't mean it—I mean, that's basically what I said. I don't remember exactly what words I used, but it was something like that. As I said, though, it doesn't matter really, and anyway she didn't buy it.

Now, though, I could tell her about Plato. I could tell her about the cave and the shadow: The shadow is kind of like a Rorschach blot, if you think about it. You can interpret it however you want and you won't necessarily be wrong. But the thing throwing that shadow, it's only like itself, it only has one way of seeming. (Or, wait. Maybe that's inconsistent? I want to say that Plato would say that we only interpret the shadow, not the thing throwing it—that that thing is a kind of absolute or essence—but then I wonder if the shadow is already that interpretation and I feel like I'm in over my head with this metaphor.) I could tell her about the orange. I could tell her: For instance, honey, the thing that probably a lot of people miss in that book I was telling you about, Bioy Casares's *The Invention of Morel*, is that the people on the island are also the missing passengers of a freighter later discovered adrift. It's not a big part of the story, but it seems really significant to me. What could have happened to them? The crew of the freighter are found dead, without hair, without nails on their fingers or their toes, their corneas dead, their skin dead. (I remember those details perfectly, though, honestly, I'm not sure why Bioy Casares bothers to include them, since he goes on to say that these people are dead, which would seem to cover just about everything being dead, skin and corneas included. But anyway.) The boat doesn't make any sense if it has no passengers—what would it be doing out there?—but there is no mention of any passengers in the book. At least, that's what I remember. So, anyway, another boat discovers this ghost ship, sinks it, and then tells everyone back in port that the island it came from is now cursed. We're led to believe that it's Morel's invention that has done this to the crew of the ghost ship, and that, because that crew was exposed to his invention for significantly less time than the people on the island, the people who should have been aboard the ship, that those people disintegrated even further than the crew has, until they finally disappeared, which is why they aren't on the boat at the time of its sinking. Could this maybe have to do with the invention's true purpose? Not to record these people but actually to immortalize or transform them in some way? What if what happened to them just looked like death to everyone else?

I could tell her all of that. She might not listen, but I could tell her. Whether or not it's part of Bioy Casares's story, it's part of mine, I could say. The shadow's all we've got. If it isn't actually in the book, that just means that I get something different from his story than he did. But that's natural. It's like quantum physics, like how you can't measure something without affecting that measurement. Which, I think, means that you can't really measure something, you can only measure your effect on it. But wait. I'm getting off track. About the mirrors: She had read an article that said that mirrors made a room look bigger. (We lived in a cramped apartment, which . . . no, I shouldn't say it—well, OK: The boy's stuff was everywhere, and what made it worse was that these were things that he never used, things that we had been told were necessary for one reason or another, by books, television, teachers, and other parents; my wife too had her craft nook and the better part of the living room, while I managed with a desk in the hall closet.) She said, I think, that she was curious about what a mirror facing a mirror would look like. As I recall it, my feeling—which would seem to have stayed with me despite the fact that I couldn't really remember the conversation during which it was formed—was that we maybe shouldn't find out. But mirrors had been installed anyway. I was famous in our home for being averse to new things, and so usually changes were made despite my protests. (Which, in my defense, weren't exactly protests, but more like lines of questioning.) When the boy changed schools, for instance, I was the only one wondering if it was the best course of action. My wife has never particularly cared for this aspect of my character, and the boy has recently begun to question it too, which is part of the reason I indulge his fantasies—to keep him on my side. What about our son? I asked the night after the mirrors had been installed, talking in my sleep (not unusual); also, I guess, seeking answers in my sleep (very unusual). The next morning, before she too disappeared, my wife relayed this information to me and answered my question: We have no son. And she was right. He had already disappeared. But all that was after the mirrors went up.

I'd like to think that, rather than being intractable (as I'm sometimes accused of being), it's just that I want to think things through before getting into them (natural, I think, in a person who writes about his life as much as I do), and there's always a lot of thinking to do. I will admit this sometimes involves a Zeno's arrow of patience on the part of others. Sometimes my wife would rather just shoot the damn arrow, and who can blame her? Work had begun in the apartment before I was even awake from my nap. If the movers hadn't bumped

Gabriel Blackwell

into the sofa while carrying my desk out, I might have awoken hours later, in the moving van, still on the sofa. I didn't understand where my wife could have borrowed the money to pay for it all; paying for our son's school was already a challenge, given what we made. (Well, to be fair, what she made. My writing brought in very little.) But it was done in an afternoon, our home resplendent. The mirrors, however, made it extraordinarily difficult to navigate our apartment. Though I had some familiarity with the layout—I mean, we'd lived there for seven years (ever since the boy was born)—I still found myself lost, and completely so, not just turned around or momentarily confused. It happened almost immediately after the mirrors' covers were taken off. Even the act of walking across the room was a significant challenge, as it was nearly impossible to judge distance, and the boundaries of the room seemed to change with one's position. And there was the issue of my reflection, getting in the way, repeating enough to make me unsure as to whether I was approaching or stepping back from whatever was in front of me. I'm sorry if that seems confusing; it was confusing for me. Basically, every step meant that one of my reflections got bigger and the rest of my reflections (of which there were many) got smaller, except that in getting smaller, they were multiplying and so also, in some way, getting bigger. It's impossible to convey in words. It almost made me nauseous, the sight of it. Think motion sickness.

The people who had installed all of this had had to remove the furniture and everything else in order to do so, and so all that was left was one giant, room-shaped mirror. If I'd had my wits about me, I would have asked my wife why she thought this was a good thing, but, well, I didn't have my wits about me, and anyway, we were both tired from all the commotion of having the mirrors installed. We were so tired (and, frankly, so lost and confused) that we simply lay down on the mirrors and fell asleep (we wouldn't have been able to find the bedroom and there was no bed in it anyway). When I awoke (no idea what time it was; all of the clocks had been removed), we had the conversation I've already mentioned; then, at some point (again, no clocks), my wife was gone. I don't know if she had followed our son into a mirror (an absurd thought, but one that occurs to me) or whether she had left by the door (an equally absurd thought, for where now was the door? was there one?). I really can't say—it was difficult to tell, even when she was there, which her was her and which was her reflection. I don't know. You know, I'm not sure that I'd even slept next to her, or whether it was she who had answered

306

my question about our son. Which seems like a ridiculous thing to say—a reflection obviously can't answer a question—but you know what I mean. In any case, whether or not she had found it, I couldn't follow her, because *I* could no longer find the door. I wandered from place to place (unless, as I now suspect, I didn't, I simply stayed in the same place, going in circles) until finally the dizziness was too much. It felt like I was in an elevator whose cable had been cut and whose emergency brakes only worked when I closed my eyes. I sat down. I think I slept. When I stood up and stretched my legs later, I noticed a line of smudges on the mirror where I had just been lying, an outline of my body (or at least the warmer and maybe grimier parts of it) that looked like some kind of semitransparent archipelago. Or what's the one when it's just a ring? Atolls?

It occurs to me that I may be giving the impression that I sleep a lot. I mean, here I've said that I woke up, napped, and then, a few hours later, fell asleep again, and then, even after I'd woken up, fell asleep. But that's not quite right. I think—maybe a psychiatrist or a neuro-scientist could say for sure—that this might have to do with the fact that I mostly sleep now, now that the mirrors are here, and maybe memories work like dreams? So that they kind of project back to you what you've experienced most recently? I do sleep a lot now (although without a clock and without any clear indication of time passing, it's really impossible to say), but I didn't always. Because of the dizziness I've already mentioned, I spend a lot of my time with my eyes closed, and it's kind of difficult to stay awake when your eyes are closed for hours at a time. *You* try it. Unfortunately, this leads to a lot of head-aches and just aches in general—I'm not used to sleeping this much, and the mirror isn't terribly comfortable. But what else am I going to do? I either have to sleep, hold my head very, very still, or focus on that line of smudges (since everything else here just reflects back and forth and makes me sick).

They seem more defined to me, the smudges, more defined and maybe a little more filled in too, maybe just by virtue of the time I've spent lying here. I don't want to seem too gross, but I think what they really are is dead skin and follicles and sweat and grease. They are, right? So what I've called my archipelago is really kind of almost like a corpse, in a weird way. Maybe that's a morbid thing to say. Somehow, though, thinking that way makes me feel oddly like Prendick preparing to leave Moreau's island—as I recall it, Prendick does a kind of Robinson Crusoe in reverse just before he leaves, sal-vaging what he can from the island to outfit a boat, making another island out of the boat. Like Prendick, I've packed those things most essential to my survival and left the rest behind. (Montgomery, of course, smashes the boat to splinters before Prendick can use it, though Prendick does eventually get off the island. I think he also built a raft? But then the raft fell apart before he could get it to the water? Hmm. I wonder how he got off the island now. There's no Montgomery here to smash up my boat, but maybe that's because my Montgomery's already been through, with the people who did the mirrors.) As for Morel and his friends, they don't even have to worry about how they'll get off their island—they're rescued by the boat I've already talked about, though whether they reach their destination seems doubtful. I guess I mean that in the traditional way, not in like a metaphysical, Lacan's letter kind of way—they reach some destination, obviously. I must be waiting for my rescue boat, since I have nothing to make a raft out of. (*Do* I?) I *can* make waves, just by turning my head, but it remains to be seen if there's any way of crossing them.

This is a little off topic, I guess, but I think Morel gets off light, especially if you compare him to Moreau, who, say what you want, but at least Moreau experimented on animals and not people. I mean, Morel informs everybody of his reason for asking them to the island (aide-mémoire: He wanted to record them using the titular invention, a new kind of recording that, when played back, would reproduce not only sight and sound but also touch and even smell (wait—smell?)), and tells them what the effects of his invention on others have been. (Unless that was another character who told them about Morel's friend suddenly falling terribly ill and then dying? I don't remember now.) I think a few people get upset, but nobody really confronts him, at least, not from what I remember. He just kind of runs off in a huff because they don't give him a standing ovation for killing them. Probably even then, on the island, some of them are already feeling the effects of their exposure. I mean, yes, there is no indication of that in the projected version of events the refugee witnesses, but suppose that the invention worked partly by leeching more of the essence of a person as time went by, so that, even as the subject's corneas and skin die, the corneas and skin of the projection grow more and more real. Doesn't that seem likely? Maybe I'm overstating myself: Doesn't that seem possible? It would make for better recordings, since, as the people being recorded got sicker, their recorded selves would be getting better, more substantial. I'm thinking particularly of the wall that the refugee smashes open in the basement—

when the projection is running, the hole he has opened is not only closed, it is impenetrable, but when the projection isn't running, you can smash through thick concrete with a stick or whatever he uses. Not to mention that it would obey the laws of thermodynamics. (That's what I mean, right? The whole thing about matter neither created nor destroyed? I mean energy, I guess, but I think energy and matter are reflections of each other? Isn't that what Einstein's theorem is all about?) But I have trouble understanding why Morel would do this to himself, why he was sacrificing not only others' lives but his own—and for something that he would never himself enjoy. Unless he knows something that we don't. If I had been there, I would have spoken up in that meeting. It's not unusual for me to speak up. Wait. Is it unusual? I feel conflicted all of a sudden, I can't remember a time when I did speak up like that. But I feel like I would have been the one to cut through all of the passion and emotion others were displaying at that moment. (Though I suspect that if I had, my wife would have said, Well, there he goes again—never wants to try anything new. I'm not saying she would be wrong.)

I wouldn't dream of blaming Wells for the arguments my wife and I have had lately. That would be ridiculous. (I may as well blame the mirrors, or the boy.) But my son and I were talking it over, *The Island of Dr. Moreau*, hunched over a model I had made of the island and the seas around it (he was using some of his action figures as creatures, I think, and explaining to me what animal each one was), when she came home from work. This was a few days ago. First she praised the boy (was this for school? she asked), then, when he told her it was mine (he's a humble boy, and honest), she grabbed his arm—rather roughly, I thought—and took him to his room. I could hear her voice through the walls, though I couldn't tell what she was saying. I'm sure it was something reassuring, but I remember thinking that her tone would have frightened me, if I had been in his place.

My son's fascination with *The Island of Dr. Moreau* was what was to be expected of a boy his age, I think: He liked to imagine what the animal men looked like, what they *were* like. Wells too was probably interested in these animal men; I get the feeling that they were his reasons for writing the book. But it also seems to me that regardless of why Wells wrote it or what interested him in it, he nonetheless tells a more compelling story along the way, that of Moreau, isolating himself from something he loved in order to . . . Well, I'm still not sure what. Maybe it's telling that this is what I think of when I think of the book? I don't know. The scientific community has cast

Moreau out for what they consider moral and ethical offenses, and no matter what discovery he subsequently makes, it will be condemned as yet another of his enormities. (It kind of seems like there's justification for this, given the experiments Moreau's doing.) Why, then, even bother to continue as a scientist? Wouldn't it be better to simply give it up, go into another line of business? He could open a pub, or go into bookkeeping, I don't know. Is it better—for the creator, I mean, for his or her soul—to create something that he loves but with which the experts in the field find fault (or even turpitude), or to create something that he has no passion for but which the experts find satisfactory? (My wife might have asked, with good reason, whether it was my reviews that had made me wonder this, but I don't think they have anything to do with it. Reading *The Island of Dr. Moreau* to my son really affected me. I had to stop because I didn't want to cry in front of him.) Is it better to be unhappy with what one is doing but accepted as part of a group doing that thing, or is it better to be unhappy because one is pursuing what one wants to pursue, but is alone in doing so?

I know, I know, I'm getting sidetracked again. I was talking about my wife. Or the mirrors? Maybe the boy. Let's start with my wife. So, as I remember it, after she had put the boy to bed, she reminded me that our son was already doing poorly in school, that he was often distracted, and tended to ask questions that his teachers felt indicated he wasn't developing normally. They were advising a therapist, possibly drugs. I wasn't in favor of this, but, well, as my wife would say, No surprise there. During parent-teacher conferences earlier that week, my wife asked the teacher what she thought normal development looked like. The teacher explained about degrees of curiosity and avoidance and sort of implied, I think, that perhaps something at home was the source of the problem. When it was my turn to pose a question, I asked about the drawing on the wall, a big drawing on butcher paper, clearly made by her students. She informed me that it had been made by her students. I said, Yes, but what is it of? What's happening in the corner down there? Are those waves, and maybe a raft or something? My wife gave me the same stern look the teacher did, and then they continued their discussion without me. When we got home, I put the boy to bed with the first few chapters of *The Island of Dr. Moreau*. I think it was the drawing that had made me think of the book, but now I can't be sure. Maybe it was something my wife had said? I can't remember. Anyway, when he was asleep, my wife told me she had finished reading my book a few days ago—this is what I think I remember—and maybe had been trying to talk to me about it since then? I'm pretty sure that she said she felt that I hadn't been fair to her, unless I think that she said that because I think now that maybe I actually haven't been fair to her. Anyway, I'm pretty sure I said something about criticism as a creative act, and I'm pretty sure she didn't really take it the way it was intended. She said something about using this imaginary son as a wedge (I mean, how could I forget that?) and then rolled over and went to sleep. I stayed up a little bit longer, reading *The Invention of Morel*, which reading *The Island of Dr. Moreau* had reminded me of, for obvious reasons.

You know, now that I think of it, maybe the reason Morel secludes himself on the island isn't because he's worried about his friends' reaction to his explanation of his invention, but because he's already beginning to show signs of the invention's effects. After all, he would have been the one to have had the most exposure to it. He says he's recording everything because he wants this happy time to go on forever, but really, he's rarely part of it. Instead, he hides in his room—isn't that a little suspicious? Even in his room, he's part of the recording; the invention is having its effects on him. Maybe he would have been visibly sick even before everyone gets to the island. Was he wearing a wig and makeup when he met them at the launch? Gloves? If you had just watched your friend die an awful death because of something you suspect you yourself may be suffering from, what do you think you would do? Would you become afraid of infecting others, even if you knew that "infection" was impossible? Wouldn't you try to somehow get away from them? It must have been terrifying. Maybe Morel's friends don't scream at him because they pity him. But here I am again, talking about something that's not even in the book. (Unless it is?)

I remember once telling my wife about the feeling I had about finishing some book, it might as well have been *The Invention of Morel*, that I felt somehow more lonely, as though my entire group of friends had all suddenly moved away together, or as though, completely unprepared, I'd been taken out of my home and set down in the middle of nowhere. Maybe it's a stretch, but couldn't that be how Moreau felt? On his island, having shut the book on London, on science? Or did I actually tell her that? Maybe I just thought it but didn't say it. Maybe I'm thinking it now but didn't think it then. I think she said something like, It's fine to think about these things when you have time, but there are also lots of things we *have* to do in order to have that time to do that kind of thinking. She would have been right in saying something like that, but I worry that I'm not being fair to her in attributing that thought and those words to her. What if the wife I'm remembering isn't my wife? I guess what I mean is: What if what I remember is just a really small slice of the life we actually lived together, and I'm forgetting all the things that made me want to live that life? Or what if I was the one who thought that, who said that, and she just agreed? What would it mean if I remember her this way but she was, in fact, in life, some other way entirely? Was she much kinder? Was I much crueler?

At first, when I realized my wife had gone, I called out repeatedly—my wife's name and my son's name (at least, that's what I remember doing). But the strange thing is—and you can try this if you don't believe me—the strange thing is that when you say something over and over, it starts to lose its meaning. Maybe even worse, when you say something over and over and it starts to lose its meaning, you start to doubt whether it's even what you mean to say, especially when it doesn't have the desired effect. I haven't used my wife's name here because I don't really know what it is anymore, or I don't know that I know anymore. At one time, I think, I thought I knew, but now I think I don't. But I don't know—I might be misremembering that I once knew her name. I can't say. I've lost my son's name too, and I've started to doubt my stories about him even, and if you think that isn't a tough thing to handle, well, it is. When I think of the things I think I know, I'm now more conscious than ever that that person thinking those things isn't me, is only more or less like me, like the me I see in the mirror, except, in my head. See, if I sit perfectly still and look straight ahead, I can open my eyes without feeling dizzy, and so that's usually what I'm doing when I have my eyes open. What this means, though, is that I'm looking straight into my own eyes, which has become, by now, disconcerting. (Is that what I mean? Yes, I think that's what I mean: disconcerting.) Because, I think now, maybe, partly, because those eyes belong to a past me, not the me whose eyes look into them. It is a past me; it must be, right? Because light travels at the speed of light but still isn't instantaneous? So the me I'm seeing is a person that doesn't exist anymore. In a way, this makes perfect sense, since the same thing can't occupy more than one space (if it does, it's two things, one that occupies one space and one that occupies the other)—so, for me to be able to see myself, I must be looking at another thing that is not myself—but it must also mean that what we think we know about ourselves isn't so. Our brains work even slower than light moves—I mean, light is the fastest thing there is, right? We can't know ourselves, in other words, we can only know what we think of ourselves, which is really another person entirely thinking those things, the person we think of when we think of ourselves. Maybe I'm making too much of this, but sitting in a room lined with mirrors will do that to a person.

I almost never dream here, but last night (actually, just last time I slept—I have no idea if it's night or day), I did. In my dream, in a room I couldn't get to—which could be any room, since I can't seem to leave this one—maybe by whatever process light makes its way to me here in this room, I saw my wife and son leaving through what looked a lot like our front door. (How *does* light get in? The only thing I can come up with is that maybe it was let in before the final mirror was installed, and now it just bounces from one surface to another, endlessly. Is that possible? It's probably not, but I really couldn't say, and, anyway, it's all I can come up with. On the other hand, if it *is* possible, I'm not sure how my wife and son would have gotten out without also letting out this light. (Is *that* possible? Can light, which is both a wave and a particle (right?), leak like water or sand?) And I'm not sure what it means if my wife and son would then have disappeared, leaving no traces in these reflections. And then I have to remind myself that it was a dream. It was a dream, right?) I wanted to call out, but I had forgotten their names (which, as far as it goes, is as real as anything else here, so maybe it wasn't a dream). Nothing at all came out of my mouth. I stood up, and the room shifted as it always does, and I felt my stomach drop, and I staggered toward where I had just seen the door. It seemed to be getting smaller, so I turned around, thinking I had just been deceived by the mirrors, but, in every direction, that place where I thought the door had been was receding and fading from my memory. Was it in that direction? Or that one? Now that I can look left to see right, or look down to see up, does it matter?

I imagine Morel on the boat. Somehow he's survived a good bit of exposure to his invention, exposure that starts long before everyone else gets to the island—his friend, the doctor or professor or whoever, dies, but he, Morel, doesn't. Maybe he's immune to the invention's effects; maybe he just knows better how to stay out of its way. Now, like soap under water, his friends have dissipated. The crew has watched in terror. They put all of the sickening, disintegrating people in the hold (meanwhile, on the island, the projection gets better and better—what had been wraithlike and nearly transparent is now opaque, almost solid), but the infection has spread before they could isolate them, and now the crew feel weaker, less like themselves. It is the feeling of being spread thin, of being so busy that one feels as though one has tried to be in two places at once. There were grumblings about Morel from the infected passengers when they came aboard, but, since Morel is their boss, the crew has turned a deaf ear to these rumors. Now, though, they can't ignore them. The first seaman's nails turn black and then fall off. He didn't look good a few days ago, but now his skin is turning gray. The other men lock Morel in his stateroom. Morel says nothing; he hasn't said a word to anyone since he boarded. He paces mostly. Because they have been so sick, none of the sailors has bothered to go below to check on the quarantined passengers, not for days. When one of the men realizes this, he sends another man down. That man goes, returns, and reports that there is no one there. On the island, a woman's nervous laughter breaks the silence, and then the silence returns. Somewhere, though, someone is crying. A seabird on its way north swoops down out of the sky to eat a piece of bread left out on a table next to the pool, but it can't even move the bread, much less eat it. A ghost ship looms off the coastline of the island. The waves look oddly like the outlines of sailors busying themselves with anchoring this ghost ship, but the whole thing disappears when the cloud overhead occludes the sun. Another bird flies down and takes the bread, virtually out of the first bird's beak. The first bird complains, and flaps its wings. The other bird ignores it. On the boat, the seamen open Morel's cabin. They want an explanation. Why isn't he getting sick like everyone else? Does he have a cure? He barely even looks at them; better, he looks through them. Finally, one man shoves Morel. Perhaps it is that the man is so feeble that he cannot budge Morel, who still seems to be in good health. Though it has had no effect on Morel, the sailor's act of violence gives the other men permission to act as well. A second man throws a punch, cries out at the impact, and then shakes his hand as though he has just punched the bow. He has broken bones. Perhaps it is the clouds moving, but the ghost ship off Morel's island flickers again, just a bit. Another man kicks Morel, but he too cries out and immediately recoils in pain. He sits down, hard, on the deck. The first bird flies up into the trees after the thief. The thief throws back its head, and a bit of the bread disappears. The first bird is calling, getting closer, but the palm fronds won't make way for it as they've just done for the thief. The bird hits them—they are as solid as the trunk—and falls to the ground. Someone has the good idea to get one of the rifles. The man takes aim at Morel. The noise of the gunshot in the ship's corridor is awful. The bullet, crumpled from the impact, falls to the floor and slides, wobbling, to the base of the small desk in the corner. The sailors lock the door again. Morel stands near the desk, perhaps mumbling something about the island, the invention. The boat drifts. Most of the sailors die on the same day, within minutes of each other, sparing them at least that horror. Morel, in his cabin, continues to pace. The men from the Japanese ship (I'm almost certain it was Japanese) come aboard and discover the bodies of the sailors. They are curious about the locked cabin, but they can't find the key, and nothing they say or do produces a response from inside. Given the gruesome state of the bodies they've found, the Japanese leave the boat as soon as possible, and decide to sink it despite the contention of one of their sailors that he saw a man still alive and seemingly in good health, pacing, in the locked cabin. When they ask the sailor how he could have seen into the locked cabin, he replies that, for a brief moment, it was as though the bulkhead was transparent. Actually, in that moment, he says, the whole ship was transparent. This man—the man who would have been in the cabin if there had been, in that moment, a cabin to be in—was suspended in air in the trough of the water produced by the (momentarily) invisible boat. It was, the sailor says, as though he had parted the waves. It was as though he alone on earth knew some secret.

Aftershock
Robyn Carter

A FEW DAYS HAD PASSED since I'd spoken to Simon about the blow-gun. But it was still stretched across the living-room floor, now with a fresh litter of clockworks burrowing in the shadow of its plastic throat. Built from cracked sprinkler pipes someone had abandoned in the vacant lot next door, the blowgun was the newest addition to the cache of homemade weapons Simon had been stockpiling that fall. The menace of their points and surfaces would dull with time and dust, but newly born they pulsed with savage potential, lurking around the house, webbed or stuffed with metal nerves and organs harvested from dead machines, if not to live again then for their restive beauty.

Duct tape was Simon's adhesive of choice. Almost everything he made was sheathed in the stuff, including the blackjacks posing in front of the TV, the rusty wrench at each bludgeon's core concealed in strips of dull silver that bore the unmistakable imprint of Simon's lovingly vicious hand. He had arranged the arsenal like tepee poles, handles equidistant from one another on the floor, blunt ends converging at forty-five-degree angles: a monument to thuggery. What grace! With some things all you can do is admire the workmanship.

Gum covered the surface of the coffee table, some pieces coated in Simon's saliva and sculpted into glistening gobs, others still in their powdery wrappers. He'd told me chewing gum works well as a durable sealant, but only if you chew it and let it "set" for a little while first. Just any gum won't do, though, it had to be Dentyne, and Simon swore it was the secret ingredient in the homemade pair of nun-chucks strewn across the couch cushions in a mysterious configuration vaguely resembling a Roman numeral six.

I called across the house for Simon but he didn't answer. In the kitchen I found his ghee bubbling on the stove, its righteous stench lodging itself in the back of my throat, replacing my unease about the blow-gun. I turned down the heat and knocked on the door beside the refrigerator that led to Simon's room. Isn't this stuff done yet? I said.

Marie, he yelled through the door, if you don't like the smell, that's just another sign your dosha's out of balance.

316

He went on—my afflictions are common among those plagued with stagnant pitta, have I noticed any scaliness to my skin, an unsettling new sharpness to the penetration of my gaze, the tap water's marshmallowy taste?—but I drifted from the kitchen, his voice behind me thinning to a nimbus of mild paranoia. His nonstop rambling about the benefits of clarified butter, or the tenets of Krishna consciousness, or the dangers of fluoride and Rastafarianism and the synthetic fibers they use to make cigarette filters was more annoying than his growing fascination with instruments of bodily harm; he never actually hurt anybody, and almost always lost interest in his weapons as soon as he finished building them. He lived by a predictable code he'd culled from a shoebox full of pamphlets and filtered through a psychosis he insisted was only a ruse. It's a scam, he was fond of saying, so the government will give me money.

Simon's thoughts couldn't keep up with his mouth. A lot of people have this problem and it doesn't affect them in any negative way, just everyone around them. But Simon wore a permanent wince on his face that made him seem crushed under the weight of all those fast-moving words. He also wore prescription sunglasses, even inside. His eyes hid behind round-cornered rectangles of amber-tinted glass that made me think of traffic lights. *Proceed with caution*, his gaze seemed to say, but it was less clear whether the message was directed inward or out. The lenses were to correct a vision problem I never really understood. He tried to explain it to me several times but I'd get distracted by his repeated use of the word *lobe*. Such a slow, round word. On Simon's tongue it soothed me like nothing else. The other thing about Simon was that he slept a lot, and there was a part of him that stayed asleep, usually wrapped around a teenage stray he called Feather-boy and treated with a tenderness so vile and hypnotic I couldn't look away; the truth was I wanted some of it too. There were times when the butterscotch light around Simon's eyes would lull me into a tingly-thighed stupor.

Christine was the third leg of our wobbly table. She didn't have any physical or mental health problems that I knew of, only a job that involved wearing an apron, and a revolving set of passions that ran shallow and wide. She'd say things like I'm on my moon, and slink into the papier-mâché menstrual hut she'd built on the patch of cement outside the back door. She tried on labels like gorgeous but ill-fitting shoes. In the weeks since I'd moved in, she'd dabbled in Womynhood, Witchcraft, Lesbian Separatism, Judaism, and now Zionism. She'd found God and a sergeant in the Israeli army who

317

took suggestive photographs of her posing with his M16.

But can you just *decide* to be Jewish? I asked her once. Isn't there a sort of complicated conversion process?

Moshe says it's all about commitment, she told me, with a wave of her pink-nailed hand. If your heart's in it then you're good to go.

And as for me, well, I'd only just arrived. My last home had been a desolate place that went on and on in one direction and in the other ran smack up against a wall of cattle stink and prom queens who reigned with babies on their hips and blackness in their hearts. Every spring, a new crop of girls called me slut because of what I let the wheat-haired boy do to me in his daddy's stable with all that beautiful leather riding gear. One day it all got to be too much, or maybe too little. And there was also the matter of Mama's heart. It wasn't black but it was messed up in its own way, with a murmur, it was called, which sounds peaceful and soft, but can be life threatening, and in Mama's case, especially so on account of her nubby-minded devotion to Long Island iced tea. Actually, this might not have been true in any medical sense, but I told myself it was. I know it sounds cruel now, but at the time it seemed easier to abandon a dying mother than a stranger who'd forgotten how to live.

When it was time to go, I peeked in on Mama. Drapes drawn, lamp off, *Wheel of Fortune* casting her room in feeble blue light. It was hard to tell where Mama's things ended and she began until she moved under the blankets and a few empty prescription bottles rolled down the hill of her thigh. Then from behind a scrim of smoke, Mama's thistle voice: Why do they need Vanna when it's all automatic now? She don't even turn the letters anymore. All she does is tap them.

I guess they still need her for that, I said from the doorway.

What a waste, Mama said. What a goddamned waste.

On my way out I gathered up all of Mama's unfinished needlepoint projects and stacked them in a tower beside the front door. The dotted outlines of beetle antennae and butterfly wings, the beginnings of a daisy petal, the ghost of a weathervane: Mama's desire, trapped between wooden hoops and stashed behind couch cushions or buried in piles of Hinky Dinky circulars and unopened bills.

I rolled across three big, flat states in a Greyhound bus full of sickening urgency and people destined for warmer, sandier versions of the places they'd left. They wanted fog instead of ice. I didn't blame them. I knew I was probably after the same thing. But the guy next to me thought he was after something else. He loved America and Freedom and hated Manuel Noriega so much he was joining the Marines.

318

Semper Fi, mutherfuckers! he'd say between swigs of Hennessy. *Semper* fuckin' *Fi!* Periodically, I'd glance at him and smile through the sound pouring into my skull: songs dubbed off tribal radio I'd been playing over and over in my Walkman. Bent-up words that might've been cursing or broken prayer. I think those Indians were spinning the records backward. Lakota Sioux airwaves were the kind that wiggled right through the legs of the FCC.

Bones a-wobble, mush-minded, and tired, I emerged twenty-six hours later into a city that had just fallen down. The earth had torn itself apart at the seams. *Seven point one on the Richter scale,* someone's car radio was saying, and people clung to this number like religion because it was the only pure and clean thing for miles around. I wandered through jaundiced air, my eyes sopping up the misery of strangers, my ears still cottony with the backward sounds of the Lakota Sioux. This made me feel light and invisible but then voyeuristic and perverted. The newly dispossessed floating past me, the hurry-up-and-wait of a bus station nudging their grit-covered bodies back and forth over the same prongs of twisted rebar. There was a dog with its head screwed on wrong and someone's canary was loose. One of the few buildings in sight that still seemed to be standing was a Laundromat flanked by pear-shaped ladies wailing Spanglish at impossibly tidy piles of chaos: neat pyramids of brick and shale beholden to a force so wicked or sublime it canceled out the laws of physics. I looked through the storefront's shattered windows. Soapy gray rivers were filling its aisles, but the bulletin board was still attached to the wall, its messages dry and sacred:

Macramé Lessons–My Home or Yours
Cuarto por renta para una persona sin vicios
Room for Rent (sort of), $170/month, call for details.

I dialed the number from a pay phone a dozen times before the call finally went through, and when Simon picked up, sirens blared at both ends of the line. His directions were full of landmarks that were missing or only half there. Later I would learn this had nothing to do with the earthquake. Still, I made it to his porch and he answered the door in a bathrobe covered in darned-over holes. I followed him inside and looked in the direction his crooked yellow finger was pointing. Through a gash in the skin of the house you could see bone. Welcome to the epicenter, he said, fingers rippling along the cracked plaster, stroking the lath underneath like oh Jesus fuck this is beautiful. Then the floor danced beneath our feet and I made a small, sharp sound and thought of Mama. Aftershock, Simon said, and shuffled through the kitchen toward the back door. The vacant room is actually a toolshed out here, he said, leading the way. A drizzly wind sobbed through the gap beneath its door and the whole structure listed away from the rest of the house with a cockiness that welcomed me home.

Christine stalked past the blowgun with a pious scowl on her face and a plastic cutting board in her hand. Ghee still simmering, Simon and I were slumped on the couch, watching *Cops*, his homemade nunchucks nestled between us like babies. The episode featured a drug bust in our own neighborhood; as far as we knew, it was Santa Cruz's debut on the show, so we were glued to the set, basking in our fifteen minutes. The camera zoomed in on a cholo kid handcuffed to a fence, a blurry oval where his face should have been, the boardwalk glittering behind him. *Spit it out,* one of the cops said, cupping a palm beneath the digital smear.

That's Feather-boy's cousin, Simon said.

I was about to ask how he knew this when Christine's hand darted at the power button and the cutting board went clack, cheese crumbs tumbling across the coffee table's sticky topography.

What the fuck is this? Christine said to Simon, gesturing at the cheddary streaks coating the board's surface. Thousands of times, it seemed, she'd told Simon that she used that cutting board for meat and it was not to come into contact with dairy products.

Walgreens has tons of those for a buck ninety-nine, Simon said, then got up and turned the TV back on. The screen flashed with rock-throwing kids and Israeli soldiers. *Details at eleven,* a chirpy blonde announced. Then a commercial for the Psychic Friends Hotline. *All new, all improved, all knowing.*

Christine stepped in front the screen, blocking our view. Her filmy skirt clung to the glass with an exquisite crackle, voltage climbing up her thighs, through flesh and muscle to the tip of her index finger, now poised at Simon's neck. When he yelled at her to move she tapped the swell of his jugular vein with an audible zap that bent his perpetual wince into a look of mild perplexity. Simon lowered himself to the floor, slowly, as if reluctantly answering a summons from deep underground. Kneeling before the blackjack tepee, he took off his glasses and for the first time showed us his naked face. The light made his eyelids flutter obscenely, then flop shut and lie there above his cheekbones like two purple-streaked artichoke leaves.

Come on, Simon said, eyes still closed, his voice a wisp of sound. They're gonna go to Xenia next. *Cops* never goes there. Get outta the way. He opened his eyes and pinched a clump of tobacco from a bag of Bugle Boy, spread it along the crease of a rolling paper. I knew a guy from Xenia when I lived in Philly, he told us, brushing tobacco from his fingers. He was way more fucked than anyone in that whole damn facility. Once he grabbed a syringe full of Thorazine from one of the nurses and said he was gonna stab her with it if she didn't let him outta there, but three orderlies pounced on the guy before anything happened, and that was the last time I saw him.

I want you out of here, Christine said.

They had hot holes in the walls of that place.

Out.

For guys to light cigarettes.

Your name's not on the lease, Christine said.

Simon licked the edge of the rolling paper and smoothed it in place with his thumb. No matches allowed, he said, pointing his amber gaze at me.

I picked up the nunchucks, desperate for a prop, some weight to throw around, but all I managed to say was, Come on, Christine.

She donned her apron, still muttering, Out, out, out, as she knotted its strings around her waist, but Simon's shades were back in place and he'd glassed himself off from the sound. He blew smoke rings at Xenia and said, If you're not wearing a shirt when the cops show up, you're going to jail. That's how they decide.

Christine stomped out the front door as Feather-boy blew in the back, all swirly black curls and limbs made of air. Simon rose from his spot on the floor and followed his hands to Feather-boy's luminous skin, yellow fingers tracing full lips like oh Jesus fuck this is beautiful. Then man and boy shuffle-flew into Simon's musty-walled lair, slate-gray bird sounds traveling through the radiator pipes, stroking my ears. Busy-fingered, I listened on the couch.

Hours later the three of us pooled into the kitchen like a mirage, shiny versions of ourselves made of heat. Feather-boy fixed himself a bowl of Christine's Cheerios and carried it back to Simon's room, shutting the door with a demure little click. Simon had forgotten about the ghee and it had simmered itself into a black-bottomed gloss. He switched off the burner and peered into the pot. There's something you don't know, he said, something that you need to take into account.

What? I said.

I took a test.

What kind of test?

At the nuthouse in Philly. They gave me a test, and it said I had the mind of a twelve-year-old.

Oh, I said, staring past him, at the door to his room.

It's math, Marie.

Over the next few weeks Feather-boy withdrew into a listless fug, his arms and legs noodled by something the curandera on Riverside could not drive away with herbs or spells, so his cousin tried to beat the sickness out of him even though we still didn't know if it was AIDS for sure. When neither belt nor fist seemed to work, Feather-boy's cousin sent him to church. Lalo's making me go to confession, Feather-boy told us in the dank safety of our kitchen's late-November chill. He could barely walk but insisted on standing. I pressed a package of frozen kosher corn to the side of his face and he stood at the stove, prodding the burnt ghee with a wooden spoon, a gesture darkened by the effort of living. It exhausted him completely and he collapsed onto a chair with the spoon—its first time out of the pot since Christine's outburst. Simon hadn't touched anything in the kitchen since. And neither had Christine. For almost a month the ghee soured and the cheese hardened, pot and cutting board governing the house in a fragile détente. You don't have to do anything that asshole tells you, Simon said, bent over the table, its pocked wooden surface sparkling with screws and VCR guts. Feather-boy raised his face, eyes skittering from the floor to the rubber-handled pincers in Simon's trembling grasp, and beneath the glossy down that skimmed the boy's lip: Lalo's message swelling blue and ugly.

Through a hole in the ceiling of the sanctuary you could see an almost star-shaped piece of sky. The earthquake had shaken a beam loose and when it fell its bolts took a chunk of roof with it, so now seagulls came to Mass. Their droppings clung to the pews and dripped from the altar, hardening into an icing of ripples and florets. If you ignored the smell and let your eyes get lazy, the impression was that of an ice palace. We crossed its threshold as if on skates, gliding through its airy expanse to the row of booths built into the opposite wall. Confessionals are not really designed to hold more

than one person. Still, we piled in. Feather-boy and I sat down on the
little bench and Simon stood, wedging his feet into the sliver of floor
space between the bench and the door. The screen's wooden lattice-
work cut the priest's face into a jigsaw of wary eyes and capillary-
webbed jowls. He didn't mention any rules about occupancy limits
and skipped the formalities I had expected. Can you guys excuse me
for a minute? he said, and Simon said, You're the boss, and the priest
opened the door on his side of the partition and disappeared into an
envelope of sunshine. Simon leaned against the screen and from his
jacket pocket produced a little machine made of parts from the
insides of cameras or tape players with wires attached to an on/off
switch that looked a lot like the one from the radio on our kitchen
windowsill. I asked what it was and Simon said, Watch, and pressed
the wire to his neck and when he flipped the switch a soft buzz jan-
gled his brain. I could tell because after that words seeped from his
lips in the liquid tones of the almost dead or very sleepy. Wanna try
it? he said, and I asked him what it did, and he said, You know, not
everyone who's struck by lightning actually dies. A small percentage
survive. And you should see their skin. It's not always charred like
you'd expect. Sometimes, the electricity leaves a pink print, like a slap
from a monster with tentacles shaped like lightning bolts. Feather-
boy touched the bruise on his lip and said, I didn't know about that,
and I said, Neither did I. Well, Simon told us, holding up his machine,
this works like that, except instead of the lighting bolt–shaped tentacles slapping your skin, they tighten around your veins and nerves.
Is that better? I said, and Simon said, A thousand times better, and
the priest returned to his compartment and sealed himself into the
darkness with us, and Feather-boy said, Forgive me, Father, for I have
sinned, and Simon pressed the wire to his neck and flipped the
switch, and a mismatched pair of man-boy palms found the flesh of
my thighs, and I sucked in gray air and held it, pictured it reddening
to blood, as if this wet slip of an instant would stretch without snapping as long as my lungs refused to drain. An invisible fist closed
around my windpipe, floating my arms, setting my fingers to work
on Feather-boy's beads, the plastic ones that look like bone dangling
from his neck. Breathlessly, I ticked off Hail Marys and Our Fathers
and the Joyful-Luminous-Sorrowful-Glorious Mysteries of the Rosary.
Feather-boy had schooled me in preparation for our visit: the Agony
in the Garden, the Scourging at the Pillar, Resurrection, Ascension,
Descent, Assumption. The lurid colors, the danger and pain and tor-
tured bliss of each holy enigma were there in that breath, hot on

the shell of my thoughts, the throbbing surface of my thighs, but underneath, at the center of this swollen moment, a clotted sense of loss and home and Mama, a flare in the ache for the wheat-haired boy, the hunger of lost purpose. Exhaling, I looked up at Simon, desperate for his little machine, but his glasses were off again and his eyelids were artichoke leaves and he couldn't see anything. My eyes swept the dark for Feather-boy's gaze but it was tied up with his words, communicating sins—all made-up sins (would Lalo check?), convenient and uncomplicated: stealing, cursing, coveting thy neighbor's wife—and Father Cabrera was delivering his sentence, almost an afterthought, his putty-colored eyes on me, on my face, appraising the flush dampening my cheeks, the trance parting my lips, the thrilling trespasses beneath my skirt, which he did not mention explicitly but seemed to be addressing when he said, What about you, young lady? Do *you* have anything to confess? Through the jigsaw holes I watched his eyebrows creep along his forehead like inky black caterpillars and then I said, No. Not right now. Right now, I am perfect.

Feather-boy's sins forgiven, a prayer candle pocketed as dubious proof, we hurried straight to Simon's bed and in hallowed silence worked each other's clothes off with fingers and teeth. Multiple welts seethed on Feather-boy's ribs, and the worst one seemed to deepen with his breathing, the slit skin glistening as his chest rose. My impulse was to lick the wound, but Simon had me pinned, his palms locked around my wrists, cocooning my hands in prickly sleep, his naked face and switched-off voice condensing his presence, stripping it down to a cosmic and primordial essence that pressed his knee into my collarbone and filled my mouth with his dusty, green taste: Ice Plant and Rock Rose and starry-flowered Devil's Grip. I wondered if Simon had been rubbing his cock with the same juicy-leafed succulents I'd grazed on as a child, waiting for Mama with sour on my tongue. Long afternoons where diesel fumes would collude with the sun, burnishing the sky a white so strangely viscous and unlike the pretend blue ceilings of TV outsides that I thought of the colorless stretch above as something else: a membrane that grew between days, a marker of time more than space. That the two were connected was beyond me, and the moment I learned how—that we are constantly spinning and revolving and there's no way to stop—my nose bled from brain-hurt, but there on the sagging shoulder of the interstate, beneath a plasmatic sky, these killing facts hovered out of reach.

The sun had shifted and now tongues of light darted through the window's rusting blinds, stenciling our bodies in rows of golden blanks that brightened the center of Feather-boy's gray-edged fatigue, surging through his fingers as they wiggled off my skirt. The teeth of its zipper bit my hip but the sting sweetened beneath his touch. I told myself it was a sign of recovery, and licked the tang of highway weeds from my lips, let go of my hands as numbness erased them from my body.

The next day broke sallow skied and bitter, the gilded air in Simon's room gone along with Feather-boy and the fragile détente. Christine came home with a new cutting board and Simon sliced himself a piece of cheese. Christine called the cops, and from a drawer in the kitchen crammed with twisty ties and old power bills, she unearthed the lease. Come on, Christine, I said, come on. I'm wearing a shirt, Simon told the cops, tugging its fraying hem, but they charged him with trespassing and confiscated the nunchucks and blackjacks. They saw the blowgun too but left it alone. That falls within legal limits, the younger cop said, lacing Simon into a disposable pair of zip-tie handcuffs. Are those really necessary? I said, and with a wincy smile the cop told me it was protocol and called me ma'am, a word that seemed to rouse the older cop from the mean-eyed dream he was having in the middle of our living room, his glare plowing through the meadow of aluminum and plastic life around him. On his way out he paused in the doorway and asked me how old I was. I answered him truthfully, and he ran a hand over his missing hair, saying, Nineteen is a small and damn idiotic number.

The charges were dropped but Simon's eviction was part of the deal. Soon after he moved out, Christine changed her name to Shoshanna and announced she was marrying her sergeant and moving with him to a settlement in Gaza. I asked her why she called the cops on Simon if she was planning to leave anyway. It's the principle of the thing, she said. I didn't know what she meant by this but it made my hate for her grow into something lifelike and threatening that I carried around out of a stupid sense of obligation I'd never felt before. I put it down the day she left, long enough to help her pile her things into a cab. The unusually humid morning slapped us with hot, wet sheets of air and as the car sped off, a hard rain began to fall. I gave Christine a little wave that I curled into a dirty-finger gesture and held above my head as I turned back toward the house. The torrent was melting her menstrual hut into a slurry of flour and glue and pulpy newspaper, its color the same divine and empty shade of lavender as the lightning-dyed sky.

I ended up inheriting Christine's apron and the job that went with it, which turned out to be at Kinko's. Now I spent my days making copies for libertarians and socialists and a dour revolutionary named Rocky Stone whose paranoia was legendary, even by Santa Cruz standards. *Head for the hills!* his fliers would say. *Another injustice is upon us.* Now I can't recall any of the injustices in particular, or whether they were particular at all. The job's repetition got to me. I'd always thought seeing the same things over and over again would make you remember them. But, actually, the opposite happens. They disappear.

As I collated and stapled and cropped and bound, I'd think about how since Christine was gone, Simon and Feather-boy could've come back, but I didn't know how to find them. Maybe Simon was so spooked by the cops he decided not to risk returning for his stuff. Just some clothes and the blowgun, but still. Maybe it was that Lalo had discovered where he lived. I figured I'd never know and told myself to accept it, but wondering took root and longing unsealed itself in wet, messy ways. The anxious film on my palms posed a workplace hazard: Once, my soggy fingers smeared a fresh stack of Rocky's latest manifesto. He eyed the damp spots and leaned his bark-skinned face over the counter, swallowed me up in his stare. That's right, child, he whispered, the coppery fear on his breath burning my lungs. I wiped my hands on my apron and said, What's right? but he didn't answer; he had already fallen back into the scattered grist of his thoughts.

It was almost a year after their exodus, and by then I'd quit looking, but I did find them. Simon was pushing a shopping cart full of crumpled-up Feather-boy, all rubber-doll eyes and gloom-colored skin, rusty power-saw blades clanging in the rack up top meant for toddlers and purses. They were rattling down River Street, past the clock tower, its hands stuck since the earthquake at four minutes past five. Simon's shuffle had slipped into a limp, his right leg fighting his left in what appeared to be the same hopeless pursuit of harmony that forced his face to hate his words. He was yelling *Hare Krishna* at those Rasta dudes and their dirty, glassy-faced white chicks—the ones with parrots on their shoulders and bird shit in their hair—his old wince scalding his temples and brow, and all I could think about was the pictures of Christine with her boyfriend's M16 between her breasts. She'd flipped through the stack and passed me each print one by one and when she got to an out-of-focus shot that made her eyes look gentle and high she told me her plan was to shave off her hair when she got married, and not wear a wig like other Orthodox women do because she thought that was cheating. Now Simon was wheeling Feather-boy into the almost-gone sun. I followed them down Front Street, watching them for a while, and then I watched the sky where the sun used to be, the pink-orange dregs of day rearranging themselves until they were Christine's bald head searing itself above the horizon, the same way your face eventually melts away if you stare at a mirror in a darkened bathroom and say Bloody Mary a hundred times. There was Christine, a shiny-headed alien, the contours of her scalp carving out sexy slopes and arcs, the machine gun's barrel grazing her ear, her missing hair somehow fortifying the weapon; it seemed deadlier in a beguiling and underhanded way, like it would ease you into complacency, then kill you slowly cell by cell.

Simon and Feather-boy had shrunk to a tiny gray mass vanishing over the levee, and up ahead, beneath the rising moon, the Ferris wheel spun, slow and round and made of light. We'd ridden it once, Simon and Feather-boy and me—squeezed into a rocking metal cradle—on a Tuesday night when rides cost a dime. I was terrified about leaving the ground, but Feather-boy scooped up my broken nerve and whispered it to health: *Sana, sana, colita de rana*, and Simon said, Lobe, lobe, lobe, and his burnt ginger stare was working its tingly magic, but I wanted to crawl under Mama's moldering blankets with her, watch the Wheel of Fortune spin its easy hope our way, its golden axle anchored to solid ground. *What a waste. What a waste.* Hands wrapped around the cold steel bar, Feather-boy's coo warming my neck, mechanical lurch, heavenly suck, and there we went, the clatter and roar of the boardwalk below giving way to the drub of my heart. My gaze latched itself to the Slushee-spattered asphalt and I didn't notice the sky until it was draped over my lap, and we were as high as we could go without actually flying, swaying atop a flickering neon shrine to corn dogs and black-tar heroin and the things in between.

Si no sana hoy, sanará mañana.

327

I scanned the levee for the shopping cart's glint, but Simon and Feather-boy had moved on. I could've gone after them but I didn't. I turned and walked home, back to a house I'd filled with strangers—in a nod to tradition—its lease still jammed into the twisty-tie drawer, the names listed there primitive history. Christine never wrote down the landlord's phone number, and when I tried calling Mama's, a recorded voice told me the line had been disconnected.

The loll-headed girl who moved into Simon's room had piled his belongings up along the living-room wall with the blowgun he'd left behind. I sifted through ratty T-shirts and flip-flops and his collection of pamphlets until I found his little box of lightning. Pressing its wires beneath my jaw the way I'd seen Simon do, I held my breath and flipped its switch, and then: a bright lick of pain—intense but stunted and flat—and me thinking, I'm probably doing it wrong.

NOTES ON CONTRIBUTORS

Legendary French poet CHARLES BAUDELAIRE (1821–1867) is the author, most famously, of *Les Fleurs du mal*. His translations of Edgar Allan Poe have been credited with provoking the birth of symbolism, and his prose poems were a major influence on such writers as Mallarmé, Rimbaud, and Verlaine. He was also a notable art critic, essayist, addict, and misanthrope. Although he was well known in his lifetime—he and his publisher were convicted of moral offenses for the erotic/thanatic content of *Les Fleurs du mal*—many of his works were published only after his death.

GABRIEL BLACKWELL is the author of three books, the most recent of which is *The Natural Dissolution of Fleeting-Improvised-Men: The Last Letter of H. P. Lovecraft* (CCM). With Matthew Olzmann, he edits *The Collagist*.

Six of CAN XUE's books have been published in English translation, including *Blue Light in the Sky and Other Stories* (New Directions), *Five Spice Street* (Yale University Press), *Vertical Motion: Stories* (Open Letter), and *The Last Lover*, which will be published by Yale University Press in July. She lives in Beijing.

H. G. CARRILLO's piece in this issue is from "Black Male Bodies with Spanish-Speaking Tongues: An Essay." He is the author of the novel *Loosing My Espanish* (Pantheon and Anchor); his short stories have appeared in *Conjunctions, Kenyon Review, The Iowa Review*, and elsewhere. He teaches at George Washington University.

ROBYN CARTER's writing has appeared or is forthcoming in *Playboy, Ninth Letter, Switchback, Storyglossia*, and *Echo Ink Review*.

MAXINE CHERNOFF was a 2013 NEA fellow in poetry and the 2009 winner of the PEN USA Translation Award. Her new collection, *Here* (Counterpath), contains many poems that previously appeared in *Conjunctions*.

GILLIAN CONOLEY's new and seventh collection, *Peace*, is just out with Omnidawn. City Lights will publish her translations of three books by Henri Michaux, *Thousand Times Broken*, in the fall of 2014.

BRIAN EVENSON is the author of more than a dozen books of fiction, most recently *Windeye* (Coffee House Press) and *Immobility* (Tor). A new story collection, *A Collapse of Horses*, is scheduled to appear from Coffee House Press in 2015. He lives and works in Providence, Rhode Island.

ROBIN HEMLEY is the author of ten books of fiction and nonfiction, most recently *A Field Guide for Immersion Writing* (the University of Georgia Press) and the story collection *Reply All* (Break Away Books, Indiana University Press). Formerly the director of the nonfiction writing program at the University of Iowa, he is now the writer in residence and director of the writing program at Yale-NUS College in Singapore.

BRIAN HENRY's most recent book of poetry is *Brother No One* (Salt Publishing). He is the translator of Aleš Šteger's *The Book of Things* (BOA Editions).

CHRISTIE HODGEN is the author of *A Jeweler's Eye for Flaw* (University of Massachusetts Press), *Elegies for the Brokenhearted*, and *Hello, I Must Be Going* (both Norton). The recipient of a Pushcart Prize, she lives in Kansas City.

EDIE MEIDAV is the author of the novels *The Far Field: A Novel of Ceylon* (Houghton Mifflin/Mariner), *Crawl Space* (FSG/Picador), *Lola, California* (FSG/Picador), and the forthcoming *Dogs of Cuba*. She teaches in the MFA program at UMass-Amherst.

STEPHEN O'CONNOR (www.stephenoconnor.net) is the author, most recently, of *Here Comes Another Lesson* (Free Press), a collection of stories.

LANCE OLSEN is the author of more than twenty books of and about innovative writing, including three appearing this spring: the novel based on Robert Smithson's earthwork the Spiral Jetty, *Theories of Forgetting* (FC2); *How to Unfeel the Dead: New & Selected Fictions* (Teksteditions); and *[[there.]]* (Anti-Oedipus). He teaches experimental narrative theory and practice at the University of Utah.

JOHN PARRAS is the author of *Fire on Mount Maggiore* (University of Tennessee Press), which won the Peter Taylor Prize for the Novel, and the chapbook *Dangerous Limbs: Prose Poems and Flash Fictions* (Kattywompus Press). He teaches at William Paterson University and edits *Map Literary: A Journal of Contemporary Writing and Art*.

MATTHEW PITT's collection *Attention Please Now* won the Autumn House Prize and Late Night Library's Debut-litzer Prize, and was a finalist for the Writers' League of Texas Book Awards. His work has appeared in publications including *Oxford American, Southern Review, Epoch*, and *Best New American Voices* (Harcourt). He teaches creative writing at Texas Christian University.

MARTIN RIKER's writing has appeared in publications including *The Wall Street Journal, The New York Times, The Guardian*, and *London Review of Books*. "Samuel Johnson's Eternal Return" is from a novel in progress.

Cover artist CHIHARU SHIOTA is based in Berlin. Among her many recent exhibitions have been shows at the Museum of Art in Kochi, Japan; the Maison Rouge in Paris; the National Museum of Art in Osaka; the Neue Nationalgalerie in Berlin; and the Biennials of Venice, Seville, Lyon, and Moscow.

RICHARD SIEBURTH's most recent translation is a collection of Louise Labé's *Love Sonnets & Elegies* (NYRB/Poets). His edition of *Late Baudelaire* will be published next year by Yale University Press.

Slovenian poet and prose writer ALEŠ ŠTEGER (www.alessteger.com) has published *The Book of Things* (BOA Editions) in English translation by Brian Henry. He is the editor in chief of Beletrina Academic Press.

PETER STRAUB's many novels include *Ghost Story* (Orion) and *In the Night Room* (Ballantine). He has won ten Stoker Awards and four World Fantasy Awards, among other honors.

ARTHUR SZE's most recent books are *The Ginkgo Light* (Copper Canyon Press) and, in collaboration with Susan York, *The Unfolding Center* (Radius Books). *Compass Rose* is forthcoming from Copper Canyon.

LAURA VAN DEN BERG is the author of the story collections *What the World Will Look Like When All the Water Leaves* (Dzanc Books) and *The Isle of Youth* (Farrar, Straus and Giroux), which won the Rosenthal Family Foundation Award from the American Academy of Arts and Letters. Her first novel, *Find Me*, is forthcoming from FSG.

ANNELISE FINEGAN WASMOEN is an editor and literary translator. Her translations include short stories by Jiang Yun, Lu Min, and Wang Meng, as well as Can Xue's novel *The Last Lover*, forthcoming from Yale University Press in July.

WIL WEITZEL is currently at work on a novel set in Pakistan's Hindu Kush range. His stories have appeared or are forthcoming in *Conjunctions*, *New Orleans Review*, *Southwest Review*, *Kenyon Review*, and elsewhere. He teaches at Harvard University.

MARJORIE WELISH is the author, most recently, of *In the Futurity Lounge / Asylum for Indeterminacy* (Coffee House Press). *Of the Diagram: The Work of Marjorie Welish* (Slought) compiles papers given at a 2002 conference at the University of Pennsylvania devoted to her writing and art (https://slought.org/resources/of_the_diagram).

PAUL WEST is the author of fifty-three books, most recently the novel *The Ice Lens*, forthcoming from Onager Books. He has received numerous awards, among them the Literature Award from the Academy and Institute of Arts & Letters, the Aga Khan Prize for Fiction, and the Order of Arts & Letters from the French government.

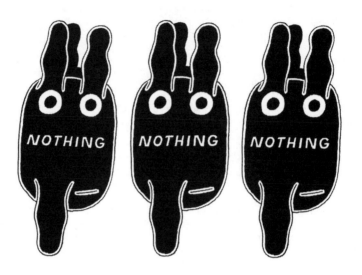

Jena Osman:
Corporate Relations

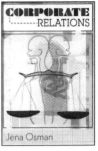

A work between essay and poem tracks the constitutional rights granted to corporations in landmark Supreme Court cases since the Civil War. It asks, if corporations are persons, what are persons? machines? "Osman's a canny operator whose intelligence is that of a literary sharpshooter: She never misses her mark, but the damage done is often not (or is simply much more than) the damage you anticipated."—Seth Abramson, *Huffington Post*
Poetry, 80 pps, offset, smyth-sewn, orig. paperback $14

Farhad Showghi:
End of the City Map

[translated from the German by Rosmarie Waldrop]
Showghi's prose poems take us into a place where apparently simple everyday scenes turn, by a little stretch of language, into the unpredictable und strange.
"Cool beauty on fire."—*Neue Zürcher Zeitung*
"A most stimulating labyrinth of language, whose corners hold touching surprises."—*Sand am Meer*
Poetry, 64 pp., offset, smyth-sewn, original paperback $14

Claude Royet-Journoud:
Four Elemental Bodies

[translated from the French by Keith Waldrop]
This Tetralogy assembles the central volumes of one of the most important contemporary French poets. His one-line manifesto: "Will we escape analogy" and his spare, "neutral" language signaled the revolutionary turn away from Surrealism and its lush imagery.
Poetry, 368 pp., offset, smyth-sewn, original paperback $20

Gérard Macé:
The Last of the Egyptians

[translated from the French by Brian Evenson]
Macé explores Champollion's twin interests: Egypt and "America's savage nations," his deciphering of the Rosetta stone and the Indians' deciphering of the forest. He finally follows Champollion to the Louvre where he set up the Egyptian galleries, encountered Indians of the Osage tribe, and felt the sadness of their slow song.
Novella, 80 pp., offset, smyth-sewn, original paperback $14

Orders: www.spdbooks.org, www.burningdeck.com

NOON

A LITERARY ANNUAL

1324 LEXINGTON AVENUE PMB 298 NEW YORK NY 10128

EDITION PRICE $12 DOMESTIC $17 FOREIGN

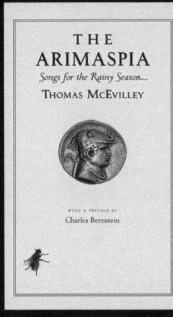
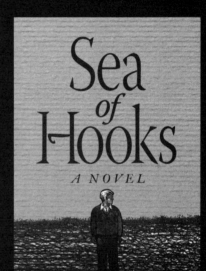

BROWN UNIVERSITY LITERARY ARTS
A HOME FOR INNOVATIVE WRITERS

Program faculty

John Cayley
Brian Evenson
Thalia Field
Forrest Gander
Renee Gladman
Carole Maso
Meredith Steinbach
Cole Swensen
CD Wright

Joint-appointment, visiting & other faculty

Angela Ferraiolo
Joanna Howard
Gale Nelson
John Edgar Wideman

Since 1970, Literary Arts at Brown University has been fostering innovation and creation. To learn more about the two-year MFA program, visit us at http://www.brown.edu/cw

THE ONLINE **MFA** APPLICATION DEADLINE IS **15 DECEMBER**

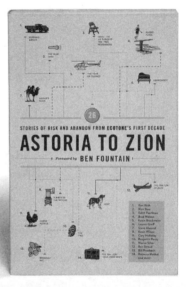

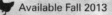

FC2 & The Jarvis and Constance Doctorow Family Foundation

present the

FC2 Catherine Doctorow Innovative Fiction Prize

Winner receives $15,000
and
publication by **FC2**

Entries accepted
August 15, 2014 - November 1, 2014

Submission guidelines
www.fc2.org/prizes.html

Fiction Collective 2
1974|2014

Jarvis &
Constance
Doctorow
Family
Foundation

FC2 is among the few alternative, author-run presses devoted to
publishing fiction considered by America's largest publishers to be too
challenging, innovative, or heterodox for the
commercial milieu.

The Ronald Sukenick/FC2
Innovative Fiction Contest

entries accepted
AUGUST 15, 2014 – NOVEMBER 1, 2014

$1,500 & *publication by* FC2

submission guidelines:
WWW.FC2.ORG/PRIZES.HTML

Fiction Collective 2
1974|2014

FC2 is among the few alternative, author-run presses
devoted to publishing fiction considered by America's largest publishers to be
too challenging, innovative, or heterodox for the commercial milieu.

Bard's unique summer-based MFA in Writing focuses on innovative poetry but also welcomes students working in sound, performance, and other short or mixed-media forms. In this interdisciplinary program, anchored in the theory and diverse practices of contemporary art, students work with a distinguished faculty of writers, artists, and scholars, and are in close dialogue with faculty and students in Film/Video, Music/Sound, Painting, Photography, and Sculpture.

Photography by Peter Mauney '93, MFA '00.

2014 Writing faculty include:

Anselm Berrigan

Robert Fitterman

Renee Gladman

Paul La Farge

Ann Lauterbach

Anna Moschovakis

David Levi Strauss

Roberto Tejada

Dana Ward

Matvei Yankelevich

Bard MFA

MILTON AVERY GRADUATE SCHOOL OF THE ARTS

mfa@bard.edu • 845.758.7481 • bard.edu/mfa

CONJUNCTIONS:57

KIN

Edited by
Bradford Morrow

"These fictions, essays, and poems address the familial bond from a variety of angles. A mother takes her boys sledding while contemplating the mysteries of the numerological universe. A daughter crosses over to the afterlife, where she encounters both her mother and herself. An adopted boy given to delinquency examines the naive love his suicidal mother has for his distant father. An uncle begins a process of mythic transmogrification. An urban father protects his young daughter from cranks and characters on the subway, even as he begins to realize he cannot shield her forever. A suburban mother who is losing her teenage daughter to a dangerous high school friend drugs the girl and herself in order to share a desperate moment of togetherness."—Editor's Note

In *Kin*, twenty-eight poets, fiction writers, and memoirists unweave the tangled knot of family ties. Contributors include Karen Russell, Rick Moody, Rae Armantrout, Octavio Paz, Ann Beattie, Peter Orner, Joyce Carol Oates, Miranda Mellis, Can Xue, Georges-Olivier Châteaureynaud, Elizabeth Hand, and many others.

Conjunctions. Charting the course of literature for over 25 years.

CONJUNCTIONS
Edited by Bradford Morrow
Published by Bard College
Annandale-on-Hudson, NY 12504

To purchase this or any other back issue,
visit our secure ordering page at www.conjunctions.com.
Contact us at conjunctions@bard.edu or (845) 758-7054
with questions.

CONJUNCTIONS:60

IN ABSENTIA

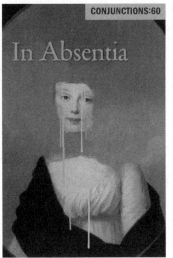

Edited by
Bradford Morrow

Things gone missing. People vanished or changed beyond recognition. A once-bedrock belief now so alien as not to seem believable anymore. A woman's threat of suicide. A man's phantom limb. Another who comes home from prison only to find that home is no longer what it was, friends no longer who they were. Love gained, love lost. A promise forgotten. A couple gone off the grid into the woods and ghost-plagued madness. An exceptionally ill-timed death. These are among the many scenarios explored in the pages of *In Absentia*, a literary compendium about the presence of absence. From Joyce Carol Oates's story of a young protagonist whose devotion to working with bonobos at a zoo leads him on a journey far beyond the normal districts of primatology to Karen Hays's essay on a wide spectrum of subjects—not the least of which is the metaphysics of the fourth dimension—these works attempt to observe the unobservable, to see what isn't quite there.

Conjunctions:60, In Absentia, features work by thirty literary artists, including Charles Bernstein, Robert Olen Butler, Robert Coover, Brian Evenson, Benjamin Hale, Ann Lauterbach, Carole Maso, Yannick Murphy, Joanna Scott, Frederic Tuten, and Marjorie Welish. Don't miss this haunting, revelatory exploration of the black holes in our everyday lives.

Conjunctions. Charting the course of literature for over 30 years.

CONJUNCTIONS
Edited by Bradford Morrow
Published by Bard College
Annandale-on-Hudson, NY 12504

To purchase this or any other back issue, visit our secure ordering page at
www.conjunctions.com.
Contact us at conjunctions@bard.edu or (845) 758-7054 with questions.